THE BLAZING

CHIEF

Book Three of The Deschembine Trilogy

BY

MATT SPENCER

BACK ROADS CARNIVAL BOOKS,
BRATTLEBORO, VERMONT

BACK ROADS CARNIVAL BOOKS
mattspencerauthor.wordpress.com

Digital ISBN: 978-0-578-62829-5
Print ISBN: 978-0-578-62830-1

Copyright © 2020 by Matt Spencer
Cover art © 2020 by Luke Spooner

For David Pierce,
In Loving Memory
(1981-2003)

This book's been a long time coming, largely due to the strange, troubled publication history of the first two volumes in the series, *The Night and the Land* and *The Trail of the Beast*. That's a nice way of saying that the original publisher accepted all three books, with contracts signed and everything, but only published the first two before getting bought out by incompetent jackasses who ran the company out of business. Due to a lot of contractual vagaries and other publishing-world-related nonsense, the first two books languished in semi-limbo for several years, while this, the final book, sat around in, well, just limbo.

It was a disheartening, infuriating time for me as a writer, but in the end, it turned out to be a blessing in disguise. In the intervening years, you see, I'd worked with editor Garrett Cook on two new stand-alone novels, both set in the same universe of this first series, building on the groundwork of the mythology I'd set out therein. Eventually, I reacquired the rights and set about getting the first two books back into print, with an eye on the conclusion of the trilogy finally seeing the light of day. In the years between first writing whole damn thing, seeing the first two thirds of it published, and getting the rights back, I'd changed considerably, both as a person and as a writer, as one does (one likes to think for the better). While going back over the first two, though, I discovered that I still love this story and its characters—yes, even some of the despicable ones. It continues to pick up a growing, enthusiastic readership to this day, and I can't express enough love and thanks to readers who've continued to ask, "So when the hell's the third one coming out, man?"

So for both all those readers and myself, I seized upon this second opportunity to pull out all the stops in this final installment...to give the intertwined journeys of Rob, Sally, Sheldon, Janie, Remelea, Jesse, Zane, and Puttergong the thrilling, cathartic send-off they deserved. With Garrett's tough-love, two-fisted editorial guidance, I feel like I've done just that, bringing this tapestry of horror, adventure, action, romance, tragedy, triumph, surprises, and just plain ol' weird shit to vivid life in ways that never would have otherwise occurred to me. The esteemed Mr. Cook, it must be said, in case you don't already know, is also a powerhouse of a dark fiction author, whose work I wholeheartedly recommend, though as with my own, not to the squeamish.

Mad thanks are also due to my darling wife Laura and our cats Marlowe and Pixie, along with Amanda Fish, Bill Hillburn, Cyndal Ellis, Emyli McGrath, Holly Brewer, Ian Bigelow, Jessie Cross-Nickerson, Kay Lemay, Luke Burke, Matthew Gomez, Sheryl Westleigh, and the Brattleboro Historical Society. It's been a ride. Catch you further on up the trail, folks.

THE BLAZING

CHIEF

"I am in blood stepped in so far that should I wade no more, returning were as tedious as go o'er."
- *Macbeth*

PROLOGUE:

THREE MONTHS AFTER

THE SOLAR STORM

At nineteen, Ronald "Fishhook" Fairbanks figured he'd seen it all. Over the back end of Summer, he'd seen a whole lot more. For one thing, he'd never expected to see a dude get chopped in half with a Goddamn sword. By the end of the early Autumn day, that wouldn't even be the weirdest thing he witnessed, or the worst.

That morning, he woke up in a ditch, under a blanket of leaves. He couldn't remember his dreams, but he knew they'd been bad. He sat up, brushed most of the leaves out of his face and hair, blinked his eyes clear, and looked at the sky. He almost panicked, because it wasn't the same sky anymore. So what if he should be used to it by now? It still freaked him out, whenever he woke up looking at it. It never had gone back to normal after the solar storm, never lost that weird, sickly, purple-orange tinge.

Fishhook twisted the worst of the snap-crackle-pops out of his body, hoisted his bag over one shoulder, shuffled to the edge of the road, and stopped dead in his tracks. A little kid stood on the other side of the road, staring at him, four or five he guessed by the height, dressed even shabbier than himself, in plain brown shirt and britches with legs and sleeves falling to the knees and elbows, with dirty bare feet. No, wait, hold up. That wasn't a kid. It was a fully grown, evenly proportioned adult, except only three or four feet tall.

Fishhook blinked, made sure he was seeing this right. "Hello?" he shouted. "Hey, what's up!"

The short fucker just kept staring, past Fishhook. When he looked around, another face peered out of the bushes, on the other side of the ditch. It was shaped like a human face, but it sure as shit wasn't human. It wasn't staring *out of* the bushes, either, but rather was *made of* them. Branches and leaves jutted and twined together, pressing against each other at just-so angles, so they formed a jaw, eyebrows and forehead. Knotty clumps formed the chin and cheeks, with the leaves from two parallel horizontal branches for lips, two budding pods that hung in twin hollows for eyes. The breeze drifted through the bush, fluttering the face so it moved, like it was talking to the short fucker across the road. When the air went still, so did the face.

Fishhook spun back around. The short fucker was gone. When he looked again, the bush still had a face. Plants could play tricks on the eyes at funny angles, sure, but such illusions usually faded once you looked closer. The more Fishhook looked at this one, though, the clearer he saw it. Its gleaming seed-pod eyes looked right back at him.

He shivered, muttered, "Well, fuck you too, then, you freaky bitch," turned, and hurried up the road, doing his best not to look off into the woods. He didn't want to see more plants with faces, or something even freakier.

At sixteen, Fishhook's birth-family had kicked him out of the house for being queer. Well, *kicked out* wasn't technically accurate. More like he'd left on his own, because his piece-of-shit stepdad would have beaten him to death for it otherwise. Since then, he'd found his brothers and sisters of the road and the rails, and he'd been to plenty of their funerals; all in nice, neat funeral parlors, with open caskets displaying serene, well-dressed, made-up mannequin-like young corpses, of boys and girls who'd died of overdoses, stabbings, shootings, beatings, or exposure. Anyone who showed up who'd known the departed—*really* known them—might think they'd wandered into the wrong place. More than once, Fishhook had wondered, when his time came, how many of his real friends would show up and ask, *Who the fuck is Ronald Fairbanks?*

Fishhook hadn't touched any drugs in months, yet ever since the solar storm, it seemed like the whole world had overdosed on bad acid. He hadn't seen any of the others in a while; Shipwreck, Scags, Skunk, Stonewall, old Boxcar, Abby, any of them. He usually caught up with folks on the rails, and he'd been avoiding trains like the plague lately. Where the trains still ran, folks said, those railroad bulls had cracked down, gotten twice as diligent and four times as mean. They didn't even bother to arrest you anymore, just beat you to death, lucky if they didn't pull a train on your ass first, and that's if the freaky people—the *things*—didn't catch you first.

Who the hell had Fishhook first heard about the *things* from? Skunk? Yeah, probably. Of course that crazy motherfucker would believe something like that. Except Skunk had never had that much of an imagination. The last time they'd ridden the rails together, though, he wouldn't shut up about *the people from another dimension who you had to watch out for now.* Then as the weeks passed, Fishhook heard more folks spouting the same shit...the same strange words and names...

Schomite. Spirelight. Crimbone. And finally, *High Natural.*

Since the solar storm, cell phone service had come back in some places, but WiFi was a thing of the past. That threw a wrench in anyone keeping up with anyone. The last time Fishhook had seen Abby, she'd mentioned she'd be in Chattanooga in a few weeks, visiting some cousins. If he'd kept track of time right, she should be there by now. So that's where he was headed.

When the solar storm happened, there'd been a lot of train wrecks, all at once, all over the country, along with plane crashes, prison riots, riots on the streets of major cities…Hell, some people claimed the military had turned on and eaten itself, which was why not even the National Guard had swooped in, to either save everyone or just fuck everything up worse. Nowadays, the back roads were the closest place left to safe. Chattanooga sounded too densely populated for Fishhook's liking, but if he could just get there and find Abby, maybe he could get his bearings. She'd given him her cousins' address. If he could just find her—find anyone he trusted who was left—then maybe…

Whenever he heard a vehicle whirring towards his back, he stepped a little further off to the side and stuck his thumb out. A few cars and trucks blasted past him. There were fewer of them these days, and hitching was always a crapshoot, more so in some parts of the country than others. Here in the middle of the damn Bible Belt, you got fewer motorists willing to take a chance on a dude with ratty dreadlocks, with ears and a face full of piercings, including a big septum ring, wearing a beat-up leather jacket covered in radical political buttons. To be fair, they had more reason than usual to be suspicious. Maybe they thought he was one of those *others*, never mind that he was five-five and weighed a hundred and forty pounds soaking wet, probably less by now.

Something big and clanking slowed to a stop behind him. He turned and saw a long, gray pickup with a rattling U-Haul trailer hooked to the back. Two people sat up front within the truck, which had a backseat in it, to Fishhook's relief. The U-Haul had a dinosaur painted along the side, advertising some resort out in California that probably didn't exist anymore. The truck pulled over onto the shoulder. Fishhook hurried up alongside it and yanked on the right rear passenger door. He found it locked. The front passenger window cranked down.

"Just a moment, son," crooned the driver. "Before we let you in…do a little dance for us. You know what I mean."

Until a few months ago, Fishhook would have gone, *You gotta be shittin' me.* A year or so back, he'd spent part of his winter on the streets of Manhattan. He was only half black, and usually passed for Caucasian. That hadn't stopped the NYPD pigs from pulling over to harass him for a laugh, to make him *do the chicken-dance.* For all the stereotypes about the North and the South, the racist bullshit he'd encountered in Tennessee had nothing on what he'd gotten from the New York pigs. Except he'd heard the driver's tone, and he knew that wasn't the issue here. He still froze up.

The driver leaned over towards the glove box. A knob turned and it dropped open. Fishhook heard a pistol cock. "You know what I mean," the driver repeated.

Fishhook's extremities tightened. His heart pounded while the edges of his jaw quivered with deer-in-the-headlights dread. He wanted to tell the driver to fuck off, wait for the next ride, but lately, that might still be an invitation to get his head blown off. He let his pack slide off his stinging shoulders, then he hopped like a bunny, waving his arms around like some poor bastard in a stupid costume spinning a sign outside a tax-return office.

"Okay, that's good enough. Well, go on now, Fran. Let the boy in."

The front seat passenger twisted around, reached back, and pulled the lock up.

Fishhook hoisted his pack, opened the door, climbed in, and tossed the pack across the other side of the long back seat. It smelled like a thousand years of stale dust and wood chips in there. It reminded him of his dad's truck when he was a little kid, before his mom had won the custody battle and hooked up with that right-wing scumbag who'd become his stepfather. Fishhook bit back on the urge to break down sobbing. His real dad had always been a kind man, fuck what his mom had told the judge. Would he have still been a kind man if he'd been around long enough to find out his son was a queer? Fishhook liked to think so.

He noticed another smell in here, like old rotten eggs. He fumbled around 'til he found the seatbelt strap, then buckled up. The driver up front looked absurdly small, almost a midget, coming up barely high enough to see over the dash. Fishhook remembered the other weird little fucker from earlier, but no, this guy was just a really short dude. He had big, pale, bespectacled bug eyes, with silky salt-and-pepper hair cascading from beneath a dark blue ball cap, around a narrow, weather-beaten, stubbly face. His jaw and cheeks had that sunken quality, from the bone-deterioration that happened after smoking too much meth. He wore a checkered green and white shirt, with sleeves that were too big around his gnarled, spidery hands. He put the pistol back in the glove box and returned both hands to the wheel. Next to him, there sat a woman with pasty, pillowy arms, beneath a sloping, wrinkly neck, supporting a wobbly head that looked too small for the rest of her, covered in pale, patchy, stringy hair. She smiled at Fishhook, showing off more black gaps and tortured red gums than teeth. Looking at the two of them side by side, Fishhook got the impression of an insomnia-crazed Kermit the Frog and a googly-eyed, lobotomized Miss Piggy.

The truck lurched back onto the lonely highway and sped off through this world that wasn't the world anymore. Fishhook only just now noticed a tiny ceramic crucifix dangling from the windshield mirror. *Great. Jesus freaks. Just my luck.*

"Sorry I had to scare you like that, son. I had to make sure. You understand."

"Make sure of what?" Fishhook got the gist, but he had to make sure too. There were a lot of versions of the story going around. Fishhook still didn't know what to believe, but someone else's ideas about it could mean the difference between life and death.

"That you're a man. That the bones beneath your flesh move the way a man's skeleton is supposed to move. That you don't *move* like one of the *abominations*."

"Yeah, I get it. A Crimbone, you mean."

The old guy nodded, keeping his eyes on the road. "What's your name, son?"

"Fishhook," said Fishhook.

"No it ain't," hiccupped the old bastard. "That's not your *real* name, is it?"

"That's what everyone who knows me calls me."

"But that's not the name your loving parents gave you, is it? It's okay. You don't have to tell me if you don't want to. My name's Norm. This is my wife Fran."

Fran looked back at Fishhook, gave him that infected, gappy smile again, and waved with a hand like a speckled, flesh-colored Mickey Mouse glove. "Hi!"

"Hi." Fishhook waved back, even though her high-pitched voice made his skin crawl.

"You want some coffee?" said Norm. "You're shivering like a leaf back there." He pulled a thermos from a drink holder and held it back.

"Yeah, that'd be great. Man, thank you so much!" He grabbed the thermos and unscrewed the cap. Steam wafted out. The first gulp burned his tongue. He almost gagged, then tilted the thermos, blew on the liquid's surface, and sipped slower. It tasted like shitty gas-station coffee, but he didn't care. The warmth flooding his veins reminded him what true relaxation felt like.

"Where are you headed to, son?" said Norm.

"I'm trying to get to Chattanooga. I've got a friend waiting for me there. Or at least she said she would be, before…well…all this craziness."

Norm nodded. "A girlfriend, then?"

Fishhook glanced at the cross dangling from the dashboard mirror. "Yeah."

"Chattanooga is on our way. The place used to be a good, God-fearing city. These days, though…I still own land up in the north, son. That's where we're going, where we hear things are still good. You and your girlfriend could come with us…"

"Maybe. I'll have to see what she wants to do."

'We'll be stopping in Rock Spring soon. This highway takes us straight through the center of it. Have you been to Rock Spring, son?"

"I don't think so."

"Lovely little town. God-fearing people there. At least I hope that's still the case. We'll have to stop for gas there. If the Lord is on our side, there will still be a gas station open. Amazing that there are still gas stations open anywhere, when you think about it, isn't it?"

"Yeah. Yeah, I guess it is."

"That's why people don't realize the end times are already here. They all expected it to happen at once. After the sky let the fire loose on us, you'd think that would be that, but no, it's still happening slowly. Lots of people still have electricity. They still go out to eat, would still go to the movies if there was anyone out in Hollywood still making them or shipping them to picture houses…act like this big old world keeps spinning on as always. But I take one look at you, boy, and see that you've seen it too."

Fishhook sipped more coffee from the thermos. "Yeah. Yeah, no shit, right?"

"You know, further down south, there is the town where I grew up. I courted and married Fran there." As if on cue, Fran looked back at Fishhook, smiled and nodded. Thankfully, she didn't open her mouth this time. Maybe that meant there *was* a god. "Fran and I here used to have a program, on the local radio station, talking of the word of the Lord. When the Lord unleashed the wrath of the sun, he spared our radio station, so we might continue to preach our ministry to whoever was still out there listening, right when more people needed to hear it than ever. Except the people no longer liked to hear us tell what the good Lord had to say. I was forced off the airwaves, for speaking the truth of our Lord. Even now, while society falls apart, people still find ways to tell themselves that our civilization has not already abandoned us. Soon, only one civilization shall remain…that of our Lord's making. That will be the Kingdom. It was censorship, plain and simple. People don't want to give up the evils they think define them. You can't be one of the drug-addicts, in *the Kingdom*. You can't be a fornicator in *the Kingdom*. You can't be one of the homosexuals, in *the Kingdom*."

Fuck, Fishhook couldn't get out of this truck fast enough. *The guy's being nice. So is his wife. He doesn't have to know who you are. No one's making you suck their dick for a hit, or anything like that. Count your blessings. It'll all be over soon enough.*

Fishhook also noticed that he really needed to piss. Damn, he should have done that back on the roadside. He tried to will the contents of his bladder further up through his abdomen, away from his aching dick. "Yeah, I know, right? Say, how far are we from…wait, which town, man?"

"Rock Spring. Just another mile or so."

Even with the windows up, the closer to Rock Spring they drove, the more something smelled like burning pork. It didn't exactly cancel out the rotten egg smell, but it made Fishhook pay a lot less attention to it. The truck rounded a bend, and he saw all those *little boxes made of ticky-tacky* buildings of downtown Rock Spring, Tennessee, nestled in the shadow of the Smoky Mountain ranges. Half the town was on fire, including a red caboose in what used to be the yard of the local historical society.

"Norm?" squeaked Fran. "What's going on? I don't like this."

"I don't like it either, hon. Just sit tight. Now what in the world…"

"We should turn around."

"We can't. This is our route to where we're going."

"So we can find another route! Come on, honey, we can find one that doesn't…"

"Doesn't what? Make us to look in the eye what the Lord hath placed before us? No, my dear, many are those who would avert their eyes, and look where that's gotten us."

"Man, seriously," said Fishhook, "listen to your wife. This is no good."

"You're speaking out of turn, young man. I don't recall asking—"

The nearer the center of town drew, the louder the screams echoed. Fishhook twisted around against the seatbelt in rising agitation. "Dude, look, I know when I'm in a bad place that it's time to get clear of, and this—"

"We will be clear of it soon enough. Now hush." The truck sped up.

Far ahead, a soot-covered woman ran screaming out of a burning municipal building. She tripped, fell, got back up and shambled a little, then sprinted across a big, green common-area lawn. What she ran from came from every doorway, alleyway and corner, converging towards her…bodies that *did* move with superhuman speed and agility, like they didn't have real human skeletons under their filthy, scarred skin. They weren't dressed like Fishhook or any of his old train-hopper buddies. Some of them weren't wearing clothes at all. They all looked like *those others*, some with the mottled, swirly skin folks now called *Schomite* or *Crimbone* or whatever, others with the gleaming, pearly, whiter-than-white elf-like builds of those called *Spirelights*. It didn't matter anymore. Some new master had united them, under a banner of rape, murder and plunder. None of the safeguards of so-called modern civilization were left to do shit about it.

The fleeing girl must have had a good thirty feet head-start. One of the Schomites stretched out its gnarly clawed hand and grabbed her, like time and space folded between them to close the distance. It tackled her to the ground, ripping her clothes off, its teeth tearing and worrying into the flesh beneath.

Something hit the side of Norm's truck. The whole world spun through the air…

~

Blood stung Fishhook's eyes. When he wiped at it, his arm screamed.

Oh fuck, oh fuck, don't let it be broken, don't let it be broken…

Shattered glass blanketed him like sharp snowflakes. Some of it stuck in his face and hands. Someone kept screaming. At first, he thought it was him, then he realized it was Fran. His jaw felt like someone had popped it off and stuck it back on upside down. All that came out of his mouth were huffs and grunts. The whole world screamed, along with every nerve in his body.

One of his eyes still more or less worked. Except every time he opened or closed it, he saw something different. There was Fran up front, shrieking and gyrating. Next to her, Norm stared blankly, over the steering wheel embedded in his chest. Through Norm's window, Fishhook could see the top of the police car that had broadsided them. The red and blue lights still spun and flashed while smoke rose from the mangled hood. One of the cops moved like a drunk toddler while he tried to pull his partner out of the wreckage. He was gray with ash, except where scarlet streamed from his scalp, down his side. The wrecked cop car wasn't the only siren blaring. It sounded like there were a lot of them, for miles around.

~

A grumbling *whoosh* sounded somewhere. Flames licked out of the edges of the twisted hood of the truck, small and pale at first, then dark with smoke, puffing out thicker and thicker. They leaked past the border of the shattered windshield, into the truck. Norm didn't appear to mind, probably because he was dead. Fran shrieked louder and thrashed furiously. Her seat rocked and banged against Fishhook's knees.

Fishhook tried to bolt, but his seatbelt held him in place. He tried to unbuckle it, then shrieked because he'd just used his fucked-up arm. Yep, it was definitely broken. *Shit!* He took a few deep, rapid, whistling breaths to get himself under control. His good hand shook as it found the button. The belt snapped and slithered away. When he tried the door handle, it refused to budge. The whole rig was twisted around him. He rammed the door with his shoulder. Bigger flames were filling the front seat. Fran squalled like a bobcat caught in a trap. Parts of her face turned red, bubbling up with welts full of boiling white pus It smelled a lot worse than the rotting-egg scent from earlier. Fishhook drew up sideways across the seat and mule-kicked the door, once, twice, thrice...

The hinges gave, so the cold air spilled in on him...

~

Concrete pressed against his shoulder, shoving chips of broken glass through his coat so they bit into his arm. Every time he thought he'd gotten the pain under control, it seemed, another part of his body moved funny, so his whole being lit back up with grinding, shrieking raw nerves. He smelled more burning buildings, more burning flesh.

I have to move. I can't, though. I don't want to. Why am I even conscious? Can't I just go back to sleep? Just let all this go away...

~

His eyes opened and closed, opened and closed...

Someone let out a furious howl. At first, Fishhook thought it was one of those things, closing in on him. Then a dark shadow passed overhead. He shifted sideways and tried to crawl under the truck, but the rising fumes sent him scuttling back the other way.

His eyes opened and closed, opened and closed...

~

Everything blurred in and out of focus. His fucked-up arm felt just as bad as before, but it seemed further away now. He got a grip on the next overturned car and pulled himself to his feet.

An echoing clash shook the earth, of metal striking metal...with a chime that reverberated through the concrete, beneath his feet, a sound that pulsed through his whole being. At first, he assumed it was another car accident, but that was wishful thinking. No, it was the clash of otherworldly matter against otherworldly matter…something that shouldn't even exist in this world, yet there it was.

When his eyes snapped back open, he saw the center of the town lawn. Two of those freaks had just slammed into each other, howling with elemental bloodlust. What the hell was Fishhook watching? This was nuts! It looked almost like a kung-fu fight in some Jet Li movie on TV, but the more his vision cleared, the more it looked like two wild animals ripping each other apart, quicker than the human eye could follow…both of them swinging long, curved blades of black metal, 'til one deflected the other's downward chop and sidestepped him with a diagonal slice. A meaty crunch sounded. The loser split open and hung in two directions like a blooming flower, his insides gleaming and gushing…*because another man had just chopped him in half like a head of cabbage, with a fucking sword. A sword made of unearthly black metal. Fuck!*

The winner righted himself, let out a joyous growl, then looked at the split-open body, which was somehow still standing. He gave it a boot to the ass so it fell over, spilling its insides across the grass. That's when Fishhook noticed the whole lawn alive with a melee from some other reality, an even weirder one than the last few months. Fishhook couldn't even tell who was on whose side…until the swooping shape descended…

Fishhook's eyes opened and closed, opened and closed…

~

More meaty crunches sounded, as blades cleaved through bones and organs, everywhere. From where he leaned, Fishhook still heard Fran shrieking. The burning truck wasn't that far away, still somewhere to his left. He was no badass, that was for sure—and now that he saw all those otherworldly mutant freaks hacking the shit out of each other in the distance, he realized he didn't want to be—but there was no way was gonna leave someone to burn to death like that, not if he could help it. He lurched, righted himself, hobbled halfway over to the truck. Then the heat of the blaze pulsed in his face, repelling him like a wall of pure, hot energy. Fran stopped screaming. Fishhook's guts turned to liquid and tried to fall out of his asshole.

Plenty of other folks kept screaming, people who lived around here, while the otherworldly marauders dragged them out of their homes and jobs, while they laid waste to the infrastructure. Big, greasy rednecks came out brandishing shotguns, pistols, semi-automatics, automatics, you name it. At first, they looked happy as pigs in shit to finally get a chance to act like the local militia against the invaders…until they started shooting, and it didn't do a squirt of piss worth of good, except to get the things' attention. Fishhook couldn't tell if the creatures moved fast enough to dodge bullets, or if the bullets just didn't hurt them. Either way, they swarmed in on the gunmen. Before Fishhook knew it, the shooting had stopped, replaced by more blood, guts, hair, teeth and eyeballs flying all over the place.

Out on the lawn, a strange sort of circle had formed. Somewhere in the middle of all this, Fishhook had gotten a sense of the two sides fighting each other. The ones who'd attacked the town were made up of both those dirty, animalistic freaks and those…pale, gleaming, whiter-than-white elf-like fuckers…*Spirelights*; that was the word for them, right? Except weren't those two sides supposed to be fighting each other? What the hell were they doing, ganging up on this town together? The ones who'd come to fight them all seemed to be the other kind, the beastly ones…*Crimbone?* It was like they'd swarmed in out of the hills, as though to defend the place…baited into a trap, apparently, one which must have worked, given how few of the latter were left, and by the way the leader strutted back and forth like a rooster in a henhouse.

Fishhook couldn't make sense of the leader's appearance. It looked like a cartoon animal version of Axl Rose or Kid Rock or one of those assholes, the cap of its head tied up in a dirty red bandana, but with a jutting, deformed snout like a dog's face, with big dragon wings fanning out on either side. And it was dripping in blood, from head to toe…blood, and who knew what other fluids.

"Okay," the creature's voice boomed, while it rubbed at its crotch, "this is where the Daddy told me to git shit rollin'. Can't tell why just yet. Place looks like a shithole to me. Still, I gots ta say, not a bad Goddamn start at all. Ain't that right, bitches? Why, just look at all these bitchass so-called Crimbone we got here to start replenishin' our ranks with." The creature cast an eye around, at the last of the gnarly defenders who'd been herded into the circle. "Why, it's almost like they all swam right up to our *fishhook*, ain't it?"

In that moment, it might have been Fishhook's imagination, but he swore the monster peered across the expanse and looked him right in the eye. That's when he quit pretending not to be a coward, when he booked it, quick as he could, back behind the nearest wrecked vehicle that wasn't on fire.

"Not as big a haul as we'd hoped for, but that's okay. Shit, this won't do at all. No, wait, let me check." A crunch split the air, followed by another shriek, along with a wet, ripping noise. "Gah, peh, these here Earth-line bastards an' bitches get more rancid every stop! Oh well, catch as catch can. Nah, nah, nah, boys, you take 'er easy with the good folks of this cute little town. The meat tastes better when you get it off the bones alive."

PART ONE:

WHAT'S LEFT OF

THIS WORLD

THE UNITED DESGHEMBINES

ONE

Janie traced the words across the dimly lit page. The building was so quiet that her sliding finger sounded loud enough to wake someone rooms away. Among this Deschembine crowd, she'd discovered, that wasn't an unreasonable worry. By now, she might be the last survivor of any other crowd. Funny to think, not so long ago, she hadn't thought there were so many *crowds* around.

Janie, the last Earth-line girl. All because a turncoat Spirelight Secret Police boy had a thing for her, and by whatever whim of the lands, he'd turned out to be a big deal in this whole mess. When the world fell apart, he'd grabbed hold and held onto her and this little floating sliver of a vagabond society that hadn't slid off into the abyss yet. It was better than being *Janie, one more dead Earth-line girl. He* made it better…most of the time.

Right now, she was a little less than halfway through the prong-bound volume, with its text that looked like it had been banged out on an old-fashioned typewriter with a spotty ribbon. Sheldon had given it to her back in Virginia. He'd presented it like a Valentine's Day card or fresh-picked flowers. At first, she'd liked that a lot. Sheldon didn't care about things like Valentine's Day. The way the world looked, maybe no one else would, either, ever again.

"I've skimmed it," he'd said. "It's a compilation of Deschembine history…of my people and the other Deschembine races in this world."

She'd flipped through it. To her relief, it all looked to be written in plain, dry English.

"I…well, anything that helps," he went on, shuffling his feet. "So maybe you'll feel more at home, the more you understand about us."

At the time, he hadn't mentioned that the book had belonged to Claudette. When he did, Janie had said, "You mean she wrote it?"

"Not exactly. More like she compiled and translated it. Most of what she was working from would've been…well, written from the perspectives of the different races."

"*Biased*, you mean."

"That's oversimplifying it, but yeah."

Janie's lips tightened. An *Earth-line* oversimplification, he meant, *because all those Earth-line people were just so stunted and ignorant about how things really are.*

"When did she give you this?"

"She didn't. I just found it a few hours ago."

"You went through her things?"

"Yeah. They're gonna seal her room, and we'll be leaving soon. I had to make sure to save anything potentially useful."

Something sank in Janie's gut. "I'm not supposed to have this, am I?"

"Not really, no." He kissed her cheek.

Her arms fell limp at her sides. "You're taking shit from your dead friend, without asking anyone. What are you gonna say if they find out?"

"I don't care what they think, and I don't wanna deal with their bullshit about it. We don't have the luxury of running a museum. That's why I snuck it out to you in secret. Get it?"

"Yeah? So what *do* you care about? 'Cause the longer I'm around your crazy ass, the more I wonder—"

He'd grabbed her by the shoulders and stared into her eyes. "You," he said. "I care about you."

In Spirelight culture, the bodies of the dead were disposed of without ceremony. The essence of the gods had left them, taking the individual essences, to blend as one with the gods in their pantheon. They laid the deceased's belongings to rest instead, everything the departed had kept and cared for in life, imbuing the items with their spirit.

"So why are we still here with them," said Janie, "the United Deschembines?"

"'Cause it's the best chance we have right now— some chance at all, to survive. They let us stay 'cause of some crazy messianic ideas they have about me and my sister. Oh, right, and I helped 'em win one battle. If it works for them, it works for me. That work for you?"

Janie had spent that battle locked in a basement while the slaughter raged overhead. To hear some folks tell it, it was Sheldon's strategic contributions that had almost gotten everyone killed. "Sure," she said. "That, and you have family here." *Some family still alive, anywhere.*

"Right."

"So are you gonna tell *her* about the book?"

"Sally? Yeah, maybe. Not just yet, though."

Janie wouldn't either. She wouldn't heap more stress on Sally if she could help it. She knew those weren't

Sheldon's reasons, though. He did the job these people had handed him, so that he and Janie could stay with them. If they didn't like how he got the job done, they were welcome to kiss his ass and leave him the fuck alone. That's how he saw it. His fellow Spirelights were the problem. He'd made that pretty clear to her. He harbored a latent, simmering scorn for them, particularly the ones who still tried to practice their faith reverently.

"Give 'em a break," she later tried to tell him, after some time on the road with everyone. "They're hangin' onto whatever they have left that keeps 'em going." She lowered her eyes. "They've got more left to believe in than me..."

"Since your mom, you mean."

"Yeah."

At that, he'd enfolded her into his arms and they'd stood there swaying, holding tight like a pair of orphans.

She almost got lost in the way he ran his fingers through her hair. Then he just had to go and say, "You know, the man who killed Annie was a *proper follower*, like these fucks here trying to hold onto all that old—"

At that, she pulled away and slapped him, hard. For a second, she saw his whole body flare with the instinctive violent reaction, bred into him by his upbringing since he'd been old enough to walk. He never let it out on her, but she still saw it, so she shrank away.

Sometimes when she glimpsed that side of him, she was ready to dump him on the spot. Except how did you dump someone when you were stuck together in the little cramped group trying to survive a world that looked more and more like a Goddamn *Mad Max* movie? *Could* she leave Sheldon if she wanted to?

When the tension cooled enough for them to speak, he said, "I was supposed to die when the beast stabbed me. The essence of Spirah left me like it was supposed to, but it left the rest of me in my body. Or I just hung on stubbornly and the essence went on without me, because I'd changed. Maybe it was the connection I'd made with you and Annie. The Spirah gods don't want their people forming connections like that with people outside the coterie, you know. Anyway, the gods can keep their divine essence. They can keep their fucking pantheon. All I want to join as one with is you."

They'd all left Virginia not long after that, in a battered old bus Zane had salvaged from a scrap yard or something. At least that's how Janie liked to think Zane had gotten the bus. You never knew with the Crimbone.

That had been late July. Now it was November or December. Or did anyone even still go by that old calendar? Claudette's book mentioned a Deschembine calendar, but there were no illustrations, so Janie had no idea what one looked like.

At least she knew it was three in the morning, thanks to the clock on the wall. Not even the wind blew outside, through the abandoned military base in Western Canada, where the United Deschembines had shacked up. Janie stared for a moment at the dull concrete floor of the barracks room they'd cleared for her. They'd left the desk and a stack of bunk beds. Only the lower half was ever used. The desk-drawers had been cleared of whatever the last soldier to sleep here might have left—*the last* Earth-line *soldier to sleep in this room*. Had that soldier kept a journal or anything? If so, Janie wished someone had left it behind for her. It would be nice to be able to read some Earth-line thoughts that weren't hers. The last Earth-liners to live in this room were probably dead.

By now, she was on her third or fourth reading of Claudette's book. Too bad Claudette hadn't left the biases in, tried a little harder to translate the true voices of where her people came from. Janie bet she could've understood a lot more than anyone gave her credit for. At least she felt a little closer to keeping all the different eras and important figures straight in her head. The book mentioned a lot of countries, continents, regions and landmarks from old Deschemb, with weird names like *Ghestruland, Wallutia, Valaka, the Razor Ranges*, in stories of people adventuring from one place to another, and almost no damn sense of where anything was, geographically, in relation to each other. Would have been nice to have a map, like in those fantasy novels she used to read in high school. She had a slightly better sense of how many years or centuries passed between the big events. At this rate, she ought to find a pen and paper so she could take notes.

She marked her place, then flipped ahead to the part about the earliest Schomites to *cross the great, black ocean*, from Deschemb to this world. Maybe she should start on more familiar ground, so to speak, and work her way back.

Apparently, a pair of Schomite sorcerers had met and realized their kind's days were numbered if they stayed in that world, so they gathered what wandering tribes they could and *led their followers to the farthest shores of the coldest land. Those who'd survived the journey looked out across a deeper, darker ocean than anyone had ever seen. Clouds hung low and black, like a stone ceiling that blocked the sky. On those shores, the tribes built their boats on the lands' instruction, then set sail across the dark ocean. At the end of their journey, they washed up on the shores of this world. The two sorcerers came ashore first, to commune with the spirits of the new land. They asked to negotiate their people's stay. The lands answered. The sorcerers gave up their own physical forms and fused as one with the native spirits, to speak to their people through this world, to teach them its language.*

That, Janie gathered, was who the Schomites meant when they spoke of the *Old Lords*. From there, the text went on for a while about how the Schomite refugees migrated and scattered, how they adapted to blend in with the native humanoids, how some groups intermingled more than others, how they'd combined the ancient knowledge they'd brought over with the tools of this world's people to build some glorious, mythic civilization the likes of which the world had never seen before or since. That had ended when the Spirelights showed up, out of the same phantom ocean, bent on giving this world to their gods as they'd tried to do to Deschemb, and the whole thing went crashing down, like…what, Atlantis or something? The text was just as vague about the geography here as that of Deschemb. So was any hint of just what phase of prehistory this had all happened in.

Christ, how was she supposed to feel *more at home*, by finding out more and more how everyone around her was full of so many extra senses and superpowers beyond her comprehension?

At these quiet hours, she could almost pretend the rest of the building was a house like the one she'd grown up in. The inhabitants of the town around the base must have run away scared when Crimbone fledglings stationed here had made their Second Calls and turned on the brass.

I keep telling you, Janikens, Mom always used to say, *you'll know everything you gotta know when you just watch, when you just listen. You'd see and hear all kinds of things you never thought could be there, but you listen to too much of the noise on the surface.*

"*Earth-line girl…*" The creeping hiss came from the door she hadn't heard open. She still seemed to feel the cold breath of the words on her neck and spine.

In the doorway, there stood the lurching, hollowed-out shape of a man who should have died in Virginia. In fact, everyone had thought at first that he had. Then someone managed to identify the barely breathing gob of meat hooked up to respirators in the infirmary under the Renaissance Kingdom. They'd found him under the corpse of the Spirelight Secret Policeman who'd died hacking him to bits. Before the attack, Claudette and Deacon had led the United Deschembines. Claudette had, alas, stayed dead. It was hard to argue with a severed head. Sheldon had told everyone he'd seen Deacon die. By the time the mistake was cleared up, Jesse and Zane had taken up leadership duties.

Now Deacon shambled into Janie's room. His left arm swung uselessly at his side, under a dank, leathery coat that made the uneven contours of his broken frame look like the twisted, moss-covered roots of a dead tree. His right leg dragged in a heavy brace that clunked and scraped across the floor. He must have made quite the effort to sneak down the hall to Janie's room.

She spun out of her chair and pressed her back to the desk. It made her feel stupid and weak, letting this broken creep scare her, which made her even madder. She straightened up and hardened her eyes. "What the hell are you doing in here?"

"What are you doing up, Earth-line girl?" His dead leg dragged forward, leaving little scrapes in the floor, no longer bothering to be quiet. His head lolled so his lopsided jaw almost touched his right shoulder.

He's not dangerous anymore, she reminded herself. Sure, she'd heard about what a badass he used to be. She'd also heard from Sally how stalwart he'd acted in front of the people who looked to him, how it was a different story once he got you alone, if you happened to have tits. Sally was a hardass who knew how to put a prick like that in his place. Janie wasn't. That didn't matter, she remembered as she stared at Deacon. He was just a broken, pathetic asshole who lacked the motor-functions to fend off a small dog.

"None of your damn business," she told him.

"Electricity's a luxury these days," he said. "We're lucky the generators power half this base. Maybe you shouldn't waste it."

"Tell me what you want or get out."

He scuttled towards her like a cockroach. Cold sweat cooled her. Taut strength still rippled through his extremities, even the ruined ones. He'd spent his life learning to use it violently, complete with augmented muscle and bone structure she lacked, and she was still a scrawny teenage Earth-line girl who didn't belong here. So maybe that made them equally matched now? She controlled her breathing, bared her teeth, and held eye-contact with him.

Deacon's half-dead face moved closer. His body sagged lower sideways, 'til he looked past her at the desk. His yellowy eyes widened. "Where did you get that?" he spat.

"What the hell's going on here?" There was no passion in the new voice, only steely authority, laced with cool sadism. Melting snow slicked the new shape in the doorway, from the short-clipped blond hair, around the pale, angular face and icy blue eyes, over the leathery black-blue duster coat, down to the tight, worn steel-toed boots. You'd never guess the shape belonged to a sixteen-year-old boy.

Deacon spun on his good leg. "You…you disrespectful little…"

The shape strode forward. "I asked you a question, you dickless fuck. You've got three choices: answer it, get out, or get beaten uglier than you already are."

Deacon shuffled away from Janie, but didn't get any closer to the shape in the doorway than he had to. He still stabbed out a crooked finger. "You…you're nothing but a reckless, ignorant monster. Yeah…a monster who calls a great woman his friend, then defiles her remains."

"Get off it, Deacon. It doesn't concern you."

"My friend's memory concerns me." Deacon's eyes watered. Something caught in his throat. "My friend's *faith*—"

The shape shot forward and locked a hand around Deacon's throat. Deacon's back slammed against the wall. His body stretched the straightest it had been since climbing off the infirmary cot. His feet dangled. He wiggled grotesquely. The tip of a pocketknife pressed into the soft, withering flesh under his chin.

Janie shut her eyes tight. There was Mom in their house back in Brattleboro, head thrown back with her neck yawning open and a lake of blood still spreading across the kitchen table. Janie opened her eyes and saw her boyfriend pressing that same knife—the one that had cut Mom's throat—against someone else's throat.

"*Sheldon, stop!*"

Sheldon dropped Deacon, closed and pocketed the knife, then looked at Janie. The blue eyes were softer now, recognizably human…if *human* was what you'd call him in the first place…what you'd call anyone within a hundred miles of here, except Janie.

Deacon lay against the wall like a clump of stiff, moldy rags. "You've never brought anything but ruin with you. Either of you."

Sheldon glared down at him. "I said get off it."

"Reckless, blasphemous, *destructive*–"

"I'm on my watch, and I just caught you harassing a resident in her private quarters. I catch you trying any more of that shit, I'll kill you."

"If I tell the others what you've stolen, from Claudette, what you've *given to your Earth-line*—"

Sheldon kicked Deacon in the ribs. "You make me wanna puke. *You're a fucking Schomite*, and now you wanna justify your sleezy sniffing over piety for *Spirelight beliefs?*"

"My friend believed, and I—"

"Your friend. Heh. You mean your boss who made smart use of your limited usefulness, which you're all out of. Save it. She was a deluded hypocrite. So are you. It's your kind of thinking that'll kill our chances at survival. You spout all that shit about how we're *not abandoning our coteries and heritage, but moving them forward.* Wake up! Those coteries and heritages are what's fucked us in the ass this whole time. Just like the gods behind them. Now get out."

Deacon scuttled backwards into the hallway like a crab. "Born of the Spirelight Secret Police…*That's what you still are,* one of the Secret Police, you and your sister. The Crimbone and the Secret Police, *that's* what's fucked us. You're the one who's out to finish the job, just like I tried to tell Claudette."

~

Sheldon slammed the door and heard Deacon drag himself away. Maybe the bastard would crawl outside to hide in the dark and freeze to death. No, Sheldon wasn't that lucky.

He turned back to Janie. "You okay?"

"I'm fine."

He hugged her tight then eased up when she didn't hug back. "What's wrong?"

"What do you think?"

"Right. Look, he won't bother you again. I'll—"

"He saw the book."

"So let him tell whoever he wants. Anyone who makes a stink about it, they'll get the same treatment he just did."

"Right. Just like anyone who *makes a stink* about anything you do, huh?"

"Well, yeah. Look, I can get away with shit like that now. We've got a good thing going here like that. Gotta take an upshot where we can find it these days, right?"

"So when do you start giving me that kind of treatment?"

"Why would you even say that? Look, don't worry about what he saw. Jesse and Zane are the only ones fit to do anything about—"

"And your sister."

"What about her?"

"You answer to her, too, don't you, like you do Jesse and Zane?"

"I said don't worry about it! Me and Sally are on the same page. Jesse and Zane won't give a shit. Hell, I'll tell 'em myself, how I kicked Deacon's ass—"

"Right, sure, *laugh it up over some beers*, about how you beat up a miserable cripple. Big tough men."

Sheldon had to grit his teeth for a second. Apparently, there was nothing he could say that she wouldn't twist around, like she *wanted* him to turn out to be just like all those asshole Earth-line boyfriends who'd treated her like shit. Maybe she'd find that comfortably familiar, in some sick way.

Instead, he said, "I'll do whatever I have to do to keep you safe." He ran his hand up and down her back. "Please, trust me."

"I do," she whispered. "So do the rest of these people here. It's not just me you're supposed to be protecting. You can't abuse that power, even for me."

"You're the only reason I'm doing this."

"No, I'm not. Otherwise, you'd find some other way." She turned, closed the book and held it out. "Here, take this back. I don't want it to cause more trouble."

He pressed her grip more firmly around the binding. "Keep it. Keep reading. Keep learning."

"That's what I've been in here doing, and yeah, I *have* been getting an idea about your heritage, and I *do* respect…"

"Claudette would want to keep doing good for this group...real, *practical* good, with what she left behind—"

"Is that why you just called her a deluded hypocrite?"

"Look, if I'd respected that old custom, this book would be rotting in a sealed room, under an abandoned amusement park." He stroked Janie's cheek. "What I do for them is for them. What I do for you is for you...for *us*. So is it okay if I stay in here for a little while and pretend all that out there doesn't exist?" He nuzzled his face in her neck while his hands glided up her back, beneath her shirt.

"That'd be good." She lifted her arms, pulled off her top, grabbed his hands and pressed them against her breasts.

Tensions around here had just gotten worse as word from elsewhere trickled in. Not all of the United Deschembines acted so willing to stay united. What food or supplies anyone had, had been scavenged or stolen from elsewhere, so it hadn't taken long for people to start stealing from each other, or worse. Plus there were still a few Earth-line people running around in the area, scared crazy with no idea what was going on, and some of them had guns. So Sheldon and Sally took turns patrolling the base and the surrounding hamlet, using their detection skills as former Secret Police to sense out situations, hopefully before they got out of hand. Most days and nights, one of the siblings worked while the other slept— or in Sheldon's case, stayed with Janie. That only involved as much sleep as she wanted. Jesse preferred that only one of them—Sally or Sheldon—be in harm's way at a given time. Jesse wouldn't have inherited Claudette's belief in Sheldon and Sally's significance, except that he saw how important they were to the people. Helping folks hold it together was everything. Sure, Sheldon got that.

Tonight, though, there'd been word of trouble in a town several miles out. Jesse and Zane had gone with that

Crimbone fledgling that followed them around, along with a few others. Sally had insisted on joining them. Sheldon didn't worry for her, any more than he did for Jesse and Zane. He just stood here with Janie, the two of them holding and rocking each other gently back and forth, their body-warmth holding off the blistering cold that seeped in.

Janie shoved off Sheldon's coat and ran her palms up over his scrawny, gnarled chest, beneath his dingy shirt. Against his hips hung two large, curved knives in shimmering scabbards, completely unlike the knife he'd threatened Deacon with, even older than the black metal of Jesse and Zane's weapons.

He remembered when Janie had taken him home for the first time when they were kids. He'd pulled a rusty old machete from a tin vat in her back yard, started going through motions with it. She'd teased him for playing like a little kid, had called him Sir Lancelot, though even then, she'd sensed he wasn't playing around at all.

Now he squeezed her ass and pinched her nipple while she gnawed on his neck. She undid his belt. The long knives thudded on the floor, along with his coat. She kissed him with deeper hunger, a little violently. They sure weren't kids anymore.

TWO

A forward-curved serrated blade licked out of a winter coat, through misty night air. It punched, slid through muscle, sawed a rib in half and speared a heart. When it hissed out, a pulsing, misting squirt chased after it. The corpse fell sideways with a numb thud. The man still standing was Crimbone. So was the dead guy—just meat now, no glow to drink. A guy had attacked him, so his black blade had turned living meat into dead meat. Mister Deadmeat's black weapon crumbled to ash, floated and sank into the blood and snow.

*One more ghost for the ghost-town…*A few such ghosts had checked in tonight, some Spirelight, some Crimbone, a civilian Schomite or two, the odd Earth-line straggler. One of them had been a Crimbone fledgling. Even in this icy gale, the smell left Jesse Karn a little nauseous.

Howling winds drowned most noises, but Jesse still heard the cocking shotgun as though the barrel was right at his ear. His bulk shifted in time with the tightening trigger. The blast shredded the left flap of his coat. He spun and sprang, clearing the snow-choked road in three lightning-fast strides. A fresh shell pumped into the chamber. The Earth-line man must have held out here for months. Now he crouched between two buildings and aimed again. Jesse closed the distance. His blade reappeared as the trigger tightened again. The blade made two clean strokes and blood jetted between arms and shoulders. The arms thumped like logs in the snow. The shotgun sailed up out of the dead fingers and struck something just right, so it went off. The shot boomed out. Flecks of wood sprayed from a building and bounced off the back of Jesse's bald, scarred head. He swept the blade down again, completing a single motion, splitting the man in two.

Jesse wiped his knife clean before sheathing it. You never had to clean the black metal after killing Spirelights. You just sheathed it and let the metal drink up the blood. That's how you kept the black metal strong, supple and sharp, as the glow did the same for your body and soul. If you killed anything else with the black metal, you'd best clean it, or it would rust and get dull, same as a normal blade. There'd only been a few glows in this rabble.

Jesse walked out of the alley. A female Spirelight ran at him, solidifying as the frosty mist fell away behind her. To any normal eyes, she'd look like nothing more than a bundled, hooded scrawny girl-shape hurrying through the snowy wind, incongruous in her death-strewn surroundings, save for the homemade spear clutched in her gloved hand. The spear was forged from an iron pipe and a foot and a half of razor-edged carbon steel. Someone's insides soaked the blade, running down over where it was bolted to the pipe, so it pooled on the top of her gloved fist. She skidded to a halt several feet from Jesse. He sighed and shook his head. He knew she could control that brandished weapon, but he was still glad when it stopped shy of his face.

"What the fuck are you still doing here?" he growled. In the shadows of early dawn, his eyes gleamed like spinning coins.

"Making sure the van's running and no one comes along and tries to strip the fucker."

"You were supposed to take off in it."

"I heard a gunshot. Who—" She spotted the armless corpse. "Oh. Where's Zane?"

"Around here somewhere. Get back to the van and take off."

"Why? Everyone's dead. We should see how much good looting's left."

"Maybe. First, I'm gonna find Zane and we're gonna see if we can figure out who these assholes were and what they were doing here. You drive back to the base and check on Sheldon."

"How the hell are you supposed to get back?"

"There's gotta be something around here we can hotwire."

"What's the point? We both know damn well, the only *danger* Sheldon's facing right now is being the first Spirelight on record to knock up an Earth-line girl."

Jesse shrugged. "My son's mother was an Earth-line woman."

"That's different. It's Crimbone—" She flinched. "Sorry. I didn't mean—"

"Yeah, you did." He shrugged.

"Stop that shit!"

"What?"

"Always assuming I'm *thinking like a Spirelight*, that I'm judging you the way—"

He growled out exasperation. "We really gonna talk about this here?"

"We just agreed everyone's dead, right?" She glanced around, to make sure. "So yeah. Get it through your skull. I don't think like that. I just think like me."

"Yeah. You do." *And last I checked, you're a Spirelight.* Jesse knew better than to expect countless ages of religious and cultural conditioning across two worlds to just go away in one person, no matter how unique they thought they were. This young crowd these days sure thought they were something special.

She wasn't wrong, though, about looting the place. The base was good on rations at the moment, but they could never be too well supplied. There weren't many hunters in the group, nor was there enough local game to feed everyone, especially this time of year. Jesse, Zane, Crawler and Sally had taken to scouting out and raiding any nearby towns they could find. Funny enough, they hadn't found this one 'til tonight. Crawler's Familiar had showed up with the news of trouble to the east. They'd piled into the van and followed the creature as it soared between the treetops ahead of them, 'til they found themselves here.

Another shape darted up the street, opposite the way Sally had come. This one was tall and broad and bald like Jesse, black as the snow was white. Gore and bits of splintered bone clotted the head of the spike-capped battle-hammer in his left fist. "Where's Crawler?"

"Dead," said Jesse.

"How?" asked Zane.

"A small hemorrhage."

"The words *small* and *hemorrhage* don't go together, man."

The news of the death of one of their own hung heavy over all three of them. Sally finally said, "Who else bets the name Balthazar goes with this shit?" She waved her spear at the seeping heaps that darkened the white street in spreading pools.

Those attackers had once been Crimbone, Schomites and Spirelights, but they hadn't been any of those things for a long time, or anything else recognizable. Jesse didn't have a word for the surgical mutilation that had refashioned them. "How'd you guess?"

Sally thumped the butt of her spear against the ground. "So why were they here? We're that way." She cocked her head at the road leading back to the base town.

"They weren't after us," said Zane. Jesse and Sally both looked at him in confusion. He gestured for them to follow.

On their way sat the red van with a massive snowplow blade rigged to the front. Zane yanked on the ice-crusted handle so his door crunched open. He snatched the jug of liquor they'd been passing around earlier. He took a deep swig, felt the liquid warm his throat and guts, then held out the jug for Jesse and Sally. A shrill scream of burning rubber shredded through the stillness. Jesse and Sally sprang backwards onto the sidewalk. The headlights of a pickup truck closed in.

A drawn-out nasal hoot sounded, *"Time for some Dessembeen roadkill, motherfuckers!"*

Zane growled irritably and ran at the headlights like he was playing chicken. His arm cocked back. The jug sailed through the air and collided with the windshield. Both shattered in a shower of glass. The truck spun out of control, then flipped and plowed into one of the abandoned storefronts. A booming thunderclap rolled from the demolished porch like a shockwave. Twisting metal and snapping wood shrieked and barked. Zane trudged into the cloud of sawdust and splinters that mingled with the snow. The driver had come halfway out, on his back, spine and guts crushed at the waist between the truck and the porch boards. Half his face was too much of a mess to tell if the left eye was still there. The other eye widened, swollen and bloodshot. He gurgled red foam. Zane's hammer swung down like a croquet mallet, splattering the skull across the porch.

It never stopped weirding Jesse out, hearing Earth-line people more or less speak Old World language. Sheldon's Earth-line girlfriend was the one exception, he guessed. It helped that she'd never tried to kill him.

Jesse and Sally sprang off the porch. "You asshole," Sally shouted at Zane, grinning. "That's alcohol abuse!"

Another, fainter noise drew them all up sharp. The grim humor bled from Sally's face. A chorus of dragging feet came from the direction in which Zane had been leading them. Some of those feet were trying to run. It wasn't happening. Zane motioned for Jesse and Sally to stay cool. Apparently, he'd found some friends, about a dozen of them. In the first faint glow of morning, the approaching figures grew hazy gray outlines. They still had that special spring in their step, the kind you don't find in Earth-line bone structures. They were all torn clothes and bloodshot eyes, splotchy bandages and gimp legs. Sally hung back. Her face turned to stone and her spear shifted in her grip. Jesse didn't blame her, no matter how broken down these unknown Crimbone looked.

Jesse peered harder at the man and woman in the lead. He could see more of their faces than the rest, partly because they were closer through the mist, partly because they were less bundled up than the others, like they'd given some of their clothes to the less hardy of their number. Then he recognized their hard, bright young eyes within sunken, element-hardened faces. It had been five months since he'd seen them. By the look of them, it might have been twenty years.

"Sam?" he shouted. "Anya?" He trotted towards them.

"Who's that? Is that Jesse Fucking Karn?" That hadn't come from Sam or Anya. It came from a yellow-skinned Crimbone man with a high, shrill voice. Dredded white hair fluttered around his face from beneath his hood as he shoved forward.

Jesse glanced at Zane. "Why'd you make it sound like the fighting was done?"

"Hear 'em out, man," said Zane.

"Sure, just give this one a sedative first." Jesse pointed at the white-haired Crimbone.

Zane looked from Jesse to the upstart. "Looks like you two assholes are already getting along better than ever."

"We'll get along fine," Jesse growled, "soon as he goes back and tells the Cabinet to go fuck itself."

Zane sighed and rolled his eyes. "Damn. Now I wish I still had that jug."

Sam Cash stepped up, past Byron. "No one's here from the Cabinet." His voice was deep like Jesse remembered it, though raspier, with less of the no-

nonsense, cocky stoicism of youth. "There *is* no more Cabinet. There's Balthazar."

"Fuck," Jesse muttered. It was a lot easier to keep his cool, now that Byron wasn't the one in his face. It was also harder, because someone had mentioned Balthazar. "Guess that answers the question who those other assholes were after."

"Yeah, we made it two months without a run-in with 'em," said Anya. Her words slurred sleepily, though she held herself steely as Sam through the shivers. It wouldn't do, to let those they led see how close she was to falling flat on her face. "I'd really started to think we lost 'em."

"That's probably what they were waiting for," said Zane

"Yeah," said Byron. "Sorry to crash your party with our shit."

"You ain't, yet," said Jesse. "How widespread is it?"

"Far as any word comes or goes these days," said Byron. "How far out of the loop are you guys?"

"About as far as we could get. That was sort of the—"

"How long have you guys been hiding in this frozen shit?" Byron yelled. "What did you do, decide to get off the trail and hide someplace so godawful no one thinks you're worth a squirt of piss bothering over?"

"For right now, yeah, pretty much," Zane answered before Jesse could. "Figure by the time this shit thaws out, we'll have something better in mind than waiting around for Balthazar to come out of nowhere and stomp us into sludge."

Jesse didn't have to look to feel Zane's eyes on him. Since they'd staked their ground, Jesse's focus had been on holding it. The longer the stasis held, the more fidgety Zane got.

Sam stepped up. "What do you know so far?"

Byron pointed at Sally. "Looks like they're keeping Spirelights with them, for starters. Arming them, too, no less."

Sally and her spear only twitched a little.

"We finish playing catch-up after we get out of this fucking cold?" said Zane.

"How you wanna do that?" screeched Byron. "Stuff us all in that van of yours? You two assholes still rattling around in that heap…you and your Spirelight bitch you saw fit to arm?"

Zane stepped close to Byron before Jesse or Sally could react. "Look, you don't like them, and they don't like you. While we're being honest, I've never much liked you either, but fuck all that for now. Cool? *Cool?*"

"Yeah," Byron finally said. "Cool. Didn't you say something about finding some damn warmth?"

Zane climbed the porch of the storefront next to the one with a truck in it. He swung his hammer through the deadbolt and knob. The door swung on its hinges. "Figure there's someplace to build a fire in there."

The crowd drifted towards the door. Nostrils flared as they passed the squashed corpse with the shattered skull. Some of them actually bothered to glance at it. Many nostrils were too clogged and crushed to smell anything, which to a Crimbone felt worse than blindness. No wonder most of them moved like they *had* gone blind, or were suffering from some kind of brain damage. Sally kept to the fringes, legs braced, gripping the spear with both hands.

"It's okay," Sam said in Jesse's ear. "We all know who she is."

Jesse figured Sally overheard. He looked at her anyway. She nodded in a way that told him she had her shit together. He looked at the arrivals. Only Byron, Sam and Anya even seemed aware of her. The others looked so worn down and hazy, it was a miracle they figured out what direction to stumble in. Sally followed everyone onto the porch, but not inside. She stood by the door like a sentinel, her spear more or less relaxed. That was probably best, Jesse figured; no sense inviting the bull into the china closet. Not to mention, when folks inside weren't talking about Balthazar, they'd talk about Rob. Sally didn't need that right now, not with her duties to focus on. Neither did anyone else, frankly. Jesse went in, hopefully to make the best of matters.

If Rob Coscan hadn't made a name for himself first, people might think the thing called Balthazar *was* the High Natural…especially since the real High Natural had dropped off the map.

Jesse hadn't expected to miss Rob Coscan. The damn kid was a war criminal, simple as that. In the ancient feud between the Crimbone and the Spirelight Secret Police, qualifying as a *war criminal* took some effort. Rob had gone above and beyond. Jesse would still have preferred Rob Coscan to Balthazar, as the threat everyone now had to think about.

Jesse glanced at Sally. So what must she think by now, about Rob? It wasn't a matter of how she *felt* about him. That was obvious. She still loved the sonofabitch. Those two crazy kids had spent five years happily married, Jesse gathered…happy as anyone could be, stuck together, hiding from the world in the most secluded backwater Florida shithole of a town they could find. Then someone had found them anyway and abducted her. Rob had stepped back in amongst his own kind, stepped up to the role he'd been groomed for, and led them on a genocidal rampage in the name of rescuing his lady love. Stupid fucking kids. That had something to do with how shit had spiraled out of control, into the world everyone lived in now. Jesse had stopped trying to puzzle out the blame. He just had to keep his little band alive. So now here was Sally, side by side with him and Zane in this ugly new world. Where the hell was Rob? No one knew.

How you feel about someone and what you rationally realize about them are two different things. Lately, though, something in Jesse's blood kept pulling Rob Coscan to mind. Jesse would probably hear about the kid soon…hopefully before he met Balthazar face-to-face.

Not everyone even agreed that Balthazar was Crimbone. Some people claimed, he not only fought with the black metal, but had fused it with his body. Others said he was some kind of reptile-man or Frankenstein-monster. The latter suggestion jumped quicker to Jesse's mind, considering the state of the guy's minions. It depended on who you asked, whether he was a dwarf or a giant. Either way, he sounded not so much like a wielder of weapons as one big weapon himself…a fearless, relentless, *thinking* weapon that dropped it like a bomb wherever he appeared. Then he vanished. Within hours, he'd show up hundreds or thousands of miles away, wash-rinse-repeat. He mostly targeted Crimbone and Spirelight Secret Police encampments. Civilians caught in the radius didn't often walk out.

Between the solar flare and the mass awakening of fledglings, most high-tech modern military threats had been nipped in the bud. Balthazar had finished off any stragglers there. Obviously, bullets didn't stop him. He liked to whittle the field to half the best fighters, then beat them into submission. After breaking his alpha-rivals bodily, he had them taken prisoners, awaiting his torture. From there, he finished off their minds and set to refashioning them, inside and out. They next appeared wherever he did, in ever greater numbers. If you met Balthazar, your best hope was that he *allowed* you to die fighting. He never chose higher numbers than he could handle. *What he could handle* grew while civilization shrank. His scattered minions must be pushing into the thousands by now. That was just on this continent. Overseas communications had grown spotty to say the least, especially since the Internet went away.

Zane once mused over drinks how Balthazar had done more for getting Schomites and Spirelights to work together than the United Deschembines ever had. They'd first heard of Balthazar two months after the shit hit the fan in Virginia. That's when the world started doing somersaults, or at least when everyone started noticing.

In a funny way, the United Deschembines had probably saved Jesse and Zane's lives. Without the big happy family to look after, what else would they have done? Go back to sniffing for Rob's trail 'til Balthazar caught up with them? Defending spoiled rich assholes from what they had coming to them, in the name of Earthline "tolerance"? Indeed, this rocky, icy waste had kept them out of sight and out of mind, 'til tonight.

THREE

This building they'd broken into turned out to be a spacious secondhand shop. Zane dug out a table, chairs, and finally some candles. Once everyone was gathered, he said, "How many more of Balthazar's troops are on your tail?"

Anya Summers ran a hand back through tangled, graying hair that had been bright red and straight five months ago. "That's the last of 'em we've seen, and you haven't even had a look at 'em in daylight yet. They first hit us all the way back in Virginia."

"How long ago?" asked Jesse.

"After you left, the land felt right to everyone, as a place to hold out 'til there was something else to do. We'd have just hit roadblocks any direction we went anyway, so why not camp out for a while, right?" She smirked bitterly.

"No more direct trouble from Earth-line law?" said Zane.

"Not as bad as you'd think. We had some luck striking up good relationships with the local Earth-line civilians. Only Crawler didn't stick it out. He decided to try to catch up with you guys."

"He did," said Jesse. "He was doing well, 'til about twenty minutes ago."

Sam and Anya both nodded, understanding. "Not long after Crawler made it out," said Sam, "some stragglers slipped in. I guess we're still a little prettier than those guys. They told us the first stories of Balthazar. Then the winds started sounding different through the tree leaves—that dissonant whistle you hear trees make now, right, when they really don't like the wind blowing through 'em? Turned out, they meant to tell us Balthazar was on the way."

Jesse and Zane exchanged a short, sharp look. "How'd you get away?" Jesse asked.

Sam's face sank and paled, like a man's will when he's about to say something he's not proud of. "Anya and I were the first Crimbone on record to make both the Second and Third Calls at once, right? The way Balthazar recruits, we knew he'd be coming for us. We decided not to hand him that asset."

"So you ran," said Zane. "Got it. I hate to say it, but we should all probably say thanks."

Sam continued, "About half our pack decided to stay and fight. Who knows, someone might get in a lucky stab, right?" He shook his head. "Anyway, Balthazar didn't follow us, but we kept running into his creatures along the way. Whatever vehicles we could hotwire kept not lasting long, so we've spent a lot of miles on foot. Then we met up with Byron and his boys and girls."

"These are all my guys," Byron said. He shot a look at Sam and Anya. "None of theirs survived."

"Byron, shut the fuck up," Jesse said.

Byron sprang to his feet. "Yeah, so let's hear it from you guys, before you start barking orders. According to Sam and Anya here, you found the High Natural like you were supposed to, then you let him slip. Again. Last I heard, you were out bumming it with the folks you were supposed to help him kill, the ones who provoked that corpse-orgy that clusterfucked Virginia."

"We only got there for the tail end of it." Jesse smiled humbly.

"How many are in your group?" said Byron.

Jesse was about to say *None of your business, asshole*, then Zane said, "About fifty, I think. Hard to keep track. There was less than twenty when we left Virginia. We picked up more along the way. A lot of them have died since."

Byron looked at the door, which someone had propped shut with a block of wood. "No one told me the tainted Spirelight girl was still with you."

Jesse leaned back. "You know, Byron, when you guys came through the mist, I saw Sam and Anya in the lead, with you sniffing their asses."

"Do you wanna step outside, Jesse Karn?"

Jesse grinned wide enough to swallow the room whole. "Why Byron, I thought you'd never ask."

Zane got up and clamped a hand on Jesse's shoulder. "Forfucksake, Jess, look at the man! At least wait 'til he's fit to tangle. Byron, sit your yellow ass the fuck down."

"Get it out of your systems while you can." The haunted, almost trancelike voice was Anya's. "Expect a lot more like us coming this way, too…whoever's left…"

"What, you mean to our little home sweet frozen shithole?" said Zane.

"Isn't that why you're here? Be glad it's frozen, while it lasts. Balthazar's not the only thing we have to worry about. 'Cause once the ground thaws and drinks up all the blood the melting snow's been saving for it…I'm not looking forward to what'll sprout and bloom from the lands by then."

Jesse and Zane exchanged looks. By a scan of the other weary, haunted faces, it was obvious the girl wasn't just talking crazy. Even Byron's bravado drained from him, now that she'd reminded him of whatever they'd all seen out there.

"Okay," said Zane. "Jesse, Sally's probably freezing her ass off out there, chipped shoulder and all. I'm getting hungry enough to eat that dead trucker's splattered brains, and I don't wanna think how long it must've been since these guys last ate. Now that we're out of the cold, though, my nose is thawing out, and some of those festering wounds of theirs stink almost bad enough to kill my appetite."

Jesse stood up and nodded. "You're right, brother. Let's go find some food and medical supplies."

~

Jesse stepped out onto the porch. Sally wasn't where he'd left her. His eyes darted everywhere. She came so silently from the right, he almost didn't spot her. Through all the snow and mist, he knew it was her because of the spear she carried.

"Relax," she said, "nothing came out of the dark and ate me. Figured I'd load some goods up in the van. Did you come out here just to check on me?"

"Guess I did."

"Asshole."

"Yeah. Any supplies left around here still good?"

"Oh, yeah. I ain't been wastin' time."

"Good. Let's go check for any you missed."

"You wanna take a look in the back of the van first." She cocked her head sideways.

Jesse followed her. Along the street, the icy air kept all the corpses from smelling too bad. Fresh snow already layered all the red spatter. Sally pulled open the van's rear doors so the overhead light cut on. Across the bare metal floor, to the right of several boxes of canned food, pasta, and any other food that would still be good, there lay a shape wrapped in tarp, like a giant blue burrito with something dark, hairy and juicy sticking out of one end. Something rolled up and down in Jesse's throat.

"One of Balthazar's…things," Sally said. "We've seen 'em up close now—well, more or less, in the dark and all. Now's our chance to dissect one."

"*Dissect* it?"

She shrugged. "Any better idea about 'em can't hurt."

And she hates being reminded that she's still a Spirelight. Jesse couldn't help smiling. The hills had just damn well better let them reach the base before the fucker thawed. "You can stash that, now." He nodded at the spear. "Got a sidearm handy?"

"I have a pocketknife." She tossed the spear in next to the tarp.

"When did you get another one of those, anyway?"

"Took it off a dead agent back at the Renaissance Kingdom." That's where the spear came from, too. She'd taken it off the corpse of the same renegade who'd kidnapped her in Florida. It was heavy enough that she'd doubled her arm strength and coordination, just practicing with it.

They started on towards the buildings she'd raided. "Whatever happened to your original pocketknife?" he asked. "The one your parents gave you."

"You took it away from me."

"I did? When was that?"

"The first time we met. I had a concussion, and I tried to slit your throat 'cause I thought you'd come to rape and murder me."

"Oh, yeah. Time flies, huh?"

"Sure does. Got any ideas what we're supposed to do with this vagabond Crimbone pack?"

"Don't worry, we ain't giving any of 'em a lift back to the base."

"Damn right, we're not. So what are we doing with 'em?"

"Making sure they're set to see to their own wounds and fend for themselves here for a while."

"You mean let them set up here like we're set up at the base."

"If they decide to. They don't have wheels, and none of 'em will be up for following the snow-plow tracks on foot any time soon. 'Sides, if the lands let any outsiders find their way through Zane's maze, that's some serious love-at-first-sight."

Calling the roads back to the base a maze was no metaphor. When Zane had first rigged the van with the plow, Jesse had grumbled, "Great, why don't you just put out road-flares leading straight to us?" Zane had grinned, gunned the engine, and taken them on a special twenty-square-mile drive surrounding the base. He'd seemed weirdly picky about which back roads he did or didn't take, which he joined with off-road trails, which he'd follow then turn around halfway. That had taken all day. When he was done, he'd said, "Okay. Now get out and take a walk along the roadside in any direction. Go on. See if you don't get lost. Try it."

Jesse had tried it, and it was true. Only certain folks at the base had been trained on the subtleties of finding your way in and out of a Crimbone-carved maze, or how to maintain it with all the right detours in or out.

Sally now said, "So you don't trust 'em, but you're sentimental enough not to leave 'em to die."

"Byron I know not to trust. Sam and Anya...I wanna say they're on the level. We need 'em, either way."

"Hows that?"

"Sam let on more than he realizes. Reason they've kept ahead of Balthazar so long is he knows how to hear the air warning him about an attack. Between him and that cadaver you scored, this looks like one profitable little jaunt."

They reached a store awning where the letters still spelled *General Store*, almost legibly. They scrounged out anything left that Sally or other scavengers hadn't picked clean. Jesse had a Bunsen-burner setup in the van they could cook with. They'd stop and grab that.

On the way back, Jesse said, "What we talked about earlier...about how you're worried I see you, with your Spirelight heritage and all..."

"It's cool." Sally stared forward and walked a little faster. "So what about the Spirelights back at the base?"

"They're the people I'm looking out for. That makes 'em my people."

"But a Crimbone's people are Schomites, and you defend them from Spirelights. Last I checked, by killing Spirelights."

"Check again," he said. "That was some other world."

LOUISIANA

ONE

Louisiana's main roads and highways were still too active these days. So were the deep swamps. This piney stretch of back roads worked just right, though. The old motel was mostly empty, dark except for the oil lamps that glowed in the windows of Room 28, so the woman pinned to the bed could scream as loud as she liked. Her nails dug into the scruff of the man's neck and tore his back apart, which just drove him crazier.

The last time she'd tried getting him in bed, he'd thrown her against a wall, though not in the way she'd had in mind. For a while, that had been that, no matter how often she spied him eyeing her in the right way…until tonight.

As they settled together, he cradled her and stroked her hair with a gentleness she'd forgotten he could show. She held him inside her for as long as she could, scared to wake up from this dream. Her body relaxed into a limp quiver. He slid out and collapsed next to her. She lay her head on his chest and snuggled closer, stroking the scars of wounds she'd stitched. He rubbed her shoulder. His other thumb brushed hair from her face and stroked her eyebrows.

She purred and rubbed her cheek against his bristly chin, drifted in and out, then asked, "So what brought that on?"

He grumbled. His arms didn't so much hold her anymore, as just sort of lay across her. *If he starts whining, all guilty and shit, I really* am *gonna kick his ass.* Of course, she understood. She'd met Sally, after all—*lucky little Spirelight bitch.* No, Sally was more than that. That was the problem.

By the time they'd hit Louisiana, Rob had still been a physical wreck. During the drive down, the world around them hadn't been so bad…well, no worse than usual, not yet. They both knew how to avoid attention from their own kind. That was good, because they no longer had a pack backing them up, and they probably weren't so popular with, well, literally anyone else. Her worst worry was that their faces had somehow become known to Earth-line law enforcement, that someone would recognize them while they stopped for food or gas. Normally, between the two of them, they could have easily handled that situation. At the time, he'd have been worse than useless in a fight. Her nerves had been so shot to shit from looking after him that she'd hardly have fared much better.

The whole way from Virginia, it had been sleeping in the car or in cheap motels. Finally, they'd found a little out-of-the-way fishing village, about twenty miles from Lake Pontchartrain, where they could lay low for a spell. They holed up in a room above a little diner, with the back half of the building stretched out across the river on stilts. The old Cajun lady who ran the place didn't usually let out rooms upstairs anymore, she said, but Remelea and her husband had kind faces. Everyone called her Delphine. Best of all, she didn't ask too many questions. Remelea said Rob was her war-veteran husband, recently medically discharged. Delphine understood. Her late husband had come home from Nam and died from Agent Orange. Times were tough all over, and she was glad for the extra help around the diner, first from Remelea, then from Rob as his strength returned.

Delphine never once let either of them wait on customers, restricting them to dishes and food-prep. Remelea hadn't done such drudging, menial Earth-line work since before her First Call. Neither had Rob since Postville. There was a surprising comfort to it. Maybe she just appreciated it better because she knew deep down that these were the last peaceful, lazy days she'd ever know.

She'd been keeping them afloat with cash she'd filched from the corpses back at the Renaissance Kingdom. She hadn't cleaned out half bad, though the bloodstained bills had sure gotten her some odd looks from store clerks and such. It was one more thing Delphine never asked her about.

Something in the Louisiana air swelled Rob up with fresh vitality, like nothing else ever had, short of drinking the glow from a Spirelight in its death throes. Fucked if Remelea knew what it was; the town just smelled like dead fish to her. Before long, he started talking about getting back on the road towards New Orleans...towards Talino.

By then, the rest of the world *had* changed, creeping in around them 'til they couldn't ignore it anymore. Remelea had missed too much 'til it was too late, like a frog letting itself cook in a slowly heating pot of water. *Sort of like falling for this asshole called Rob Coscan.*

The *water*, it turned out, was where the problems started. The fishermen talked about the strange critters hauled up in their nets, like no fish they'd ever seen or heard of. *Except like something out of a nightmare*, some said.

One time, a fisherman brought a *nightmare fish* into the kitchen, through the back door, telling Delphine she had to check this crazy shit out. It was shaped like a fish, still flopped around with its gills puffing torturously. Except instead of scales, its skin was somewhere between humanoid flesh and the slick hide of a salamander. From its eye ridges to its fleshy lips, its gasping face bore an undeniably humanoid stamp, except with no nose. Rob and Remelea got so caught up looking at the thing, they didn't realize Delphine had gone and grabbed the meat-tenderizer 'til she shoved between them and beat the thing on the head 'til she'd splattered its brains all over the counter. She brandished the blood-and-brains-drenched tenderizer at the fisherman, told him to get that thing out of here, and to never bring an abomination like that into her place again. Once he and the nightmare fish were gone, she'd shouted at Rob and Remelea to get back to work and clean the mess up. She'd refused to speak of the incident afterwards.

Over the next couple weeks, word went, such abominations were practically all the fishermen caught anymore. It was fishing that kept the little community's economy afloat, so it wasn't long before shops started shutting down and emptying out overnight, so the place looked more like a ghost town every day.

The morning Rob and Remelea planned to leave was the morning the whole town went crazy. She awoke to the sound of shit breaking downstairs, and Delphine screaming. Remelea was halfway down the stairs when a soggy crunch sounded and the screaming stopped. When she reached the parlor, the first thing she saw was half of Delphine's brains splattered all over the counter, the other half leaking out of her smashed skull across the tiled floor, just like she'd done to that drowning nightmare fish. The parlor was full of mad-eyed, frenzied locals tearing the place apart, along with whatever customers had already come in, who the strange infection hadn't claimed.

"You don't understand," one invader shrieked over and over, like he was the one being attacked. "We gotta. We gotta. Lay down and let it happen, Goddamn you, or everyone else is fucked! It can't leave here. It can't."

For a frozen instant, Remelea panicked for leaving her hook upstairs. Then the shrieking man jumped the counter and came right at her. His neck opened, Remelea got a jet of hot blood to the face, and he dropped spurting at her feet. Her hook *was* in her hand, and she'd just torn the man's throat out with it. Apparently, she just hadn't noticed herself grab it on her way out of the room. Hey, at least that meant the quiet spell hadn't dulled her reflexes. Nor Rob's, apparently, because there he was, already in amongst them, his twin blades sailing about him, painting the walls with the men like they were a squad of Spirelight Secret Police.

Remelea didn't remember much after that. She and Rob had fought their way to the car, through more frenzied locals. She remembered their eyes, how the whites had gone yellow, how veins bulged all over their sickly, fish-belly-pale skin in unnatural hues of blue, black and purple. Maybe someone had gotten hungry and desperate enough to fry and eat a nightmare fish. More likely, it had happened from drinking the same local water through which the critters swam. After getting back on the road, it turned out the same thing had happened everywhere nearby, with nowhere to retreat to but into the swamp.

Since reaching Louisiana, they'd encountered no fellow Deschembines—neither Spirelights nor Schomites, Crimbone or otherwise. As it turned out, the next band of Earth-line hunters had. They were the first Earth-line people Rob or Remelea had seen all day who hadn't been driven mad by the weird new infection. They'd gone a different kind of crazy, a lot more on their game. They'd *recognized* Rob and Remelea, as *them abominations that brung all this down on us.*

In the skirmish that followed, she'd gotten her leg ripped open, from knee to waist, so this time it was Rob who'd had to get her out of there, to look after her while she recuperated. Somehow, he'd found this little abandoned motel. He'd spent the next three months tending to her 'til she could get around on her own.

It had been the most miserable, humiliating time of Remelea's life since her cast-off days; being an invalid at someone else's mercy, cooped up in the dark motel room with no electricity or running water, never leaving her bed except to hobble outside on crutches to relieve herself. All while the big strong man went out to hunt for food and supplies, patrolling the surrounding woods for threats. He found a nearby creek, from which he hauled back clean water and fish. The fish he brought home looked like that nightmare critter they'd seen in Delphine's kitchen, except smaller. Once he raided the motel's staff kitchen for some spices, fried the fish up in those, they'd tasted halfway edible. At least they hadn't come down with whatever infected those assholes back in the fishing village. The water tasted fine…more than fine, in fact, like it flowed from some new spring, just for them.

Maybe drinking the water had something to do with it, but either way, for the first time, Remelea tasted it: whatever it was around here that had rejuvenated Rob so quickly. In that dark room alone, she'd smelled the sweet rot of the swamp out there, calling to her…taunting her, driving her into fits of panic, twisting her brain around 'til she'd dread his return like that of a jailor.

She'd see him come through the door, back at his full strength, stalwart and able, his lean frame outlined by the light behind him…the light of the deadly outdoors that had once been her playground, which she now had to hide from. She started hating him for the power he didn't realize he held over her. It didn't matter that it wasn't his fault. Part of her always saw her foster father standing there. Her foster father was dead, she reminded herself, because she'd gutted the glad-handed sonofabitch years ago, right before she'd made her First Call.

Why do I still even remember that? I've been fully fledged since before Rob was in diapers. We're supposed to shed those memories of our castoff fledgling days.

To think, not that long ago, she'd been the one stuck nursing his half-dead gimp ass back to health. All the same, it had been his unwavering care—that *decency* he refused to let his demons drive out—that had made being stuck with him so torturous…until tonight.

Over the last two months, she'd gotten back on her feet, rebuilt herself. They were back on equal footing, side by side, out here in the wetlands, fighting their little guerilla war, against both the scouts who came out of New Orleans and the remaining local Earth-line survivalist nutjobs. They'd stopped trying to take the scouts alive for questioning. The bastards just laughed themselves to death under interrogation, the crueler, the better, it seemed. Some of them got hard and creamed themselves as they died, their tortured laughter breaking into gasps and grunts of ecstasy, right before the life rattled out and their eyes went glassy. It was like someone had jacked with their nerves, so they could no longer tell the difference between agony and ecstasy. When Rob and Remelea stripped and examined the corpses for clues, the ugly ritual scarification might have explained the madness…'til Rob had the bright idea to cut some of them open and look around inside. That's where things got weird. The scouts' guts had been *rearranged*, with the tubes cut and grafted, some organs altogether missing, organs without which no humanoid body ought to be able to function.

They got more coherent information out of the Earth-line nutjobs. The rest of the world kept getting stranger too, like it was trying to catch up with this place. Through all that, it was just them, the two Crimbone and whatever wanted to kill them. If Remelea knew anything better than causing lovely mayhem, it was a man packing an adrenaline-boner. If anything proved Rob Coscan to be superhuman—a dumbass, sure, but superhuman nonetheless, even by Crimbone standards—it was how long he'd held out against their natural chemistry. As they'd prowled the swamp together, she'd listened to its voices, constantly reminding herself to listen for the important information, to not keep asking it how he felt about her, for it to boil his brain just a little more 'til he saw sense. She'd pretended tonight wasn't inevitable.

By now, life in the wetlands had burned everything out of Rob Coscan's slender body that wasn't hard, spring-cord strength, intensified by his growing oneness with those lands, to a degree even Remelea found scary. You'd think it had boiled everything from his mind and soul that wasn't savage, efficient purpose. She knew him better than that, though.

Tonight, they'd both been on their last nerves after the bad scrape in the marshes. Once they'd gotten back to the motel, she'd screamed at him that it was time to quit pussyfooting around and get a move on. He said for the umpteenth time that the moment wasn't right, that they didn't know enough about what they were walking into. The moment would present itself soon, he promised.

"*Just like you've* promised *a million times* already," she said. "What did you used to say? *I tell you when we get there, I tell you when we get there.* You asshole, we've spent half a Goddamn year at the enemy's doorstep, eating nastyass human-faced fish, while whatever fucked-up energy's leaking out of this swamp seeps into our damn brains!"

"The fuck you talking about?"

"Oh, sure, *you* don't notice it! Hell, here you are, happier than a pig in shit, right at home. *This* is what you came looking for, isn't it? Figures, for a basket case like you. I should have my fucking head examined, for ever listening to a Goddamn thing you said."

"Look, if you're so champing at the bit for whatever's waiting in New Orleans, why don't you just go ahead without me and—"

"Oh, right, *New Orleans, New Orleans, New Orleans. I wouldn't be here in this shit if it wasn't for you and your...your...*"

That's when she'd lost it, started punching, kicking, clawing and biting at him. She couldn't stop herself, so he stopped her, by wrestling her down onto her back...onto the bed, it just so happened. She bit at his face and neck like a snapping turtle, and he bit back 'til his mouth found hers and stayed there. When he tried to rise, she held him there, so he went yanking off her jeans and undoing his own. What the hell had finally flipped this switch in him? Not that she wasn't complaining.

Now that they'd finished, he stared at the ceiling. "Something's different," he said in a strange voice.

"I'll say." She hugged him tighter, loving the soft, sweaty quiver of their naked flesh pressing together.

He sat up, staring farther into someplace she couldn't see.

"You okay?" she asked.

"I need to go out, listen to the night." He looked back as though just now noticing her. She no longer recognized his eyes, or his voice, at all. "I'll be fine. It's just...something weird's happening. I need to figure it out alone. Just me and the night. The night, and the land. Please."

With a jolt, she recognized what was happening. *When—what—how—the hell…? Is it because we just finally fucked and got it over with? You've gotta be shitting me.*

Yeah, that was it. It was ludicrous, but it made sense if you knew him like she did. *Yeah, that's right. I gave him this, because those Crimbone balls of his finally boiled hot enough for* me, *a pure Crimbone woman, hot enough to make him forget* her.

Remelea allowed herself that much good ol' fashioned savage feminine pride. Rob had married Sally Wildfire. Earth-line fashion or no, not a day had passed since then that he hadn't held those silly vows sacred. For the last five months, though, he and Remelea had blazed their own trail together, in the manner of a true *Crimbone* husband and wife. The only thing missing was either of them calling it what it was…well, that and the sex…because of what he couldn't let go of, what had stood between him and his truest Crimbone self…until tonight.

"Go on," she whispered. "I'm here if you need me."

He opened the door, letting in the chill of a Deep Southern winter, then closed it behind him.

Two

Rob looked at a different swamp than the one he'd come in from. The same twisting, twining Cypress and Tupelo trees greeted him as before, stretching out over glistening stagnant water, downhill from the parking lot. It was what dwelt *within and beneath* the rocks, trees and shrubbery that now bubbled out, telling him new stories. Every mossy surface and shade showed off a new world, coming together into something he understood much more clearly…not in the language of squalling, hooting wilderness noises that anyone could listen to if they tried, but in some higher, weirder language that made more sense to him than anything this world had ever tried to tell him, through anyone or anything. The swamp welcomed him back and taught him secret lessons.

When he'd first stepped out, there'd still been room in his head for a personal life. Less than half a year ago, he'd been in Florida with his wife, happy to think they'd never be anywhere else. Then something else had crept into their world. He'd fought through hell to make his wife safe from it. Once she was safe, he'd left her. Because of something that other world had told him, something that made him the worst danger of all to her. But how? All he knew was that he'd bolted up out of his coma and found himself splayed out on the table Jesse and Zane had strapped him to, surer than he'd ever been of anything in his life. He'd read it in a book, in the ancient Spirelight temple…The lands had led him from that moment to this…like he'd asked them to. The animals, and the land, the swamp…and something beyond it all, a world he found in his dreams, one that never completely went away when he woke up.

Ever since, Rob's only constant company on this trail had been the one fellow Crimbone who hadn't betrayed him. She was also the one woman to ever turn his head from his wife. It figured.

The passage to that other world was hidden somewhere in this one. To find it, he first had to find the man called Talino.

Out here in the night, for a moment, everything was clear and peaceful. Something within him melted away. He'd felt a similar catharsis twice before, both times back in Brattleboro, Vermont, going on six years ago.

"*Bong-chicka-bowa,*" sang an overhead voice, "*Bong-chicka-boowwaaaaaaaa…*"

Rob's eyes trailed to the potbellied bat-like shape perched on a nearby heavily leaning branch. "Where the fuck you been, birdie?"

"Waitin' for the show you two crazy kids just put on in there. Should'a given me more of a head's up, Biter-Boy. I'd'a gone for some popcorn."

"Did you just come out of the woodwork to rub it in?"

"There you go, Biter-Boy, hurtin' my lil' feelin's. Naw. I jus' came to say goodbye."

"Goodbye?"

"That's right, kiddo. My business by you just got wrapped up. When you blew yer load in there, you blew out the last of the fledgling in you, too."

Rob's gaze dropped reflectively.

"Aw, don't get all bashful. 'Fore long, I's gonna start all discorporealatin', get sucked back to the ephemeral realms. So I wanted to make sure to tell ye, it's been a hell of a time. Watchin' you evolve towards bein' the most badass Crimbone sombitch I ever shown in. Shit, look at me, gettin' all weepy-eyed. Hell, I'm proud of you, Biter-Boy."

"You're *proud of me* for cheating on my wife. Figures."

"There you go, talkin' like ye still got yer head stapled up inside your own asshole. Nah, to be honest, I's a little disappointed about that. Way you held out for so long, with all them miles an' months between you an' sweet lil' Sally-Poach, even with that fumin' Foxy-Girl fire-crotch bobbin' in yer face the whole time, I actually got to thinkin', *Shit, this here's the one damn Biter-Boy out of ten-million with the will to actually keep his blade where his mouth is.* Oh well. Shit happens. Plus, I wanted to send you off with a last lil' bit of advice."

Rob sighed. "Okay, go ahead, shoot."

"What's happenin' now is you're seein' the world in all its true shinin' glory for the first time. It's teachin' you the true ancient language of the Crimbone. You'll be speakin' it out loud 'fore ye know it. Just be careful when you decide to switch over from plain ol' English, bad English, or whatever, into the real language of your blood. That Old World Crimbone talk is *powerful* talk. You don't wanna jus' go 'round shootin' yer mouth off or sayin' *Hey dude, pass the beer* in it. You get in that habit, even I don't wanna see the crazy shit you'd stir up."

"So when *am* I supposed to use it?"

The voice went high-pitched and coquettish. "Oh, Biter-Boy, you can *use it* every chance ye get. Oh right, the ol' Crimbone language. You'll know, long as you remember to listen to your blood."

"Thanks, Puttergong."

"Ain't a thing."

"I meant...for everything."

"Aw, you're jus' gettin' sentimental. Now I *really* know it's time for me to skedaddle." The bat-like shape beat the air with its wings, tore through the foliage, and rose into the night sky beyond. Rob was about to say one last thing, then it swerved, mingled with a flock of birds, and passed out of sight.

Rob stared at the stars for the first time. The door opened behind him. Remelea whispered, "Rob?" He turned. She lingered in the doorway, still naked.

"Get dressed. It's time. We're heading for New Orleans."

She gasped. He'd just spoken to her in Old Crimbone.

THREE

Puttergong soars out over swampland, watchin' the stars and moon ahead. Any minute now, he won't see 'em no more…*Any minute, any minute*…After quite a few miles, he notices he's still smellin' the stink of the swamp below.

Now what in the Sam-hell fuck? It ain't never taken this long to get back to the ephemeral realms after sayin' goodbye to a fledgling! He done everything he was supposed to do, and over a shitload more time than it ought'a take, too. After   uerrie' up with all Biter-Boy's bullshit, Puttergong's earned a fuckin' rest. He'd like to give someone a not-so-pretty askin' about why he ain't I' it yet. Trouble is, anyone who could answer him is back in the ephemeral realms. His wings is I' tired, too. He ain't sure why. It ain't like he's flown that far for a Familiar.

Puttergong flies down towards the lights of Earthline skivi-lie-zation, what's left of it anyhow. Earlier, he munched on an egret while he watched Biter-Boy an' Foxy-Girl goin' at it. Maybe after some more comfort-snackin', he'll be able to think straighter. He sniffs for tossed off bits of food, the nearest dumpster, maybe more birds. Richer aromas float up from what's left of a steakhouse, like a bunch of assholes are busy ruinin' a bunch of perfectly good fresh-killed carcasses, cookin' all the blood out of 'em, drownin' 'em in all that sweet an' sour gunk. Tiki torches light the parking lot (ain't so much electricity goin' around these days). Genuine ol' fashioned cowboys an' cowgirls go in an' out of this here dive. Maybe they's in there gatherin' for some kind'a *How the fuck we supposed to pull together and live through this shit?* Powwow. Or maybe they's cookin' out and boozin' up, tryin' to pretend for a few hours that reality's still what it used to be.

Earth-line skivi-lie-zation has held up best in spots where there was the least of it to begin with. Probably 'cause that's where the real shit was always closest to the surface anyhow. Eh, let the Earth-liners enjoy it while it lasts. The fucked-up thing is, Puttergong's facin' the possibility of bein' here to see it with 'em.

So what the fuck's a Crimbone Familiar to do, once he ain't got a fledgling to look after no more, but for some reason, he ain't findin' his way home?

"Oh, what to do, what to do," he mutters, and lets out a cackle.

"Who the fuck's sittin' up there?"

Puttergong looks at the sidewalk an' parkin' stretch beneath. There's a couple good ol' uerri boys millin' around drunkenly, starin' up his way. Let 'em stare. If they ain't too drunk to see past the torchlight, all they'll see is the egret he ate last.

"Oh, no one here but us birdies...*Hehehehehe*..."

"Who's that crazy fucker up on the roof?" says one of the podunks. "Hey, man, you smokin' the dope or uerrier '?"

Before Puttergong can answer, the second uerri taps his buddy on the chest and points. "Holy shit, Phil..."

The one called Phil peers up hard, into the darkness above the steakhouse sign. "Holy fuck, it's one of them *things*."

The other good ol' boy grabs a rock and chucks it through the air. It misses Puttergong by a mile and bounces off the bricks somewhere. Puttergong's saw-tooth jaw drops open at the end of his long horse-like snout.

"Git out of here, you ugly little Satan-monster," shouts the one that threw the rock. "Git, an' take your big, people-lookin' Satan-monsters with you!"

They can see him. Hot damn, tonight's just I' weirder an' weirder.

"Don't chase it off, man," says Phil. "I'm goin' to the truck to git the shotgun."

The one who threw the rock watches his buddy head for the truck. "Huh? How'm I supposed to keep it there?"

"Hell, I don' know. Talk to it, or   uerrier '. Man, I'm gonna be the first to bring down one of them things, mount a devil-monster trophy on my wall!"

Puttergong don't much feel like I' mounted by Phil, so he lets out a screech and dives off the steakhouse roof. Puttergong's jaw locks on Phil's neck, yanks him high in the air, then bites that tasty juicy throat clean out in one razor-sharp chomp. The body drops and slams on the truck's roof. Metal screams and sprays shattered glass everywhere. Puttergong circles while the other   uerri starts screamin', then he sticks out his haunches for a hawk-style dive. Claws stab shoulders,   uerrie' round some collarbone. Back up Puttergong goes, pullin' this one kickin' and screamin' into the air. He lets go right as the body slams into what used to be a big ol' neon sign. It makes a big ol' show of shatterin' glass.

All sorts of folks pile out of the steakhouse. They flip their shit as they see what's what. Puttergong's enjoyed this bit of public fun that he wasn't allowed to do before, but he's had enough antics with Earth-liners for just now. Before them two started   uerrier' him, he'd done some reflectin' about the last five years, plus back over lots of the eons he's been through before that. By now, he's got him a sorta theory as to why he's still here.

Part of him hopes it's all just a big wild pigeon chase, but he's still got that Familiar's idea of duty hammered deep in his skull. It'd be a fucked-up new kind of duty, but if that's what he's been matched up with, he'd better check it out, in case he has to hop to it right quick. Hell, could be fun. Might just lead to a chance of watchin' a little more of Biter-Boy's development, too. If Earth-line podunks is seein' Familiars now, the world's gotten even more interestin' than Puttergong figured it would. There'll be plenty of miles 'tween here and there to enjoy life as this world's first ever Free Familiar.

With all this neat new shit in mind, Puttergong flies north.

FOUR

The chirping bugs and birds guided them as they darted through the marsh. You had to go fast in the swamp, even with a highly tuned instinct for where to put your feet, and not stop 'til you were where you wanted to be. Otherwise, even solid spots sank under you, so you'd sink right along with them before you knew it. Scuttling muskrats, lurching snapping turtles, fluttering cranes, all hooted, yawned and rustled just a little louder from the right direction. Rob and Remelea's indrawn breaths seemed to pull a slight breeze through the brush and reeds, swaying them like pointing fingers. They kept side by side, except where the way forced them to move in single file. Their duster coats sailed out behind them like fluttering reptilian tails. Whenever he glanced at her, the dynamic power and blood-flushed life in her eyes and limbs made him fall in love with her all over again.

All over again…Shit. Who the hell had he been kidding? Even moving at this breathless speed, he still smelled her all over himself, and not only the hot sex they'd just had…

The life *in you, in your body, in your soul…That's why I know I can cut my way through anything. I had to force myself to keep going, 'til you looked me in the eye and believed in me. That's what made all this real. I still don't even know if it's right or wrong. I don't care anymore.*

Through the trees ahead, there stood a small fisherman's cabin. Behind it stretched the banks of Lake Pontchartrain. Within the cabin, Rob recognized the scratchiness of an old-time record player…*Jambalaya*, the original Hank Williams version. He'd last heard that song less than a week before the Spirelights showed up in Postville. There'd been some kind of community jamboree, out in a field somewhere. The beer kegs had been running dry, all the bands had packed up, and someone had set some ol' country greats pumping through some speakers. The last celebrants had milled through the litter that volunteers would soon collect and stuff into garbage bags. Rob had still been having fun mingling. He'd spotted Sally creeping off into the trees, in one of her moods. That always poured cold water on his good time. Still, the breathless impulse to comfort her had taken over, where making her smile was more important than anything. He'd followed her into the brush. In the light that spilled through the leaves, she sank to a spread of dry earth.

"You okay?" he'd asked, maybe followed it with "Wanna get home?"

Her eyes had gleamed up at him with kittenish serenity. She'd leaned back on the earth, squirming and shifting languidly, then tugged him down slowly and teasingly, flexing her hips up at his. As Rob had settled over her and kissed her deeply, ol' Hank serenading them from the speakers, he'd thought, *My life can't get any more perfect than this.*

Now he pushed all that away…as far as he could with that damn song playing. Here he stood at the banks of the watery border to New Orleans. The old fisherman on the porch reminded him of Chet Carter, the orange farmer who'd rented the trailer to him and Sally in Florida. That was a little funny, since this fisherman was black, and Chet had been a bit of an antique southern racist.

The Spirelights had killed Chet. It was probably a miracle the renegade Crimbone running this area hadn't found and killed this fisherman. Since the world had started rearranging itself, lots of Crimbone had gone renegade. It was a wonder they hadn't started a wholesale slaughter of civilian Earth-line people as they had the Spirelights. Even this deep in the swamp, rumors filtered in, how the last desperate Spirelight Secret Policemen had panicked, cutting losses by hunting down and executing the Earth-line businessmen who'd unwittingly bankrolled them. Powerful Earth-liners *with* some idea who they worked for had thrown their own fits, putting hits out on anyone who asked too many questions. None of them lived to see the contracts carried out.

Rob and Remelea hurried towards the shack. The old man got out of his rocking chair and limped off the porch, peering through the moonlight.

"We need to borrow your boat," Rob said.

"What'cha need ma boat for at this hour?"

"To get across the lake, to the city."

"Why not take de bridge?"

"The bridge is no good these days."

"We can pay you," Remelea cut in.

The fisherman let out a scratchy laugh. "*Pay me!* With what? Who's money, huh? What's left to buy with de money, what this swamp can't provide?"

"Maybe the swamp sent us," said Rob.

The old man took a closer look at them. He cleared his throat and spat out a gob of sludge. "The swamp sent me some little cracker bastard and a spic bitch...the kind who move like dey don't even have the right bones under de skin. To what, kill me? You think the swamp thinks I want that? You can go fuck yourselves, de both of you. Life's still sweet, even to an ol' busted-up fi uerrie like me. So my boat."

Rob held the man's gaze. "Maybe we're not offering payment. Maybe we *are* the payment…from the swamp." The words rolled up out of his throat…from that other place that was and wasn't him.

The old man shrank back. His half-toothless mouth hung open. For a second, he looked ready to shit himself. Then he smiled mirthlessly. "You think you de one in control here, *High Natural*. Over me. Over dis swamp. Over de madem'selle uerrier at your side. *They* all in control of *you*, always has been, and de dreadful thing is, they don't know what they doin' with you any more dan you do. You *are* de one folks call de High Natural, de one everybody waitin' for. Ain't ye?"

It was Rob's turn to freeze and stare. "I guess I am," he said.

"You goin' to see da man folks call Talino, been bringin' out de devils in everybody?"

"Yeah."

The fisherman trembled and shrank up. "Dat devil-man Talino, lot of folk say he de one called up de High Natural, dat de High Natural's de worst devil yet. Other folk say other things. What you want wit de devil-man Talino, High Natural?"

"I'm gonna kill him," said Rob.

The fisherman chuckled and looked to Remelea. "You think you serve the High Natural, madem'selle *uerrier*?"

"I don't serve anyone," she said. "Not anymore. He's my friend."

"So you say, cherie. Very well. Take de boat. Help *your friend* kill de devil-man Talino, if you think dat will be de end of it. Sorry I call you spic bitch."

"I've been called worse by better," she said.

"You a powerful   *uerrier,* cherie. You take your power wherever you please. I now worry, though, that you be holdin' yourself back, robbin' yourself and the rest of us of what you might be, what you might have to give…stayin' stuck to this one here."

"Yeah, well, you wouldn't be the first to call me a dirty thief, either."

Remelea glanced at Rob. His eyes were doing that weird, distant thing again. The two of them headed around the shack, then out onto the narrow, rotting dock. At the end was a small metal boat with an old-fashioned gas motor. When Rob and Remelea climbed in, it swayed precariously. Remelea untied the rope then pulled the cord 'til the engine chugged to life. The boat lurched into motion, abruptly enough that she grabbed the rims to steady herself. Rob sat up front. He stared out across the water as it rippled in the moonlight. The shore looked so far away, it felt like they'd set out on the ocean. Its lights still sent a fluttering shimmer all the way out to them, like silver blades on the waves. The twang of the record player was the last sound from the shore to fade away behind them.

As they bobbed and coasted across that shimmer, Remelea said, "We really should try to get this boat back to that old guy when we're done. How far off is that damn shore, anyway?"

"Twenty-three miles."

"Will this little rig get us that far?"

"It'll get us there. You know, I got my first real taste of my Crimbone nature in this city?"

Remelea nodded. "When you were living here with Jesse's son."

"Yeah. Too bad I didn't know what we were really going through. Could've appreciated it better."

"I still think it's weird he didn't tell you. Y'know, with him knowing, while you didn't. Man, I'd be pissed."

"I used to be. Hell, it wouldn't have made any meaningful difference. It makes sense, if you knew him…Y'know, I used to be pissed about a lot of things, and now I…can't remember why I ever thought they mattered so much." He looked back at her. "Is that…normal, after the Third Call?"

Remelea didn't answer. The boat bobbed along beneath them.

NEW ORLEANS

ONE

They came ashore in Metairie. The suburbs around New Orleans proper stretched out black and dead around them, a moldering necropolis. Everything stank of swollen, pulpy death-rot. Feral dogs and cats ran by everywhere, weaving between their feet, sometimes snapping at their heels, otherwise sparing them only the briefest resentful glances. Little remained of what humanoid population hadn't gotten out in time, other than some rotting corpses. The rest skulked and stared like starved toads, from darkened doors that hung rotting halfway off their hinges, at the back of half-collapsed porches.

After three hours of walking through that maze, Rob and Remelea hoofed it up the high overpass that wound down into the thick of the city. New Orleans was nothing but a swamp letting a city stay there, Rob used to say. Now its old sounds and smells said *Hi* to him as though he'd never left…except they weren't the same sounds or smells anymore.

The city hadn't been *taken back* by the swamp. Rather, it had become a living, breathing embodiment of it …except it now embodied something else, too.

Bonfire glows pulsed from the streets ahead, between buildings into the night, to the beat of a thousand thundering drums. Their rhythm was the swamp's rhythm, as would be that of the savage dancers around the final corner. Rob already felt their stomping feet thundering up through the pavement, beneath his own boots.

Jazz, Blues and Zydeco had once been the embodiment of the swamp's music. Rob remembered the magic the musicians in Jackson Square used to share with everyone. It was like the musicians breathed it in, lived through it, and sang it out as beauty. The swamp's tune had changed and taken the human music with it. It was still beautiful, though. It must be, because Rob had never felt more alive...*never felt thirstier.* The sensation livened him, so his blades pulled thirstily against his hips.

He and Remelea brushed open their dusters as they stepped off the overpass. Their hands twitched towards their weapons. Remelea's weapon resembled a big, black meat hook with a horizontal grip, hammered into straight lines, sharpened on the inner edges and the last third of the outer edge. It never looked practical for combat 'til you saw her use it, requiring a very specific style and coordination of movement, one Rob had never seen in anyone else. He'd watched her wield it often. His own twin blades were the oldest of the black metal, wielded originally by the first Crimbone in the Old World...later by Magur Sevi, the first High Natural.

The drumbeat thrummed with gleeful malice, a contempt for everything it touched. It rippled out to them, through the pavement under their feet, up through their legs so their guts churned, trying to shake their nerves loose, 'til every step became an effort. Rob would have expected his new state to fortify him against it. Instead, the new sensitivity only made it worse. Remelea's hand brushed his. He almost closed his fist against her, thinking he should prove himself as the High Natural by making this hardest walk alone.

Prove what? There's no sacred rule book for the High Natural. You're nothing but a perfect storm of natural phenomena and circumstances. Want to know what the High Natural's good for? Decide for yourself, starting now.

When they rounded the last corner, Rob said, "Remelea, meet Talino."

"Where?"

"All this shit."

Between two wide lanes, there ran what used to be the streetcar line. Nearby, one of those streetcars lay on its side. Two drummers perched atop it, one at either end. On their backs at the drummers' feet lay mummified corpses. The corpses had been hollowed out from behind, part of the spines removed, with broad hollow metal cylinders shoved up through them, stretching their dried abdominal flesh, stapled around the top edges. Such were the drums the creatures beat. The sound echoed down through the cylinders. It filled the streetcars and thundered out through the broken windows, flooding the streets. Fifty feet down was another overturned streetcar with two more drummers, two more dead people turned into drums. It ran like this all the way up and down the avenue, for as far as Rob or Remelea could see. The dead-eyed drummers stood naked, painted in clotting blood, much of it their own. Their legs were flayed and cauterized, their feet nailed to their perches. Barbed wire strapped them to metal rods that held them upright. Their wide, crazed eyes told you they were happier than pigs in shit…or had been hypnotically convinced they were.

In the streets, the dancers writhed, jerked, and tossed themselves this way and that to the drumbeat, deaf to everything else. The drumbeat seemed to yank them on invisible hooks, through a perverted puppet show 'til they died of exhaustion or puked and shat out their own guts. A few strewn, trampled corpses had already done that.

Those who didn't dance writhed and seethed through more intimate perversions, through streets paved in slimy bone and viscera. Two men bashed each other up and down the sidewalk with nail-studded two-by-fours. Shreds of their faces and torsos dangled from each other's weapons. They didn't even try to block or dodge, just worked each other over at a frantic rhythm, almost like they were taking turns with their strikes, eager for each other's punishment. They kept it up 'til one of them backed into a flaming metal can and went over with it. The spilling flames engulfed him and spread to a couple rutting on the curb. The couple screamed as they caught fire. They thrashed at first like they hoped to get clear, then just stayed there humping while they roasted.

A nearby body had been thrown from a window and impaled on the spikes of a wrought iron fence. Its lower half dangled into the street. A man came along, lifted the legs, and started fucking it. While he was going at it, a naked teenage girl hopped the fence and thumped the skull on the bars like a monkey with a coconut. When the skull broke open, she smeared brains all over her face and neck and breasts, between her legs and through her hair. The guy doing his business at the other end didn't seem jealous.

All Remelea could say was, "Why?"

"You've heard the same shit I have about Talino, right? This is what he gives them once he's taken everything else, which is nothing some part of 'em ain't thought of."

"So what's he got 'em celebrating?"

"Me showing up."

"I'm gonna hate myself for asking, but…how the fuck do you know all this?"

Rob smirked mirthlessly. "I'm the High Natural."

"I liked it better when I was the one constantly having to explain shit to you."

Some of the revelers had once been Crimbone, some civilian Schomite, some Earth-line. It barely mattered now. Somewhere around here, there'd be Crimbone who were still themselves…Talino's Crimbone, kept lucid by drugs and shielding spells.

From atop the streetcar, one of the drummers spotted Rob and Remelea. Apparently, the drummer hadn't been castrated, judging by how his eyes sparked at Remelea. The flesh was flayed from half his mouth. What were left of his teeth showed in a ragged, gummy permanent grin. Something about that look just set Rob off, so he sprang through the crowd. He flung his arms wide to knock the celebrants aside. They tumbled and crashed against each other. He felt and heard their bones snapping. The disruption just fueled their joyous fury, like the ugliest mosh-pit he'd ever seen.

Rob jackknifed himself up onto the overturned streetcar rim. He almost fell through one of the broken windows. He found his balance and slung the hardest punch he'd ever thrown at the drummer's neck. At the end of the punch was one of his black blades. He hadn't noticed himself draw it. The drummer was such a mangled mass of gore that the bloody spurt didn't appear to come from within. It was more like the neck's flesh exploded across Rob's hand and arm. The spray puttered off. The neck was still there. The head lulled back against the blade that had severed the spine. Rob ripped the knife free. The upper body swayed away. The metal rod kept suspending the lower half.

Some flicker of respect touched Rob, for the man who'd once been there, for the identity that had been stolen to create whatever thing he'd just killed. His blade flashed again and severed the wire. The corpse slid free, dropped through a broken streetcar window, and thumped somewhere within. Rob looked up. Maybe he'd kill the other drummer. Its hands had fallen at its sides. The silence spread. The writhing bodies shambled to a halt. Their eyes rolled everywhere in search of the disturbance. Rob sheathed his blade and scanned the crowd for Remelea. When he spotted her, her hook was out and ready. Those close to her backed away, like they sensed her connection to the disturbance. Blocks away, other drummers still went strong. So did their dancers. Rob sprang off the car and hurried back to Remelea's side.

The crowd parted for them as they walked down the avenue together. Palm trees had once flourished along the median where the street cars now lay. Some of the palm trees had been reduced to scorched stalks. Others had withered and dried up top, while their trunks had swollen and split open, giving birth to slimy orange clumps of some new alien plant life, like it had impregnated the trees through their roots, from the mystically irradiated soil, so it now snaked out in veiny patches in all directions, pulsing with slick, white, tough-shelled fruits like cancerous growths. Rob and Remelea reached the next fallen streetcar. Its drummers now also fell silent. The revelers kept settling down, like someone had unplugged them. They still quivered and hissed beneath the slick red and brown muck that drenched them. Every block looked like a repeat of the last. They walked a little closer together.

So here's hell, Rob mused, *the one from that Earth-line religion I grew up having shoved down my throat. Someone's painted it over the city I loved...the swamp I loved. Funny. After everyone I've killed, all I had to do to get to hell was cheat on my wife. Here I am with the woman I did it with.*

After another mile through hell, the revelry thinned and fell away. By the time they reached the intersection of

Saint Charles and Napoleon, the streets were nearly as dead as Metairie had been. No fires burned, except in some windows. Across Saint Charles was the restaurant where Rob used to work as a cook. The glass was smashed in. Shrouded, ghostly figures moved and sat about within like the place was still open. Across Napoleon, there stood the gutted remains of the Rite Aid where he used to buy beer and shoot the shit with the security guard. The memories now felt like catalogued facts, things he'd read in a book about someone else's life, background information on these parameters. On the next corner, there stood a church.

"He's in there, isn't he?" said Remelea.

Thick vines covered the face of the building, binding the doors open. Tiny pods speckled the vines, glowing from within like firefly tails. Those pods could get as big as basketballs. Some of the ones inside would be, grown that way because they'd be the only remaining light source. Old World plant life…something that shouldn't be able to survive, let alone thrive in this world. They'd been fortified with equally alien magic. Lightpears, they were called, loosely translated from the old Deschembine. 'Til hours ago, Rob would have needed Remelea to remind him of that. Now it felt more at home in his head than memories of how this city used to be.

Greenish yellow light shown from within the church, almost neon but softer, as only natural light can be. Rob and Remelea entered a gilded foyer and gazed through another doorway, into what had once been the chapel. The network of vines stretched floor to ceiling like prison bars, forming a winding maze. At the other end, there shown little shards of an open room. Someone stood at an altar like a priest, wrapped in the white flutter of holy vestments, no less.

Through the maze of vines, there came another shape. It approached, wispy and silent. Rob's eyes widened. His heart fluttered as he thought he recognized it. A stranger turned the corner.

"Welcome to the new City Hall." The teenage girl curtsied like a Victorian chambermaid in her sparkling evening dress.

"Who are you?" asked Remelea.

"I'm Kimberly. Your host has instructed me to lead you to him, through the garden."

Remelea looked at the vines blocking the way. "Fuck this maze bullshit." She shoved Kimberly aside and sprang. Marble floor showed through the vines, everywhere but the first turn.

Rob yelled, "Remelea, no, wait!"

Her hook sheared through the green bars in her path. Gel-like plant blood sprayed everywhere. The severed vines lashed and flopped on either end. The lower ones shrank downward, zipping away beneath Remelea's feet. Her legs kicked into the air like she'd slipped on a banana peel. The other vines beneath her slithered aside. The giant black mouth in the floor swallowed her.

TWO

The vines closed like lips as Rob dove at them. Both of his blades seemed to leap free into his fists as he sprang. He slashed the flora aside and tumbled into darkness. After a long, breathless drop, he barrel-rolled through putrid, sopping earth. When he sprang to his feet, the weight of the muck on his duster nearly checked him. The smell hit him next, so rancid it was almost solid. His eyes squeezed shut against the sting. He willed them open and blinked furiously. More vines slithered into place and closed over the hole above.

Basements weren't exactly all the rage in New Orleans, for the same reason cemeteries were all above ground. A cavern had been dug through the church foundations, reinforced mostly with more vines. Rob spread his feet and crouched. His boots sank deeper into the mud. Tiny lightpears lined both concrete and earthen walls like a galaxy of greenish yellow stars. He didn't spot Remelea 'til he saw what else was down here. Yards away, she shambled left and right, her hook lashing at the four men who hemmed her in. At least they looked like men 'til Rob's eyes adjusted. Vines fettered them to the walls. No, they were *one with* the vines, which threaded them inside and out. Scorched flesh and muscle moldered and sagged on their naked bodies. Bones gleamed through the sagging flesh. Clumps of plant life inhabited their ribcages. From what he could tell, they had no lower abdomens left to speak of. Their mouths grunted and gibbered, eyes ablaze with the rudimentary intelligence of working brains still stuck in those skulls. Plain kitchen knives had been bound crudely to bony fingers that bobbed and twitched at the end of whipping arms.

The knives lashed at Remelea, so quickly and plentiful that she was losing ground fast. Whenever her hook almost cut one in half, the vines jerked the body clear while another fighter swept at her unguarded side. The poor, soggy footing down here didn't help, either.

Rob lunged with his twin blades in the lead. Their tips pulled him into it like a pair of magnets. His body turned into a spinning, ducking, lashing, pivoting machine, the center of a cyclone of deadly razor edges. He made no series of moves, just one continuous, fluid attack. A set of legs flew away. The body sank to its waist, held erect by vines rooted to its back and shoulders. Rob slashed them free. The body splashed on its face and sank deeper, still squirming. His other blade unseamed an attacker from the crotch to the cap of its head. The skull split like a yapping hand-puppet with a vertical mouth. Brains melted out of the skull in rotted clumps. The body splashed in the muck and stayed dead. Not so the first one he'd felled. A new set of smaller vines came loose from the wall and reconnected the appendages. It came back at him before he realized it. The knives on its fingers gashed his shoulder. He howled. His injured arm sheathed its blade, grabbed the attacker's wrist, and twisted. Simultaneously, his other blade hacked at the skull. The neck lashed backward, then went back, and back, and back, slithering away like a snake, carrying the head with it.

Rob's next strike chopped the ribcage down the center. He wrenched the wrist so hard that the attacker's arm popped off at the elbow in a greenish-brown spray.

The knife fingers dangled from his shoulder like splinters. He jerked them loose and flung them as far as he could, in the opposite direction from their owner. Someone else's knife-fingers stabbed him in the ass through his coat. He thrust his hips forward so his flesh slid free of the points. He still felt them caught in the coat. He redrew the other blade and whipped around, his feet pivoting furiously against the mud that sucked at them. The ass-grabber's head flew from the neck. His next strike severed the offending arm so it dangled from his coat by the tips. When he moved, the knife-tips tapped and plucked at him.

In a frenzied glance, he saw Remelea holding her own against the remaining attacker. It danced around her tauntingly, getting in little jabs here and there, wearing her down.

Rob slid out of his mud-sopped coat. It splashed in the mud and sank beneath the severed arm. Three thin vines came from the walls, wove themselves with the bones and muscles in the shoulder, then pulled it free and away. He sheathed a blade. Reached out, and yanked Remelea back by the scruff of the neck. She thrashed before she realized it was him, then she went with his maneuver. The thing she'd been fighting shot at them both, letting out a harpy screech. Rob held up his knife so the thing's open mouth swallowed it and the blade punched through the back of the skull. The jaws champed on the black metal, splintering its teeth into jagged shards. Its arms came in twin rainbow arcs at Rob's face. He wrenched his blade loose, yanked his foot from the muck, and gave the creature a high kick to the chest that sent it flying. The knife hands clapped inches from his nose, before it splashed and floundered.

"Who the fuck are these guys?" Remelea panted.

"Dead Crimbone."

"*What?*"

"Yeah, with just enough gray matter for Talino to resurrect and—*Shit, look out.*"

All three bodies were back up and reassembled, though not quite like before. What they'd become had no regard for symmetry or selfhood, parts treated as merely parts. A head Rob had severed had attached itself to a body Remelea had decapitated. An arm she'd cut off stitched to a stump he'd pruned, and so forth.

"They wanna wear us down," she huffed.

"All those vines on the walls are their supply line," Rob growled. "Make a circuit cutting those off. I'll cover you."

The walls were getting closer to naked, but fresh growth kept slithering in from above to fill the space. Remelea leapt at the supply line, as Rob called it. He kept the three stooges away from her while she worked. That was tough, considering each of them could attack him with one limb or set of jaws while they semi-detached another and made a grab at her. He barreled into the one in the middle and launched back into a continuous spin attack. All three monsters came apart, exposing their torsos and limbs to him, the better to keep their skulls in one piece. Over and over, they redoubled their speed and resilience, 'til it felt like he was fighting an endless, lightning-quick army. His limbs burned and throbbed.

When there wasn't mud in his eyes, they watered from the stench. His every muscle screamed so loud, he could barely tell where his wounds were anymore. He could no longer see Remelea.

The things weren't regenerating quite so fast anymore. Rob spun low. Five serrated edges scraped his skull. He cut across a pair of calves, before slicing off two more pairs of legs at the knees. Blood ran through his hair, down his forehead. He wiped at it with the back of his hand before it could reach his eyes. As he rose, he noticed how dim the cavern had gotten. The majority of the little lightpears had fallen from the walls on severed stalks. They sank in the mud.

A torso with a lolling head rose from the mud like Dracula from the coffin. A pair of legs slithered by like eels, on their way to rejoin with the shape. Rob swung at the head. The teeth of his knife caught in the side of a skull. He dragged the teeth back, finishing the sideways sweep. The top of the skull came off like a jar's lid. He didn't wait to watch the body fall, instead spun and lunged at the other shapes.

His legs dragged harder than ever through mud. It felt thicker, from so many dead things sinking through it. His blades came down in twin cleaving arcs, catching one face while the other target squirmed back. The latter towered nearly to the ceiling. The vines no longer bound the limbs to the torso, so much as extend akimbo towards them. Knife-fingered hands clenched and clicked at the end of arms that looked like tentacles. They shot at him like a flock of birds of prey. He stood ready, but the knife-nailed hand of the other remaining thing grabbed his leg beneath the knee. Its edges sank in and dragged back. Rob's left blade spasmed, chopped and cleaved the skull. He twisted 'til it split wide open. The other knife hands came at him from two directions.

A wet chop echoed. The knife hands flailed skyward as the body spilled back. It splashed at Remelea's feet. She hooked it through the chin and yanked. The head popped off and flew loose from her hook. She caught it midair with a sharp crescent-kick so it splattered like a melon on the concrete wall.

Rob and Remelea sheathed their weapons and staggered. They collapsed against each other then sank into the muck. All they had strength left for was to hold each other above the surface. Only a few lightpears remained. The hole in the ceiling now showed bare. Light spilled in like a finger of sunlight through thick clouds.

So there were still lightpears up there, fully grown ones, which meant more vines. Those vines weren't coming down here anymore, though. The remnants down here twitched and squirmed nervously along the walls. Their pointed ends hovered above the muck, as if tasting the air like snake tongues.

"What are they waiting for?" Remelea's voice was almost trance-like with fatigue.

Rob's chest burned and pounded. "For the last strength to go out of us, I think, so they can come in and strangle us."

"So what now?" Remelea panted. "Wait for 'em to come then do our best to take 'em with us?" It sounded almost like a suggestion.

Rob fixed his eyes on Remelea's with fresh fury. What she saw jolted her full of fresh energy. He let go of her, grabbed the hanging vine, then yanked himself to his feet with it, onto shaky legs. Remelea teetered back blearily.

"Come on." He grabbed her hand and pulled her up. "I ain't allowed to lay down and die, so neither are you."

"So what now?" she slurred.

Rob shambled drunkenly to the nearest wall. Several vines dripped from where they'd been hacked in two, now stuck to the walls by tiny hairs, as inanimate as any Earthline plant life. He grabbed one that ran in from above, and strode back, ripping it loose as he went. It squirmed in his grip, but it was too bled out to put up a real fight. He held it out to her. "Ladies first."

"Fuck you," she said. It twitched as he handed it to her, so she looked at him doubtfully. "You honestly think we'll be able to handle whatever's up there?"

"No, but like you said. We'll do our best to take it with us."

THREE

Once Remelea grabbed the ledge, Rob put his palms under her feet and pushed. Once she pulled herself out, he started climbing. Once or twice, he was almost sure he'd lose his grip and fall. She caught his arms and pulled him up into the chapel. They collapsed next to each other. Mud, blood, and Old Lords knew what else seeped and ran out of their clothes and hair onto the cold marble. Their last strength was in their hands, which clutched each other desperately.

When Rob lifted his head, the maze of vines was almost completely gone. A bare shining chapel spread around them. From the sandstone borders, it looked like the stained glass windows had been freshly installed. Didn't he remember them from the outside when he'd lived here, though? Early morning light showed through them. Rob's vision was just blurry enough that he couldn't make out the images.

The dead girl still stood there. Jesse and Zane had told Rob about her. He also remembered her from Sally's story. Up close, she made him think of Sally. Old Lords, he could see it…Sally had been force-fed some of this girl's dead flesh, in the ritual that had *altered* her. The dead girl knelt and tilted Remelea's unconscious face up, to pour liquid into her mouth from a polished chalice.

Rob's hand swatted impotently. "*Get away from her, you rotten cunt.*"

"I wouldn't try that," said a crisp male voice from the other end of the chapel. "Not unless you want your friend to die where she lays."

Rob rolled onto his side. He saw the man at the altar. In his right hand, there shimmered a jewel-hilted scimitar of the black metal. Yeah, Jesse had described it, but Rob now felt like he personally recognized it.

It's the blood memory of the High Natural. Many Crimbone have wielded that blade through the ages, and they all go on through me. For them, this blasphemer holding it has to die.

Talino waved the scimitar absently at his side like a child's plastic sword. He didn't wear his priestly vestments like leadership garb, either, more like something he'd thrown on as a housecoat. Rob squinted 'til he knew he saw right, then groaned and rolled back the other way. The dead girl was pouring liquid down Remelea's throat. Remelea spasmed, coughed, then shoved herself frantically onto her hands and knees. She spilled right back over. Rob drank when the dead girl brought the chalice to his lips. It tasted like bitter tea, only thicker. When she drew back, Rob snatched the cup savagely and kept drinking. He'd have chugged it all, but he heard Remelea's rattling gasp, spotted her staring pleadingly. He passed the cup over and let her have the rest. Fresh vitality already heated his veins. He felt every open, stinging wound, all over his body, and noticed that his bleeding had slowed up considerably.

The dead girl slipped the cup from Remelea's fingers. "That will do, Kimberly darling." Talino paced absently. "Now go wait in the foyer."

Kimberly smiled, curtsied and obeyed.

"You can both stand up whenever you're ready," said Talino. "Sorry for the rude reception. I wanted to make sure you were in the right mood for a civil interaction."

"Not quite," said Rob.

"Sure, but you're too worn out to kill me, so we can at least say what needs to be said. After that, you can decide what you really want to do."

"You can take your chances if you like."

"That's fine," said Talino. "Remelea—that's who you are, right?—would you excuse us, please?"

"Whatever you have to say to me," said Rob, "you can say to both of us."

Talino's face lit up warmly, as though watching children at play. *"Mister Coscan, I do declare!* Are you trying to play the…what's the word…*feminist?"*

"I just like it better with two of us and one of you."

"If you say so. I really should warn you, though, you won't hear everything you've come looking for, unless it's between just the two of us."

"No, it's fine, really," said Remelea. "I've had enough weird shit for one night. Rob, you came all this way for this perfumed prince asshole, you can have him. I'll just go hang out with the zombie. Or something."

Before Rob could object, she turned and strode back through the chapel. He limped towards the altar. His shoulder stung annoyingly, but it was his ass—the left cheek, specifically—that really hurt like a sonofabitch. No matter what this fuckhead had to say, he had it coming for getting Rob stabbed in the ass by Crimbone swamp-zombies.

In the rising sun outside, the stained glass windows grew clearer. Yeah, those images definitely hadn't been there the last time Rob had set eyes on this church. One showed Magur Sevi, the first High Natural, climbing the hillside arduously, bleeding from his score of wounds, the mists from the deadly valley rolling back behind him...the same image as that old drawing of Louis's, same angle and everything, except in the style of the Earth-line middle ages. Rob liked Louis's version better. The next image showed some other ancient hero of Crimbone lore, standing before an altar in a sacred place not unlike this, except with some huge alien creature seated there, fettered like a withered captive god. In another, a dark, cloaked figure strode through lashing snow and winds, a pair of long knives in hand that looked like the twin blades of Magur Sevi. In the rising sun, though, they shimmered white-hot silver instead of black. For some reason, they reminded Rob of the Spirelight glow. Above and behind the figure, there flew a dark, winged shape like a Familiar...like Puttergong.

Rob looked back at Talino. "How can you wield the black metal?"

"Maybe I was born of the Crimbone line. Maybe I decided not to make the Calls, so I might channel my energies elsewhere."

"That doesn't explain how you have it, or that you can hold it without it making you fumble so you cut your own dick off."

Talino chuckled like Rob had just tossed off a friendly joke over a few beers. "Your mad blood visions aren't the only way to touch the ephemeral realms." He stepped from the pulpit as though taking a morning stroll through a tranquil garden. "The elder Crimbone do it all the time, when they first receive the weapons that will soon be sent to the latest fledgling."

Rob flinched. He circled slowly. "The elders work with the energies sent to them, to refortify metal that's been ephemeral, for work in this world..."

"Right. All so a Crimbone can channel the truest self, the purest intent, through the black metal. Have you noticed how few Crimbone even do that anymore...aside from you and maybe your little fuck-buddy out there? They can't. Whether they realize it or not, they've *taught* themselves that three voices aren't enough for a Crimbone. They need a puppeteer. Some find it in you. Others find it in me. What's the difference?"

"Anyone answering to your call, they ain't real Crimbone." Rob snorted through blood-clogged nostrils and hissed murder through clenched teeth.

"You still talk about the others with reverence, like you talk about this weapon I shouldn't be able to handle." Talino's blade wove idle figure-eights in the air. "It doesn't matter what I've had to do so I can, or how much nobility you think its matter embodies. I'm the one holding it. When I swing it, I decide what it cuts. The wielder reveals the weapon's true nature, not the other way around. You've met Crimbone who answer to me. You probably met plenty of them when you lived here. Didn't you notice, back when you tore out of Pittsburgh, building your pack as you went? It was always the ones who joined up along the way, who were quickest to rally the others to believe in you, wasn't it? The best among them, anyway. Ah, now I see, you're putting it all together! Oh, come on, don't look so hurt. Plenty of it was still you. *No one* does that much on their own, though."

"Whatever," Rob snarled. "It doesn't change shit right here or now."

"Except how you'll always look at every fellow Crimbone you meet, for the rest of your life. You have to now. You can't afford to convince yourself wholeheartedly that I'm lying. Growing up, when they thought of the evil they'd been born to fight, I guarantee they visualized men like us. You're right, those elder Crimbone still reach through doorways that have lingered open for them. You're about to learn to open the doors they've left locked, or are just too scared to open themselves."

Rob's fingers slid around a blade's handle. "Where?"

Talino looked at the image of Magur Sevi in the stained glass window, then back at Rob. "Old Lords," he whispered, "Maybe lightning *has* struck twice."

Rob followed Talino's gaze. "He'd have wanted to kill you, too."

"Obviously. I won't lie. I'd like to live to see everything you'll become, what you'll do. It really doesn't matter, though. Why *do* you want to kill me so badly?"

"Damn, I thought you were just evil, not a fuckin' moron."

"What's your definition of evil? No, really, I'm honestly curious."

"You tortured my friends. You killed my dad. You had my wife raped and tortured. Hell, you raped her yourself, just with your damn magic instead of your dick. You did it with that girl out there, before you turned her into a zombie so you could keep…" Rob's speech dissolved into a growl. Blood pounded so hard and hot through his head, he felt like the veins in his temples would burst. Yeah, *now* he was ready for another fight! That elixir was great stuff. He took a deep breath and lowered his hands from his weapons.

Talino actually looked a little nervous. His voice stayed calm. "You ran away from your father because he tried to stunt you, like he stunted himself. When he came to me, he was looking for you, trying to take you back to that closed little world so he could keep stunting you. When he described you, I saw all your potential without even meeting you. He'd have denied you that potential. I'm the one who decided to help you realize it. I gave you the love of your life. You should know as well as I do, you *couldn't* have loved her before my…enhancements."

"Bullshit."

"When she ran away from her people to this city, do you know what she acted on? Simple childish rebellion. That's all. Same for Spirelights as it is for Schomites or Earth-liners. It smacked her in the head, like such impulses tend to do. You did the same thing. You just had more justification than most. The Spirelights? They're just conduits, like those animated corpses I sent to wear you out; an endlessly reproductive army that channels your true enemies. That's what they'll keep doing, 'til you strike at the true source."

"What, I'm supposed to go punch out the Spirelight gods themselves or something?"

"We're getting ahead of ourselves. You can reason with enemies who act on their own. Reason doesn't work on a puppet. Good thing you know what does work." Talino nodded at Rob's twin blades. "If you'd met your cute little wife like that—before I cut her strings—you'd have killed her like any other glowstick…because you *haven't* yet figured out how to strike at the true source.

Right now, there's nothing for you to do but kill as many of that source's agents as possible, like weeding the flowerbed. I *let* her be something more than just another pawn. Those people you saw out there, on the street? That's who they really are, the essence of how they've always treated each other. All I did was strip it on a drumbeat, down to the guts and bone."

"So what, you expect me to become your puppet or some shit?"

"Maybe later, you'll realize that *I've* been *your* puppet this whole time. Your so-called friends meant to lead you back into a world your father would have denied you, but they'd just do the same thing he tried to do. They can't imagine anything but treading water. They don't know if they could handle the transition. You went and set the transition rolling anyway, though. All you have to do now is ride it the rest of the way through. You couldn't do that within their structure."

"If you wanna give me so much, start with some fucking answers."

"Go ahead and ask. I'll see what I can do."

"How do I find these doorways? So I can strike at the source?"

"You'll make your second true beginning where you made your first."

Rob's head spun. His gaze dropped to the scimitar in Talino's hand. He'd seen the weapon before, he was sure...up close, somewhere in this lifetime.

The pommel was stamped with a symbol he knew, because it was stamped on the pommels of his own weapons: two vertical slashes with upward-pointed teeth on the outer edges, a straight slash running across them...the seal of Magur Sevi.

Once as a child, Rob had wandered into his parents' room, looking for Dad. Dad had been out working the farm, on his way in for an air-conditioned break, it turned out. By the time he came in, Rob had already spotted something amidst the clutter on the upper shelf through the open closet doorway…wrapped in an old blanket, the handle sticking out invitingly, unmistakably that of an antique sword. He'd moved towards it, mesmerized. He hadn't been tall enough to reach up and pull it out, but he'd been trying to think of a way to get to it when his father came in. When Metaiew Coscan saw his son looking up into that closet, he flew into a roaring rage, grabbed Rob by the arm and flung him into the hallway against the opposite wall. Still roaring, he slammed the door, like he'd caught the kid playing with a loaded gun.

Talino now gripped that same sword handle.

"Got anything more specific to tell me, asshole?" said Rob.

"Nothing comes to mind…nothing a smart boy like you oughtn't be able to figure out."

"Then I guess we're done here."

One of Rob's own knives jerked free. His eyes didn't leave Talino's sword hand, even as his blade sailed for Talino's neck. The arm didn't have time to move and block. Instead, it phased out of physical existence at the owner's side, back in higher to catch Rob's strike. Old World metal clanged and locked with Old World metal, the scimitar's edge between the saw teeth of Rob's long knife. Talino's face stayed calm and sure. Rob's wrist twisted so the teeth held the scimitar. His free hand shot up and grabbed Talino's wrist. Talino's eyes weren't calm anymore. The pounding blood in Rob's temples bled through his vision, into the sweet old crimson swirl. He pressed with the saw teeth 'til the scimitar's metal strained. It cracked in half, right as Rob snapped Talino's wrist. The whirring, vibrating song of Old World metal breaking was like no sound Rob had ever heard. Energy spurted from both halves of the break, like blood from a severed limb. It hurt Rob's ears and shook the building so hard that the stained glass shattered with a deafening pop. Harsh sunlight poured in on them like fire, mingling with the giant lightpears above. The lightpears shook and flared.

Talino stumbled backwards. The broken blade clattered between them. He tripped and fell against the altar, as much from the shaking floor as agony. Rob sheathed his own weapon and picked up the remains of his dad's sword. It rebelled against anyone else touching it, vibrating with the captive essence of Metaiew Coscan…an essence Talino's magic no longer held in check.

Just a little longer, Dad… Now leave this one to me.

Talino seethed through clenched teeth, pale and damp with sweat. Rob stalked forward snarling, dragged him upright by the hair and pulled his neck back, making sure their eyes met as he lifted the broken blade. It felt heavier with every movement. He fought it, guided it, and let the edge drop. The deep wet chop reverberated up both of Rob's arms. The body thudded against the altar. Rob rose. Talino's head swung by the hair from his fist. The broken blade of Metaiew Coscan turned to ash in Rob's hand and floated away.

Lightpears shook and blazed above as he carried the head out of the chapel.

FOUR

The dead girl followed Remelea out onto the front step, then just stood there staring at her…if you could even call whatever went on behind those blank eyes *staring*. Remelea's fingers twitched towards her hook, thinking to put the girl out of her misery, or whatever unnaturally prolonged state in which she existed. Something kept staying her hand, though…fascination, maybe? It sure as hell wasn't the bitch's smell, which was like a rusty trashcan full of rotted vegetables and dead feral cats.

Remelea edged a little further away, keeping an eye on the thing. "So…Kimberly, right? How's New Orleans life these days? Time yet for the Saints to come marching in?"

The dead girl's eyes widened a little. "Saints…Two *saints* of this church came marching in today…"

Remelea edged a little further away. "Wait, you don't mean…Me and Rob? Girl, I hate to break it to you, but there are a few problems with that idea."

"Maybe later, you'll realize I've been your puppet the whole time."

Remelea wished this dead bitch would shut up. She sounded like someone talking in her sleep, reciting her end of a conversation happening elsewhere. The flat affect made it even worse. Except for a moment, she'd sounded close to actual inflections.

"What the hell are you talking about now?" said Remelea.

"Go ahead and ask. I'll see what I can do."

Remelea looked away, back up Saint Charles. The Avenue was even emptier than they'd found it. "Look, take it up with Rob. This whole shitshow visit was his idea. Half the time, the bastard makes even less sense than you do."

"How do I find these doorways? So I can strike at the source?" Had the girl just done an impression of…Nah, couldn't be. "You'll make your second true beginning where you made your first."

Was it Remelea's imagination, or had the bitch just started stinking even worse? She turned further away from it. "Look, I just wanna get this over with so we can get the fuck out of here, hopefully to some place that doesn't smell like shit!"

"Desert air…"

"Right. The desert air would be nice right now. Nice and dry."

"Remelea."

Remelea turned and jolted. The dead girl had slipped up right next to her. "*Gah*, Jesus! I swear, you sneak up on me like that again, I'm gonna—"

Their eyes met. The thing looked alarmingly close to facial expression. "Sanderson."

For a moment, Remelea couldn't form words. "What did you just say?"

The girl's mouth moved as though to speak again, then her whole face froze, like someone had just hit pause on a video.

"*What the fuck did you just say?*"

An explosive crash echoed out of the building. It rolled through the stone beneath their feet. Remelea steadied herself and looked up the steps, to the front doorway. Here came Rob. The heat of an immense, spreading blaze rolled out after him, licking the archway with a swarm of pale yellow tongues that licked the stones and left black stains.

"What the hell were you doing in there?" She spotted the severed head snarled to his fist by the hair. "Oh."

"We should leave," he said.

"Just a Goddamn second," Remelea growled.

She lunged at Kimberly. The girl had turned away from them, her shoulders slumped morosely. Remelea's hand closed on one of those shoulders. 'Til now, she'd instinctively avoided touching the creature. Now that her fingers sank in, she realized she'd made the right call. Through the cloth of the dress, the flesh sank like wet papier-mache against the bone. Remelea spun the girl about, then froze at the sight of those eyes. A moment ago, they'd been blue. Now they blackened putridly, sinking back into the sockets like those of a dead cat stretched out on the side of the road.

Rob touched Remelea's shoulder. "She's almost gone. Let her find her own way out." There was a soothing, sonorous quality in his voice she'd never heard before

"Yeah," Remelea muttered. "Old Lords, c'mon, baby, it's fucking cold out here!"

FIVE

The Avenue was peaceful in the early dawn, except for the blazing church behind them.

"So did you learn what you came here to learn?" said Remelea.

Rob's adrenaline had subsided to a simmer. His body felt increasingly heavy, especially where he'd been bashed and gashed. The heat of the blaze washed out after them, into the street. Strange, hitherto invisible energy wafted from frosty surfaces into the air like dust clouds. In those clouds lived echoes of the shapes that birthed them, catching the light in an alien color spectrum. He'd seen that spectrum before, in dreams that weren't exactly dreams. The mirages looked and felt almost more real to him than this street. For a delirious moment, he felt like he *almost* knew how to step sideways at a just-so angle, so he'd pass completely into the dream realm. Again, he noticed Talino's head dangling from his fist. He wasn't sure why he was still holding onto it. It dripped at his feet.

"I can strike at the source," he whispered. "I can bring the true enemy to their knees."

"Rob, please," said Remelea. "Can we talk about this later?"

All of this—countless ages of genocide over two worlds—can be over, really over.

He made himself focus on the dimensions of reality he shared with her. They reached the first overturned streetcar. Nothing was left of the crowd but the mess they'd made.

"I don't reckon you know any detours around all this shit?" said Remelea.

"As a matter of fact, I do," he said. "Right this way, m'lady."

"Robert Coscan, if you ever call me *m'lady* again, Old Lords help me, I'm gonna bite your dick off."

They took one side-street, then another, back towards the overpass. After another few blocks, they saw the first new person. A black man, average looking except for the stains on his clothes, shuffled from the direction of last night's debauch. *Talk about the Walk of Shame.* The man halted when he spotted them, eyes widening.

"What's that asshole's problem?" Rob grumbled.

"The fact that you're carrying a severed head around might have something to do with it," said Remelea.

More stragglers ambled into sight at the approaching intersection.

"This is becoming not okay," said Remelea.

A party of five broke through the crowd. They approached with the upright, unified purpose of a Crimbone pack, except only three of them were Crimbone. The other two were Spirelights, clearly former Secret Police. The worlds lined up in front of Rob's eyes. He saw the tendrils in the air between the party, binding them. It looked nothing like the bonds of love and camaraderie he felt between himself and Remelea, keeping them from falling in a heap with the rest of the corpses littering the streets. These three Crimbone felt no less inclined than natural to gut the Spirelights at their side and drink their glow. Something crueler than bloodlust weighted them all down, driven through them like rusty nails. Something worse kept their legs and backs straight…a fear that outweighed the spectral shackles…*Puppets*, like Talino had said.

Rob and Remelea closed the distance and faced the three Crimbone and two Spirelights.

"Both of you, come with us," said one of the Crimbone, "to answer to the charge of these lands for the disturbance you've caused."

Rob lifted Talino's head. "You mean this charge?" He tossed it like a bowling ball so it rolled at the speaker's feet.

"We didn't answer to him. These degenerates here were his playthings. Our true leader is stronger than any High Natural."

"He in walking distance?" said Rob.

"Sure, if you have the strength left to get to the French Quarter."

"Sure," said Remelea. "Just one thing first…" Her hook ripped from her belt. The two Spirelights drew weapons as she closed with them. Rob nearly sprang to her aid, but he'd seen her eyes. All she could see right now was the glow. Its taste was the sweetest thing on the air, especially as she ripped the Spirelights open and drank deep. She needed it more than he did. By the time she settled down, the Spirelight puppets lay at her feet in a lake of entrails.

Rob's left blade stuck out at arm's length, its edge resting against the throat of the lead Crimbone, who'd skidded to a halt just in time to keep his windpipe closed.

He eased backwards. The other two Crimbone froze in their tracks, as Rob brandished his other blade. They blinked and looked at each other, the way Earth-line assailants usually did when they saw a Crimbone move— or rather *didn't* see, thanks to the blinding speed.

"Sorry," Remelea said. "I was getting distracted."

"Just remember to share next time," said Rob. His eyes returned to the rival Crimbone. "Like you were saying, guy. Lead the way."

SIX

Hanging moss had overtaken every surface in the French Quarter. Kudzu vines snaked up walls and wrought iron railings, entwined with more of that veiny, sickly orange plant matter Rob had seen spilling from the ruptured palm trees. He didn't have a chance to slow down for a closer look, but he kept spotting those pale, bulging growths, the ones he couldn't tell if they were puffing fruit or cancerous growths. More than once, he swore he saw screaming faces pressing up from beneath those growths…faces from somewhere else, screaming either in eagerness to burst free, or in warning to any onlookers, about whatever waited on the other side from which they came.

A small cluster of tag-alongs hemmed Rob and Remelea in. The three other Crimbone led the way. They reached a stone dock on the bank of the Mississippi. A massive, multi-tiered heap of metal floated alongside them, one of those old-fashioned tourist-trap gambling boats, now overgrown with rust and more maliciously crawling plant life, none of it native to Louisiana, or this world for that matter.

The lead Crimbone stopped, cupped his hands to his mouth, and gave a bullhorn bellow. "*All hands on top deck. Great Balthazar has been sent for. We need witnesses for his audience with these blasphemers.*"

A metal gangplank extended out on clanking gears and pulleys. It settled on the edge of the stone dock. Rob and Remelea followed the three local Crimbone up the ramp, leaving the entourage behind. Soon as they stood on board, the plank rolled up behind them. Their hosts led them through a dilapidated, moldy-smelling casino hall, to a metal stairwell that went up four stories. The Spirelight glow pulsed powerfully throughout this boat. The higher they climbed, the thicker it grew.

They stepped out of the stairwell, onto the upper deck. Before them spread what had once been a lavish dance floor beneath the open sky. Fifty or so slaves waited, Crimbone on one side, the Spirelights on the other, like two families at a wedding. No one smelled like they'd washed in a while, unless you counted splashing around in the gutters like drunk pigs in shit. At the far end of the deck, there waited a wide, empty space. The three Crimbone obscured that view as they headed down the center. Rob and Remelea followed. The wind stirred strangely. The three Crimbone stopped abruptly at the end of the walkway. Faint shifting sounded. They stepped aside.

At the head of the deck, which had been empty a second ago, a short, stocky man now strutted like a rooster. He wore a torn shirt and blue jeans cut off at the knees. His head was wrapped in an oversized speckled bandana with the tied flaps falling over his left shoulder. Similar cloth bound his lower arms and legs, like bandages covering hideous wounds. His gnarled feet and hands were bare, showing off clawed, misshapen fingers and toes. His skin looked like tanned leather. His mouth and nose were thick and elongated like a pit-bull's snout. His drooling mouth opened and showed off sharp, jagged teeth. Beady yellow eyes glittered with a malicious simplicity that might be either stupidity or distilled, focused hyper-intelligence of the deadliest kind. Maybe both. He stormed towards Rob and Remelea, champing and stamping, the drool turning to froth. The crowd receded from him on either side, as though for some revered holy man.

"Who these fucksticks?" shrieked the abrasive voice from a mouth that didn't look built for human speech. The voice sounded scratchy and wet, like gravel grinding through putrid honey. "Colt, why you had me called from the good work to look at 'em?"

The lead Crimbone smiled. "This man claims to be the High Natural. He doesn't believe me when I tell him you've replaced him."

"I tol' you, boy, don't go talkin' at me like one of them hotshot fancy big-city business cocksucker types." Those drooling jaws looked ready to literally bite Colt's face off.

Somehow, Colt didn't shit himself. Or if he did, Rob didn't smell it. "Sorry, great Balthazar…I meant to say—"

"I know what you fuckin' said. I just don't like the sound of it. Like you're talkin' down at me, like maybe you forgot where you come from, *like maybe I can't depend on you.* So shut up." Balthazar spun, strutted over, and got in Rob's face. "So this here's the famous big, bad ol' Rob Coscan, huh. And here I was, thinkin' I should expect somethin' fancy. Boy, to me, you just look like another scarred-up Crimbone bitch. Don't even start with that ol' song an' dance about them two pig-stickers you got there, or who else used to sling 'em around."

Rob turned his face to the side. This guy's breathe smelled like he'd been sucking moldy beer through a dead dog's ass. "Well, for starters, shorty, I just killed your boss."

Balthazar squawked out an ear-piercing laugh. "Silly rabbit! I run the show 'round here, like I'll be runnin' it all over this rottin' little globe pretty soon. Folks answer to *me*, like you'll soon be doin'. *I* ain't got *no* boss!"

"Not even Talino?"

"Heheh…heh…Hear that, Colt? This feller's a real joker, huh? Here he goes, tryin' to make me think he's killed the Daddy! Like he could…like *anyone* could…"

Every tooth in Colt's grin was like a blade twisting in a wound. "I'm afraid he's not joking, Great Balthazar. He cut the Daddy's head off. I saw the head a little less than an hour ago, so I figured you should meet this guy."

Balthazar's next ear-piercing squawk was one of disbelieving agony. He struck like a snake where he happened to be pointed, which was at Colt. Gnarled clawed fingers caught Colt under the chin, hoisted him skyward and jerked loose. The momentum sent Colt a few inches higher, like an upside-down yo-yo. Balthazar spun with a heel-out, groin-pulverizing kick. Colt's back smacked the railing with a crunch. His body tipped backwards, slid off the railing, and splashed somewhere below. Balthazar headed back towards his guests. His claw lashed down, not at Rob, but at Remelea. With a panicked roar, Rob's blades sang free. His right swooped up and caught Balthazar's forearm inches from her face. Cloth binding shredded…and metal clanged against metal.

Rob's eyes widened. This fucker moved faster than anyone he could remember…yet the movements slowed in his strange new double-vision. Wherever Balthazar's limbs went, an otherworldly mirror seemed to hover above them. In that mirror, the next move always came a second or so sooner, so Rob's reactions happened accordingly. It gave him just enough of a lead to hold his own. With a dripping grin, Balthazar pistoned a splayed palm at Rob's sternum. Rob drove the tip of his other knife at the palm. Remelea, of course, had already pulled her hook. She swung it at Balthazar's leg, which was already coming at her midsection. Midway, the kick changed course. It went under the hook and caught her hip. She rolled with it, but still doubled up as she went backwards. She thudded and tumbled across the metal deck. The crowd on the Crimbone side scattered for her. She tried to sit up and doubled forward.

Balthazar's palm closed into a fist and sailed just shy of Rob's edge. Their knuckles smacked each other. Rob's hand flared like he'd just punched a brick wall. Balthazar's other leg came in a sidekick. Rob darted backwards, chopping with his uninjured hand. The leg retreated from the blade. The arm with the freakishly hard edge backhanded Rob in the face. Rob's back smacked the floor. He rolled out of the way of a bare, clawed foot that stomped at his face. The stomp made the whole deck vibrate. Rob came back up and spun to face the monster. When Balthazar unleashed punches and kicks, Rob went into a spin. Balthazar's graceful bobs, weaves and sidesteps looked like a folk dance. Rob's knives aimed again and again at the vitals, kept clanging against knees, lower calves, and the undersides of forearms. The knife handles rippled against his palms and up through his limbs, like the kick of a gun, 'til his fingers felt numb and flimsy. Over and over, his ears recognized a special clang. *What the fuck*—

By now, Remelea had strutted painfully to her feet. She rushed Balthazar from behind. Without looking back, Balthazar grabbed Rob's wrists and slung up his haunches into a mule-kick. Remelea took both feet in the chest. She let out a deep hiccupping sound and tumbled away.

Rob's feet left the ground. The world spun like a kaleidoscope as his body stretched out a-dangle. His shoulders strained in their sockets. Wind flattened his clothes against his skin. Balthazar's hands squeezed his wrists tighter, then let go. A hollow metal wall slammed into Rob's back. It strained and scraped him as he slid to the deck.

Somewhere, Balthazar screamed, "*You ain't killed the Daddy, you ain't killed the Daddy, you ain't killed the Daddy!*"

Rob rolled forward onto his hands and knees. This must be how insects splattered on windshields felt. He'd dropped his knives somewhere. His fingers quested for them. He couldn't find them.

Remelea was back up. She rushed Balthazar again, in a low crouch. Her hook sailed through a maneuver that would unavoidably gut anyone but this freak. The cloth on Balthazar's limbs hung in shreds, so Rob saw most of what had been blocking him: long, pointed exoskeletal cylinders like curving tusks. They shimmered in an unmistakable shade of black. Balthazar's right fist swung at Remelea. The tusk parted from the arm, tearing away the last of the cloth, revealing a fan-like spread of flesh.

Remelea evaded the worst of it, but still caught some knuckles on the side of her neck. As she went sprawling, her hook licked out and grazed Balthazar's midsection. He squawked and hopped away, then danced around like someone had dumped fire-ants into his boxer-shorts. The last of the cloth fluttered away from his altered appendages. The black metal hadn't been strapped to him like armor. It was grafted through his flesh, who knew how deep. The horns on the arms were rooted just beneath the palms. The metal capped his knees in slats that ran down the sides of his legs, looped his ankles, then came up behind in more horns. The horns opened and closed slightly, reflexively, showing off their fans.

Rob shook his head as clear as he could manage. He'd landed against the outer stairwell wall. Next to him, the door to the stairwell swung open and shut in the breeze. By now, most of the spectators had panicked and fled through it. Others darted around the deck, trying to watch while keeping out of the way. Some of them had gotten trampled. Others still tried to reach the door. A Crimbone ran past Rob. Two Spirelights were close behind.

Since his First Call, Rob had never forgotten about the glow while around Spirelights, 'til today. He remembered it fine as these ones approached, because he could seriously use the boost right now. His senses flared towards the scent. Balthazar and Remelea looked far away and hazy.

Balthazar punched Remelea again, this time in the face. He lifted her off the ground by the neck. She hung limply from his fist. By her heaving, terrified breathing, Rob could see that she was still conscious.

"*Fuckin' High Natural who kills the Daddy,*" shrieked Balthazar, "I'm gonna whip you out'a that pretty shape of yours. Then I'm gonna whip you back into shape and add you to my gang, once you know who's boss. First, though, I'm gonna break your bitch here into itty-bitty pieces so there's no puttin' her back together. Then I'm gonna fuck what's left!"

Rob pistoned himself up and almost fell right back down. Another Spirelight ran past him, for the door. Rob threw himself sideways and tackled it. The Spirelight bucked and kicked. The glow already flared up through Rob, feeding his fury, which fed his strength. His teeth latched onto the Spirelight's windpipe and worried left and right. He wrenched back, spat out a gob of meat and trachea, and plunged his face into the gushing fountain. Wave after wave of maddening light electrified his veins, as he sucked down mouthful after mouthful of blood, all in a few seconds. He shoved the heap aside and sprang back up.

Remelea's arm was twisted behind her back to the snapping point as he closed the distance. His palm edge swung in a chop, onto the joint of the arm bending hers. Balthazar's arm let go and swung wild. Rob evaded it as he launched his other fist in a jab to the chin. Remelea dropped away as Balthazar staggered in surprise. Rob's old boxing instincts kicked in. Motherfucker, he'd hammer Balthazar's elongated snout so far in 'til that ugly fucking face was shaped *normal*. He gave a left, a right, then an uppercut, saw the weakening counters coming, pulled a rope-a-dope, then launched a sustained chain-punch. He grinned as he finally saw Balthazar staggering.

Remelea, meanwhile, fumbled around 'til she found her hook, then shambled as she chased down another fleeing Spirelight. Her shambling was almost as good as an average person at full strength, and her prey was panicked.

Striking Balthazar's jaw and cheeks hurt almost like getting punched. Rob braced his wrists and kept slinging, concentrating on the nose and other soft spots. Cartilage turned to squirting pulp. It gloved his hands and arms in lumpy gore. For a moment, Balthazar appeared to totter helplessly, then he straightened up, grinned and snorted out a bright red snot-rocket the size of a grenade. Rob sprang away so it splattered on the deck between them like a gob of rotted fruit. Balthazar launched one punch then another. Rob crouched and bobbed between them, then locked his hands around Balthazar's neck. It was like squeezing a tree trunk, until his thumbs found the windpipe. Balthazar grabbed Rob's shoulders and sank his claws in. Rob held fast and bucked both elbows, knocking

Balthazar's arms wide. This time, the clawed hands closed on Rob's wrists, squeezing and digging and pulling, the strongest hands Rob had ever felt. Blood streamed slickly over his forearms.

Balthazar started kicking, so Rob's heel stomped on both his feet and kicked him over and over in the shins. The guy's bones obviously weren't all made of metal, but they were damn sturdy. Every attack on them sent back shots of pain. The two of them spilled backwards together. Balthazar twisted sideways so Rob went under him. Rob's ribs strained, smacked between the metal deck and Balthazar's bulk. Balthazar cocked back a fist aimed at Rob's face. That's when Rob saw something out of the corner of his eye, just out of reach. He wrenched sideways. Now his hips rather than his torso were pinned under Balthazar. The punch broke two of his ribs instead of his face. His fingers closed around what he'd been reaching for.

Balthazar's fist cocked back again. Rob twisted around and lunged up, arm out. At the end of the arm was one of the black blades. It skewered Balthazar between the ribs. Balthazar froze and looked down at his bleeding torso. Rob yanked the blade out, ready to stab again. Balthazar leapt up and away, howling and yelping like a little kid with a bee sting. Blood gushed down his side, painting his abdomen and jeans, spreading out across the deck around him like he'd pissed himself.

By now, Remelea had finished with her Spirelight. She stalked back in with her dripping hook, still sore and cautious.

"You little shit, I was fightin' fair!" Balthazar turned left and right, still hopping around. Dark, wet red painted his shirt. "Next time you run into me, I'm gonna fight dirty, you little fucksticks, hear me? An' I'm gonna fight even *dirtier* while we away from each other!"

The deck blurred and tottered around Rob and Remelea. Balthazar was gone. "Where'd the freak go?" Remelea slurred. "He was just here."

"Yeah," said Rob. "So were a lot of assholes." By now, the deck spread empty around them.

"Yeah. Cool. That makes sense. Smart assholes. That guy, though…What the fuck…It's like he just…then he was…Holy shit, what a…" She put her palm to her forehead. "Damn, what a fucked-up morning."

Rob sniffed and listened to the air. "He'll want us at our full strength before he takes us on again."

"So it'll be a while. Cool. Once we're out of this city, I say we sleep for a week."

"No arg—*Ah!*" Rob curled forwards, clutched his ribs, and rasped, "Yeah, no shit."

SEVEN

It's pretty dead back up the Avenue, except for the burning church, which is mostly a blackened stone shell by now, with just a few blades of pure yellow still licking the inner edges of the gutted windows. If anyone's watching, it's from behind the darkened, shattered store and restaurant fronts, telling themselves its safe there 'til the coast is clear enough for them to go out scavenging for food. Most of those skulkers are likelier to *become* food and/or pieces of ass for someone or something else, but that's their business.

One minute the street's empty. Then the air moves all weird through some nearby trees, and a tired, battered thirteen-year-old boy appears in the middle of the intersection. His bloody face twitches and contorts as he stares at the smoldering church. Anyone watching ducks for cover.

Balthazar winces and rubs at the gash in his side. It's already closed up, but his hand still comes away red and sticky. He stares at his red palm, trying to remember the last time someone got one in on him so bad. The wound still throbs so he wants to sit down, like the black metal's still stuck in him, coursing through his bloodstream like bad drugs. It's the first time a wound has tried to put him out of action since his earliest years on the farm.

Balthazar can't sit down. That'd be weak. Weakness would disappoint the Daddy. He had to see where the Daddy died, though, before he gets on with the good work, keepin' it up 'til the world the Daddy wanted to make is up and runnin'. Except how can it get there without the Daddy? Balthazar don't know if he's up to fillin' those shoes, even if he could fit his big ugly clawed feet into 'em. It's weird, how his whole body smarts from a beatin', like he just got as good as he gave, for once. He tries to sniff, but his snout's all clogged with clottin' blood. He huffs out a giant gob that splats in the street, then snorts a few more times 'til he can breathe in and out through his nose. He still don't smell the Daddy. There's nothing left of the Daddy to smell in that charred church.

No, wait, there's still a faint trace of the Daddy on the air. It lingers on the rotting gob nearby, the one that used to be the Daddy's girlfriend. That nasty High Natural and his nasty bitch partner just left her like that, spendin' her last minutes scared and lost and alone, 'cause she didn't have the Daddy's love-magic to keep her goin' no more.

The daddy's girlfriend used to be an Earth-line girl. Then she gave somethin' from herself so the Daddy could make a perfect girlfriend for the High Natural. She helped out so good that the Daddy loved her and made her so she'd live as long as he did.

The Daddy told Balthazar all about the High Natural and the High Natural's girlfriend. Lately, he told Balthazar all about the bitch the High Natural's with now. Before even touching the deck, Balthazar smelled that those two been fuckin'. So now the High Natural ain't even with that nice, perfect girlfriend the Daddy made for him. The Daddy made that girlfriend for the High Natural so he could become the big ol' badass he is, and he up an' left her, and he paid the Daddy back by killin' him!

Balthazar knows the Daddy weren't his real daddy. He's pretty sure he was made in the ritual only a year or somethin' after the High Natural's girlfriend. His momma was a Crimbone fledgling, doin' work for the Daddy out in the swamps. But she fucked it up somehow. The Daddy had already had the idea for Balthazar in his head for a while. So he had the momma be the momma, as a way to make amends for failin' him. Balthazar's real daddy was her Familiar. *The* Daddy fixed 'em both up with magic, made it so they could make a little Balthazar right there on the altar. Kinda like how he made the High Natural's girlfriend, only different. Balthazar's not quite either kinda thing—his momma or his daddy—so he's never been able to get a girlfriend, from either species.

At the farm, when he was good, the momma used to bring him girls from the town. She'd throw 'em in the pen and tell him they could be his girlfriend. He always tried bein' a nice boyfriend, he really did. Momma kept tellin' him how quick he was growin' up, quicker than any normal boy. He should feel proud to already be gettin' girlfriends, she said. If he didn't make them girls his girlfriends, she kept tellin' him, he'd be too wound up the rest of the time to learn proper.

It never worked out, though, between him and those gals. Oh, he'd tried, even managed to get it in far enough once or twice so it felt nice, but they always kept screamin' and clawin' at him so he screamed and clawed back, so by the end, it always ended with a big, clumpy, smelly mess to clean up. Finally, Balthazar stopped tryin' to be a boyfriend. He even got to feel bad about tryin' so hard. After that, when Momma tossed the girls in, he'd just stay in one corner of the pen while they cowered in the opposite corner. Momma always had to clean out the cage, once Balthazar finished. That always made her even more pissed off, so she beat him worse.

Balthazar still ain't quite sure what Momma did with the girls he *didn't* touch. He's pretty sure she gave 'em to the men who came to teach him to fight. Sometimes he recognized those girls' smells on those guys, like that.

There were folks who came to be other kinds of teachers, to tell Balthazar all about the world. He guesses they treated him like a student nice enough, even though he could tell they were scared to be in the pen with him. They taught him to read, told him all kinds of stories, about military history, how battles were fought and won, with or without any of the big, fancy equipment. They told him about how big an advantage he'd have, how he'd be able to make the whole process of war real simple like, when he was unleashed on the world, because of all the things he could do that no one else in history had ever been physically capable of, and because of all the things about the world the Daddy had told him.

Then came Crimbone men. They visited him in his cage. At first Balthazar thought they saw him as somethin' to beat up on. Then he figured out they was there to teach him how to fight. Obviously, they found him scary and disgusting like Momma did…like the girls Momma gave him always used to. Once he figured out how to fight back, though, the ones who stayed alive liked him even less. Even the ones who lived wouldn't be fit to fight for a long time. That's why a different bunch came every week.

Only the Daddy didn't think Balthazar was disgusting or scary. The Daddy was only around some of the time, though. The Daddy called Balthazar beautiful. The Daddy loved Balthazar, so Balthazar loved the Daddy. Balthazar asked, why did the Daddy make him stay with all these mean people? The Daddy said he'd like to take Balthazar away from here, back to the swamp-city where he was born. Balthazar would'a loved that. He'd love to have the Daddy for his real daddy. The Daddy's girlfriend could be like his real Momma. But Balthazar was turnin' into somethin' more powerful and beautiful than anything else, something that'd be able to tear this nasty world apart and put it back together nicer, once the Spirelights, the Schomites, the Crimbone and the Earth-line folks have all been knocked into line together, into their proper place.

Then came the last time Balthazar's momma chased him into the pen with the stick. It must'a been a few days since the last bunch of Crimbone came to give him his fightin' lessons. He hadn't left a one of 'em alive. He guesses by then he was too used to fightin'. On that fateful day, something clicked on automatically in his brain. Momma didn't look like the momma no more. She just looked like some bitch who kept hittin' him with a big stick. So he took that stick away and beat her with it 'til she was splattered all over the pen. When he went out, all them other folks on the farm was rushin' to fight him too. He beat 'em with the stick 'til it broke. After that, he used his teeth and claws. That was also the first time he used the metal horns on his arms an' legs—the ones the Daddy had drawn an' sculpted from the ephemeral realms, so he could make 'em part of Balthazar's body with magic.

Once everyone on the farm was good and splattered, Balthazar got scared. The Daddy would be pissed, probably wouldn't love Balthazar no more. So Balthazar went and huddled in the pen with the Momma's splattered remains.

Eventually, the Daddy showed up. Turned out, the Daddy wasn't pissed at all. In fact, he was pleased as punch. He'd known Balthazar would eventually do that, he said. It meant Balthazar was finally ready to leave the farm. For a while, Balthazar lived with the Daddy in the swamp-city. He mostly wasn't allowed to go out, except some nights when the Daddy snuck him out to the naked swamp. That's where the Daddy taught Balthazar what them black metal horns on his arms and legs was really for, taught him how to really use 'em.

The Daddy would take out that big curved knife and tell Balthazar to fight him. At first, Balthazar was scared to. He remembered what happened to everyone else he'd fought. He didn't want to do that to the Daddy. That's the only time the Daddy ever got mad at him, talked mean like the people at the farm, told Balthazar he'd stop lovin' him if he didn't fight. So Balthazar did what he was told. He never hurt the Daddy, though, 'cause no matter how mad he got, or how fast he attacked, or from which angle, the Daddy's big curved knife was always right there to block him. The Daddy told Balthazar all the different *ways* to attack, kept havin' Balthazar practice 'til he got every last one of those moves just right. That took a while. There was a lot of moves for Balthazar to get *just right*. By the end of it, though, he sure knew plenty of 'em.

Balthazar still wished he could go outside more, like maybe during the day some. Otherwise, those was the happiest times of his life. Then shit started happenin' out in the world, on account of the High Natural. That's when them two old Crimbone came from the north, to a party at one of the Daddy's other houses. They tried to kill the Daddy. They burned down the Daddy's house. After that, the Daddy came and said it was time to start the good work full force. He taught Balthazar all about how to go about it. That's all Balthazar's been doin' ever since. He's been even happier than when it was just him, the Daddy, and the Daddy's girlfriend...all 'til last night and today, when the High Natural stopped hidin' in the woods and hit the city.

The Daddy always said they'll all like Balthazar fine, once they realize it's him who gave 'em the nicer world they got comin'. Balthazar don't yet know where to start without the Daddy, though. Ever since he was set loose, Balthazar knew when he got there just what to do...every place, over and over. He always had the Daddy, waitin' for him back home, to tell him *where* to strike, and when. That's the one thing Balthazar don't know no more, though. Good for him, he knows just where to go to find out...even though he don't wanna, had been hopin' never to have to look at that place again.

All the same, he sucks it up, spreads his wings, and takes to the air one more time, out over the swamp-city they used to call New Orleans, then over the tangled, rottin' wilderness surroundin' the place. Before long, he spots the little soggy island, covered up top with an old rotten farm, rotten wire cages...and a rotten little cabin, hanging halfway out over the mucky water at the back, with gators swimmin' around the bottom of those stilts. Balthazar don't wanna walk inside that stilted cabin, but he do. He knows what he's gotta find there, and he knows just where to start lookin'.

The few times Balthazar was ever allowed inside this ol' shack, it was the one place that ever felt like what most folks must call *home*. That was always only ever when the Daddy visited. It was always not too cold in there, not too hot, but just right, full of paintings on the walls, nice furniture that smelled like sanded wood and oil…somethin' about it just always too nice to not soothe the mind and heart, no matter what ugliness you'd just walked out of. And always there, in the back room—*the study*—was the Daddy's desk, where the Daddy used to sit over lots of old books and maps, copyin' down words and lines, into a big ol' book of his own.

The Daddy always put on his long, lightly woven, bright green coat before he sat down to work. The Daddy always seemed like he could relax for a while, forget who the rest of the world wanted him to be, whenever he put on that long, bright green coat.

That long green coat must feel really comfy, Balthazar remembers thinkin'. *I hope the Daddy lets me put it on some day.*

"This is where I'm mapping these lands, Balthazar," the Daddy once told him, "so by the time you're ready to spread your wings and fly out across the world, I'll be able to tell you where to go, so you'll know where to spread the Good Work."

"But how do I work the Good Work, Daddy?" little Balthazar asked.

"Oh…by the time you're ready, and I've pointed you in the right direction, you'll know." With that, the Daddy reached over, ruffling and scratching at Balthazar's big, pointy ears.

That turned out to be true, sure enough. Except now that the Daddy's dead, Balthazar don't know what to do no more. He don't know *where* the Daddy next wanted him to go, for starters. But the book where the Daddy wrote everything down, all his plans that Balthazar now needs to follow, that's *gotta* still be here. Doesn't it?

The first thing Balthazar notices, when he walks in, is that all the furniture has been taken out. The boards sag with wet rot beneath his feet. All those paintings he used to love starin' into for hours, they're all still here, but they've fallen off the walls, their frames busted, so they sag sideways, with mold creepin' up out of the boards, over their faces.

When Balthazar walks into the study, the Daddy's desk is still right where it always was. When he pulls open the top drawer, the whole desk whispers wetly, then one of the legs gives out so it collapses sideways. One of the floorboards splits beneath it, so it goes even more lopsided. Bathazar gasps, draws back, then leans in and looks into the open drawer. There it sits, the Daddy's big black book of notes and maps. When Balthazar picks it up, though, it falls apart between his fingertips into wet papier-mache, like a wheat cracker someone's been sucking on for too long.

Balthazar throws his head back and howls at the molderin', saggin' ceiling, "*What am I gonna do now?*"

He sinks to the floor and feels the boards sag beneath his knees. Hell, he can feel the whole building saggin', closer to just breakin' loose and crashin' into the swamp. With his eyes squeezed shut, he starts to visualize the swamp, as it spreads out for miles around. Through that swamp, there shoots a single zig-zaggin' beam of light, like a glowin' snake, right up into Bathazar.

"Who are you?" Balthazar whimpers.

I'm the voice—the true *voice—the one your* Daddy *always answered to. All those answers he sought in that soggy, rotted book…Don't worry, I'm here to give them to you anew, as not even he ever knew.*

"So you're…you're…Is this the lands themselves talkin' to me, directly like, at last?"

I am the one who has flowed in the lifeblood of these lands since the Deschembines first set foot upon these shores. I'm the only reason the Schomites were ever able to listen to the voices of the lands in the first place. All this time, the Schomites and the Spirelights *have waged their ideological wars, never realizing that I was the one they were really fighting over, this whole time. They could never hear me, though…except for a few, those like your Daddy, the ones who learned how to* truly *listen.*

"But…how is it *I* know how to truly listen? The Daddy never taught me how."

He didn't need to. You hear me now because I've chosen to speak to you directly, starting here and now, as I never did for him or the others. I've waited a very, very long time for someone just like you, Balthazar. That's the real reason I helped your Daddy…so we could create something beautiful and perfect like you. Soon, you will be the one to unite the rest of them, as I've always known you would, dear one. Don't you worry. I will show you how.

"How to what? Kill off the Spirelights and their gods?"

Oh no, my boy. I'm here to tell you how to take the gods themselves *as your slaves…to take their power as your own. Listen to me, and I'll lead you to where you need to be to claim it. I'll lead everyone who needs to be there to the appropriate place, at the chosen ritual hour. They'll do your bidding and think it was their own idea, until it's too late.*

THE GOSPEL ACCORDING

TO PUTTERGONG

ONE

Many lights burned in the base, but only one in the little town surrounding it. Naturally, those lights were in a bar—all candles, oil lamps, and a fireplace. The generator Zane had rigged didn't have the juice for the whole town.

Hours earlier, two Crimbone, two civilian Schomites, and one former agent of the Spirelight Secret Police had walked into that bar. One of the Crimbone had dealt with the locked door, with all his usual subtlety. That meant they'd have to prop the door shut with a chair against the snowy wind. The place hadn't been raided dry, because everyone except this crowd was too scared to go out scavenging this far. They took turns playing bartender. Right now, it was one of the Schomites. She put two Heinekens and two Guinnesses in front of everyone else, while her husband plucked magic from an old guitar, singing in a soft, dark, reflective murmur.

The Spirelight shouted, "Hey Lilly, grab yourself a beer and get your ass out here with the rest of us!"

"No way." She swigged from a bottle of Jack Daniel's. "Beer's for pussies."

"You are who you hang with, sweetheart."

She winked at him. "It's okay. I like pussy."

Tiger sat to Sheldon's right with the guitar. It wasn't dark yet, according to Bob Dylan in Tiger's voice, but it was getting there. Sheldon glanced at the window. He agreed with the second part. Jesse and Zane sat to his left.

"Any altercations on your watch last night?" Jesse asked.

Sheldon realized Jesse was talking to him. He filled Jesse in on the incident with Deacon. "So where's Sally now?" he asked.

"Taking a look at that carcass we hauled back," said Zane.

"After what she just went through with you guys," said Sheldon, "she should lay off her watch a little. She's earned it."

"Yeah," said Jesse, "and you ought'a take yours more seriously or quit volunteering for it."

"Fuck you, I'm drinking here."

Jesse sniffed. "Like you stopped off to fuck your girlfriend while you were still on your watch?"

Tiger's next pluck on the string faltered, so the sound died off in a dissonant twang. Sheldon felt every eye in the place zeroing in on him and Jesse.

"How'd you—? Oh, right." Sheldon pounded half his beer in one chug, then set it down hard. He ignored Tiger's audible gulp. "Yeah, sure. Then I went and caught back up afterwards, and guess what? *Nothing else had happened!*"

"You sure about that?"

Sheldon could only think of one other older man whose laconic manner could shift so little, while letting so much more threatening severity bleed into the atmosphere. For the first time in years, he remembered his father, in the Common Ground, right before the asshole had damn near knocked his brains out against the edge of a countertop. He now drew a deep breath through his nose. Jesse Karn wasn't his father, and he wasn't eleven years old anymore.

"Yeah, Jesse, I'm sure," said Sheldon. "I was trained as a detective from age five, remember? And without being able to tell who's been fucking who by sniffing at 'em like a dog. It ain't like there's a big stretch of turf for me to cover, either."

Jesse's stern, cold eyes stayed on Sheldon. "Right, and the civilians living on that turf have a lot to be nervous about, every damn waking minute of their lives. That makes 'em prone to do stupid shit. You think your Earth-line girl's the only one who might run into trouble from someone acting like Deacon? You being there could make all the difference between—"

"It's never led to a damn bit of difference since the first few weeks, *because these people never know one way or another*. They *think* I'm out prowling around, that I'll drop out of nowhere and fix everything if they get in trouble, like I'm…who's that guy in all those Earth-line movies and picture books, the one with the pointy ears?" He looked at Tiger. Tiger always remembered shit like that.

"I think you mean Batman," said Tiger.

"Right. Well, guess what? I'm not the Goddamn Batman, and I'm fucking sick of people who should know better pressuring me to live up to something I never agreed to be."

Jesse pointed to the knives on Sheldon's belt. "You picked those up when they were offered to you."

"Ah, fuck you, you've got even less of an idea what these are than Claudette did." He slapped both handles. Everyone but Jesse and Zane tensed, like they thought he was about to draw them. He rolled his eyes. "Hell, that dead headless bitch could've been offering me a couple Hbombs for all she knew…Shit, fuck this. Hey, Tiger, why'd you stop playing, man? I was enjoying the song."

"I'm all set for now," said Tiger.

An awkward silence followed. Once Tiger started plucking chords again, everyone relaxed back into reverie before they knew it. His melodious voice—so strong, yet still so sensitive—murmured, *"As you look around this room tonight…Settle in your seat tonight…"*

Tiger *would* play that song now, wouldn't he? Before Sheldon knew it, he relaxed back onto his stool, murmuring along with the lyrics. Except he wasn't singing along to Tiger's rendition. He sang along to the original recording, the first time he'd heard it, flopped on Janie's beanbag chair in her bedroom in Brattleboro when they were kids. *What do you want from me*…He'd thought he wanted to ask that question back then. Ha! How did the original version of that song go again? It was one of those Earth-line classic rock bands Janie liked. She'd know. He wished she was here, with him, having fun with these guys. That's what he wanted from her, just to see her having fun again. Her life back in Brattleboro—with her mom, with her friends—had seemed pretty fun. Then he'd showed up.

When Tiger sang the closing lines, Sheldon sighed, "If any of the Earth-line folks out there make it through this, Old Lords, let it be the music-makers."

Jesse and Zane glanced at each other.

"I'll drink to that," said Zane. Everyone agreed. "A lot of great Earth-line artists got Schomite blood in their ancestry, you know. Most of 'em live and die without even knowing about it. There'll be artists who survive this. Deschembine and Earth-line." He leaned on the bar, gazed off, nodded slowly to Tiger's bluesy guitar rhythm, and smiled. "They'll be the ones who tell the truth folks'll know about all this shit. Sure, the historians'll fuck it up."

He elbowed Jesse and they exchanged a wink. "They always do. It's the music-makers who tell the truth, the one people'll figure out."

"Think so?" asked Sheldon.

"Crimbone live longer than other folks, kid," said Zane. "Got better memories, too."

Sheldon straightened his back, stood up, and suddenly felt sober. His face contorted violently. His hand went to his solar plexus. He swayed, ready to keel forward over the bar. Jesse and Zane rose and stepped to either side of him. He snatched the bottle of Jack from the bar and chugged hard. Lilly was up and had her hands on his shoulders. Her gentle touch could soothe a rabid badger. Sheldon lowered the bottle. He hardly noticed when she slipped it from his hand. He wiped a glistening smear from his mouth and held her hand desperately to his shoulder.

"Sorry," he shuddered.

Tiger had a hand on Sheldon's other shoulder. "It's cool, man. We've got you."

Sheldon's free hand grabbed Tiger's arm. "Jesse, Zane. You got your weapons, right?"

At those words, everyone was up and ready. Their eyes followed Sheldon's to the front door. It flew open, sent the chair against it crashing, and smacked the wall. A blast of arctic wind carried in a big, dark, winged shape, on a gust of snow that hit everyone in the face. Jesse and Zane answered Sheldon's question by pulling blade and hammer respectively. The wings settled well shy of them on the edge of the bar, folding and shivering around a potbellied bat-like shape.

"*Whoooooooooooooo-eeeeeee!* I jus' flew in, and hot damn, is my wings tired…Yeah, I know, that'n's a moldy-cheese oldie, but that moldy cheese is good eatin'."

Sheldon rubbed at his midsection through several layers of shirts. The pain faded now that its source sat in plain view. He still wasn't sure how that worked. The High Natural had given him the burning black trail through his gut. 'Til now, he'd assumed the connection ran exclusively there. This attack hadn't felt like the others, though. Those times, it was like he'd been ripped right out of himself and *into* the High Natural, sharing the bloody rush of the beast, its blades, and its victims, all at once. It had felt like getting raped by a thousand blades of icy flame, while at the same time *being* those blades. When he'd realized he'd survived the beast's attack, he'd felt severed from the rest of existence as he'd known it. He'd felt a lot of things since then, but the desire to give that pain back, to any asshole who gave him an excuse, had always guided his survival instinct. Until he'd found Janie again.

Everyone stared poised at the Familiar as it perched on the corner of the bar.

"Jesse, Zane," Sheldon muttered. "Crimbone Familiars are bound to their fledglings, right? Like, within a certain physical radius?"

"That's right," said Zane.

"This Familiar's fledgling is nowhere near here."

"You sure about that?" said Jesse. His grip tightened on his blade as he stared at Puttergong.

"Oh, yeah," said Sheldon. "I'm sure. That's not supposed to be possible, is it?"

"No," said Zane. "Yet there sits the little fucker."

"So do you still smell the connection between it and Rob anywhere?" said Sheldon.

Jesse and Zane looked at each other, then back at Sheldon, then back at the Familiar. They both said, "No."

Zane went on, "That's *supposed* to mean the Familiar's returned to the ephemeral realms and come back for a new fledgling. But I don't smell any fledglings, either. Which is pretty far the fuck out of what I like to call possible. Jesse, should that be possible?" He pointed at the grinning Familiar.

Jesse took a pull on his beer. "Nope."

The Familiar shifted its ass onto a barstool. It shook snow from its body, stretched out and wiggled its talons. "Brrrrrrrrrrrrrrrr, damnit, I say *brrrrrrrrrrrrrrrr!* Whose idea was it to let that fuckin' draft in? Oh right, that was me. Hell, I's gettin' all comfy now, while you dingbats is all up an' buzzin' like you're about to shit yer diapers. So how 'bout one of y'all go close the fuckin' door, huh?"

Tiger moved mechanically. He took a wide path around the Familiar, shut the winter out, and propped the chair back into place. From there, he edged his way back to his barstool, never once taking his wide eyes off the creature.

"Good boy," said the Familiar. "Howdy, Ripper-Man. Thumpy-Bumpy. Hey, Cop-Boy, ain't you a sight! All growed up, wearin' yer big-boy panties, plus yer big ol' coat an' yer jackboots over 'em, so nice…" The creature waved its claws at Sheldon, then sniffed. "Brings a tear to my eye, it truly do. Why, seems like jus' yesterday, you was nothin' but a lil' beanpole, shoutin' *Lead me to yer beast, you ugly familiar!*" Puttergong looked around. "This sure is one weirdass party, but I got shit to say to all of y'all, so thanks for savin' me the pain in the tail."

Jesse and Zane kept their weapons out. "Don't thank us yet," said Jesse.

"What do you want to tell us?" said Zane.

"'Fore I say shit, everyone sit the fuck down. You bitches is makin' me nervous. That means puttin' up the pig-sticker and the bopper, too."

Jesse and Zane put their weapons away and sat down. They nodded for everyone else to do the same.

"What's a Familiar gotta do to get a drink 'round here?" It grinned and batted its eyes at Lilly. "Aw, an' you got purty saloon girls, too! Shit, you thought of everything. Hey, Purty Saloon Girl, mind servin' me up some'a that there Jack-be-Nimble?" It nodded at the bottle of Jack Daniels she held.

Tiger leaned in protectively towards his wife. Before she could answer, Zane got up, stormed behind the bar and slammed a bottle of well whiskey in front of the Familiar.

"Well, you ain't so purty, Thumpy-Bumpy, but thanks for the drink. Since you're over here, can I get a smoke?"

Zane flicked out three cigarettes in front of the creature then walked back to his seat.

The Familiar lit the smoke with a bar match. It puffed on the cigarette and ashed on the counter without asking for an ashtray. "Okay, cool, I think I'm all set now." It threw its head back and poured a third of the bottle down its throat in one chug. It said in a bad impersonation of Marlon Brando as Don Corleone, "I'd like to call thith meeding tho orda." It continued in its normal voice, "Now what you all wanna know first off, I reckon, is how I'm here an' Biter-Boy ain't. That's just the start of how me bein' here at all's some weird shit."

"When is you-being-around *not* some weird shit?" said Sheldon.

"You got yerself a point there, Cop-Boy. Jus' so happens, it's weirder than usual lately. Anyhow, I ain't figured out the rest of it any more than y'all have. Not quite, that is. So don't ask." It grinned at Sheldon. "I got me a theory or two, though."

"About what?" asked Jesse.

"Purty Saloon Girl, Ripper-Man, Thumpy-Bumpy an' Cop-Boy! Y'all can jump up an' shriek Hella-loogie-ah! Our widdle High Natural has finally done gone an' made his Third Call." The Familiar waved the bottle around in a drunken toast, then swigged a little slower.

"Where's Rob?" asked Zane. His voice was blank, but a strange light gleamed in his eyes.

Puttergong took a slow, deep drag. It gave off a shrill hissing sound as it exhaled smoke through its saw-teeth. The acrid cloud wasn't quite the same shade as anything that came out of humanoid lungs. It smelled a lot worse, too. "Right where his lil' ass belongs: on the move."

"Towards what?"

"Well, Thumpy-Bumpy, that's somethin' we's all just gonna have to wait and find out."

"Quit fucking with us, Familiar," said Sheldon. "Don't talk like we're all in this together. You're—"

"Speak for yourself, Cop-Boy." Puttergong grinned wider.

Sheldon went livid. His hands dropped to the knives on his belt.

Zane clamped a hand on Sheldon's shoulder. "The kid's got a point, Puttergong. Everyone here's on a different playing field than we've ever known. Looks to me, that includes you now."

"Well, yeah, 'cause my fledgling went and made his Third Call, and here I still am, stuck with all you fuckers."

"So you're saying your way home ain't opened." Zane still almost sounded relaxed.

"Hey cool," said Puttergong, "someone's gettin' the idea." Its eyes fixated briefly on Zane. "*I wonder why, Ripper-Man.*"

"Hey, hold up," said Sheldon. "Jesse, Zane, correct me if I'm wrong…" He eyed Puttergong hard. "By proper definition, Puttergong, that means you're not even a Familiar anymore, doesn't it?"

Puttergong slouched and shrugged. "Hey, thanks, Cop-Boy. Here I was, thinkin' I'd have to explain that shit to everyone. You ain't half so dumb as you was last time we hung out. Remember that shit, Cop-Boy? Yeah, that was a cool night, huh?" The creature splayed and clacked its front talons on the countertop. "So let's agree, we's all playin' a different game than we was before."

"Sure," Zane answered, with that special decisive sharpness he only used whenever he made sure to speak before Jesse did.

"Right," said Puttergong. "So if any of us wanna figure out what we're supposed to be now, we have to be straight up with each other."

Zane leaned backwards and muttered at Jesse, "Sounds like the little fucker has a point."

"Cut that shit out," said Jesse.

"What shit?"

"I'm the one who notices that scary shit. You're the one who keeps me from going off the rails, remember?"

"Y'all two are so cute." Puttergong batted its eyelashes. The thing had eyelashes. That was weird to notice right now. "Anyhow, you ain't half-wrong, Thumpy-Bumpy. Good, we's all on the same page, far as we need to be right now. As to everything else…" Puttergong grinned at Sheldon "That ain't just everybody's business to know quite yet." The creature tossed the glowing cigarette butt over its shoulder with a low raspy laugh. It flapped up above the barstool, flew at the door, didn't even seem to break rhythm to open it, then disappeared into the snow and wind outside.

TWO

Sheldon's brain wanted to swim out of his ear, across the counter where the side of his head lay plastered. Where was the light in here coming from? It had burned low, whatever it was. There was still too much of it, and it couldn't even make itself useful by warming the place. He hadn't taken off his coat, he noticed, so the chill wasn't too uncomfortable to ignore for a while longer.

Where was everybody? No one had left right after Puttergong's departure. He remembered that much. That would have been panicking. Whenever he'd passed out, Tiger and Lilly must have moved to haul him home. Jesse and Zane would have said, *Nah, let the little punk think about it later when he drags his own hungover ass home through the icy wind.*

The barstool next to him groaned as it swiveled. "What walks on four legs in the mornin', two in the afternoon, three in the evenin'? *Bzzzzzzz*, time's up! The answer to the Familiar's Riddle is: a Cop-Boy that wakes up with a screamin' hangover, a Cop-Boy who's done some soberin' up, then finally a Cop-Boy that gets fallin' down drunk all over again but can still pop a huge enough boner to hobble home on it."

Sheldon lifted his head. The front door was propped shut again. Someone had fed and tended the fireplace recently. A couple oil lamps still burned nearby. Puttergong's talons hooked the opposite edge of the bar, legs cocked downward so the rest of the body balanced upright like a helpful barman.

"What'll it be, stud?" For some reason, the lighting made the Familiar's eyes look green.

"I think I need some water."

"I don't think you wanna drink the tap water in this place."

Sheldon's stomach did a few extra somersaults at the thought of more booze. He still said, "Fine, whatever."

One clawed foot unhooked from the counter, dipped sideways, and brought up a bottle of Bud. Sheldon shrugged, unscrewed the cap, and swigged warm mule-piss amber.

Puttergong fluttered up and backwards, snagged a bottle of better whiskey, then came back to the barstool next to Sheldon. "So you figured out what you an' I have to do with each other right now, Cop-Boy?"

Sheldon took another gulp. "You haven't gone back to the ephemeral realms because your connection to Biter—to Rob Coscan—hasn't been completely severed."

"*Bingo*. Know why?" Puttergong swigged.

"It's the link between him and me. Because of your link to him, you and I ended up tied to each other through him. Whatever I've turned into by surviving the connection…"

"'Cause of that time you survived a Crimbone blade in the gut, you mean."

"Right. You've settled your end of things with him, but not with me."

Puttergong drank deep. Its bulbous gut swelled like a veiny, leathery balloon. "Damn, Biter—er, I mean Cop-Boy—you really thought this shit through, ain't you?"

"It's how I spend my alone-time lately, when I still have any."

"Ever quite figure how I'd play into it, 'til I showed up tonight?"

"No."

"Technically that was yesterday anyhow. So what'cha think that is…my end of things with you?"

"An accident? I don't know. I gotta say, for someone who likes to talk like you know more than anyone else, you're doing a lot of fishing for answers."

The creature twitched backwards, like Sheldon had touched a nerve. "Like I said, Cop-Boy, you smarter than you look…which is still wasted stupid. So since I's here, let's put our noggins together and try to figure some shit out. Let's say, for all practical purposes, you an' me's connected like a Crimbone fledgling and a Familiar generally is. Which makes my question for you…what do you want?"

"Huh?"

"What every Crimbone fledgling wants—once they make that ol' First Call—is to be a full-fledged Crimbone. A Familiar's there to help 'em get it. Biter-Boy wanted a lil' more than that. But we ain't talkin' 'bout what Biter-Boy wants. We talkin' 'bout what Cop-Boy wants. And don't give me all sorts a' shit about wantin' to live all happy ever after with yer lil' Injun girl, or whoever you're stickin' that third leg in these days. So pull your head out'a your drunkass dickhole long enough to say what you really wanna see happen, as in the big fuckin' picture."

"Same thing everyone else wants. I want to make all this bullshit stop."

"Who don't? Ever bother thinkin' about whatever you want instead of all the bullshit? Seems to me, that's what most folks forget to take a real look at. Everyone just keeps actin' like a bunch'a bulls shittin' all over the china shop, though. The only way you ever gonna make bulls stop shittin' is to go 'round killin' bulls 'til there ain't none left to shit. Then you still gotta wait 'til their death-relaxed asses has leaked dry of everything they had stuffed up in there. Someone's always still gotta clean up that mess, though, huh? So either you wanna go 'round killin' everyone 'til there ain't no one left to kill each other— which ain't so far from what some other folks is fixin' to do—or you wanna make it so whoever's still kickin' don't feel like killin' each other no more."

"Right. Good luck with that."

"So either we can sit here an' sing coon-bisexual-ya-de-ya 'til everyone else gets the pieces-an'-lovin' idea an' starts prancin' 'round holdin' hands, or we can go make some luck for ourselves."

"Got any brilliant ideas?"

"Maybe I just do. Follow my lead, *lil' brave*, and you can make all this fightin' stop cold. That's right, just kick everyone out'a the saddle at once, then let whoever can pull 'emselves back up start over, and not even have to kill anyone else to do it. You jus' gotta take away the reason for it." Puttergong cocked its head at the knives on Sheldon's belt.

"My knives are the reason for all this shit?"

"Them knives was *made* by the reason. They might just be the one damn thing strong enough to kill that reason, too. Yessir, they contain the purest central concentration of that source you'll find in this world. They's also what you gotta take with you *outta* this world, to the *real* source, where it really lives, and you gotta stab them blades *right into the heart of it*. Same heart a Crimbone blade stabs a little piece of, every time it comes out...same heart Biter-Boy's blade was *really* stabbin' at when he barely missed yours."

"The Spirelight glow..."

Puttergong nodded. "Boil it down, Cop-Boy, that's all this whole mess has ever been about. The Crimbone are addicted to Spirelight-killin' 'cause that glow just tastes too damn fine. They was made that way 'cause of what that glow's a piece of. What that glow's a piece of is why the Spirelights started beatin' up on the Schomites so the Crimbone had to show up an' do some killin'. So what happens if the glow ain't there in the Spirelights no more?"

"They wouldn't *be* Spirelights anymore. Just like I'm not."

"So what'd be so bad about that?"

Sheldon rubbed his head. "It's too *big* a thing, is what it is, too…cosmic to process. Maybe I'm just still too drunk."

"Nah, it'd feel just as big if you was sober as ol' Oedipussy when he woke up and realized he just banged his mom. It's as big a thing as there ever was, and it's small as them blades on your belt…small as you an' me sittin' in this here bar, somewhere in the middle of this big ol' world. Everything's that big an' that small all at once. Which really means there ain't no such thing as size when ye think about it."

"*Not the size that counts but how you use it*, huh, little birdie?"

"*Awforfucksake!* Here I'm bein' all sincere for once, and you gotta go makin' dick jokes."

"Now you mention it, I'm curious…You Familiars…I'm gonna regret asking, but…"

Puttergong's front talons slid down and lifted its sagging belly, showing what the bulge normally hid. Sheldon glanced down and caught a good look at Familiar genitalia. He was right, he already regretted asking.

"Anyhow," said the confirmedly male Familiar, "what *does* mean shit is the *shape* of things. That's what gives anything meanin', what keeps worlds turnin', an' how they fit together. What *you* gotta do is find the shapes that match up with them blades, an' you gotta fit 'em together."

"So there's a shape to the glow, and a shape to the Spirelights, and those need to be severed by these blades?"

"So far, so good."

"Sounds like you're saying I have to stab the gods."

"That's right."

"The hell…?"

"Did I stutter, bitch?"

"How am I supposed to *stab the gods?* If all this shit's made one thing clear through the ages, it's that the Gods of Spirah aren't in this world, except through the Spirelights. We always figured they wouldn't show up 'til we'd claimed this world for them."

"Well…that's sorta close too, but not quite right. Lemme spin a funny lil' yarn for ye. Stop me when you think you heard it. At least one of the Spirah gods found its way here once. Or some fleein' glow from a dyin' Spirelight didn't get drunk up by a Crimbone and didn't flee back to the Spirah pantheon or nothin'—sorta like my new situation, now's I think about it—and got itself some sentience. See, back then, in the first ages after the Spirelights showed up an' spoiled the whole Schomite-Earth-line lovey-dovey party—"

"Wait, what?"

"You tellin' me you ain't caught up on that? Never mind. Story for another time. Anyhow, Schomite relations with the Earth-liners hadn't been totally fucked to shit yet, so this glowin' Spirah god, Spirah sentience, whatever the hell it was, it gets hold of some Earth-line bozo while he's trippin' balls on somethin' or other out in some desert…and through that one balls-trippin' bozo, this Spirah glow infects the dude's whole crew an' spreads. This god, it told this feller all sorts of crazy shit—or maybe it was a few different fellers, one for every flavor. But it weren't never interested in makin' strong-arms of the Earth-liners like the rest of the pantheon did the Spirelights. Didn't bless 'em with all the science and magic you Spirelights use to carve whatever world you're in into the shape of the gods. All it wanted to do, best we can figure, is confuse the hell out'a the Crimbone as to fuck up the diaper-plomacy, which it did.

"One minute, you got all these Earth-liners and civilian Schomites, all clustered together, all *Hi-didly-*

fuckin'-ho, neighbor. Then this Spirelight god does its thing. So as an answer from motherfuckin' nature, you got all these Schomite kids wakin' up, realizin' they're Crimbone. Right as they have all these Spirelight glows flyin' at 'em from every direction. That sorta drove 'em all a lil' crazy. Of course, the Crimbone eventually caught wise. By then, though, the last scraps of Schomite-Earth-line lovey-dovey skivi-lie-zation was done. The taint of the Spirah gods cooked up a whole new batch of watered-down Earth-line variations on the same ol' shit. Call it the Earth-line idea of organized religion, if you wanna.

"So you got lots of different bunches of Earth-liners tryin' to strong-arm each other, just like Spirelights has always tried to strong-arm folks, only goofier. The spirits of some lands took a shot at correctin' things, by reachin' out and talkin' through this one Earth-line magic man, so he figured a way to suck the Spirah taint out'a his feller Earth-liners. To work up the energy for that, though, he first had to get enough of 'em marchin' to his beat. To do that—most Earth-line folks bein' stupid and not makin' much sense in their thinkin' an' all—he had to tell 'em he was speakin' *for* that bit o' glow-blow that'd been jerkin' their strings. He told everyone the glow had changed its mind, didn't want 'em goin' 'round actin' like bloodthirsty nutjobs no more. Then he went an' sucked that Spirah taint out'a all of 'em and into his self. Then he went an' pissed off the wrong folks on purpose so they gacked his ass, in a big ol' public-execution jamboree. Once his body got gacked, his spirit took away that glow with him.

"Since then, the Spirah gods don't come 'round this world so direct-like no more. They figure it ain't worth messin' with, 'cept through the Spirelights, the ones originally sent over from ol' Deschemb. But that Earth-line magic man, that guy who tried to help…all them stupid Earth-liners kept on spreadin' his talk. They built a whole new rulebook for livin', based off a bunch'a shit they hadn't even seen or felt or talked to directly, just smoke blown up their asses. 'Cept to get their point across, they went right on doin' all that bullshit he told 'em to quit doin', worse than ever, in the poor fucker's name, no less. They went wipin' out skivi-lie-zations left an' right so they could put up new ones they thought'd work better...or make more do-ray-me for the assholes in charge. It was like the whole Earth-line race *had* turned into Spirelights after all."

"Gonna try telling me the Schomites have been any better?"

"Heh. It ain't about bein' *better*, Cop-Boy. All it's been about for the Schomites and the Crimbone is stayin' alive, not gettin' stamped out under all the bullshit the Spirah gods brought about. While they're at it, wipin' their asses with everything their aggressors stand for, makin' sure them aggressors feel sticky an' stinky from it. Only way anyone's thought of to do that is fight dirtier than dirt. But fuck all that with a big ol' donkey dick, 'cause we got us another option now. It's time to move on, and you got it in you to do the pushin'. So I's here to help you with that."

"Why?"

"Huh?"

"Why would a Familiar want all this to end? Isn't all this shit your reason for existing?"

Puttergong let out a shrieking laugh. "You think my kinda critters wasn't around before there was Crimbone for us to Familiarize? We been other things. Familiars is just what we gotta be while there's gotta be Crimbone around. It's been fun, no lyin', but I reckon the forces we work for'll find somethin' even funner for us to do next. While I'm bein' honest, I kinda like the idea of gettin' the credit."

"So what forces do you work for? Bigger gods?"

"Heh...*Bigger*, shit. Take size out of the mix, the gods ain't nothin' but another sack of assholes fuckin' with folks. So Cop-Boy, what do you do when you see a bunch of assholes fuckin' around with folks? You go kick their ass, right? So go stick yer foot up some gods' asses!"

"Let's say you're right. Where do I find these gods?"

"Back in the Old World, of course."

No one even thought of Deschemb as a real place anymore, Sheldon realized for the first time. To the descendants of the Deschembine refugees, it was a concept that embodied their heritage beyond this world. Spirah was the idea for where the gods waited.

"How do I get to the Old World?" he finally asked.

"You already been right at the harbor gate. One of 'em, anyhow. Yep, you sat right in kickin' distance of the shores of the shrouded ocean—and I mean that literal as it gets—and you didn't even notice...I'm guessin' 'cause you didn't exactly have the blood in your brain to pay attention. When you see what I'm talkin' about, I wanna be there to watch you shit yourself. Stick with me for now, Cop-Boy. I won't be goin' with you past the harbor gates, though. That's the point where my connection to you cuts off for good...you an' Biter-Boy both."

Sheldon almost knocked over his drink. "Wait a second. How's he fit into this?"

"You didn't think you could just step off the boat onto the shores of Deschemb and ask directions, did ye? There ain't but one critter in this here world with the instincts to even start gettin' around through the Old World. And when I say *instincts*, I don't mean like they was trained or conditioned into him like all your Cop-Boy knowhow. I mean he was born with 'em in his blood. I'll tell you somethin' funny about Biter-Boy. Woken up like he's gotten, his brains is so full of other people's memories, from another world, that half the time, he can't tell the difference between that and his own self, here an' now. That's why he's such a nutty pain in the ass. This, though…It's what this world's been primin' him for his whole life…to help you reach the gods so you can stab 'em. He just don't know it yet."

"Are you telling me…this whole time, the reason a High Natural even exists in this world, is to play tour-guide to a recovering Spirelight in the Old World?"

"Sure is startin' to look that way, ain't it? Anyhow, time for you to get used to the idea of shakin' hands with the feller who gacked your family and run off with your sister and stuck a connection 'tween you an' me in your gut. 'Cause you an' him's gotta take a lil' trip together."

This time Sheldon did spill his beer. The bottle rolled off the other side of the bar and clattered somewhere. A ring of cold glass pressed his lips. That was Puttergong, holding and tilting the whiskey bottle for him. He grabbed it, swigged, and slammed it on the counter.

"Now, Cop-Boy," Puttergong went on, "I ain't sayin' you gotta accept this here idea right here an' now. Just make sure you have by the time you and Biter-Boy stand face to face, so you don't go hackin' each other to bits 'fore you even get shoved off."

"What about him? I'll bet he'll like the idea even less than I do."

"Well, someone'll just have to hunt down his ass, bring him up to speed, then show him to the spot where you guys'll be meetin' up. Pro'lly me, which I frankly don't look forward to. Amazin' as this'll sound, Biter-Boy can be an even bigger irritatin' stubborn pain in the ass than you."

Sheldon swigged more whiskey. "So we have to journey to the land of Deschemb, across the same hidden ocean between the worlds that our ancestors took over here." He whistled. "So what about once we get there?"

"Once you step onto the shores, Deschemb will recognize the both of you as its own. The air you breath will do its thing in your lungs just like the air of this world. But only the High Natural will be able to properly recognize it back. He'll ask directions of the land there, just like he does here, except for the first time in his miserable lil' life, he'll be in the right place, so he'll be hearin' directions he's actually supposed to understand. The lands'll also tell him what you both need to know about dealin' with the folks an' critters you find. Where you gotta go is the birthplace of the Spirelights, the Kingdom of Spiralla, or whatever's left of it by the time ye git there. One thing I guarantee you *will* be left is the original Spirelight temple…"

Sheldon thought, *What used to be the temple of the Gods of the Dark Lands.*

Puttergong continued, "…That's where the first Spirelight—"

"Bathshire."

"Right, that guy. Anyhow, that's where he made the original pact with the Spirah gods, so he could lead his people against them Dark Land gods. It was on the altar in that temple that the Spirah gods forged them there blades you're wearin', Cop-Boy. They put a lil' of 'emselves in them blades like they done the Spirelights, so this feller they'd made their head bitch could use 'em to lead the Spirelights out to reshape the world in the image of the gods. That's the funny thing about gods. I never seen it fail once. Whenever they step in on someone's behalf, they tell 'em they're settin' 'em free of whatever's holdin' 'em under. But folks never realize they're just swappin' one slave-driver for another. They jus' got 'emselves upgraded to be proxy slave drivers. 'Cept once these particular gods sent ol' Bathshire and his people out with them blades, they weren't expectin' them blades to ever find their way back into that there temple, to that altar where they was forged.

"*That's where the gods is vulnerable, Cop-Boy*, 'cause they left the door cracked between the realms, y'might say. So you take them purty shiny knives of yours, and you stab 'em right into that Spirah altar. You do that, you'll be good as fuckin' the gods right up the ass. Once you done that, while you still stand at that altar, there won't be no more barriers to hold you back. Not size, not space, not gods, not race, not even the big, shrouded ocean 'tween this world an' that. At that point, if what ye really, most wanna do is cut the folks here loose from their influence, all you gotta do is reach on over and do it."

"You make it sound easy."

"Gettin' there won't be easy, but once you're there…"

"Aren't you forgetting one big problem?"

"What'd that be?"

"If I take away the Spirelight glow, and somehow manage to send the message back for all the fighting to stop…Well, this dumb fucking war isn't about just Schomites and Spirelights anymore. This Balthazar asshole, he's got both Spirelights and Crimbone swarming in it, to make way for his new coterie. Long as he's in action, this isn't just about the glow anymore."

"You leave that fucker to me, kid. You an' Biter-Boy do your part there, I do mine here, everything'll go off without a hitch. Once you got your blades up the gods' asses and you reach across back here, believe you me, everyone here's gonna hear you when you talk to 'em. You'll have their undivided attention. You got any more dumbshit questions?"

"Just one. You mentioned that stray Spirelight glow, the one that got loose in this world, that the Earth-line magic-man had to put down. Once that guy cast it out of everyone else, where did it go?"

"Shit! Y'know, now you mention it, I never did think of that. Fucked if I know! Aw, hell, look at the time! Hey Cop-Boy, you sit in here a while, then get yourself back to your nice warm bed, get yourself laid, get done whatever you gotta do. Then get your ass on the road, towards the border back into the You-Es-o'-Anus."

"The what?"

Puttergong sighed. "America. After that, wait for me in the first border town you find, the skuzzier the backwash-water, more full'a John-Wayne's-cock-suckin' assholes, the better. I'll see to my own damn business, then I'll catch up with you there, to lead you to where you gotta get. Be watchin' for me."

Sheldon jolted backwards as the Familiar spread its wings and beat the air, upsetting its barstool. Puttergong didn't bother with the door this time, just crashed right through the window.

SPLITS IN THE TRAIL

ONE

Deacon's feet left swerving smears in the snow. The cold gnawed on his twisted bones, especially the ones that hadn't healed right, no matter how many layers he contorted himself into. It felt better than the bruises Sheldon Wildfire had left on him the other night. Before he'd gotten so crippled and ugly—before Sheldon Wildfire—Deacon could have knocked on any door he wanted around here, for a piece of ass, a place to sleep, whatever else he wanted.

No, wait, not *around here*. That had all been another life, back at the Renaissance Kingdom. He used to be able to keep track of shit like that, before that massive skull-fracture messed up his brain, when Sheldon Wildfire left him in a dog-pile of Secret Police agents, all slashing and stabbing and punching him. The more he tried not to think about that day, the more he relived it in his nightmares. That was one silver lining about never being able to sleep for long, because he always rolled the wrong way, waking himself up with a fresh burst of shrieking agony, half the time to the realization that he'd pissed himself.

Before that day, Deacon's people had listened to him. They'd looked to him as a proud, upstanding, handsome speaker who could rally them to hold together. Now whenever they saw him lurching and hobbling towards them, they turned away, dropped their conversational tones to embarrassed whispers, and tried to pretend he wasn't there. Good for them. They could keep pretending the man he'd once been was dead, that it wasn't Sheldon Wildfire's fault they were in the fix they were in, that two out of three of the pregnant women they'd set out with hadn't given birth to corpses, that four more children hadn't died of exposure between there and here, that they hadn't seen their new heroes Jesse and Zane butcher and pillage their way through other traveling groups, because everyone would have starved otherwise.

No, if they wanted to see how ugly their lives had become, without blaming themselves, all they had to do was look at Deacon. Every shrieking step made him feel ready to split in half. The agony lived everywhere in him but his dick, which now felt nothing, even though the medics had managed to save more than half of it, along with one of his balls.

"Ya hate dem all, don'tcha, Twisty? All dem an' all dis around ya."

Deacon didn't recognize the voice. He knew what kind of creature it was, though. The accent sounded like an offensive caricature of some far-away regional dialect. What the hell was it doing around here? Wasn't the token Crimbone fledgling dead? Deacon only knew that by eavesdropping, because no one talked to him. Except now some Crimbone's Familiar was talking to him.

He spun to look for the creature. His twisted foot slid out from under him, so he crashed flat on his back in the snow. He tried to get up, but his arms were full of dead nerves so he couldn't push them under himself properly. Whenever he tried to plant his palms flat on the ground, his hands felt like a knotted cluster of broken fingers that wouldn't unclench. Even when he managed to sit up, ice still seeped through his coat and hair. His eyes trailed through the dead night sky, around the edges of the buildings on either side. Wings beat the frosty air, descending towards him. Steely talons settled on his chest, no doubt to rip out his ribcage. The creature's hot, rancid breath puffed in his face.

"I not here to kill ya, Twisty. I here to let ya give death to dem ya hate so bad."

"How do you know who I hate?"

"I been watchin' ya, Twisty. Ya'd like to kill dem all, wouldn't ya? Answer me honest. If ya lie, I know it. I fuck ya up even worse, even uglier wit more pain."

"Yes," Deacon rasped. It felt good to finally say it to someone. "Yeah, there was a time, when I could have killed them all for disrespecting me like they do now."

The thing chuckled. "Dere's folks nearby, who could do dat killin' for ya, but dey can't find y'all. Should be easy, but dem keepin' watch, dey plowed a maze all about these parts. I can take ya to dem...*up*, over da maze. You tell 'em de way, dey come here an' dey do de killin'...*kill de two here ya hate de most, Twisty.*"

"Stop calling me *Twisty*."

"Whatever you say, Twisty."

"Fuck you. Why don't you just lead 'em here yourself?"

"De sonny-mon—de one you call Balthazar—he don' like me talkin' to his followers direct. It hurt his image, if ya get me, dem seein' he still got his daddy-mon de Familiar showin' tings 'round for him. So I take ya to dem, an' ya speak for me."

"Balthazar...death..."

The Familiar cackled quietly. "Ya...Ya, Twisty, death."

The talons left Deacon's chest. They tightened in his shoulders 'til they pierced his flesh. It actually didn't hurt so bad, compared to what he was used to...not 'til they jerked him up and erect, stretching his shape straight. It hurt even worse when the Familiar pulled him skyward. The higher they went, the deeper the cold bit into him and the harder it grew to suck in air. It bit through nerves he hadn't realized were still there, as the Familiar carried him away through the night, zigging and zagging over the moonlit forest floor below.

Looking down, he saw the maze Jesse and Zane had plowed, between the base and everywhere else. He remembered every twist and turn he'd need to know.

TWO

The scant light in the medical lab spilled like an icy cone over Sally and her cadaver on the table. Jesse came in and approached silently.

"Hi, Jesse," she said without turning around. "C'mere, check this shit out."

He stepped up next to her. In the antiseptic light, her angular face and hands looked hard as the metal table. Deep creases that hadn't been there five months ago now stood out on her face. Silver streaks ran through her tied-back auburn hair.

Her nostrils flared as Jesse reached her. "Are you drunk already?" she asked.

That still startled him, how she possessed senses like that...Crimbone senses, not Spirelight Secret Police senses. "Yeah, a little, sure," he said.

"Should we do this later?"

"No, let's get it over with." That went both for whatever she had to say and what he wasn't looking forward to telling her.

"Haven't seen my no-good brother anywhere, have you?"

"Yeah. He's not so fine. Will be in a few hours, I figure, hopefully a little less stupid."

"You're more optimistic than me. He got drunk and passed out, didn't he?"

"Yeah. Too much to hope you've got a better idea than me about this mess?" He waved his hand over the cadaver.

"Probably. I ain't heard your ideas yet."

Somehow, the cadaver looked more alarming stripped and splayed out than it had in life, when it had been trying to kill him. Jesse remembered this guy—this thing—coming at him in a leap, fifteen feet in the air, right after it killed Crawler. Crawler's death had probably saved Jesse's life, getting a better look at what he was up against before it closed with him, like the younger man hadn't. Jesse hadn't managed to take it down right away, either. It had never stood upright once it landed. In the gloom of early morning, he'd figured it just liked to fight in a low crouch. Now he saw that the joints had been broken and rebuilt at the groin and ankles.

Sally's rubber-gloved fingers peeled back the flesh next to the right knee. "Check out these extended hamstring tendons. They run like that throughout the whole body." When she'd noted his buzz, he'd at first taken her tone for chiding. Now he recognized a hard, clinical fascination for whatever she observed. Her eyes gleamed obsessively. Her icy detachment was almost alien, like she might show no more qualms with such mutilations and experiments on a living captive's body. "There's Humanoid-Deschembine DNA properties grafted with botanical mutations from…I don't know what the fuck, yet."

Sometimes Jesse forgot about Sally's medical background, what she'd learned from her mother in her youth. "You're saying that's animal matter grafted with plant matter."

"Yeah," she said.

"Scientifically, I'm pretty sure that makes absolutely no fucking sense."

"Scientifically, this plant life shouldn't be able to survive in this world's atmosphere. Then again, neither should we."

"Hang on…"

"You didn't know that?" She looked up at him. "Yeah, bet there's a lot of discoveries Spirelight scientists have made, shit that'd fry your brain if it leaked out. My mom was part of the research project that hit on that little doozy. There's things about the ways our lungs and circulatory systems process oxygen, nourishment, you name it, that shouldn't be able to handle any of those things in this world the way the bodies of Earth-line creatures do. You could chalk that up to adaptability and evolution, except those things have stayed the same within us for thousands, maybe hundreds of thousands of years…and yet, here we still are. We haven't managed to pinpoint whatever bridges that gap, by any known physical or metaphysical laws."

"Call it a little Old World magic." Jesse smiled.

Sally didn't. "We do. This is some Old World magic I've never studied, though. The outer flesh on all four limbs is skin-grafted from someone—or something—else. Four different someones or somethings, of escalating levels of toughness. Feel how tough that left arm is? Good thing that ain't on his chest, huh? A little tougher, it might slow down even your blade."

Jesse looked around and spotted the box of the kind of powdered rubber gloves Sally wore. He pulled on a pair, then felt and looked over the different portions of flesh she'd indicated. A fusion of flesh from five different creatures, and no scarring…like the flesh had liquefied and resolidified at the joining points.

"Look at these coloration patterns from the chemical tests on the exposed tendons." She prodded and pointed with her scalpel. "This was done over time, and there's marked evolution in the results."

Jesse peered closer. "Yeah. Check out the age of these battle-scars. There was continuous work done on him between trail-work. Our boy here was a work-in-progress. Balthazar's bio-engineers are evolving."

"Balthazar, huh?"

"You think of anyone else who'd have freaks like this for minions?"

"Yeah. Whoever Balthazar answers to. You and me, we once compared notes on New Orleans, remember?" She just tossed it off, like they'd traded funny vacation anecdotes and shown each other pictures.

Jesse thought of her voice on that tape he'd replayed too often for his own good over the years, keeping himself pissed and crazy for whenever he met those fuckers she'd talked about. Finally, he'd gone to New Orleans and met those fuckers. He'd taken sweet, savage revenge on men who'd raped, tortured, and experimented on a teenage girl. That girl's voice was still stuck in his head. This woman sounded like she'd never met that kid.

"Come on," she went on, "don't tell me you ain't thought it. About what that asshole's creating to throw at us, I mean."

"Say his name."

"Talino," she said. Finally, there was some emotion in her tone. "Can you imagine what kind of shit this could turn into, with just a little more work?"

"No, I can't, and that's what scares me. I'll bet they weren't throwing their best at Sam and Anya's pack, either. We'd better go back there tomorrow, grab a few more of those bodies, see what else we can learn."

Sally's shoulders tightened. "You can make that run without me, if you don't mind."

"Not at all." He had to admit, it was a relief to see her icy demeanor crack. "Wanna put this guy on ice for the night? Zane and I brought back some beer. You're gonna want one, trust me." He met her eyes nervously and gestured at the cadaver. "Tonight's big developments didn't stop with this guy."

THREE

The high, bright ceiling really put the zap on Sally's head, especially after the dim closeness of the lab. Bright, open places had never agreed with her. It was part of why she'd freaked out so badly when she and Rob had found Postville, a place so flat and open, so *bright* and *safe*. She'd never trusted that sense of safety, and in the end, she'd been right.

For the longest time, surviving for its own sake had formed her comprehension of existence. These days, she guessed, she survived for others, folks who still held out hope for something better.

In the ruins of the Renaissance Kingdom, she'd pried the spear from the pulpy, sun-rotted fingers of Vencie's severed arm. It was the purest, deadliest distillation she could find of the evil that threatened her survival, what she carried into the close, shadowy madness wherever she found it. Part of her would always be touching that evil, ever mindful of it, so she could turn it on itself every chance she got. The United Deschembines thought she was the ultimate embodiment of one thing. All she felt like was a cold manifestation of the other, drained of everything else, redirected against the threat that had spawned her. Part of her knew better…the part Rob had introduced her to, within herself.

So here she sat with Jesse and Zane. She broke the long silence. "What do we do now?"

The guys lifted their eyebrows like they expected her to know.

"We're all worn out." Zane straddled a chair ass-backwards, his arms folded across the top, his massive shoulders relaxed forward. "Figure we ought'a rest up, get our heads clear before we make any big decisions."

"Quit trying to fake it, man." Jesse leaned back with his feet propped on the table. "You're the one who's been stewing about it worse than anyone."

"Okay, Mister Mind-Reader," said Zane, "what exactly do you think I'm faking?"

"You've already decided what you think we should do. Quit stalling and spit it the fuck out."

"Okay, fine." Zane cast a look at Sally. "It's time we struck out to find Rob."

"I don't know where to start telling you how that's a bad idea," said Jesse. "Puttergong didn't even say where he is."

"Exactly. You think that weird little fucker's gone far? I think it wants to lead us to Rob."

"Right," said Sally, "'cause doing what Puttergong says always turns out great."

"You weren't there, Sal," said Zane. "Earlier tonight, I mean."

"*Well excuse me, then,*" she blurted. "You gonna go there? *You weren't there* the night my brother tried to kill me, because of how that little monster just wanted him and my husband to fight to the death. I don't *need* a reminder. I got it right here." She swept her hair back from the scar across the side of her head.

"Look," said Zane, "going where a Familiar wants you to go and doing what the damn thing expects you to do are two different things. Either way, now that the High Natural's fully fledged, my bet is he won't be hard to find for long."

"Say we go looking for him," said Jesse. "Say we take the United Deschembines with us. You thought about what we'd be throwing them into? Didn't you hear what Anya said, about…whatever the fuck the world's changing into out there?"

"Who said anything about taking them along?" Zane scowled. "Will you two quit looking at me like I just kicked a puppy? Look, we've got 'em off to a good start. With everything else heating up, everywhere else, no one's gonna give enough of a fuck to bother 'em, long as they stay off the radar—"

"Right," said Sally, "'til someone worse than those freaks today just happens by, and we ain't around to catch 'em ten miles out."

"They got better chances here than most places."

"Unless Anya's right," said Jesse, "about what's gonna happen once everything thaws."

"So we're supposed to shelter 'em forever? Look, we've had five months to get it together. We're set for this as we're gonna be. You said it earlier, Jess. We've been waiting for a sign from the lands. A whole fuckin' bag of signs just fell in our lap."

"You forgotten how Rob was running that pack of his last we saw him? Yeah, he's the High Natural, but what does that mean in this world now? All the time we spent watching for one to show up, we had no idea what to expect. We were thinking about it in the old ways, of the Old World. The High Natural's the ultimate unchecked manifestation of Old World Crimbone power. Everything happening now, *that's* what having a High Natural in this world means."

"That's why we gotta find him," said Zane. "He needs people who understand him, who know him as Rob Coscan *and* have some idea—any idea—about the High Natural."

"Zane, *I don't think there's any place in this* world *for the High Natural's energy*, not with what it'll become once it reaches its full strength. If he's allowed to live long enough to get there, he'll –"

Something broke in Sally. "Jesse, stop it, please! *Don't* say we have to—"

"I'm not saying we should go do anything."

Zane ground out his cigarette on the table. "Right. Just sit here circle-jerking each other, waiting for the world to burn."

"No, I'm saying we should keep doing what we've been doing, for these people here. That's what my blood tells me."

"And *my* blood tells me something else," said Zane.

Jesse took a long look at Zane's eyes. So there it was, and that was that. He gazed at the tabletop, at Zane's ground-out cigarette. He braced for a self-inflicted wound. "Do what you gotta do, man."

What Zane had to do was lunge to his feet so his chair crashed over behind him. Jesse glanced up. Zane kept staring like he expected a bigger reaction. There was nothing left to say, though, and they both knew it.

"Sally, you coming?" Zane asked. She looked at him like he'd spoken in a language she didn't know. He growled, grabbed his coat and stormed out. He closed the door quietly, which was somehow worse than slamming it.

After a long silence, Jesse said, "He's gonna do it, you know. Probably tonight."

"Do what?"

"Take off. To find Rob."

"Just like that. Out of the blue. Your best friend, after you two've been together…?"

"A long damn time. You heard him say it, though. It's what his blood tells him to do. You've been around enough Crimbone to know what that means. You still wanna find Rob? You can still catch Zane before he books it. Now's your chance."

"Heh. What would be the point, other than get myself killed? Rob's the one who left me, remember?" Before that can of worms could open any further, she asked, "How long *did* you guys share the trail together, anyway?"

Jesse started to answer, then something in his throat hitched. "Since I was a noncommissioned officer in the Union army."

"Hold up. *That* Union army?"

"That's the one. I'd already made my Second Call. I wore my blade like the commanding officer wore his saber. I'd've caught shit for it, probably have had to desert to survive, except the other soldiers had seen me fight with it. The sight of the black metal freaked the hell out of the other troops—those Union *Earth-line* troops we served with. I hardly even used my rifle. The shooting would start, and I'd slip out of formation without anyone noticing. I'd just get right in among the rebs and start shredding, missing all the friendly fire I pleased. None of the guys in my regiment could figure out how I did it. A couple of times I took a bullet, so yeah, I'd be out of action like any soldier. A medic once made the mistake of saying my arm had to come off. I broke his arm in three places. I never got gangrene, always healed up and went right back to fighting, even though it was an Earth-line cause that never meant shit to me."

"It should've."

"Huh?"

"Who do you think the Confederacy's biggest silent backers were? The Tribunals realized you guys had good things in sight, the way this country was coming together…Hell, the Earth-line whites hadn't even cocked up their treaties with the red-skins so bad by that point."

"You mean Janie's ancestors? I think they like *Native Americans* better now."

"A lecture on Earth-line political correctness from a Crimbone. Ain't that some funny shit. Anyway, yeah, when all that North-South friction revved up, the Spirelights thought, *Hey, perfect way to shake all that down a few pegs*. Plus…well…there were a lot of dormant Crimbone among the slaves…a lot of really beaten-down, angry men and women who our Tribunals didn't wanna see have the chance to reach their full strength. Slavery was an Earth-line institution that benefitted the Spirelight agenda."

Jesse's eyes narrowed. "I know all that, now. As a matter of fact, you might have guessed how I'm getting to that. It ain't why I enlisted, though. Fledglings aren't privy to those kinds of political machinations."

"Why, then?"

"'Cause I was young and stupid enough to think some little Earth-line war would be a fun way to flex my Crimbone muscles. It was a different story for those Earth-line troops I served with. I don't just mean what war's really like, as opposed to what stupid kids think it is. I got the same nasty wakeup call as the rest of 'em. I took to it better than they did, 'cause I was born to be a predator and they weren't, but still..." He shook his head. "For them, it was one of those things folks go through but never talk about, serving with a creature like me, I mean. Those who go blabbing about it are called crazy, get denied by their fellows all three times before the rooster crows. You won't find any records of me in the Earth-line history books, even the ones they don't show their kids in school, no matter how many major victories I pretty much handed to ol' Honest Abe, along with fistfuls of severed heads." He noticed Sally's expression. "No, not literally. My point is, most of the other soldiers were too nervous to even sit with me by the campfires. It was a nice power trip for a skinny, scrappy fledgling like I was."

Sally eyed the hulking beast seated across from her. She tried to picture him as a skinny fledgling. It wasn't happening.

"Zane was born to parents straight from Haiti," Jesse went on, "Crimbone who'd somehow been guided to these shores from their own...not by the will of the slave trade, but by the will of the lands. They were passing themselves off as freed slaves or something. Then he got cast to the world, and he wound up toiling on a plantation as a slave anyway. He made his First Call at sixteen and ran away. It was in...shit, where was that? Tennessee, I think, where my regiment picked him up. He volunteered, so we fixed him with a gun and a uniform. Last thing I expected out there was to run into another fledgling, let alone a runaway slave. I mean, sure, I'd heard there were those of the Crimbone bloodline being kept down south as slaves. Even heard rumors of other, older Crimbone fighting in other regiments, sent in silently by the Cabinets, but I didn't believe it 'til I met Zane. Shit. For him, it turned out, it wasn't much different in the army than with the *massahs*. Except this new bunch let him kill and loot and pillage with them. He took to it pretty enthusiastically.

"The poor dumb bastards…Now they had *two* spooky, lightning fast, damn near unkillable killing machines at the fire with 'em, even though Zane didn't have his hammer yet. They didn't get why I took to him, even though we both acted and moved and fought the same, did things they couldn't, things even our Indian scouts couldn't explain. They still told themselves I was the same race as them, 'cause of my white hide. They called him the nigger. Fuckers, to us, *they* were the niggers. We played along while that worked for us.

"Anyway, one night I caught my commanding officer whipping him. For trying to desert, Zane told me later. I gutted that fucker like a fish, only slow. Here's how it is. A Crimbone can fight and fuck and joke around over beers with Earth-line folks, but the minute you see one of your own under the lash of one of theirs, all that shit goes right out the window. Your blood just heats up, so you remember who and what you really are, who and what *they* really are."

Sally shrugged. "You've seen me kill a few Crimbone since we started getting along. Here we are still drinking beers together with my guts still inside me."

"One more way times are changing, I guess. Anyway, by the time the last light slipped from the commanding officer's eyes, he knew everything he'd ever need to know about me and that weird black blade I carried. Obviously, Zane and I both had to desert after that. I was pissed that he'd thought to go without me, but he told me he'd figured I'd follow along when I got fed up with that bunch of Earth-line crackers. He was probably right. Anyway, we hadn't been on our way long when I fell into a state."

"A state?"

"You've taken some funny drugs in your travels, I'm guessing? Had 'em kick in with more than you've bargained for so you turned into a drooling nitwit so you could watch and feel yourself shambling all over the place, but you couldn't pull yourself together enough to stop it?"

"Sure. Go on."

"Zane carried me through it like a sport, that's for damn sure, kept us deep in the thick brush, out of sight of the torches of the search party already on our trail. I slowed us up so we almost got caught." He met her eyes. "Do you know what that state was?" She shook her head. "In stepping to Zane's aid, I'd made my Third Call."

"How?"

"The Third Call comes when a Crimbone fledgling makes a choice, some ultimate test of loyalty, between their Crimbone brethren and whatever they've been devoting themselves to throughout the fledgling days. I just told you, how it is, between Crimbone and everyone else."

"Right. So wherever Rob is, what choice could he have had to make like that?"

"No clue."

"Bullshit." Sally remembered the cellars under the Renaissance Kingdom, finding Rob strapped to that table. She'd cut him free and he'd left. *I need to get as far from you as I can*, he'd told her, because he loved her so damn much and was scared of himself on her behalf. So who'd he left with? "What was that Crimbone bitch's name? Remela?"

"Remelea."

Sally pounded her beer. If Rob was sticking his dick in the Crimbone killer-woman, fine. Hell, Sally might have fucked that one herself, except she'd never felt safe getting that close and personal with any Crimbone whose name wasn't Rob Coscan, not without worrying about getting her throat bitten out, or worse. She couldn't even get mad, considering her own affair with Lilly.

But no, her thing with Lilly was nothing but two friends who knew one more way to make each other feel good, at the end of days full of so much pain and hell. Since Rob and Sally had gotten together, his ideas of monogamy had bordered on the puritanical. He'd act guilty for noticing that another girl was cute. *What are you embarrassed about?* she'd say, *I noticed her too.* It was delusional and unnatural, even creepy, but it was part of who he was. It was part of how he loved her. She'd loved him back all the more for it, in spite of herself.

Whatever Rob and Remelea were going through, wherever they were, Sally couldn't very well hold it against them if they'd decided to fuck the pain out of each other, if that's what they needed. But if it meant something to Rob that triggered his Third Call…

After whatever's happened between them, if Rob caught me and Remelea in a fight, he'd jump in on her side. He'd kill me for her if it came down to it, because she's a Crimbone like him and I'm a Spirelight, and that's what his blood tells him now.

"Shit, Jesse, didn't he say I was the first woman of his own kind he ever met? Yeah, the *closest thing* to a woman of his kind. So once he saw me again after spending some time around the genuine article…I guess I just don't measure up anymore."

Jesse reached over and squeezed her shoulder. "Hey, c'mon, kid, you know that's bullshit. Rob loves you. He's a lot of things, but that ain't gonna change."

She shrugged him off, hunched forward, squeezed her eyes shut, clenched her teeth, and slammed her bottle on the table. That was satisfying, but not as good as going berserk like she felt. "Fucking bastard…*Goddamn backstabbing little prick!*" She grabbed two fresh beers, slid one over to Jesse, and drank half of hers in one chug.

"Hey, whoa, take it easy there!"

"Don't fucking tell me what to do. We ain't on duty." She took another deep pull.

"Now you sound like that pain-in-the-ass brother of yours."

She almost smiled through the streaming tears.

"You know," said Jesse, "chances are, Zane's already off the base and on his way by now."

"That quick, huh."

"That's how quick things tend to shift in Crimbone life, once you and your blood make a decision."

"I've started to notice," said Sally. Given how long a Crimbone life could apparently last, that was a lot of shifts.

Jesse sighed and settled back in his chair. "I remember…Years after the war, we'd walk down streets and see old men sitting and talking on porches. You'd be surprised, how often we'd recognize faces through all those wrinkles and fallen out teeth, men we'd fought next to…or against, the ones who surrendered fast enough, that is. I still wonder if any of 'em recognized us, with all the bulk and scars we'd put on. I found myself wishing I'd given 'em more of a chance than I did when we were all young and strong together, really gotten to know some of 'em, y'know? It didn't matter anymore. They were the lucky ones. They'd lived through their war. They'd made it to where they could just sit back, relax and wait for the end. I remember thinking, *Zane and me, we'll outlive all those old bastards and still be strong and smooth as we are now.* The Crimbone ain't made to reach that reward, to be able to sit back, know we've survived everything we'll ever have to survive. A Crimbone's built to get tougher to kill with age, 'til sooner or later someone gets in a lucky shot."

Sally sighed and smiled. "But you liked the *idea* of that, didn't you, of reaching a day when you and Zane could just turn into dirty old men on a porch together."

"Yeah."

"…Something to hang onto, to fight towards other than the *bigger picture*. Even if you know it's bullshit, it still got you through every fight you shared with him, didn't it?"

Jesse gave Sally such a haunted, vulnerable look, she worried for a second that he was about to try to kiss her. Instead, he settled back and shook his head. "I guess everyone in this kind of life finds an idea like that. No, actually…I looked forward to whenever I finally slipped up, or Zane did. Once we came into our own together as Crimbone, it seemed like he was the one always reeling me in, 'cause I was the one always rocking the boat. I was the one who might piss off the lands or the Cabinets we answered to and get us into more trouble than we could get out of. Now I wonder if I've just been scared of letting him rock *our* boat, the Jesse-and-Zane boat. I think things changed between us a lot earlier than I let myself see it. He always knew my mind, on everything. Now I realize, I don't think I ever knew his. Doesn't matter anymore, I guess. Here we are, and he ain't."

FOUR

Zane made a few rounds through the streets, then stopped by his quarters and threw some supplies into a bag. There was a lot of walking ahead for him, he figured. This place would get along fine without him. It would be tougher for him, once he found Rob. He already had a plan in mind for that, sort of. Usually, whenever he made plans, he'd been able to talk them through out loud, have Jesse help him smooth out the details. It couldn't be that way this time, though.

Zane passed the Big Red Beast, as he and Jesse had taken to calling it over the years. He had a mind to hotwire it out of here. Nah, the van was Jesse's baby. So what did that make Zane, its wet nurse? It was his wizardry that had kept it running all these years, reinforced it all over into the indestructible monster that had carried them through so many weird scrapes. He'd fixed the front of it and a few other sturdy-enough vehicles with the snowplow blades, along with chains on the tires, so everyone wasn't trapped in the little radius of their shelter, in the middle of these frosty Rockies. There were six functional vehicles here besides the van, all communal, all ones folks had found when they arrived, all running thanks to Zane. Funny, considering how little love he had for machinery. He was cursed with a gift for it, though, so he applied it wherever it helped his pack. The van's emptiness now loomed at him through the windows.

Well past the gates, near the base town's borders, a set of headlights broke through the darkness. Zane didn't stop walking. The car slowed to a crawl next to him, and the window rolled down. He said into it, "This you guys' idea of how to sober up?"

"This is my idea of how to work out a hangover," said Lilly from the driver's seat.

Tiger leaned out of the shadows of the front passenger seat. "Figured we'd go on a scouting run, clear some of the mess of that earlier bombshell *without* getting drunk again."

"Well, keep your eyes peeled."

"For those other Crimbone in the next town downhill?"

"You'd better not, 'cause you'd better not go anywhere near 'em."

"Hell," said Lilly, "I don't even know where they are. From how you and Jesse talked, I don't think these snow tires would get us that far anyway."

Zane walked alongside the car to where buildings gave way to white trees. "Got your CB working?"

"Yeah."

"Good. Stay within Sphere Three of the maze tonight. Don't veer southeast."

Zane set a good example by walking southwest, back towards whatever was left of the United States by now. He didn't plan to keep to the maze.

FIVE

Sam Cash stood watch on the porch. He hadn't seen or smelled any more trigger-happy Earth-liners, not live ones anyway. He sucked in the icy gusts and listened to the wind whoosh through this snowy, misty ghost town, shoving buildings 'til the wood strained, ricocheting through alleyways. It was an uncomfortable voice, but it didn't have anything to say to him. The lands never told you anything your blood or your blade could tell you first. There was nothing to do with his blade right now, strapped to his leg under his coat, so he slowed his breathing, held it 'til it grew hot within his core, let it out slowly, and listened to his blood. The frozen dead jutted here and there from the snow like long, jagged rocks, for as far as the streets showed. The closest corpse was the guy still pinned under the truck that had totaled the porch next door. Sam had no plans to still be here when spring warmth thawed out the corpses so they stank everything up…when the Canadian Rockies birthed their own new flora and fauna.

His coat seemed to hold out less and less icy air by the minute. Anya was somewhere inside, doing the real watching. Good thing they didn't have to talk about it out loud. It wasn't just their natural attunement as a Crimbone team, though there was that. Sam used to joke how he was amazed that any woman had ever consented to sleep with him. Looking back at himself before his First Call, he was even more amazed.

Anya, though…she never ran out of ways to make him go, *Cross that off the list of things I figured some hack made up for bullshit romance novels.* If the Cabinet—when there'd still been one—had called and asked for a written transcript of their on-the-job conversations, they both could have filled out identical word-for-word reports, without having to compare notes. Half of it would consist of things they hadn't even said out loud, and it would still match up. It was like the rhythm of their bloodstreams was just that well synced up.

She knew what she was doing up there, he reminded himself. No matter what species of male you were, though, or how tough your female companions had proven themselves, there was still a lot of caveman left in your protect-the-little-woman instincts, he guessed. That was Sam's one lingering objection to Jesse and Zane's decision to leave them out here with Byron's pack. Otherwise, he'd have preferred this setup, especially after hearing about life on base. That, and being back on a military base sounded at least comfortingly familiar. Except no, he guessed, it wouldn't, at all.

It wasn't his discomfort with the idea of the United Deschembines—though there was that—or that he wouldn't trust himself among them. He would, at least as long as Sheldon and Sally Wildfire stayed there.

When Sam had first heard about the United Deschembines, it had sounded like a recipe for disaster.

He'd been all for hunting them down. If anyone could hold something like that together so it might actually work, it was Jesse Karn and Zane Rochester.

Growing up in the Deep South, Sam had been raised on the legends of Jesse and Zane, as only a castoff Crimbone kid could be. Once, when he was thirteen or fourteen, he'd gone on one of those guided tours of an old plantation. He hadn't even put it together, the true significance of where he stood, 'til the tour guide let something slip about a runaway slave who'd come home and started an uprising, during the civil war but before the Union troops pressed in that far. The guide hadn't gone into many more details than that. It wasn't the sort of thing the local historical societies liked to lean in on too heavily, not when it came to selling the good ol' romanticized image of the antebellum South to the tourists. In that moment, though, young Sam had known exactly who that returned runaway slave had been, along with his lone white companion, and just how bloody that two-man siege had gotten. He also knew that the two marauders had taken off for Vermont afterwards. Something had clicked in his brain, so he'd seen through the meticulously glossy restoration of the old mansion. He'd seen and smelled things long painted over, tasted the old screams on the air, felt the ghosts telling him secrets that would make the other tourists shit themselves. That's when he knew, beyond a shadow of a doubt, that he would one day make all three calls and live the life of a fully-fledged Crimbone.

After being cast to the world, it hadn't taken Sam long to get himself arrested as a homeless juvenile delinquent. Of course, when they processed him, they discovered any record of any family he'd ever belonged to had gone missing. On paper, he didn't exist. They still threw his little ass in juvie, because what the hell else were they gonna do with him? Someone pulled some strings behind the scenes, so he went swiftly from there to military school. Military school led to the Marines. His stint as a Marine led to his career in law nforcement.

"Boy-yo-boy, Jackal-Juggler," Sam's Familiar Hornigulp had exclaimed, "some motherfuckers sure must got some high hopes for your tight lil' ass, huh?"

"How?" Sam still remembered, he'd been busy unpacking, face scrunched against the faint bleach-piss smell in his bunk mattress. That soon out of juvie, he'd still been braced against anyone with interest in his *tight lil' ass*.

"Someone with Crimbone Cabinet influence smells somethin' special 'bout you, kid."

"Who arranged it?" Even at fifteen, Sam's voice had been a constant deadpan of strained patience. His parents used to say, he'd been born with an *I'm too old for this shit* look on his face. His dad was an old Navy man who'd been a young private at the Gulf of Tonkin under the command of Jim Morrison's dad, so that was saying something.

"Some rich recluse wacko down in Louisiana, has folks all over who owe him favors. Always up to all kinds of fancy middleman bullshit, like anyone'd give that much of a rat's ass over him anyway. But hey, *fuggettaboutit*. Anyway, get this. Here you are, all the way down in Hickville, get sprung from juvie into fuckin' Earth-line military school, by your own kind. But the guys with the paperwork on you, had to make all them fancy phone calls? All the way up north! Go figure, right? So who's the fuckin' Cabinet send to do the muscle work for ya? Jesse Fuckin' Ripper-Man Karn and Zane Fuckin' Thumpy-Bumpy Rochester."

Not that Sam had met them personally back then. He wondered if they remembered his name. Legends of Sam's boyhood heroes had inspired him to walk the trail he'd carved as a fledgling, the kind of trail that didn't leave one's head much time to float into the clouds. That trail had stretched so far, though, that he'd started to wonder if his chance to pick up his blade had passed.

Then came the day at the blockade. He'd lived his fledgling days serving his country. Now he served his lands. He'd never apologize for either. The more he understood the difference, though, the more it hit home how the former didn't exist anymore. Neither did the world he'd been groomed for, a world for legends like Magur Sevi or Jesse Karn or Zane Rochester…or Sam Cash, as he might occasionally daydream.

Now Jesse and Zane were men Sam had shaken hands with, stuck in the same shit-pit as him. They were obviously extraordinary men, men he was proud to work with on the same side, but still just men.

Sam had now met both of the *tainted Spirelight* siblings. He'd met the brother back in Virginia, the sister here. With both, he felt the truth in what people said about them. The boy had been nearly dead from some hell of a fight. Sam had been one of those who'd hauled him up and gotten him to what had passed for an infirmary back at that place. When he'd spotted the kid lying on the ground, bleeding from a leg wound that had barely missed the femoral artery, he'd assumed at first that he was helping out a fellow Crimbone. He hadn't learned 'til later whose life he'd helped save. Moreover, that's what he'd smelled. He hadn't gotten so much as a hint of the glow. The girl was another matter. She still *glowed*, all right, but it didn't draw out Sam's killing urge. Rather, it sent a cleansing breeze through him, so he felt almost like he'd never need to kill for the glow again. In a way, that's why he was glad to stay off base. Even if he didn't need to drink the glow, he'd still have to kill Spirelights again eventually, because there would always be Spirelights who'd try to kill him and his. He'd survived this long by accepting such facts unmoralistically.

The problem was, it sounded like the United Deschembines were trying to create an illusion of civilization for themselves at that place, built around a few people who held them all together…or rather the idea of those people. Since the Renaissance Kingdom raid, Sam had seen less and less of what could be called civilization, and too many pockets of people trying to sustain the illusion of it, with less and less success. He'd always felt most at home out in the wilderness, anyway. He could think better without the noise, hear the true voices better. Hornigulp used to tell him he needed to grow out of that. A Crimbone needs to hear the right voices no matter what superficial noise clogs up the air. So Sam went with Earth-line law enforcement to work on that. Go figure, he'd ended up patrolling the Virginia pines. So had Anya. It turned out they'd been in the Marines at the same time. She was younger and had done a shorter stint, and was champing-at-the-bit pissed that the lands kept steering her away from Spirelight action, wouldn't give her a window to the blades.

At first, Sam thought her fledgling days would have been better spent punked out on the streets, beating on crackheads with nail-studded baseball bats, likely to get arrested by a cop like himself. He told her so when the department assigned them together. She'd responded with the obvious handcuff jokes. On their first patrol together, she'd pulled the cruiser over into some trees, wrestled him into the back and showed him she hadn't been joking…except she'd been the one to slap the cuffs on him. So there went any dumbass Earth-line regulations about fraternization. She was the first and only Crimbone woman to have him—not a minute too soon in life, because in his limited experience, Crimbone sex and Earth-line women didn't mix well.

Over these last couple days of R&R, such as it was here, they'd both healed quickly. These weren't exactly ideal accommodations, but compared to the freezing hell everyone had been trekking through, it was *Shangri La*. The problem was, their companions had recovered just as quickly. The more those guys got their strength back, the more they showed their true colors little by little, the less Sam liked them.

A black shape passed overhead. Far away, something landed with a thump in the snow. Sam stayed planted and listened. A moment later, there came another thump, louder but still soft, around the corner in the alleyway to his right. Sam slipped silently inside. He smelled his way through the darkness, to the stairwell. His first impulse had been to investigate the noise outside. Instinct drew him to fetch Anya, instead. It wasn't 'til he reached the second landing that he saw the glow of candles. He heard the others shuffling about. A candlelit sliver outlined the door to the wide bare top room where most of the pack had camped out. Anya stepped out into his path.

"Is it my turn to go on watch already?" she said in her sweetest casual voice. She stepped into the stairwell with him. Her face stopped matching her tone.

Sam nodded and rubbed her shoulder. "Not yet, hon. It's all dead out there anyway."

"Well, if you insist." Her hungry kiss was quick and desperate, like sleep lately.

"You guys want we should clear the space for a few?" some clown shouted from within the room.

"Nah, man, it's cool," Anya shouted back "We're headed downstairs." Once they were down in the store space, she whispered, "Byron slipped out the window. Everyone saw him and pretended not to notice." She said more quietly, in the private language they'd developed between them, *"The rest of them are in on it. I think I'm the only one who wasn't* supposed *to notice."*

"In on what?"

"Did you know a Familiar just showed up?"

"What the fuck? There's no fledgling here."

"I know."

They slipped outside. Sam had seen the direction the dark shape had taken. Anya knew which window Byron had used. They hopped the right railing, landed and crouched silently in the snow, then pressed their backs to the alley wall. Their ears adjusted to the howling wind.

The whispering voice didn't come from a Familiar, and it wasn't Byron. It was raspy, hissing, agonized. "...After that turn, you'll see two chopped-down posts sticking out of the snow. That's where the sign used to be, when we first got there. They chopped it down, 'cause they didn't want—"

"I get the idea." That was Byron.

"It's a straight shot after that. Be careful about those extra two...not part of the plan...Be ready to use what's strapped on your belt."

"I'm not drawing black metal on my fellow Crimbone." Byron's voice was a low, squealing hiss.

"I've heard different about you."

"It's not the same! I've been on the trail with those two. We've fought side by side. We've—"

"Save it for the memorial moon-songs. Do what you like. You're making things harder on yourself, though. There's other Crimbone between you and the ones you're *really* supposed to kill. Think they'll think twice about drawing on you?"

"Oh, don't worry. I'll draw on Jesse Karn. I've waited for an excuse to punch that asshole's clock for a *long* time."

"Good. You were on the trail with those others for a while only because Great Balthazar matched you up with them. You're at the end of that trail."

"You smug glowstick rat! I should kill you just for talking at me about shit like *the trail*."

"Please do."

"Ha! Nice try, you ugly little turncoat. Fuck you. You wanna pussy out, find your own way. Hey, cheer up! Between how you're shivering and how those shoulders are bleeding, you ain't got long anyway."

Sam and Anya went back around the side of the porch. As they came back in, the rest of the pack filed out of the stairwell and spread out into the room: seven men, three women. A woman in the lead said, "You guys decide to go fuck in the snow? Too cold for my ass, but whatever gets you off."

"So what'd you guys all come down for?" Sam put himself between them and Anya. "You wanna watch?"

"We're not the ones into invading people's privacy."

Anya stepped up. Natural authority flowed through her stride. "I don't like your tone, bitch."

Sam watched the others file out, circling up. None of them made to draw, but Sam saw their arms ready to swing.

Steady, casual feet climbed the porch. Byron stepped in and clapped once for everyone's attention. "Okay, folks. I've listened to the lands. It's time to stop hiding in this hole like outcasts."

Sam turned. "Whatever do you mean, Byron?"

"The lands have spoken to me. I'm taking back charge of this pack."

"That didn't sound like the lands talking to you outside," said Sam.

"Don't get uppity, kid. I've been at this longer, don't forget. It's not right, us sitting here on Jesse Karn's holy terms."

"So when did you guys run into Balthazar?" said Anya.

"Mister Cash," shrieked Byron, "I suggest you shut your bitch up."

"I suggest you don't call my gal a bitch again."

"Are you threatening me, kid?"

"Nah," said Sam. "See, I don't really give a flying fuck what words you throw around. My gal here, though, she's…unpredictable."

"When did you assholes throw in with Balthazar?" Anya repeated coldly.

Byron's whole body stiffened up, between Sam and Anya in front of him and the pack at his back, the latter expecting him to lead them through this mutiny. His face bled cold and blank. "I can't remember, exactly. It was a while after he finished with me, before I was ready to go to work for him. He didn't have us enhanced, like he did those dead, frozen ones outside. I suppose now you can guess why. He told me what to do and set me in your direction, though. He said the lands would lead *you* to the tainted ones, but not if your blood told you that you worked against them. He was right."

Sam's dukes flew up. He snarled and sprang. Byron leaned sideways, ripped off a table leg and swung. Shit, the guy moved even faster in a fight than he talked! The table leg splintered against Sam's head. It sounded like a thousand metal pans clanging together inside his skull. He smashed sideways into the collapsed table, rolled off it, and sprawled on cold, hard boards. He still felt his body, but it wouldn't move for him.

Anya's blurred shape shrieked and sprang. Someone's foot kicked her legs out from the side. They swarmed in, obscuring her, their boots thudding dully and rapidly all over her. Her hands were already bloody when they shot through the cluster. She got a man by the ankles. He crashed on his back and she barreled out of the barrage. She managed to break his face in a few places, his collarbone in a few more, before they dragged her back. Their boots kept thudding. Anya wasn't fighting anymore.

Move, you sonofabitch, move! Even Sam's thoughts sounded further and further away. His most vivid sensation—other than his throbbing skull—was the wetness of blood saturating his scalp. He kept falling, deeper and deeper into himself. Far away, he still heard Anya getting the shit kicked out of her.

"That's enough," Byron shouted. "*I said that's enough!* Time to move. Great Balthazar's messenger has come. We know how to reach Jesse Karn and the tainted Spirelights. Before dawn, that'll be it for the United Deschembines."

SIX

Sheldon took the road behind the bar. Down the central stretch, he spotted several shadowed bodies who didn't realize he could sense them. That was good. So was the darkness that wouldn't give them a good look at him if they did spot him. He walked with perfect posture in a straight line, even though he still felt like a greasy, sweated-out pile of hungover shit. He probably looked it, too. Everyone had to bathe conservatively these days, but he decided he'd better look to that before he took off…before he said his final goodbyes. He gulped at the thought and tightened his jaw. He still didn't want this to feel real any sooner than it had to.

He cut through an alleyway. Halfway down, a receded door hung open. A Spirelight man had stepped out into the moon-glazed snow to take a piss. Sheldon didn't see the guy 'til they were less than ten feet apart. The guy still seemed unaware of him, so he made to slip by and keep it that way. He was almost past when the guy finished pissing, put his junk away, turned slightly, and jolted.

"Ah, crap, man! Look, I don't—I just—"

"Sorry I startled you," Sheldon muttered. "Just passing by."

He planned to keep going, but the guy said, "Sheldon Wildfire?"

Shit. Sheldon paused and leaned against the wall. He wasn't sure why, except maybe it was an excuse to snatch one last moment's laziness. "Shevish, right?"

"Excuse me?"

"Your name's Shevish, if I remember right. Sorry, I'm shit with names."

"Yes, Sheldon Wildfire. This is Shevish."

Sheldon shook his head and took a deep breath. "If you wanna talk to me, just call me Sheldon. Who exactly do you think I am, anyway?"

"How—What—I…don't know how to answer that."

"It's a fair question. Everyone obviously has a lot of screwy ideas about me these days, so I'm curious. What sentiments does the *idea* of me trigger in you?"

"Before the United Deschembines took me in, there was no hope on the path I followed. Back when I lived among other traditional Spirelights, it…got around that I like guys instead of girls…after my sister snooped and followed me to a neighboring town…caught me with an *Earth-line* guy, no less. I made her promise not to tell, but I wasn't kidding myself. That Earth-line guy…It was just dumb luck I found out when I did that he'd been killed. Made to look like some kind of random Earth-line street violence, but I knew better. I knew the Secret Police would be coming for me, next."

Sheldon stared, startled. He hadn't forgotten how the Tribunals had looked on guys like Shevish, at least among the civilians…and with an Earth-line man, no less! Those within the Secret Police got away with a lot more, and he'd been too young while still among them for it to matter. He'd never gone with his family to punish one of their own kind for such transgressions, but like Shevish said, it was all just dumb luck.

Shevish went on, "It took being nearly killed to realize it, having my coterie desert me as lost then finding my way to this new one. I'd found the *idea* of hope…with my new family, you know? Then you and your sister came along and turned that idea into reality."

"Yeah? How'd we do that, exactly?"

"Before I found the United Deschembines, I thought I knew what it was to be a Spirelight. After…you know…everything I went through…everything I'd believed in looked false to me. I didn't know what anything meant anymore. I'd never really known in the first place. I just knew it had been a lie. I had nothing to go on but the knowledge that I'd woken up from a lie I'd been living. But that…without a truth to replace a lie, there's not much left, is there? Then I saw you and your sister up on that stage that night, and…and I felt the truth."

"What truth?"

"Of what it really means to be a Spirelight. I'd never felt the Spirah gods within me when I pretended to follow the beliefs of the other Spirelights of this world. When I saw you two up there, I finally got it. Those other Spirelights talk about unity beneath the gods, the one they forged with Bathshire, beneath the Kingdom that would be Spiralla…but they see it as a unity that exists only between Spirelights. Now I feel that the Spirah gods wish for that unity to exist between all people. Maybe Bathshire heard the gods' message wrong. Or maybe it was the ones who came after him who messed it up. Maybe the gods only put themselves directly into one race, as the first step to giving their love to all races. Maybe just like the Schomites say their *Old Lords* did, joining with the lands of this world, when they came over on the boat. Maybe that was the second step in the plan. It took losing Spiralla, even losing all Deschemb itself, but we've finally found that way…like maybe when you and Sally stood up there in front of us all…"

The longer Shevish talked, the more Sheldon's nerves crawled and tightened at the same time. *I swear, if this guy tries to tell me I'm the Second Coming of Bathshire, I'm gonna deck him.*

Instead, Shevish just shook his head and sighed. "I don't know what I'm saying. I guess I'm just emotional tonight."

Sheldon clapped him on the shoulder. "It's okay, man. Sounds like you're talking more about the gods in your own head, like most people do." *Even though I know for a fact that the Spirah gods are real, because of everything that changed when they abandoned me.*

"I don't understand."

"Never mind. I'm just tired. Hey, whatever keeps you going is a good thing, right?"

"I guess so."

Except what would happen to people like Shevish, if you took away the gods in their heads along with the real ones? Either way, eventually, someone would find new gods, real or imagined. Hey, at least Sheldon would surely be dead before that happened.

"Thanks, Shevish. You've helped me see a little more of the big fuckin' picture. Enjoy the life your gods give you." He walked on.

SEVEN

Two Familiars fly in each other's direction, way above the roads 'tween them Urinated Deschembines and them Balthazar-whupped fuckers who just kicked the crap out of Sam and Anya. The cold air don't bother the Familiars much. They still smell each other comin', just fine. Once they actually see each other, they settle on opposin' tree limbs.

Critters from the ephemeral realms don't usually got reason to be near or speak to each other, 'less they got a pair of fledglings 'tween 'em that's gotten close an' shit, close like Jesse and Zane, or close in a similar but more huffy-puffy way like Sam and Anya. The northbound Familiar don't even got his last fledgling still breathin' in this here realm, but he was brought closer by magic means than any Familiar's s'posed to get to that fledgling...*in the huffy-puffy sorta way*, no less, the kind that makes babies. Seemed at the time, an ordeal like that would'a equaled the Third Call for her. 'Cept the magic-man charge didn't leave her much choice in the matter when he pimped her out to a Familiar, so it weren't exactly proof of loyalty. Maybe she'd'a earned it since, raisin' the result of all that magic huffy-puffy mess, 'cept her little bundle of joy up and killed her first.

The southbound Familiar's stuck here for reasons he just got through explainin' to Cop-Boy. "I don't like seein' your kind 'round here, Lockiglock," squawks Puttergong. "Not after that hanky-panky you done. Why you wasn't jerked right back to the ephemeral realms 'fore you could blow your load, emergency-situation-like, I'll never figure."

"I wasn't jerked back to no ephemeral realms, 'cause de mon set up de hanky-panky were de one favored by *dis* realm, by *dese* lands. It de sonny-mon run tings now, an' it be de sonny-mon's trail I make clear. You de one in de way now, Puttergong."

"Aw, blow it out your ass! All your *sonny-mon's* got cookin' is a bunch'a bullshit smeared all over the *big fuckin' picture*. You might'a asked around, how I like to handle fuckers get in *my* way, when it comes to that shit."

"Now ya done it, talkin' like ya mean to knock another like yourself from dese realms back to de ephemeral realms before dem realms' choosin'."

"You mean how I's talkin' 'bout knockin' your tonsils out'cher asshole? Yeah. After that, I'm gonna go do the same to them whupped Crimbone you set hoofin' it this way. Then I's gonna go do the same to your *sonny-mon*."

"In dat case, mon, what we waitin' for?"

"Aw hell, man, I'm just bein' nice, givin' you time to back out. I mean, think about it. I get gacked, I'll get sent straight back to the ephemeral realms. Sure they'll bitch me out fierce. Ain't the first time. Thinkin' over all the shit you took part in, how ye figure it'll go for you?"

"Let's us find out."

So two big, dark shapes shoot from the misty, snowy branches at each other, talons forward like hawks in the dive. Their wings beat against one another, while scrapin' talons make nasty shriekin' noises. Then there's two Familiars shreddin' each other's bellies open while their big wings keep beatin' each other somethin' fierce. It'd be a weird fight to watch if anyone was here to watch it, 'cause it's the first time in this world that any two Familiars has gone talon to talon. They shred each other's bulbous hangin' bellies wide open, spillin' guts all over the place, an' their wings break each other all to hell. They fall together, blood an' guts splatterin' the snow. But it's Puttergong whose big saw-tooth horse-snout shoots forward first, bitin' Lockiglock's throat clean out while they's still halfway to the ground. The spoutin' blood feels like somethin' nasty all over Puttergong's face. Puttergong's always figured the blood of his own kind would taste better. Lockiglock lets out one last squawk and wing-beats Puttergong a couple more times. They both flop in roadside sludge like two snow angels.

The first thing Puttergong thinks of is when he originally faded into physical bein' this go-round. Biter-Boy made his First Call without even realizin' it, standin' 'round outside his boardin' shack in Brat-o'-burrow, suckin' on a smoky-treat, and he smelled his Sally-Girl for the first time from far off, not even knowin' what she was. Then there was Puttergong, floppin' in the grass, still so little, not strong enough yet to get off the ground. It was so dim that Biter-Boy couldn't get a good look at Puttergong, thought he was a wounded birdie or some shit. So now here's Puttergong floppin' around just as helpless, plus hurtin' a lot worse.

This'd be a funny way to end this here go-round. 'Cept where do Familiars go when they get gacked like this? Somewhere in the ephemeral realms, obviously, but not back to the big ol' tree with the other Familiars. Puttergong's watched buddies take off to this here realm, heard about 'em gettin' gacked, an' he ain't never been able to find 'em since on any of them trillions of branches.

Lockiglock's limp carcass starts fadin' into the air. Puttergong's the first Familiar he's ever heard of to kill another Familiar. He sure ain't sorry it was Lockiglock. If he ain't headed back to the big tree in the ephemeral realms, though, he sure as shit don't wanna get stuck in the same place with Lockiglock. Right now, though, Puttergong's big problem is stuffin' his guts back into his ripped-up body cavity. Ain't nothin' else to do but get himself as far out of the way as possible. He don't wanna think about how folks'll fare without him, don't particularly wanna care, but he winds up doin' both. There's shit he still needs to tell Biter-Boy first, damnit, important shit!

In the distance, along comes the feet of all them whupped Crimbone Lockiglock was leadin', trompin' through the snow like Napoleon's march on Russia. Puttergong remembers them days. Fun times. A few minutes ago, he had a mind to rip the fuck out'a all them whupped Crimbone. Now all he can do is scuttle back through the bare trees and bushes, 'til he finds a bush that's big, puffy, and soggy enough for him to bury himself inside. Too bad it's so sloppy and cold in there, though. For the first time ever in this here realm, Puttergong knows all about the cold air, feels it as more than an irritation. He curls up best he can while still holdin' his guts in.

There's other feet out here...softer, *smaller* feet, soundin' just as unfriendly, trompin' right towards Puttergong. Once he spots some of the bodies attached to 'em, he figures he's bled out so bad, he's seein' shit. 'Cause all of a sudden, there's lots of folks paddin' out'a the trees and bushes, surroundin' him. The weirdest part is, they's lookin' at him on eye-level. They ain't dressed for this weather neither, ain't dressed like Puttergong's seen folks durin' the last few times he's been sent to this here realm. The feller in the lead's wearin' buckskin legwraps, along with a shiny red coat and a stovepipe hat almost tall as he is, like some carnie master.

Carnie-Master Man takes a long look, squintin' through the snow and mist. Then he turns back to the rest of these knee-high fuckers, spreads his arms, and shouts, "No need to panic, folks. The Familiar's down. He won't be making trouble for us."

Puttergong's head clears some. *Fuckin' Lepods. How'd I miss that this here region had a Lepod infestation?* "Stupid fuckin' pinch," he squawks at the Carnie-Master leader, "I ain't innerested in makin' trouble for you dumb little bastards! *No one* gives a shit about you fuckers no more, 'cause you ain't innerested in nothin' but hidin' in your holes, comin' out to play stupid tricks on folks when you get bored. Well, I don't know if y'all noticed, but things has gotten fucked up enough that y'all won't be *able* to hide for too much longer."

Some of the Lepods has gotten all huffy over the word *pinch*, not takin' in a damn thing Puttergong's just said otherwise, which he figures just proves his point. Mister Carnie-Master Man's been listenin' fine, though. He's creepin' closer, close enough for Puttergong to swipe out a set of talons and chop that fucker up like a sausage link.

"Now, now," says Carnie-Master Man, "you're in no position to get ugly like that. I recognize it's not a position you're used to—"

"Oh, you wanna try some *new positions*, bitch? Get a lil' closer."

Carny-Master Man looks Puttergong over with hooded eyes. "Oh, I doubt you have enough blood left in you for that…which is part of why I haven't given the signal for my comrades here to swarm in and segment you up for winter meat."

Puttergong squints harder and cranes his neck forward, gettin' his snout close as he can to Carnie-Master Man. If they do get him dead, he might mention, his carcass'll just crumble to nothin' before the assholes get a taste of his winter meat. But the little fucker's gotten him worked up. "So bring it on, bitch! See how many of you lil' pinches is left to *eat me* by the time you're done."

"I'd rather hear what you have to say, see if you can hold enough of a civil conversation to convince us why any of your problems should be our problems."

"Yeah? So get me out'a this fuckin' freezin' cold, fix me up so's I can get back to my business, and I'll tell ye all about it."

"What makes you assume we don't already know?"

"You watch what just happened to me, how I got like this?"

"No."

"Too bad. It was one cool fight."

"Son, my people have been watching since before the rest of you even thought of showing up. Long before the people you serve even thought of finding their way out of Deschemb, mine made the decision to pack up and take off across the shrouded sea. We didn't even have to look for it like the rest of the Deschembines. We always knew the way here, just as we could still find our way right back to it if we thought all these stunted Deschembines could do half the damage they did to the Old World. And we'd find our way to an even farther, weirder shore than those you serve could even start to look for, making precious little difference to our lifestyle. I'd explain it, but you Familiars of all creatures should understand. But I suppose, given who you've fallen to serving, you've lost touch with such broad thinking."

"So you wanna just hop from world to world every couple epochs, 'cause you're too big a bunch'a pussies to do your part, keepin' any one world in one piece?"

"This world is in no danger of falling to pieces. Of being temporarily crippled, yes, but nothing it hasn't seen before. Those experiments we spawned from our own lesser lines...the ones the rest of you call the Earth-line people…we knew early on that they'd create their own destruction, just like the lesser Deschembine refugees. This world would have survived whatever they'd finally do to it, just as it will survive whatever your Schomites and Spirelights do, leaving it to us. In a way, I suppose we should thank you…you and and your Schomites and Spirelights, for crippling the Earth-line peoples' progress. Without the intervention of your own self-destruction, they'll do far less damage for the rest of this little world to recover from. You've all been amusing while you've lasted. We'll miss you for a while."

"Get yer fuckin' head out'a yer tiny pinch asshole! You spawned the fuckin' Earth-liners, huh? All your prattle does is show me you're just as ignorant as them. You're so busy gettin' a good laugh out'a everything happenin', you never stopped to figure how it *will* all bleed on down to y'all. You think the rest of them Deschembine refugees forgot about you? Once they's all done with each other, whoever's left is gonna start lookin' your way, 'cause they ain't so behind on gettin' shit in perspective as you think. Someone's gonna ask, *Now let me think, what we got to gain by fuckin' with the pinches?* And believe you me, they'll think of somethin', no matter how stupid it is. Whatever which way it shakes out, I guaran-fuckin'-tee, ye'll still be hurtin' fierce afterwards. Fix my ass up, I'll save y'all plenty of hurtin'."

Mister Carnie-Master looks like he's thinkin' it over. "Suppose we've already thought of that, looked at all the factors, and decided you're full of shit?"

"I'd say you might've overlooked a thing or three. Listen to me, I'll get your mind right. And hey, either way, you get in on the mix, there'll be plenty of fun you can have, fuckin' with all them primitive tall folks. First, though, get me out of this fuckin' cold and fix me up!"

"Why don't you convince us *while* we're fixing you? Looks like that could take a while."

"Fine by me."

Carnie-Master Man turns and gives some weird fuckin' hand-job signal to the other Lepods, so they all scatter. The other, bigger trompin' feet has well since faded up the trail by now. Puttergong guesses that little mess'll just have to go wherever it's goin' without him. Now the pinches is all scurryin', gatherin' the thickest little branches and twigs they can find. It hurts like a bitch when they start shovin' it all under Puttergong and his busted-up wings and slit open belly. But he grins and bears it 'til they got all them bits of wood tied together and they're liftin' him up an' carryin' him off to wherever the fuck it is Lepods hide out.

All together, the Lepods haul Puttergong off to a tunnel down into the ground, not much bigger than a gopher hole, 'cept Puttergong sees a light burnin' at the other end, a light like nothin' Puttergong's seen in this here world. When he sees the source, he figures, he'll be seein' a skivi-lie-zation for which there ain't no descriptions in these here Earth-line languages.

EIGHT

Janie read for a while, fell asleep, then woke up and read some more. Sheldon still wasn't back. One of those nights where he'd stayed out after his relief from duty. Lately, he rarely got home and crawled into bed with her 'til after she'd fallen asleep. He still always wanted her to go out with him, on nights when he wasn't on duty. She rarely said yes anymore.

"I don't feel comfortable around those people," she'd said, then immediately realized how wrong that sounded. "I mean, I can always tell they don't…They always look at me and see *the Earth-line girl*, the one who doesn't belong with you."

"What the hell are you talking about? They love you! Well, my *real* friends among 'em do, anyway. Even when you get nervous and don't say much, just all your little facial expressions and stuff…it's like you're the life of the party and you don't even know it."

"I'm glad you think so."

"It's true! I still ain't heard the end of it, from Tiger and Lilly, about how cute and funny they both think you are."

She'd shrank up and blushed. "Uh, thanks, I guess? Now I'm gonna feel even more nervous around those two the next time I see 'em."

It was weird, like he wanted to spend his leisure time pretending he was in a world that didn't exist anymore, a world he'd never really been part of in the first place. *Like he just wants to take his girl out on a date*. Who could blame him? Except the only kind of *date* left, it seemed, was to hang out with his fellow hardened killers, after they'd just spent all day doing whatever fucked-up shit they had to do to keep everyone else here alive. As if she didn't feel out of place enough already.

She read back over the chapter in Claudette's book about the first Crimbone.

A Schomite pirate vessel crashed on the rocks of a strange enemy shore. Only one young Schomite brave survived. In the pitiless, death-haunted wilderness, half-starved and alone, his intelligence bled to the purest animal cunning, he found his way to an enemy stronghold. Through stealth, cunning, and raw, blood-thirsty ruthlessness, he reached the center of the stronghold, where he discovered a captive Schomite sorcerer. Spirelight spells had been scrawled on the bars, toughening the metal. The brave used his own rudimentary working mystical knowledge to undo the bindings.

"You have prevailed, young one," said the sorcerer, "not just against our enemies, but through the most hostile of wildernesses they've occupied. The spirit of this wilderness favors you. Deep within you, it has recognized something closer to itself. Who are either of us to argue, eh? Very well. You will be the first of a new breed of Schomite, the guardians of our kind. Yours will be the refined instinct—the true oneness with the wildest forces of nature, the winds, the waves, the blazes—of the strongest, most cunning predator. Your natural enemies are the gods themselves. Your prey shall be the servants of those gods, in whom their essence dwells. You will feed, absorb that glowing life force as it flees from their bodies, as you cut it loose from within them. The more of that essence you drink, the stronger you will grow, ever more relentless, ever deadlier."

The brave came to stand in the middle of a circle, his bare feet upon pulsing red coals. His nerves sang their sweet, thirsty new song. The sorcerer gave him a pair of large, curved, serrated knives, forged of a black metal he'd only glimpsed in his wildest blood memories. Each handle bore the runic stamp of that realm.

"When a beast stalks its prey," said the sorcerer, "the body must be guided by a head and a heart that listen. You must listen to only three voices: to that of the land through which you move; to the pure, wild song of the blood in your veins; and to the voice of these blades, through which your purest self—your most uncompromising intent—must be channeled. From mind and soul come the instincts of the beast, but it is the claws and teeth that rip the prey apart."

From the same ephemeral realms, the sorcerer summoned a small, grotesque, winged creature to guide the brave back into the world, through his education as the new creature he would become. From that day on, those born to the Crimbone line matured like any other Schomite, until the day when their blood woke and sang, calling them forward. If they survived the first wave of trials, the ephemeral realms sent them their teeth and claws of black metal...

A rousing little tale of adventure if ever there was one...or so Janie would have thought, back in middle school when she'd been obsessed with Greek and Norse myths. Since then, she'd met actual Crimbone, seen a little of what *those teeth and claws of the black metal* could do. Jesse and Zane had never been anything but nice to her, yet whenever she was around them, they made her more nervous than anyone else here. Everything about their physical presence spoke of all that *purely distilled ruthlessness and cunning, of a beast of the wild.* She didn't want to think of them right now, so she shoved Claudette's book aside and reached for the notebook and pen she'd finally managed to scrounge up. Free-writing her impressions, putting some of it in her own words helped a little, like doing a book-report in elementary school. Hey, at least something she'd learned in school was still useful.

Quiet your mind, Mom kept saying in her head. *Don't pay so much nevermind to all the usual foolish chatter. Pay more attention to the voices you really ought'a listen to.*

If she didn't want to lose her mind in this insane new world, the voice she had to remember how to listen to was her own. Mom wasn't here. Janie was, but who was Janie? Not much time to keep track of that, distracted with all the cold, hunger, the months on roads that looked weirder and weirder.

Her room felt too cramped and dim right now, so she found her way to the empty mess-hall a few hallways over. There were enough high windows that the moon shone in. She made her way along the walls 'til she found a light switch. The room seemed a lot smaller than it had in darkness. Stars and frost shimmered through the overhead glass like chips of razor silver. Zane and a couple other folks with some maintenance-knowhow had gotten the heat working more or less throughout the building, so no one froze to death in their shoebox rooms. She wore her coat in the rest of the building. A few sniffles now trickled through the back of her sinuses.

Four long mess-hall tables took up a third of the space. Some guy sat at one of the outer ones. Actually, he sat *on* the table. When he stood up, he rose almost as high as a normal sized person with their feet on the floor.

His head twitched from side to side at Janie. "They're keeping one of the children people here? What a delightful surprise!"

What was with that shrill, high voice? The fact that the guy was less than three feet tall might have something to do with it. Janie approached, still bleary-eyed, still half-convinced her senses were playing tricks on her.

"Hello." She leaned in for a better look. "I'm not a child, you know."

"That's not what I meant, little long-face. The world you see these days seems ruled by the strange outer people, doesn't it? You must know this, or you wouldn't be getting your first full view of one like me."

"Who says it's my first look?"

"It is, right?"

"You're a Lepod, aren't you?"

"How do you know a thing like that?" The high-pitched voice was harder on her ears this close up. His throat flexed and strained weirdly when he talked, maybe forcing the words out at a higher pitch for someone of her size.

"I've read about you guys some," said Janie. "My people know about you more than we do the others, though most of us don't let ourselves believe you're real anymore. We have our own stories about you, though."

"You're a curious little child person," said the little man.

"Just hung around the right folks, I guess."

"Like the ones you're here with now?"

"Sometimes, yeah. Why do you call people like me the *children people?*"

"You're the children of my people."

"Are the women of your people as small as you?"

"Yes. Why?"

"Just seems it'd hurt like crazy for someone as little as you to pop out a baby of my race. I mean, seriously, *ow!*"

The little man giggled. Janie giggled with him. Hopefully she didn't sound as nervous as she felt.

"I'm not here to talk to you, little long-face girl. Certainly I'm not here long enough to go into my people's history of the birthing procedure."

She shrugged. "You're the one who struck up the conversation."

"You're the first to come in here since I arrived. I told you, I didn't expect to find one of the children people here."

"You want me to get someone else?"

"No. You'll do."

"For what?"

"To learn a few things."

"What do you want to learn about? I've been reading, so maybe I could help. Sorry, but there's probably not much you don't already—"

"I didn't say *ask questions*. I said *learn*. I've already learned many fascinating things, in just this short moment between us. I wonder already how you'll be called to use *your* learning."

"I don't think any of these folks are gonna *call on me* for anything useful, any time soon. I need to learn as much as I can about them, though, 'cause I'm stuck with 'em. The more I know, the better my chances of survival." *Plus, I'm still not completely sure my boyfriend and I aren't in an interspecies relationship*, she thought.

"You and everyone here will have different ideas about what's important and who's important than my people do, little long-face girl."

"Like what?"

"Like whether you and your friends here are important, if we should help you in your big fight, or wait until you've all killed each other, so we can have all your stuff."

"Thanks for the honesty, I guess?"

"We have a creature below, trying to tell us why we should care—a pet of yours."

"A pet?" Did Deschembines ever keep pets? Come to think of it, that's sort of what she felt like lately: Sheldon's beloved little pet.

"Well, maybe not *your* pet. This is probably a creature you haven't seen." He cocked his head at Janie and sniffed the air. "Your *Sheldon* has, though that's a bit unusual. Ask him about his missing pet, if he's noticed it's gone. Last I was at the fire, the pet was clinging stubbornly to life, arguing even more stubbornly on all of your behalf. It's a fascinating being. I didn't believe it was possible for a creature to fit so many vulgarities into a single sentence and still make sense...especially since, now that I think about it, vulgar words are the only ones it pronounces correctly, in any language, with any regularity. It was my idea to take the creature home alive. Hence the council sent me to look things over above."

"Oh."

"I like you, little long-face girl! Do you like me?"

Am I getting hit on by a leprechaun now? "Not really."

"Do you want me to go away?"

"No."

"Why not, if you don't like me?"

"Is that a loaded question?"

"You have always known more than most of your children people, haven't you, little Long-Face? About what has always been here…maybe not always *understood*, but yes, *known*. Who did you once know, who always understood?"

"What the hell are you talking about?"

The little man's features contorted, so he looked uncannily younger and more innocent for a moment. "What, can't you see ghosts too, Janie?"

"What did you just say?"

"I like you, little Long-Face," the little man repeated. He grinned, turned, and hopped off the table. Janie crouched and peered under it. He was already gone. She didn't spot any more weird little people.

Footsteps hurried through the hallway behind her, so soft that she wouldn't have noticed if she hadn't learned to listen for them.

"Janie!" Sheldon trotted in, paler and darker-eyed than even the icy air outside should leave him. He charged towards her and flung his arms around her. She still hated it when he did that, except for how delicately he treated her, even at his most unbridled, like she was a priceless treasure. Before she knew it, she melted into his embrace. He lifted and spun her, then attacked her face with desperate kisses. "Damnit, Janie, I love you so much," he breathed in her ear, still holding her off the ground.

He'd brushed his teeth recently. She still tasted a hint of stale beer on his breath. He had on fresh clothes and smelled nicer than he had in at least a week. His hair was damp like he'd just bathed. Something was up.

"I love you too. Will you set me down? You're freaking me out. C'mon, what's going on?"

"Sorry, sorry!" He lowered her to the floor. His teeth clenched and he squinted through tears. "I don't know where to start. I'm scared shitless."

"Of what? C'mon, tell me!"

"Let's go back to your room. I have to be alone with you…to make *sure* we're alone."

She thought of the little person she'd just met. "We're alone as we're gonna get anywhere on this base, hon, trust me. Okay, fine." She took his hand and led him back to her room. She locked the door and said, "So what's got you so worked up?"

"Afraid of never seeing you again."

"Why would you think of something like that?"

"Because I have to leave. It's someplace I can't take you with me, and I don't know if I'll be able to get back."

She went cold, because there was no other choice. She could have gone all frantic too, but right now, one of them had to hold it together. "Can't take me, huh? Can't or won't?"

"There's no difference."

"So make me understand."

"I'll try."

NINE

Sally wandered the hallways 'til she ran into Janie.

Janie muttered "Hi," and tried to slip past her.

Something didn't sit right, so Sally caught her by the shoulder. "What's going on?"

Janie shrugged loose. "Nothing."

The girl was such a bad liar that Sally wanted to slap the truth out of her. Sheldon would hear about that, though. It might be enough to make him revert to Plan A, as in, *all the way back to Marlboro Mountain*. Instead, she said, "Where's Sheldon?"

"I don't know."

"Bullshit."

"No, I really don't!"

"This ain't the time or place for little white secrets. What's he up to?"

Janie deflated under Sally's hard gaze. "He...I couldn't...Look, he's gone crazy!"

"We're talking about Sheldon here. Be more specific."

"He's gone off...I don't know where! I fell asleep with him, and..." The girl managed to stare at Sally's face without making eye-contact. "I woke up and he wasn't there anymore."

"Come on, girl, that ain't all that happened. You know his schedule. You wouldn't be acting like an idiot like this if something else wasn't up. What'd he tell you in bed?"

"He didn't tell me *in*—I mean, it was before we— Aw, shit!"

Sally grabbed Janie's shoulder again, this time hard enough to bruise.

"Ow! Get off!"

"Sure, once you spill it."

"I'll tell you when you let go!"

Sally thrust Janie out at arm's length and let go sharply enough that Janie stumbled into the wall. "There. Spit it out."

Janie told Sally about meeting Sheldon in the mess hall, what Sheldon had told her about his conversation with Puttergong.

"*Puttergong?* You let him take off, following advice from *Puttergong?*"

"I didn't *let* him do anything. I fell asleep with him holding me then I woke up alone."

"That conniving little shit!"

"Who?"

"Huh?"

"Sheldon or Puttergong?"

"Sheldon! Puttergong, too, but…no, I mean that sneaky little fuck of a brother of mine. Damnit, I thought he'd been *learning better!*"

"So you think it's bullshit, what Puttergong told him."

"Kid, have you *met* that critter?"

"No, actually. So what do we do about it?"

Sally gave Janie a long, hard stare. It felt strangely like looking in some time-warp mirror at her younger, weaker self…the first honest look she'd given herself in too long. Her conniving fuck of a brother had let himself get talked up by the same little monster as Rob and Zane, and they'd all run off on the same psychotic grail chase. And here was Janie, being a dick-whipped little bitch about it.

Sally stormed down the hall.

Janie hurried after her. "Hey! Where we going?"

"To stop your boyfriend from getting himself killed. You wanna come along? Go get your coat."

~

Janie might have argued. Maybe there was something to what Sheldon had told her. She thought of finding Sheldon, though—of not losing him to Puttergong's *grail chase*—and Sally's zeal turned infectious. They headed out to the nearest car Zane had rigged for user-friendly hot-wiring, to those he'd taught how. As Sally got it running, Janie felt stronger and weaker than ever all at once. Damn her, she'd thought she was tough because of all those schoolyard and street fights back in Brattleboro. She'd thought she was tough and resourceful for making it to Sheldon and the United Deschembines after Mom got killed. Hell, she'd felt like a regular badass, just for holding her own this long, among people with whole ranges of physical senses she'd never heard of, who shrugged at these deadly conditions like a cloudy day, who sometimes came in bleeding from wounds that should be instantly fatal, ready the next night to go right back out and kill more enemies like eating chips.

If she'd really been so tough, she'd have fought back when Sally started tossing her around, never mind that she'd never have let Sheldon slip away in the first place. Oh well, now was the best place to start. Sally was the real badass here, knowing just what to do and acting on it without hesitation. Why the hell had Janie needed the example? Never mind, 'cause now they were off and rolling.

Just past the gate, Sally hit the brakes, hopped out, and went to Jesse and Zane's big red van parked on the curb. Suddenly Janie remembered Sally telling her how she'd only recently learned to drive. Jesse had been teaching her, using that van. Now Sally was taking her along on a speeding chase over icy mountain roads.

Sally flung open the van's rear doors and rooted around for something in the back. She pulled out something long, dark, and evil-looking. She then opened one of the car's back doors and tossed her spear across the back seat. "Just in case. Got any weapons on you?"

"Uh, no."

Sally dug out a small, black-handled pocketknife and tossed it in Janie's lap. At least the blade was closed.

Janie did her best to ignore the fresh ice in her gut while she turned the knife over in her hand. Hell, she could use it! She knew how to throw a good punch, right? Was slinging your fist so different when there was a sharp blade at the end? Hopefully she wouldn't have to find out. They sped on out of town, through the woods.

ALIVE AND THE SHIT

ONE

The car swerved to avoid a fallen tree on the narrow. Tiger felt his side of the car tilt, heard stones go *clack, clack, clack* down the cliff side. His gaze stretched further back, through the rear windshield. The snow tires kicked up a white cloud that settled into the tracks behind them.

"Why do you think it always does that?" said Tiger, gazing out the back.

"What?" said Lilly.

"The snow. Ever notice how it seems to *know*, where to settle so it hides the path?"

Lilly's eyes brightened teasingly as she guided the wheel. "Of course it does. It's a Crimbone-plowed maze. You learn things like that, when you get certified as a maze-trekker."

Tiger had failed the test three times already. "Yeah, yeah, yeah. Hot in here. Maybe you should ease up on that heat."

"Want me to roll the windows down?"

He peered through the windshield. It had stopped snowing, and she'd turned the wipers off. There'd seemed to be more life out there with the snow. "That's not quite what I had in mind."

"Oh, so what did you have in mind, you nefarious, nefarious man?"

He leaned back and smiled. "Hey, this drive was your idea."

Their eyes were instinctively peeled as always, but they both knew this wasn't a scouting run. They were still tense as hell, but not as bad as before they'd left. Going off base always meant a reason to be tense, even within the inner spheres of the maze. The icy crags rose to their left and dropped off on their right. One false turn meant crashing and burning fifty feet down, melting some of this snow along with the flesh off their bones. Right now, though, it felt like the lazy flow of freedom.

After another mile or so, Lilly pulled off to the inner shoulder and shifted into park. "Okay, be like that. We're not going anywhere 'til you tell me."

She unbuckled her seatbelt and slid over towards him. The back of his head pressed against his window as her mouth covered his. His fingers ran through her hair. Her hand slid to his crotch, working gently 'til he was pitching a sturdy tent against her palm. The window was cold against his skull, so he eased her backwards, his hands on her waist, stroking as much soft flesh as he could find between her jeans and her coat and two or three shirts. He spread back the coat, unbuttoned the top shirt, then fumbled out of as many of his own layers as his excited fingers let him. Before he could finish, she pulled him back down so his chest pressed hers and their hearts thumped against each other. She gnawed on his neck, sending sweet fluttering madness through him. His fingers stroked and tickled her hipbones, felt the rising heat, so he started at her jeans.

Old Lords, how long had it been? A few weeks? It felt longer.

"This the real reason you wanted to get off the base?"

"Maaaaaayyyybeeeeee…"

The wind whistled softly outside. Inside, the engine and the heater purred. Neither sounded nearly as loud as their breathing. The base wasn't generally noisy, but its ambiance was deafening. It was like they'd been trapped by everything they were part of, *everything that was bigger than both of them.*

Somewhere, the ground thumped like a drum. They sat up sharply, so their foreheads struck. At any other time, their groans of pain would have dissolved quickly into embarrassed laughter. The distant sounds had already killed the mood, though.

"You hear that?" she said.

He looked around, trying to make out anything further than a few yards past the windows. "Yeah. Sounds like someone running a marathon."

She slid back into the driver's seat. "Yeah, towards us. Let's get back."

"Hold on. Maybe we should—"

She shifted into drive and gunned it, throwing him around so he had to grab the oh-shit bar. Something landed on the back hood with a booming thud. It scrambled over the top and rolled across the front windshield. A mad, snarling face flattened on the glass, staring in at them with inhuman mania. Lilly floored it, swerving as quickly as possible, trying to throw the shape off. It wouldn't let go. The car screeched against a rock wall, then spun. The shape flew away into the night, over the cliff side along with a cascade of spraying gravel. The car spun to a halt, facing the direction from which they'd meant to turn. A dozen or so more malicious shapes came at them…*Crimbone* shapes. Black weapons gleamed like swishing gashes in the white snow. Lilly sped at them so they scattered. She clipped two or three before the road widened enough for her to turn around. It forced her to slow down enough that two of them attacked the car again.

How did they keep up so fast? *Because those were Crimbone out there, and not the kind they wanted to meet.*

Something yanked open the driver's door. Lilly spilled out. Tiger almost followed her, but he remembered the Katanas in the back seat, so that's where he dove. As he wrestled his way between the front seats, his hand slid around a sword handle. He barely bothered with the backdoor latch. Instead, he just rammed his shoulder against the door, so straining metal appendages shrieked. The door flew open. He rolled into the snow.

Three dark, bulky shapes surrounded Lilly. She stayed low, dodging and kicking. Expert timing was all that kept her alive, since she sure as hell wasn't stopping any of them, or even slowing them down. Tiger rose, scraped and smarting. His sword sang free, lashing out as he dashed in. His blade struck the nearest one's neck. Between his ferocity and the sharpness of the blade, he barely felt the edge slice bone, let alone the hewing of flesh or muscle. A head flew from a pair of shoulders and bounced off the car's hood. Tiger drove the point through another attacker's side. A black club glanced off Lilly's skull and she went down. As the club rose again, the rest of the pack closed in. Tiger slid sideways, pulling Lilly with him, his Katana going up to deflect the swipe. The blade shattered under the black metal, but it sent the stroke just wide enough. Lilly shambled up through the driver's door. Tiger followed. He meant to shove her into the passenger seat so he could drive, but even now, she'd have none of that.

The Crimbone was already righting himself, so Tiger didn't have time for an argument. He slammed the door after her. Something stung his lower back, like a thorn hooking him in a bramble patch...a big thorn. He jackknifed himself over the hood, jerked open the front passenger door, and dove in.

"Gun it!" he yelled, though the car had already started moving.

The car was soon as close to full speed as it would go on this turf. The rear left door flapped open and shut, fanning in icy wind. Tiger's back kept stinging, like that thorn was still stuck in him. He leaned over and jerked the wheel for Lilly so they didn't go off the nearest ledge. The winding cliff still rose on one side of them, dropped off on the other, winding around them in a blur. Contorting like this made the pain in his back sting and throb deeper and wider. The seat grew warm and wet under his left ass cheek. Lilly's shaking hands stayed on the wheel. The side of her head was red and wet. Her eyes were bleary. And here came a pack of Crimbone chasing them—creatures they'd both been raised to see as protectors, long before they'd ever expected to have to be good enough to survive such an attack, let alone hold their own against the creatures.

Tiger gripped the wheel tighter. "Lilly, darling, stay with me! Stay awake!"

"*Ninety-nine bottles of beer on the wall, ninety-nine bottles of beer…*"

"*What?*"

"Sleepy…Keepin'myself awake…*Take one down, pass it around…*"

"You should've let me drive."

"Wanna stop and switch?"

He glimpsed their pursuers in the rear-view mirror. In this snow, the car went barely faster than the swiftest runner. "Fuck that!"

"Good, 'cause you don't know this maze."

"I know you just missed a turn we should have taken!"

"Shut up. I know all the ways...I think I still know all the ways...*Ninety-eight bottles of beer on the wall...*"

Weren't they going further from the base now, though? Tiger had no idea. No wonder he'd failed the test three times. He kept one hand on the wheel with Lilly. He reached for the CB with the other. "Base, Zane, anyone!" He heard his voice slurring. Aw, c'mon, his wound wasn't even that deep! No way could he have lost that much blood already... "Get out here! This is fucked! We're...Lilly, what are our coordinates?"

"Dashboard..."

"What?"

"The compass on the dashboard...Shows coordinates...Can't read it...Eyes too blurry..."

All the base's maze-cleared cars had special compasses attached to the center of the dashboard. Zane had broken them open, tinkered with some inner workings and replaced some inner markings so they displayed coordinates within the maze. It shook so wildly now that Tiger could barely read it. "We're in...Sphere Three, Curve Eight...No, Curve Five. I don't know, follow the noise! Someone get the fuck out here!"

"You're readin' wrong...You say it the other way...They won't..." Lilly didn't sound fit to pronounce it any clearer.

Tiger kept yelling, "Those other Crimbone have gone apeshit...Someone, get the fuck out here! They're headed for the base. They're *fucking chasing us down!* I don't know, we might be lost..."

"Not lost...I know what I'm doing..." The car almost went off the cliff again.

"We're in a car, but we can't keep outrunning 'em. *Someone, please be listening, and get the fuck out here now!*" Damn, they'd been stupid. Stupid, stupid, stupid...

Behind them, the Crimbone chased the car like dogs, only a lot faster and more purposeful…and they were gaining ground. One of them took a flying leap, caught the bumper, dragged for a while, then slipped and rolled away. The catch slowed the car slightly. The next one might get a better grip, might reach that flapping back door…

Lilly lulled left and right. The car lulled a little with her. "*Ninety-four bottles of beer on the wall, ninety-four bottles of beer…*"

Two

"How far could he have gotten?" Janie asked.

"Not too far for us to find him," said Sally, eyes dead ahead, unblinking.

"What if he took a different—*Wow, whoa!*" The car had just made a sharp swerve that took them back in the opposite direction. "Forget something important?"

"This is a maze, remember? I know exactly where I'm going. Actually I have no idea, but you get what I mean."

"How've we been staying stocked on gasoline for all these cars, anyway—'specially if you have to haul it back through…all this?"

"You think these vehicles still run on fossil fuels, with Zane maintaining 'em?"

"Okay. What, then?"

"You don't wanna know. You were saying?"

"How're we supposed to pick up Sheldon's trail in this? You think he's gonna keep to the path of any maze?"

"Point taken. Doesn't matter. Hey, the lands'll guide us, right?"

"I wouldn't know."

"Yeah you would, just like I do. I just wasn't open to it before, even though that's what was guiding me this whole time, the more I think about it. Know what I mean?"

"Not really." Janie suspected she might, though, somewhere in the back of her mind, not that now was a good time to dig too deep for a closer look. Sally suddenly sounded a lot like Mom, if Mom had ever acted like a manic lunatic. A lot of Mom's old ramblings made more sense than ever these days. Most of them didn't translate like Janie had expected.

"Well, you should." Sally took another sharp turn. "Hell, you gotta be a tough enough girl, putting up with my brother. How's hearing the voice of the lands such a sweat, when we're alive like this? You're alive, and you're the shit!"

"What?"

"Oh, quit fighting it."

Janie felt a thunderclap. Sally had just slapped her knee. It had been a friendly gesture, but it sure stung. Everything was moving too fast.

"We've both been fighting it for too long, letting other people lead us around, when half the time we're probably the reason they ain't dead. What do the Crimbone say? *Listen to the lands, and listen to your blood*, right? *Right?* You know what your blood is, Janie? It's the *life*, pumpin' in your veins, letting you move so you can be who you're supposed to be. So fucking ironic. Everyone who talks about all that shit…We've been listening to 'em as guides, when we should be doing what they do, just listen to ourselves, and *run with it*. That's what we're doing now, chasing our instincts, *really doing what we feel*. And you know what?"

"What?"

"We. Are. The. Shit! Say it with me, girl. *We're alive, and we're the shit!*"

"We are alive, and we are the shit." Janie smiled, reminded how infectious Sally's new mania could be. Now she *had* to let it infect her. Otherwise, the fear and doubt would, and she'd stay useless. *No. I'm not useless. I can't afford to be. Sally's right.* She said it again: "We're alive, and we're the shit!"

Something in the car buzzed and crackled, as if agreeing with them. Janie jumped, thinking at first that the radio had cut on magically.

"Hell," Sally hissed, "Zane's fucking CB. What do they want back there?"

"*...Out here! This is fucked! We're...*" Static followed. The radio shouted a set of coordinates that sounded Greek to Janie. "*Those other Crimbone! They've gone apeshit...Someone, get the fuck out here! They're headed for the base, and they're fucking chasing us down! We're in a car, but we can't keep outrunning 'em. Someone, please be listening, and get the fuck out here now!*"

Sally almost reached for the CB but kept both hands on the wheel. The car stayed on course. Her face tightened in its resolve, to chase down her brother before she thought about anything else.

"You know where those coordinates are?" asked Janie.

Sally nodded.

"You know who that is?"

"Yeah. It's Tiger and Lilly."

"Will someone back at the base hear that?"

"No doubt."

"Can they get there in time?"

"Probably not."

"Are we any closer?"

"Yeah. Not sure how much good that'd do. That idiot can't even read the damn maze-bubble right. That's like three whole miles to pick from." The car stayed on course for another moment. Sally's eyes stayed centered. Janie hadn't thought someone could go that long without blinking. Must be another Deschembine thing. Sally's right hand let go of the wheel and punched the dashboard. "Motherfucker."

At the next turn, the car swerved left and sped uphill.

THREE

"Eighty-eight bottles of beer on the wall..."

They forgot about that tree they'd dodged earlier, 'til they both saw it coming, too late. Lilly jerked the wheel. Icy branches bent and snapped against the car. The frame groaned and bent inward. The glass next to Tiger's face spiderwebbed. He flung himself sideways, away from it, pulling Lilly to the floor with him. He reached over and hit the button that automatically locked all the doors. Too bad the flapping back door made a useless gesture of it.

Tiger scrambled over the seat as someone outside ripped the swinging door completely off its hinges. The first one in got the broken end of Tiger's Katana in the forehead. The heavy body sagged and swayed backwards, the blade driven through the brain to the hilt, pulling the handle and Tiger's arm with it. He put his boot heel to the dead man's chest and shoved hard. The body slid away, flailing back and smacking into its companions. They stumbled, shoved it aside, then crowded eagerly inward. Tiger had the advantage of parameters, but that wouldn't last long.

Overhead, something squealed, like another car skidding to a stop on the ridge above. Tiger wanted to look over the seat, check on Lilly, but two more men were shoving their way in. The butt of a black metal weapon smacked Lilly's window, sending in a shower of shattered glass. The arm that wielded it came through the broken window, the scarred, knotted fist brandishing a blade, ready to stab downward. Hanging shards cut the arm to shreds along the way, and it didn't even seem to care.

The roof thundered from some new impact, though Tiger hadn't seen any more of the ones outside leap up. This one made the roof sink deeper than ever, so it touched the top of his head. Glass shivered and sprayed everywhere, forcing him to hunch down painfully. The knife above Lilly withdrew. Prickly branches unrolled through the shattered windshield. Snow and icy water rained all over the seat. No sooner was that arm out than a bolt of lightning swept sideways into it. The arm's front half vanished, along with the weapon. A spray of crimson showered into the car, as though from a severed fire hose.

Outside, from above, something heavy whooshed left and right. The fallen tree quivered as two gutted bodies toppled into it. The two men who'd been fighting their way in had turned their attention towards whatever was killing their companions.

Tiger pistoned forward. His broken sword shot up between one man's legs. He punctured cloth, felt the blade split a testicle before plowing it through a pubic bone. He jerked it free and slashed the legs of the other climber. Both femoral arteries opened and sprayed his face, blinding him. He blinked and wiped frantically, spitting and snorting blood from his mouth and nose, sure more attackers would be on him before he could see again. The corpses thudded somewhere outside. Through a red blur, a lean billowing shape sailed to the earth, landing on both feet between the car and the remaining enemies, driving them back. The shape swung a long, carbon steel beam of death—*Sally!*

"Lilly," Tiger shouted, "you awake?" He reached down and shook her. "You with me? Lilly, darling, wake up! It's Sally! Sally Wildfire's here!"

FOUR

Out in the snow, Sally heard Tiger shouting.

Fucking United Deschembines, all wanting me and my damn brother to be their fucking saviors or some bullshit, and now they're acting this stupid. At least these two have learned how to fight, sort of. Hero's just a pretty word for enabler.

Her mind was split as neatly in two as the skull of the first Crimbone she'd met on the car's roof. The half that was here for this physical moment was a very minimal thing. It absorbed her opponents, saw their movements, tactics and strategies, told her how to counter them, and it showed her spear how to kill them as quickly as possible. Otherwise, there was nothing to think about. There weren't words to think with.

The other half of her brain was back on Marlboro Mountain with Rob, five years ago, after Sheldon attacked her. Rob had told her over and over he hadn't *missed one* this time, that he'd never *miss one* again, so there was nothing to do but wait in the cabin for Jesse and Zane to get back. She'd been more afraid of that return than any attack, even though Jesse had promised her safety. Because she'd known what it would mean, and she hadn't known what Rob would do. It meant the Crimbone would split her and Rob up, like they'd finally managed to do after all. She'd been too stupid with fear and weakness back then to know what to do about it.

She wasn't that stupid, weak, fearful little creature now, and she made sure these Crimbone felt it when she killed them.

One of them shrieked "*Tainted one!*" and lunged in at her, stabbing wildly.

The white-haired shrieker almost got past Sally's spear. She shifted backwards, retracted the shaft, skewered him in the gut, and hoisted him skyward like a trout on a pike. She swung the spear so the white-haired devil flew through the air towards the nearest cliff. A black blade landed on the shaft, inches beneath the blade. The shivering clang reverberated up through Sally's arms, through her whole body. She staggered back. At that same instant, the point of another blade drove through her lower side. She doubled up and retched, swinging the beam at this new attacker's skull. His brains splattered like water. The corpse fell, but the blade dangled in her gut. Something in her flared and drew towards it, wanting to be sucked out of herself, into the poison metal. It felt like *everything that she was* flowed towards the wound, trying to soak into the metal so it could flow into a wielder who wasn't there anymore. Her free hand slid the blade out of her body, right before it crumbled to dust against her palm.

Damn blazing trail, *right through my gut! Ain't that what you call it, Sheldon? Yeah, sure hurts like a bitch. Now we can compare notes! If I didn't think your little Earth-line girlfriend was so cute, I'd look for a nice bristly Crimbone slut to break you in right, just so we'd* really *be on the same page! Guess now I'll be altered* like you, *if I live through this, on top of my own taint. Where the hell are you, anyway, you little shit?*

Another Crimbone rushed Sally headlong. Her spear lunged out. The end caught the attacker, eager to penetrate…but it only bounced dully against a breastbone, so the attacker shambled. The beam slipped from her numbing grasp as the blazing trail through her gut sucked and pulsed, nearly paralyzing her.

The spear! The fucker who'd struck it had actually *split the pipe*. The blade was lying somewhere in the snow. *Goddamn sonofabitch cocksucker motherfucker…*

Sally's eyes darted everywhere. She spotted the blade and dove for it. A Crimbone rushed her as her hand closed around the spare inches of pipe. She whipped it around and opened his throat. A hot crimson jet hit her in the face. Just two more of the fuckers left. They closed in on her.

FIVE

High on the cliff, Janie watched in paralyzed awe. She'd seen more than enough ugliness and violence since joining up with these people, but nothing like this blinding blur of strain and flexing, every movement quicker and fiercer than human bodies could make, all geared to destroying each other—not fending each other off, not kicking each other's asses; fucking slaughtering each other. Blood and guts sprayed all over the snow, sending up a noxious smell through the icy air. And there in the middle of it stood her sister—*sister in law*, Sally, but whatever—murdering people with glee.

Janie fell to her hands and knees and vomited off the cliffside. As the shaking burn of puke subsided, the first thing she felt was the cold. The second was a new kind of heat in her blood, something she didn't know what to do with. Oh, she knew the nature of it, from every schoolyard fight she'd ever been through. Those fights hadn't taught everything, about why the blood heated up in the first place, why her forbears had learned the instinct and passed it on. People had drifted away from it, thinking all their cushy technology and intellect meant they didn't need it anymore, like they'd bought and sold their way out of nature's laws, until the latest mass shooter made the news, back when there'd been *evening news* or *mass shooters*.

Cowards like mass shooters had only *thought* they still had it, just like anyone who'd ever launched a missile strike from a computer room. All those assholes were probably dead by now. The Schomites and the Spirelights hadn't lost it. That's why Sally could still fight after getting stabbed in the gut. It was why the Deschembine races would survive everything they created for each other, sweeping the Earth-line people aside and barely noticing.

That white-haired man had almost gone over the cliff, after Sally tossed him through the air, but he'd slid on the edge, grabbed the rocks, already pulling himself back onto level ground. Hell, that hard landing he'd made should have killed him, even after Sally's stab hadn't. Yet there he was, coming back for more!

Tiger had finished wiping blood from his eyes and rejoined the fray. He nearly fell in next to Sally, but he spotted someone going back for the car, towards Lilly, so he broke and chased the fucker down. Tiger's fighting was nothing like Sally's superhuman viciousness, but he was just as enthusiastic. He leapt on the man's back, driving the broken sword in and out 'til the man fell facedown and lay still. Tiger kept hacking 'til nothing remained of the man but a set of arms and legs, spreading from a bubbling heap of dark sludge.

Sally was still bleeding all over the place, and here was Janie, staring from the cliff side, squatting in her own puke, like the weak, stupid little Earth-line girl they'd all taken her for. She was out of harm's way. Why wouldn't she be? Why would any of those fighters down there care about a stupid little Earth-line girl?

Why was she here in the first place? Because she'd fallen in love with a young Deschembine man…or at least the idea of him, so rugged and independent for his years, so unencumbered by the civilized hypocrisies she'd gotten used to. Stuck in this mess with him, she'd realized he was just as scared and clueless as her and everyone. Either way, she'd decided she was strong enough to stand with him through anything. She had no idea what *anything* meant anymore.

Hey, Sally still thought she was worth a damn. So either she was or she wasn't, right? She'd get down there, into the fray, and she'd obviously die pretty fast. Hell, it wasn't like she'd ever see Sheldon again. There wasn't a safe, cushy Earth-line world to go hide in anymore.

Janie turned and slid herself over the edge. She'd forgotten to put her gloves on, so the icy rocks turned her hands into shaking agonized stumps. She tightened those stumps on their sharp, jutting holds, shifting her boots for footing. She slipped and slid as much as scaled down the side, but she gave herself credit for not plunging to her death. Before she knew it, her feet connected with level ground, and she almost collapsed again. Behind her, the clang and shriek of the fight sounded loud as ever. It smelled even worse up close. She fought back a dry-heave, shoved her numb hand into her pocket, and found the knife Sally had given her. Mechanically, she pried it open. Her nerves heated and jangled worse than ever. Then she turned and made a shambling run at death.

Sally's blade lashed left and right, up and down, holding off a man on one side, a woman on the other. Her quivering legs barely held up, but she didn't give the fuckers an inch. Janie shambled at the man's back and jabbed with the knife's point. The tip punctured through thick, leathery cloth and plunged into tough meat. The flat upper edge slid against a rib. She cried out in unison with the man, who leapt and twisted away. He found his footing, spun, spotted her and gave her a *what the fuck* look. This gave Sally an instant to spin and slash the woman's throat.

Almost as an afterthought, Sally turned, caught the man by the hair, yanked him backwards, bared his throat, and gave his neck three hard whacks. The head came off and the body dropped at her feet. A dark lake sprayed, then pumped out of the stump around her boots.

Sally looked at the head in bewilderment like she'd already forgotten how it had wound up dangling from her fist, then tossed it away and swayed 'til her eyes met Janie's. "Holy fuck, girl, where'd you come from?"

Janie had fallen to her knees, gasping on the edge of hyperventilation. She still held the bloody knife at shaky arm's length.

Sally eased Janie's hands down and gently slipped the knife from her. "Janie, it's okay, you did great! They're dead. They're all dead! You helped me."

Janie laughed deliriously. "Thanks."

"Thank *you!* Janie, look at me. Janie, breathe. You're alive. *We're* alive. We did it."

Far to the right, Tiger shouted, "Sally, Janie, thank the Old Lords! Get up! Get over here! We're hurt bad here."

Sally didn't seem to hear. "Janie, come around, it's okay! Girl, that was incredible!"

Janie almost had her breathing under control, wanted to say thanks again, wanted to rejoice, wanted to show Sally she was tough. She muttered, "Sally...you got stabbed."

"Yeah." Sally grinned through bloody teeth. "It hurts like a bitch."

From somewhere far off, Tiger kept shouting, "Sally, Janie!"

"Janie, wake up! You're alive! You're alive, and you're *so* the shit! Janie, say it with me, girl. We're *alive*, and *we're the*—"

The tip of a blade broke through the skin of Sally's windpipe. Her eyes turned to glass. The tip disappeared, leaving an insanely small red trickle. A tiny squirt hit Janie in the face. Sally thumped in the snow.

The white-haired, yellow-skinned Crimbone man loomed up over Janie. "*Little Earth-line cunt!*"

Janie screamed. Her hand shot into the snow for the knife Sally had taken from her. A much bigger blade met and cut her fingers. She closed them on what was left of the handle. She didn't even feel herself lift it. She just saw her arm fly out of the snow, the gleaming metal extending from her shaky fist. The white-haired berserker lunged right onto the point. The blade turned in her hand and sank between his ribs.

Wow, she'd never stabbed anyone 'til today. The feeling of someone's insides twisting against her blade was an unusual experience.

Her fingers slid limply from the handle. The white-haired Crimbone man rose and swayed in bewilderment. Sally's blade stuck out of his chest. He looked at it, then down at Janie.

"*Earth-line cunt,*" he repeated, this time in a whimper.

Three new shapes descended on the white-haired man from as many directions. Two of them were Crimbone. Janie knew that because of how they moved. They didn't move like the others had, but like shambling, broken ghosts of vengeance, robbed of all grace but what guided their weapons. The third shape was undefined, attacking with full power, with two shimmering white blades. A big black blade sheared down between the white-haired man's neck and shoulder, while a black hatchet hewed the left leg above the knee. The white blades hacked through the right arm at two places so it fell away in pieces like a diced-up sausage link. The blades continued on and crunched through the chest and waist. What was left of the body landed next to Sally and twitched. All three attackers kept hacking 'til its only movement was the spreading dark flow.

Finally, they stopped, stood up, wiped and sheathed their weapons. The two Crimbone ran off to help Tiger and Lilly. The third shape fell in shock before Janie and Sally, not sure which to see to first.

"Sheldon," Janie finally got out.

He scrambled over on his knees, yanked her to him, hugged her and kissed her forehead.

Janie heard herself say, "Sally…Sally's dead."

"I know," Sheldon sobbed. He hugged Janie tighter.

"How'd you find us?"

"Ran into those guys." He thumbed over his shoulder at the two battered Crimbone, one man and one woman. Janie didn't recognize either of them. "They filled me in and we gave chase." Then in a primal, high-pitched snarl, "*Goddamnit…*"

Far to the side, one of the ally Crimbone said to Tiger and Lilly, "Fuck, you guys are in almost as bad shape as us."

Heavier wheels rumbled, from the same direction, but farther off. "The Big Red Beast," Janie muttered.

"I know," said Sheldon.

"Guess they heard the CB, too."

"I guess so."

"Stay with me, Sheldon?"

When he managed to answer, the sound was of a self-inflicted wound. "I can't."

"Tell me how to find you, then!"

"Not this time…I'm sorry. I'm so sorry."

They held each other 'til the big tires screeched to a stop. Sheldon slipped away. Jesse's feet thundered through the snow. He let out the earth-shattering scream of a dying animal. The earth quivered under Janie, and she knew it was Jesse Karn collapsing to his knees, because he'd seen Sally's corpse. He probably hadn't even spotted Janie yet.

"THE STARS ARE MADE FOR US TONIGHT"

ONE

Remelea's car rolled along a cracked, winding highway down a desert hillside. Rob blinked. He still noticed pulsating energy all through his limbs…energy the substance of his body didn't yet know how to use. *Be patient. Your body's healing, filling out with new substance, building you anew for what you're feeling.*

He barely remembered the two of them getting back to their motel, let alone leaving again, or where they were headed now. He remembered his dreams, though…all of them, clearer and truer than anything in this world had felt in a long time. The massive, twisting trees and vines of that other world, with its distant, shining temples of alien architecture, still looked and felt more real than the desert shrubs, agave and conifers rolling by through the window. He peered out at all those bushes and cacti. Had they started to bloom yet, with new, alien fruit, like what had burst from within the split, rotting palm tree carcasses on Carrolton Avenue, except without the infection of Talino's polluted magic? He couldn't tell, either because the car passed them too quickly, or because his vision was still blurrier than he realized.

He didn't feel tired, or even like he'd just woken up. He peered at Remelea. She drove just fine, as always, even though she looked three fourths dead. She noticed he was awake and silently passed him a canteen of water. He drank gratefully but sparingly. Cool water in his parched throat helped to ground him in the here and now. When he thumbed the scabs of his wounds, he still felt how deep they ran, even though they'd already tightened past the danger of reopening.

This relentless energy felt like something that wasn't his, something that had invaded him. *A Crimbone's strength is the strength of the lands. A full-fledged Crimbone is one with those lands.* He might as well blame his blood, which was all that had ever been truly his, except for the blades. Half the time, when he spoke or moved, it didn't feel like a decision he'd made...more like some other consciousness was *on* him, *in* him, *riding* him. He wasn't often privy to its thoughts or feelings, even while it shared his brain-meat.

The further they went, the more barren the plains around them looked in the baking heat. This didn't feel like Texas, or anywhere else on Planet Earth. Maybe they'd already found the way to the Old World after all. Maybe they'd passed into it without noticing, and this was what was left of it. Maybe the sun had broken through onto the fabled black ocean, drying it up, so they now drove across its scorching bed.

Nah. I'm in the wrong company for that. I'm supposed to go there with my queen...

But wasn't Remelea his queen? He closed his eyes, saw Sally's face, and his blood shrieked, *No!* Whenever he felt Remelea's warmth next to him, though, his blood said something else.

A spectral, scorched ocean floor probably wouldn't have road signs saying they were on US Highway 285, or that they were turning off onto West Oak Street. Another sign welcomed them to the town of Sanderson. After another mile or so, they rolled down the main drag of what looked like the sun-bleached ghost of an old Western movie set. There wasn't a soul in sight, not even stray dogs or cats or chickens.

"Where the fuck are we?" he said.

"Texas." Remelea's eyes stayed fixed forward.

"What the fuck are we doing in Texas?"

"Maybe nothing. Maybe just laying low to finish healing up, somewhere that ain't Louisiana or otherwise in the path of the worst of this whole clusterfuck."

"You're an even shittier liar than I am."

"Could be we're here to fill in one last gap in your Crimbone education. Mine too, maybe."

"The hell…?"

"You're not the only one who got some unexpected answers at that church." Her tightening face and shoulders said she liked being here less than he did. "*I'll tell you when we get there.*"

The main drag dropped away around them. They crossed some old railroad tracks and pulled into a big, barren parking lot, behind a sign that read *Desert Air Motel*. Remelea parked in the dilapidated lot, got out, and gazed back hauntedly at the sign. Rob got out and followed her to the main office. Inside, the heat sweltered even thicker. Stale cigarette smoke hung pungently in the air. Otherwise, the dim, cramped space seemed deserted like the rest of the town.

A gurgling grunt sounded from behind the front desk. A gangly, balding, sunburnt man in torn jeans and a wifebeater sat slumped there. His scalp was blistered and raw between the cornhusk tufts of remaining hair, like someone had scorched it with a torch. He greeted them with a rolling grin of crooked teeth between the bloody holes in his gums. "What you two want?"

"I figure we'd like a room," said Rob.

The man giggled. His eyes rolled in sockets that looked several sizes too big, like the lids were pinned open by hardened crust. "You'd like one, but you ain't got no money, do you?"

"How do you figure?"

"*No one* got money no more. Money ain't no good nowadays anyway."

Rob scoped out the wall of room keys behind the desk. "Yeah, so what the fuck are you still doing here?"

"Maybe he's got more than one job," said Remelea.

At the sound of her voice, the little man sat forward and stared. Rob just now noticed that they'd left their Crimbone weapons hanging in plain view. The clerk got up, limped forward, and leaned on the counter. He stared at the hook clipped to Remelea's belt, then into her eyes.

"I seen that piece before. Long time ago. Yeah, I remember your face too, ma'am. Figures it'd be you who'd come to finish me off."

"Yeah, so how much else did you know about me?"

The man spat to the side. "About what? You think you was the only youngin' of your kind I spotted runnin' around…" He convulsed, coughed and hacked violently, spat again, then rasped, "…*Runnin' around, makin' trouble?* Or you mean that normal family, the one took you in? What, town this size, you thought no one was talkin'?"

"Sure," she said. "Everyone talked. No one did shit."

"Hey, take it up with your own kind. *They* was always the ones watched you. Think *they* didn't know? Nah, way they saw it, I reckon, whatever you was goin' through, it'd just make you meaner and nastier in the long run, better at bein' one of *their* monsters. For when the day came. Well, look around. Here's the day. What's left for you here to do shit for us?"

Rob watched Remelea's face as the old bastard spoke. He slipped one hand into hers. She squeezed it tight. His other hand drifted towards one of his knives.

"Better leave that pig-sticker holstered, young fella…I'm *assumin'* you *are* really a young fella…closer to young as you look than she is, at least. Ah, quit lookin' at me like I'm the bad guy here. Ain't no big mystery to it. My grandma, she was half Indian, kept to a lot of the old ways. Taught me some of 'em, too. I never took to it…not that I ever had a choice, it turned out. This motel was hers before it was mine…hers and *theirs*…yours…you *creatures* who've always walked among us, look like us…'cept to those of us who know what to look for. She taught me what to look for, taught me to always let your kind come and go, use this property for their purposes. Oh, what, you're that surprised, thought there *really* weren't so many of us…what do you call us…*Earth-line*, had an idea what was up?"

Rob recalled the old fisherman on the bank of Lake Pontchartrain. A lot more old weirdos sure seemed to *have an idea what was up* than he'd ever suspected, that was for sure. He thought of Chet and Flo Carter back in Postville, how eager they'd been to take him and Sally in. Suddenly, he wondered about a lot of things.

The old man watched Rob's face and let out a wet, wheezy cackle. "I'll be damned, girl! This boy's just flat-out still wet behind the ears, ain't he?"

"It's one of his most endearing qualities," she said.

"Guess you really turned into some kinda cradle-robber, huh? Say, boy, you even *know* how many years this pretty little thing's got on you?" He leered so his hollow gums glistened more visibly. "Guess now I don't feel so bad, for the bad thoughts I used to have, lookin' at her, when she used to go runnin' wild through town with the other youngsters in the summer, that dark red hair blowin' free in the breeze, showin' off those long, smooth dark arms and legs, those—"

Remelea's face hardened. "Maybe it's time you took it down a notch."

All the humor bled from the old guy's face. "What for? You're here to kill me anyway, right? Tie up loose ends, sweep the last of your dirty little secrets under the rug?"

"I ain't here to kill you," said Remelea.

The old guy pointed at Rob. "Is he?"

"Ain't decided yet." Rob stepped towards the desk. "You were saying about your grandma?"

The old guy shrank back. "She always said we needed to be nice to your kind, that you'd protect us in the end…from those *others* who walk among us…*the shiny ones*. Lot of good you did us all in the end, huh?"

"You saying the Spirelights attacked this place?"

"Not this motel, no, but…they showed up in town…when the world started changin' shape…Since then, everyone they didn't hit, panicked and got out of here. I don't figure they got very far."

"Maybe you're right," said Remelea. "Maybe it's time I took it up with those others, the ones you say were *always watching*."

The old man sat back down. "You're a few months shy. They was already gone before the shiny ones rolled through, tyin' up *their* loose ends."

Remelea stepped up, leaned forward over the desk, and jacked her thumb at Rob. "So show him. While you're at it, show me."

"You were never one of the ones who was allowed down there. That's blasphemy, they say."

"*They're* long gone. You just said so yourself. *They* ain't gonna protect you from us."

The old man grabbed a pack of Camels and lit one, then leaned against the counter smoking silently, savoring it like it was his last smoke ever. Finally, he said, "Fine, just give me a minute, will you? You wanna see? Fine, I'll show you." He cocked his head at the door behind him and said, "Well, c'mon, this way."

Two

It was slow going, following the creaky old guy past the wall of room keys, through a musty rear office that was furnished more like a homey living room, then out into a sandy, dilapidated back lot.

"I thought it was supposed to be winter," Rob muttered, as they stepped back out into the blistering sunlight.

"It sure was in Louisiana," said Remelea. "Winter comes to Texas too, y'know."

"Could have fooled me."

"Global warming or some shit," said the old guy. "Least that's what all those liberals used to say, before everything went to hell."

Right, Rob thought. *Global warming. One more Earth-line fuck-up. Once I find where I'm going, then bring back what I claim there, they'll never be able to fuck this world up like that again.* No one *will*.

"Maybe all this heat has something to do with those new volcanoes people gossiped about," the old man went on. "Someone said one had popped out of the waters off the Gulf of Mexico like a boiling zit." He reached the middle of the lot and kicked some dust aside, revealing a metal door in the ground. He hunted around, found the old latch, tried to heave it open, then gasped, coughed wetly like a stagnant swamp lived in his lungs, and backed away. "I'm afraid it ain't in me anymore, kids. Knock yourselves out."

Rob and Remelea stepped to either side of the door, crouched, found the handles, and hauled it open. It landed with a great clang. They stared down into the hole. Their eyes adjusted to the gloom within. A steep wooden staircase led down into some subterranean mystery.

"Well, go on," said the old man. "This is what you came for, right?"

"You first," said Rob.

The old man let out a gurgling chuckle. "Well, ain't that funny! Nah, boy, I've never been allowed down there. Bet I couldn't make it on those stairs if I tried. Nah, whatever's down there now…it's all for you. Sorry to tell you this, but…whatever you find down there, maybe you'll just have to imagine it on a better day. Then again, well…careful, 'cause you just might come back up to a better day. Or an even worse one."

"What the hell's that supposed to mean?" said Rob.

"Ain't you heard? Time and worlds don't work the same anymore. Not since the solar storm, I guess. That's when everyone started whisperin' about the *High Natural*. I don't know what the hell a *High Natural* is, except it's thrown everything out of whack, makin' weird shit happen to time and space. Cross those old busted-up train tracks when you drove in here? Ain't nothin' come down 'em in years. 'Cept over these past months, sometimes at night, I look out the window and see trains passin', hear and feel them old rails hummin' like they used to. And not them modern trains, neither. Like those old steam engines, from back when this town used to be a boomin' railroad stop. I think maybe somethin' leaked out of *there*, since your people quit tendin' it." He pointed down the stairs. "You go down there, find whatever you're lookin' for, you might not come back up into the same time or place. Say you're down there just a few minutes. You might still come back up and find it's next week, next year…maybe even a couple of weeks *ago*. Hell, maybe you'll climb back up and find yourself in a nicer world, before all this. Might see a bunch of dinosaurs roamin' the earth, for all I know."

"Sounds like you know quite a bit," said Rob.

"Hah! Don't reckon I *know* much of anything…'cept how to listen. I always listened to them elders of yours, whisperin' among 'emselves, right up until they up and left. Reckon they never thought to care, what a broken-down old bastard like me heard. I ain't as dumb as they all took me for."

Rob was less worried about anything the old man had just said, more concerned with starting down into this pit and have the crazy old bastard close the door after them, lock it and leave them to die down there, either from starvation or when the oxygen ran out. He looked at Remelea. She gave him an encouraging nod.

They both descended the steep stairs into the pit. It was cooler down here, at least. With every step his boots touched, Rob was amazed at how smooth and sturdy these old boards still held.

Of course they do. Ancient Crimbone sorcerers built this staircase, probably the ones who were always there among the Native Americans of these parts. It'll hold.

Ha! Now watch, next foot I set, that'll be the step that breaks under my weight so I fall and break my neck.

That didn't happen, though. At the bottom, they found a small, bare antechamber. A dark curtain hung over a tall doorway, opposite the stairs. They spread back the curtain and stepped into echoing, hollow blackness. Remelea dug out a lighter, sparked it up, and waved it around. Countless tiny gemstones gleamed in the little flame, studded all over the walls and ceiling. When the lighter went out, they not only kept glowing, but grew brighter, revealing a fetid, cobweb-strewn chamber. At the center, there rose a plain, rectangular altar, carved from the same stone as the walls.

Rob turned to Remelea. "What is this?"

"You've seriously never seen one of these places?"

"No." And yet, he felt more at home within the gemstone glow than he had in waking life, for longer than he could remember.

Remelea took him by the hand and led him to the altar. "This hook I wear? This altar is where it first materialized from within the Ephemeral Realms, before I made my Second Call, to be blessed by Crimbone elders who then sent it back through the Ephemeral Realms, so it could materialize before me, about twenty miles east of here. This is where holy men and women of our Crimbone bloodline saw it materialize, recognized both its history and me, that I would be the one to carve out the next chapter of that history, so they could stabilize its energies for work within this realm, to begin at the moment of my choosing. The same thing happened with those twin blades of yours, except…at another spot like this. In Vermont, I guess. Did you know that?"

"Of course," Rob said breathlessly. He'd read about such chambers in a book Zane had given him, long ago. Standing within such an ancient, sacred space was something else entirely.

Remelea looked around at the glowing speckles that illuminated the room. "I've…never been in one of these places before. We're not the kind of Crimbone who usually ever get to…We're not the kind who become Holy Elders, y'know?"

He knew what she meant. As his eyes drank in the splendor of the walls, he realized why he felt so at home here…so elated. He already knew the pattern of those glowing gemstones intimately. They perfectly matched the stars and constellations of a clear night sky, as it shown down on his visions of ancient Deschemb. This was closer to the Old World than he'd ever been in waking life, and here he stood with Remelea within it. He grabbed her and pulled her close. She quivered eagerly against him, running her hands up and down his arms. The way she kneaded at his muscles made him feel stronger than he'd ever thought possible.

He gnawed on her neck and growled, "Remelea…my love…"

She gasped, nearly yielded, then shoved him away. "Later, lover-boy. Look at the stars. You need to see what they have to tell you. So do I."

THREE

They climbed back out into the Texas heat. The old man wasn't waiting for them. The sun was much higher in the sky, and it was a little cooler. The wind had well since blown away their tracks leading from the motel to the secret door. When they went back into the front office, they found a dried-out, mummified corpse in the seat behind the front desk, his head lulling back. His features had stretched back into a leathery rictus. At least the smell had had time to grow stale. Flies buzzed around the old bastard's face. In the collective buzzing, Rob heard a voice with a message that his conscious mind couldn't decipher. He was fine with that. He wasn't in the mood to hear what flies said to each other.

"How much time do you think passed up here while we were down there?" he asked.

Remelea sniffed at the corpse. "A couple weeks, would be my guess. C'mon, let's get out of here." She tugged at his hand. "Away from all this death."

As they stepped out onto the front porch, he said, "What's wrong?"

"What the hell do you think?"

"You know what I mean."

She stabbed her finger back the through the doorway, towards the hidden cellar from which they'd just emerged. "The fact that the Elders have abandoned that place, that's what! Shit. That's what I was afraid of. If this spot's abandoned, it's a good bet so are the rest. Whatever Crimbone we meet…any new ones making their Calls in the world as it is now…they ain't been tempered by the same vetting process as us."

"That explains a lot, now that you mention it."

"*Fuck!*" She leaned forward against the walkway railing. "So where do we go next?"

"Huh?"

"You're still the High Natural," she said. "What, you expect me to do everything? Go on, make a decision, bitch."

Rob closed his eyes and tried to listen to whatever this parched, shrunken place tried to tell him. Instead, he recalled something Remelea had said in the subterranean cosmos: *The same thing happened with those twin blades of yours, except…at another spot like this. In Vermont, I guess.*

Talino had said, *You'll make your second true beginning where you made your first.*

"To Vermont," said Rob. "To Brattleboro. That's where we'll find the shores of the black ocean. Back to the Old World. That's where I have to go." It came out of his mouth in the Old World Crimbone language. "The Old

World…This world…They want to be *one* world, uncorrupted by the Spirah gods, one that'll thrive like the Schomites almost had this world doing before the Spirelights showed up."

They reached the car. Rob tried to get in, but Remelea shoved the door shut and looked him in the eye. "Talino said the Spirelights are nothing but puppets to their gods. He was right. But we're puppets, too, Rob. In a way, we're puppets to the same gods."

"Now I'm really not following you."

"Ever since I picked up my hook, I've never once run from a fight with them, no matter how bad the odds. I've been in plenty of other kinds of fights, but I always had enough brains to know when it was better to take a deep breath, back down, tell myself, *Girl, this shit ain't worth it.* You ever run from a fight with a Spirelight?"

"No."

"Neither have I. But I'll bet you *have* backed down from fights with other people…with Earth-line people."

"Sure, before my First Call, but…What?"

"*Oh, can the Macho act, forfucksake!*" She pranced and waved her hands in the air like a brain-damaged child. "*Er, er, der, der, I'm the High Natural. I'm the biggest badass there ever was!* We both know that's a lie. I've seen you back down from fights with fellow Crimbone…*Crimbone you could have taken.* You ever think twice like that about any Spirelights?"

"Sure. I just never—"

"Of course not. Because *it's the thirst for the glow* that pulls us into all those fights. It overrides everything else. On that huge-ass boat in New Orleans, you took down that Spirelight so you could get the strength to help me. When you were sucking that Spirelight's life out, did you even remember I was there? Would you have even noticed if Balthazar killed me and raped my corpse before you were done?"

"No."

"Exactly, 'cause you were as much a slave to that glow as that Spirelight was before he became Balthazar's slave. He wasn't a slave to his gods when he died...but you were. You didn't have a choice. You gave up that choice when you entered the attack. We're *all* slaves, *all* puppets. What you...what I *think* you have it in you to do is give us all...it sounds cheesy, but hear me out. If you're right, you can give us all *true freedom*, freedom from the gods. That's the real reason you're doing this. It *has* to be the *only* reason."

"So that's what I'm supposed to find? In the Old World?"

"That, or you're just one more delusional cocksucker with a god-complex. Christ, I hope so." She clapped her palms to his cheeks and pressed her lips against his, hard enough to bruise. She breathed huskily in his ear, "Can I tell you a secret?"

"Go ahead."

"*I don't give two tugs of a dead dog's cock, what this world's turning into, or what you have to do with it, or what your ego tells you it's your duty to be.* I just know I've been having the time of my life with you."

Before he could answer, she turned to get back into the car. He caught her by the arm and met her eyes. "So what did the stars tell you?"

"*Stars?*"

"All those glowing gemstones, in the cavern walls, back where we just were. You said they had something to tell you. What was it?"

"Seriously? You don't know? It didn't tell you, too?"

"I guess not."

"But why would it—That doesn't make any—Oh, fuck…"

"What are you talking about?"

"Rob, listen to me. Whatever you're supposed to find in Brattleboro, I saw it, too. And you're not the only one looking for it. You've gotta be careful—we both do, now more than ever—of whatever else is looking for that spot."

"Who else is looking for it?"

"I don't know. And I didn't say *who else*. I said *what else*."

FOUR

They spotted a general store on Main Street. They broke in and raided the place for toilet paper, canned food, and whatever other sundries that would come in handy while living out of a car during the end of the world. One nice thing about a town that everyone had abandoned overnight: such shops hadn't already been picked clean.

On the way out of town, Remelea swerved onto an uphill side street. She spun the car with a shriek into the front yard of a two-story adobe-walled house. Rob spotted no more signs of life than he had back at the motel. Remelea stared at the building with a deeper, truer hatred than he'd ever seen directed against the Spirelight glow. She got out, went over, climbed the porch, kicked the door in, and went inside. He almost followed her in, but some instinct alerted him, *Whatever this is about, it's for her. Best stay out of her way this time.*

A few minutes later, flames erupted and licked out of the windows. Glass heated up and shattered, top floor to bottom. Remelea strode out while flames licked and burst from the blackening structure behind her. As she approached, Rob saw a wilder pain in her eyes than she'd ever shown him before. The glass in the windows popped and sprayed everywhere. Remelea reached Rob's side. Right as his heart started to melt for her, she backhanded him across the face, so hard that he fell on his ass and sprawled in the grass.

He started to sit up, but she shoved him back down, straddled him, and plunged her mouth down greedily onto his.

"Remelea…" he gasped.

"Shut up."

Considering how wound up he still was from his time in the magic cellar, he didn't take much convincing. She was already working herself out of her jeans and yanking at his belt. Before he knew it, she had his jeans and shorts yanked down around his knees. She drew up over him, took him in hand, arched her back, slipped him inside her.

I gotta quit doing this, he managed to think. *Too late this time, though, right? Old Lords, am I gonna survive what she's…*

Too late for what? You still think you're ever gonna see Sally again? Even if you do, you think Remelea's just gonna…gonna…

Remelea rode him there in the yard, while the flames engulfed the house, crackling ever higher against the twilit sky.

"OH COME YE LEADERS, COME YE MEN OF GREAT"

"Do the others know yet?" Janie asked the tabletop. Her teeth still chattered between words, despite the blanket someone had thrown around her shoulders.

"Let's hope not," said Jesse to the wall across the room. In one hand, he held the iron rod of Sally's spear. In the other, he held the severed blade. Deacon had died with it in his body, driven by Janie. It was scraped and chipped from base to tip…Sam, Anya and Sheldon had all hacked so fiercely into Byron's body that their own weapons had struck repeatedly off the embedded metal. Jesse liked seeing Byron's dried blood on it. He still wished he'd killed Byron himself. It was like its own strange form of grief, one more open wound he didn't know how to close.

At least he'd seen Sally's corpse. He'd never seen his son's corpse. Soon he'd make of Sally what she needed to be: a memory. Would he get a chance to look at Zane's corpse, or would news of Zane's death pass his way at random one of these days? That's what a ghost was: someone you knew you'd never see again, but you could never quite make the loss feel official, just because you'd never shared a proper goodbye with the meat that used to house their consciousness. Jesse was sick of ghosts. He had plenty of them, not just of people, but of possibilities, every good direction he'd failed to offer someone's life, everything they'd never see or do.

Something else tried to fall into place in his head, some light that wanted to break through this fog. He turned back and looked at everyone else present.

Sam and Anya sat at the table with Janie. They'd washed and put on fresh clothes. It only made their bruised, broken flesh look worse, especially in the harsh fluorescent light. At least they'd been able to answer the question of how Byron's pack had found its way through the maze, even though that made even less sense. Sam had overheard the rasping, misshapen fucker outside, selling them out to Byron. Once they'd pulled themselves up from their own beating, they'd found the broken bastard still skulking around outside.

"Sounds like that punk Deacon alright," Jesse had said. "Sheldon was right. Should've put that prick out of his misery back at the Renaissance Kingdom. How the fuck you figure his lurching, broken carcass made it all the way out there?"

"I guess we'll never know," said Anya. "I'd have taken his head for you after I chopped it off, but we had other priorities."

"Don't even worry about it," said Jesse. "Plenty a seasoned Crimbone couldn't have made that run, or helped out like that, after the beating you guys took."

At the other end of the room, a whiny whisper sounded as the door opened. Everyone but Jesse jumped a little. Tiger poked his head in. "Is it okay if…Do you guys mind if I…?"

"The hell you doing up?" said Jesse.

Tiger stepped the rest of the way in, almost fell over, caught himself against the wall, then hobbled towards the table. "I just wanted to…Hey, Jesse, it's okay, man. I'm ready to help, whatever you need."

"Get your ass back to the infirmary. There'll be plenty we need you for, soon enough, once that gash in your back heals up."

"I told you, it's not that bad, really."

As the kid walked further into the light, Jesse saw more clearly, just how green around the gills he'd gotten, in just over a few hours. Jesse scanned everyone else's faces. They all shared his concern, sure, but even Sam and Anya didn't see what he saw. He'd have expected keener eyes from them, being vets and all…except why would they know any better, given how far combat medicine had come? It was funny, how things came full circle, if you lived long enough. Aside from what was left of his and Zane's Crimbone medicinal recipes, medical resources out here weren't much better than they'd been since the Civil War. Tiger had insisted on what could be spared of the limited supply going to his wife, even though all she had was a simple concussion.

Before Jesse could speak, Janie stood up and pulled out a chair. "Tiger, c'mon, sit down. How's Lilly?"

"She's asleep." Tiger didn't so much sit as collapse into the chair. He tried and failed to hide how it knocked the wind out of him. "She was really scared, before she went out. Everyone is. Thanks for that tranquilizer you gave her, Jesse."

"No problem," said Jesse. "You should be back there looking after her."

"No." Tiger shook his head frantically. "She'd want me here, doing my part. I'll bet you all wish neither of us had lived, huh?"

"Why say a stupid thing like that?" asked Jesse.

"We got ourselves into that mess. Sally died saving our dumb asses."

Jesse walked over, put a hand on Tiger's shoulder and looked him in the eye. "She died protecting her friends. If you two hadn't been out on patrol, none of us would've known those guys were coming. That shit could have been a lot worse."

"Hey, Tiger," said Sam. "I'm glad you're here. Look, I don't know you, but…you're no Crimbone, but you're no civilian, either."

"Huh. Thanks."

Jesse hid his frustrated sigh. Sam wasn't wrong, but Tiger wasn't made to take what a Crimbone body could and keep going. That just got more apparent with every second.

"I guess you know the civilian population better than anyone else in this room," Sam went on. "What I'm asking is, when they find out they don't have Sally or Sheldon anymore, will they hold it together?"

Tiger kept trying to look tough but trembled and stared for a moment like Sam had just slapped him in the face.

"They kept it together before Sally and Sheldon," said Jesse. "In a few hours, one way or another, they're gonna know they don't have that anymore. After that, it's gonna be our job to hold them together, everyone in this room."

Jesse scanned their faces and settled on Janie's. She stared up at him, nakedly terrified. For a second, he felt bad for putting her on the spot like that. Then he remembered, just a moment ago, when Tiger had lurched in and insisted on joining them, she'd been the only one who'd thought to pull out a chair for the weakened man. Before he could assess her further, he became aware of everyone's eyes on him…looking *to* him. Because he was *Jesse Fuckin' Ripper-Man Karn*. Without a *Zane Fuckin' Thumpy-Bumpy Rochester* at his side, though, part of him felt like the biggest phony in the world, just a broken old man, as scared and useless as everyone else.

"That's great," said Sam. "What I meant was, how 'bout the inspiration to not go around killing each other?"

"I don't know, Sam," said Jesse. "Those medical responders who patched you and Anya up were Spirelights, y'know."

"I noticed," said Sam.

"So while they were making sure neither of you bled to death internally, were either of you *overtaken with the irresistible compulsion to bolt up and slaughter them?*"

"Look," said Anya, rubbing Sam's shoulders, eyes flashing sparks at Jesse, "you can back the fuck off right now, okay? We get your point."

"Don't tell me you *get my point*," Jesse snarled. "Answer my fucking question. Did you two, or did you not, kill those *Spirelights* who saved your lives, from what *our fellow Crimbone* did to you?"

"No," said Anya

"You both met Sally, right?" They nodded. "Still felt that glow from her, didn't you?" They nodded again. "What, you mean that didn't *overwhelm you with the ol' Spirelight-killing urge?*" They shook their heads. Jesse looked at Tiger again. "See, kid? That's because of what Sally gave all of us, from herself, from all the shit she went…" His voice hitched and cracked. "Everything that made her who she was. I'll say it again. Everything she *gave* us. She didn't take it with her."

"Sure, great," said Tiger, "'cept she only had a chance to give it to the United Deschembines."

"And these two here, don't forget, *these my fellow Crimbone*." Jesse pointed at Sam and Anya. "It can still spread from there, from them, from all of us in this room, from everyone on this base if we let it."

"Careful, Jesse," said a small, strong voice. "You're starting to sound like my mom." Janie smiled faintly, then saw everyone else suddenly looking at her. She started trembling again, then Jesse caught her gaze, returned her smile, and nodded.

Tiger managed his strongest smile yet, like a schoolboy looking up to his favorite coach on the sports field. "Okay, *fearless leader*, so what's—"

He leaned forward, then lurched sharply. His cheeks puffed up like a chipmunk's, right before he vomited clear, greenish-tinged bile all over himself and the tabletop. He started falling out of his chair, then there was Janie on his left, Sam on his right, catching him by the arms and steadying him upright.

"That's it, man," Sam whispered, in a gentler *bedside-manner* voice than Jesse would have expected from the stoically gung-ho kid. "Just take it easy, man. You've been tough and brave enough for one day, soldier."

"Someone get Tiger back to the infirmary," said Jesse. "Have whatever nurse is on duty do something about that infection." *Not just an infection…One from a stabwound from a Crimbone blade.* Just how were you supposed to treat that? Jesse realized he had no idea. Until five months ago, his only concern with Crimbone stab-wounds had been inflicting them.

"I've got it, I've got it," said Janie. She situated Tiger against her and adjusted her feet for his weight. "C'mon, man. Let's get you back to your wife. She's waiting for you."

Tiger mumbled incoherently. Jesse's eyes met Janie's. She'd never been able to feel at ease around him, he knew, like she thought he might go crazy and rip her to shreds at any moment, no matter how much reassurance he showed her to the contrary.

"You've got this, kid," he told her.

She nodded, then helped Tiger towards the door.

Once Janie and Tiger were gone, Anya said, "So what now?"

"We'll call everyone together once we have a plan of action," said Jesse. "One way or another, the lands just sent us that message, loud and clear. We ain't safe, hiding out here anymore, and I ain't gonna settle for some *glorious last stand* bullshit, either. You two must feel it…vibrating up from the frozen lands, through your blood."

They both said, "Yeah." Then Sam said, "So what next? And does it involve all these *United Deschembines* you've been sheltering or not?"

Jesse stormed forward and drove Sally's blade through the tabletop. Sam and Anya both jumped in their chairs. He loomed over them, snarling. "*Will you two shut the fuck up for ten fucking seconds?*" They shrank into their chairs like chastised children. For a moment, that felt gratifying; *As well the impudent pups should.* Then he realized, *No, they're fully fledged Crimbone. You won't earn their loyalty with arrogance.*

Or as Zane would tell him, *C'mon, man. We're the leaders. Try not to scare the children.*

Jesse took a deep breath. He leaned the iron pipe next to the door, then he walked out. As he trailed the halls, he thought about Sally, her attitude, all that hunted-wild-animal scrappiness. It hadn't just been her metaphysically altered presence that had changed so many people around her. It had been *her*, what the lands had made of her, what she'd made of herself. He knew this, because of how she'd changed him. She'd probably died without even realizing it. Before he knew it, he caught himself smiling, just thinking about her, like she was still right there next to him, telling him some dirty joke.

He stepped out onto an old stone loading dock. He jumped down and walked out into the snow. His arms fell absently against his sides. His left wrist fell against his hip pocket. Something crackled within. He reached in and pulled out a folded page of old wrinkled paper. Before he could unfold it for a look, several sets of feet sounded. Just some folks out for a walk, clearing their heads. They passed by without noticing him. He walked around the side of the building, into a deeper alleyway, 'til he was sure he was alone. Then he walked to the other end, to where the moonlight spilled in, so he got a good look at the paper in his hands.

The drawing depicted what was probably the most fabled moment in Schomite lore… *Magur Sevi, the first High Natural, climbing from a deep valley, an ocean of mist rolling away behind him.*

He had no idea how long he stood there, staring at the drawing, before a fresh set of shuffling feet brought his eyes up sharp. Out in the road, a small, bundled-up figure trudged along, head hung low.

"Janie?"

She shuffled to a stop and looked up at him, as though barely interested. He hurried over to her, then checked himself. She kept gazing at him.

"You get Tiger back to the infirmary okay?"

"Yeah," she said. "He's dead."

"*What?*"

"Yeah. I got him into the room. The nurse on duty was helping me with him, over to the cot. By the time we got him laid out, he just…wasn't there anymore."

"Shit."

"That's it?"

"I'm tired. How's Lilly taking it?"

"I don't know. She was still out cold when I left. What about you?

"Look, I don't know what you want me to—"

Something convulsed around Jesse's waist. It was Janie hugging him, he realized. He let his arms awkwardly enfold her while she sobbed it out. Her body felt weird in his arms. The last time he'd held someone so gently, someone so delicate and vulnerable, like a wounded bird in his palms, had been…Damn, had it really been when he'd held his son as a child? Before he knew it, he was sobbing with her. The last person he'd been this vulnerable with was Zane. He couldn't hug her like he had Zane. That would shatter her. A few buckets later, they drew away from each other, both a lot calmer.

"What's that in your hand?" she said as she wiped her eyes.

He'd almost forgotten about the drawing, still clutched in his fist. "Oh, this…? Uh, yeah, this is just…a drawing my son did."

"I didn't know you had a son."

"It's okay. My son's dead."

"Shit! Ah, I mean…I'm sorry, Jesse."

He snorted and wiped some sting from his eyes. "Why? You don't even like me."

"Uh…Look, it's not that I've ever *not liked* you, it's just…"

"No, I get it. It's cool. We're good."

After an awkward silence, she said, "Can I…see your son's drawing?"

He handed it to her. She moved it around in the moonlight for a better look, then drew back with a gasp, like a snake had just tried to bight her. "That's…Magur Sevi."

"How do you know who Magur Sevi is?"

"There's…a book I've been reading…"

"What book?"

"I'd…rather not say."

"Fair enough."

"Anyway, the guy sounds like a monster! Seriously, he made thorns sprout out of the ground that grew a hundred feet high, just so they could go up the asses of his enemies, so they'd line a shoreline from coast to coast, just so people would be too scared to…to…"

"This *book you'd rather not talk about* sounds like one hell of a good read. Sounds nice to be able to just sit down with a good book again."

Janie shivered, handed the drawing back, put her hands in her pockets, and hopped up and down. "Seriously, though, man, *who the fuck does that to people?*"

"Not someone I wanna meet, I'll give you that. Still, though, according to all the stories I ever heard, by the time he appeared in the Old World, the Schomites had been almost entirely beaten down, half of them enslaved, the others reduced to desperate savages of the wilderness. A lot of Crimbone didn't even know their own nature anymore. The Spirelights had stamped out so much knowledge, so much spirit in the blood, such communion with the voices of the lands. Magur Sevi woke that forgotten spirit back up in my ancestors, so they broke the Spirelight hold. Some folks called him a savior. Some folks called him a genocidal tyrant. Who the hell knows? Spirelights say he's why the Old World fell apart, so we all had to migrate here. Hell, so do some Schomite historians."

"Hold up, that doesn't make any sense! Didn't the Schomite flight across the shrouded sea happen at least a hundred years after Magur Sevi's lifetime?"

"Longer than that, according to most." Jesse smiled and arched an eyebrow at her. "My, ain't you quite the historian!"

She huffed and slumped her shoulders. "Shit. I wish."

"Keep at it, and maybe you will be someday."

He realized how silly that sounded, before it cleared his lips. So did she. Before either of them knew it, they were both doubled over, clapping each other on the backs, laughing their asses off.

Jesse's eyes settled back on the drawing. He read the smudged signature in the lower right corner.

Louis Karn.

He'd have recognized his son's artwork, with or without the signature. Even before being cast off at age eleven, the boy had shown moments of talent that made the Smithsonian look like a shack with drunken doodles held by magnets to someone's refrigerator. Still, Jesse looked at the smudged piece and could barely believe it was authentic. The dumbest, drunken Earth-line thug could look at it and be shaken with awe from visions of ancient Crimbone suffering and perseverance.

"Is this seriously the first time you've seen this drawing?" said Jesse.

"Yeah, why?" said Janie.

"Because Sheldon gave it to me, right before everyone rolled out from the Renaissance Kingdom. What the hell was he—"

Someone asked me to give this to you. In Vermont. Someone who says he never left the place. He said he hoped it'd help you understand something.

At the time, it had just confused Jesse worse. Now his blood rushed to his brain, bringing him a few messages, some of which threatened to knock him to his knees. He concentrated on what he could process and put the drawing back in his pocket.

"Jesse?" said Janie. "What's going on?"

"Let's get back in there," he said.

Jesse and Janie walked back in, side by side. They found Sam and Anya much as Jesse had left them. Someone had found some paper towels and cleaned

Tiger's puke off the table, at least. Sally's chipped blade still stuck out of the tabletop. The two young Crimbone looked up at Jesse like house pets waiting to be fed.

"Sam, Anya, go get everyone together," said Jesse. "Everyone needs to pack light, figure out what vehicles we can stuff everyone into 'til we can steal more. Be ready to get on the road by noon tomorrow. We're all gonna go on a pilgrimage, to the one place we're either all gonna die, or maybe—just maybe—stand a slight chance of survival."

"What happened to *no glorious last stands?*" said Anya.

"I gotta say, man," said Sam, "for one of my childhood heroes, you're not inspiring me with a lot of confidence in your sound judgment right now."

Jesse loomed over Sam. "I'm not your *childhood hero*, kid. I'm the guy telling you your options, so you can take 'em or leave 'em. All I know is this. Everything's about to converge, in a place where we're all gonna find out if anything we've been through amounts to shit. I don't know about the rest of you, but if that's about to happen, I for one aim to be there for it."

"Yeah, so where's that?" asked Anya.

"Same place it all started," said Jesse. "In Brattleboro, Vermont."

"DOWN THERE BY THE TRAIN"

ONE

Zane avoided most human contact 'til he found a truck stop several miles from the border. What scant contact he found—mostly scavengers, some people still holding out in their homes—told him what to expect when he found civilization, if that was what you'd still call it. The truckers traded in both printed money and the gasoline they'd bartered or stolen. They weren't working for the same people anymore, but they went on acting like it, getting by with the trade they knew. Some were running weapons. Others transported trailers full of clean water, food, liquor, medical supplies, whatever else they could get their hands on that people needed or wanted, in towns and cities up and down the coast.

The guy Zane took up with claimed to be a regular ol' humanitarian, the last of them as he saw it, yessiree, a regular Robin Hood of the Road, delivering relief to all the desperate folks out there in these crazy times. Zane took the lift in exchange for helping load and unload cargo.

Over the next few miles, the driver got more comfortable running his mouth, 'til he opened up about a nice rounded-up catch of sweet young pussy he planned to pick up and herd into the trailer a few stops down. Word went, a buyer waited a few stops after that, promising a fat reward. Zane waited 'til the driver decided to stop and take a piss, then he reached over, yanked the guy's arm out of the socket, broke it at the elbow, and scooted over to the driver's seat. He dug out the man's wallet before kicking him out into the snow. Later, when Zane went through the wallet, he found three hundred dollars. He didn't know why the Earth-liners still considered such currency useful, but they did, so he kept it. An hour later, he found the same border crossing through which he and Jesse had driven the United Deschembines into Canada, five months earlier. No one manned the crossing now. All the glass was smashed, both in the crossing booth and in the dark, looted remains of the Duty Free store. Zane stopped long enough to go into the latter and see if there was anything useful left. No such luck. Shit. At least he didn't find any dead bodies lying around.

Borders between lands had ceased to mean shit to the Earth-line people. *Their* borders shouldn't have meant shit to him either. As he drove back over into the good ol' US of A, though, something in the air changed. He couldn't put his finger on why or how, but it was simultaneously warmer—not temperature-wise, but more welcoming—and more electric and aggressive. *Be it ever such a hellhole, there's no place like home.*

His next step was to find as big a cluster of people as possible. He thought about that asshole he'd stolen this truck from, about those girls the guy had planned to transport between human traffickers. Yeah, in this chaotic social climate, that kind of business must be booming. It was too bad he hadn't thought to get the address of the pickup point from the guy. More of those assholes would make a great way to blood himself up, work the icy rust out of his system.

Oh well. He'd find someplace else. He'd listen to people's chatter, listen to the lands around them—*through* them—and his blood would correlate Steps Two and Three. There'd be news and there'd be rumors. Somewhere between the two, he'd sort out the truth. He'd always been good at that. *Except I used to always have someone there to help me sort it out, too, didn't I?*

Through the truck's headlights, a peeling, faded road sign announced a town, so he pulled off the lonely highway. He ditched the truck a short stretch from the town's main drag. Before leaving it, he got the trailer open and looked around inside. There were some boxes of MREs, a dozen of which he stuffed into his supply bag. The trucker had left a pack of Camels on the dashboard—Zane's brand no less; maybe the lands still liked him after all.

The town seemed dead 'til Zane reached an awning with green and white stripes. The hanging lamps inside were shaded in polished red glass. He went in and saw plants in ceramic pots and a clean, green carpet. The stained mahogany tables matched the bar counter. A little over half a dozen people sat around, most of them pretending to be at ease with each other.

Zane shrugged off his coat and shook snow from his body onto the doormat. He was the only black guy around, he noticed. After almost two hundred years, Earth-line ideas of racism were mostly beneath his contempt. That didn't mean it wasn't a practical concern sometimes.

At one end of the bar, there sat a pale scarecrow of a man, with long black hair, wearing a fraying black suit, ranting in audible gasps about the Last Days, stabbing a bony finger at an open leather-bound book. A few people clustered around him. Others, like Zane, sat as far away from the loony bastard as possible.

"And the woman fled into the wilderness, where she has a place prepared by God, so that she can be nourished for one thousand and two hundred sixty days."

It took Zane a few seconds to do the math in his brain. *Three years, plus an extra hundred and sixty-five days. That's a long time to sit around in the fuckin' woods getting spoon fed by some god.*

"A war broke out in heaven. Michael and his angels fought the dragon. The dragon and his angels fought back and were defeated, and there was no longer a place for them in heaven."

Zane recalled the Canadian redneck who'd tried to run him down in the ghost town. *Time for some Dessembeen roadkill, motherfuckers!* Were these assholes eyeing him for something other than his skin color, or for that matter the fact that he was the biggest hulking bastard here by several sizes?

"…But the woman was given the wings of the eagle…"

Zane took a barstool. His hammer swung and sagged his belt. He'd left it in plain view, without thinking about it 'til now. How long had it been since he'd done that? More often he'd gotten odd looks for keeping his duster coat on in warmer weather.

"What'll you have?" The barman's voice trembled some.

"Heineken."

"There is no more Heineken," said the barman blankly.

"What do you mean *there is no more?*"

"I mean none of the shipments have brought any in months. Where have you been, man?"

"Not here, that's for damn sure. Okay, fine, how 'bout a glass of Jack?"

"Closest we've got is well bourbon."

"That'll be fine. Save the ice. Anything to eat in here?"

"Sorry, man. Kitchen's closed. Ain't been anyone but me keeping this place open for weeks."

"Oh yeah? How much business you get?"

"You're looking at it. Folks still need some kinda place to gather as a community, right? It's this or church."

Zane glanced down the bar at the raving preacher man. "Sounds like someone took a wrong turn."

"Right."

Zane sipped his drink slowly while his senses flowed out to absorb the place. Folks didn't say much to each other, at least audibly. The only audible conversation came from the preacher man, along with the occasional companion who managed to get a word in edgewise, usually feeding him agreement. Others tried not to listen but lacked the balls to tell the guy to shut up. Zane almost did it for them. He found himself listening instead.

"And then the dragon took a stand on the seashore…And I saw the beast rising from the sea, having ten horns and seven heads, and on its horns were ten diadems, and on its head were blasphemous names."

"What are *diadems?*" someone asked.

"I think they're, like, jewels or diamonds," said someone else.

"No, ain't they, like, sacred symbols or something? Or *un*-sacred symbols?"

"Nah, the symbols are the blasphemous names. Diadems are something else, I'm pretty sure."

"No," said the preacher man, slipping out of character for a second. "Diadems are crowns. It's saying its horns are its crowns, I think. The unholy symbols—the unholy *names*—will be on its forehead, right under the horns."

How much light fell on Zane's hammer? If these folks had known how to read the symbols carved on the handle, would they call them *blasphemous names*? Probably. "Could you turn on the TV?" he said to the barman.

"No point in that, unless you like watching snow. Plenty of that outside."

"Sorry, I've been living under a rock lately, way out in the wilderness."

"Was gonna say, you don't look like the typical refugee."

"Refugee?"

"Can't think of anything else to call 'em." The barman's voice trembled bitterly. "All the big cities, they're done, man! Fallen into chaos and such, taken over by gangs...I just hear stories. It's wild. Carloads of families, bigger groups of folks, they keep passing through here. Where they came from got unlivable, so they hit the road, expecting to find somewhere better. Don't know what they're expecting to find. From the sound of it, even smaller cities and bigger towns are getting crazy. We've been lucky here, so far, maybe 'cause this town was already such a shithole that even desperate vagabonds don't wanna camp out with us. Knock on wood." He wrapped his knuckles across the countertop. "Apparently it gets crazier the further south you get, where it's warmer. You wouldn't believe some of the stories I've heard, man. At least, I don't wanna believe 'em."

The door opened again, so slow and quiet that most other people didn't notice. A pale, expressionless face appeared and met Zane's gaze without expecting to.

The little bastard was trying to sneak up on me. Then, *Where the hell did he come from, anyway?*

The figure made it to the bar and slipped off his heavy backpack without attracting much attention. *Lucky little shit.* For one thing, he kept his coat on, hiding his weapons. It also helped that he was white. As intended, the barman saw someone much older than the figure actually was. The ruse probably didn't matter anymore. It irritated Zane a little. The kid got served either way, quicker than Zane had.

"Nice to see you didn't choke on your own puke," said Zane. "How long you been following me?"

Sheldon drew up sharply. "I wasn't."

Zane loosened himself from his barstool. "Try again."

"Look, I mean, I haven't been...*following*-following you—I mean, not for long. So we wound up on the same highway across the border. Look, I didn't even know we were on the same trail 'til I found that trucker."

"Who says we are?"

"The lands, apparently."

"I guess. Where's that guy now?"

"The trucker? Frozen to death, probably. I knew pretty quick he'd run into a Crimbone, so I tried asking nice, decided to learn what I could, in case it'd been one of Balthazar's."

"And?"

"He tried starting shit, even with that broken arm, so I had to break a few more of his bones. After that, he said his other attacker was another of those freaks like me, who didn't move like a real human, except it was a giant black guy." Sheldon squirmed. "He...didn't say *black guy*, though."

"I'm sure your delicate little sensibilities must be all torn up, you little glowstick cracker. Does Jesse know you're gone?"

"I'm sure he does by now. When the hell did you leave, anyway?"

"A few days ago."

"Me too." Sheldon sat next to Zane and sighed. "I guess you left before it happened."

"Before what happened?"

"Sally's dead."

Zane stared, not sure what was harder to take in, the news itself or the boy's cold, matter-of-fact announcement about his own sister's death. *Fucking Spirelights.* Or maybe the emotionless report was Sheldon's way of keeping it together. For Zane's part, he guessed the reality of it had yet to sink in. He didn't want to imagine how Jesse must be handling it. Sally had been like a little sister to him, too...or maybe more like a daughter.

Either way, Zane thought, *he's back there torn apart by it, guaran-fuckin'-tee it, right after I picked now of all times to leave him. Great.* "Yeah?" he said. "So what about everyone else?"

"Everyone else was alive when I left, except for that pack of Crimbone from the next town. All but two of them." Sheldon told Zane what little he'd gotten from Sam and Anya when he ran into them.

"Byron, huh. Shit. Guess Jesse was right about that asshole. I gotta say, though, kid, you look like you've taken as much of the trail on foot as me, or close enough." Zane snorted. "You smell like it, too. Didn't think you Spirelights were built for that shit, even the ones who *are* hardasses."

"Yeah, well...I ain't exactly your typical Spirelight. I never have been."

"We already knew that." Zane clinked his glass against Sheldon's. "Shit, bet you're at least glad as I am to be gone from that bunch of pansies, huh."

"Actually, I'd rather still be back there."

Yeah, now that you're missing getting your dick sucked. "So why did you leave?"

The kid's face finally showed a little emotion. It wasn't much, but Zane read it just fine: Sheldon was scared shitless. "I have to go meet with the High Natural."

"That's funny. So do I." Zane recalled Rob and Sheldon's checkered history. He arched an eyebrow. "Why?"

"That's complicated. Wanna go see him with me?"

"Depends. You plan to start more shit with him?"

"Depends on him."

"That sounds too close to *you bet your ass* for my liking, but…" Zane sighed. "Same here. So what's your plan for finding him? I'm guessing this has something to do with what that Familiar had to say to you later in private."

"It does." Sheldon glanced around. "I think we need to pause on that for a second, though."

"Why?" Zane spotted the barman staring at them. They hadn't been keeping their conversation all that quiet. Apparently, the crazy preacher at the other end of the bar wasn't such a foolproof distraction after all. "Oh."

The barman said, "You guys are Crimbone, aren't you?"

Sheldon nodded sideways. "He is."

"You both don't belong. You're the ones started this whole mess."

Before they could answer, the preacher man came striding towards them. His companions followed nervously. Half the men in the bar were closing in. Everyone else either still sat tensely or edged towards the door.

The preacher man said, "And they worshipped the dragon, for he had given his authority to the beast, saying, *Who is like the beast, and who can fight against him?*"

The barman drew a shotgun from behind the bar like he was trying to answer the question. Funny, this hadn't seemed like that type of place. Sign of the times, Zane figured. The gun shook in the barman's hand, like he couldn't decide who to shoot first.

Zane noticed Sheldon grinning. He shot the grin right back.

TWO

Now the bar looked more like Zane's kind of dive. He and Sheldon sat sipping free well whiskey as they talked. Everyone else still here was unconscious, in various stages of disrepair comparable to the furnishings.

"Anyway," said Sheldon, "what were we saying?"

"You were about to tell me what Puttergong had to say, about why we're here meeting like this."

Sheldon told him.

"Sounds crazy, alright. Got any better ideas?"

"Good point. Still can't believe you trust that critter."

"I guess at some point, everything else went so crazy, Puttergong's ramblings turned into the only thing that made sense anymore. We still in this together?"

"Sure," said Zane. "If we turn out to be on an idiot chase, you ready to fight *with* me, *against* the High Natural? I'm not sure I'm exactly his favorite person right now, either."

"What are you talking about? I thought you and Jesse were, like, his heroes."

"Strapping a wounded, comatose comrade to a metal table like some damn Doctor Frankenstein lab experiment ain't the best way to inspire lasting trust."

"Okay, I see your point. And damn right, I'll fight him with you. Remember, I need him alive, though."

"Good man. Okay, let's go."

"We're not going anywhere."

"Say what?"

"Puttergong said to wait here."

"*Here?*"

"It said to stop and wait in the first town I found once I crossed the border. Said it'd find me here. I think it's gonna go find the High Natural and talk to him first, arrange the meeting so everyone walks into it on more or less the same page."

"Oh. Great."

"Hey, it's gotta be better than rushing to find him on our own, right?"

"Any port in a storm, huh. So I guess you're right, we'd best wait here. Not too long, though."

Sheldon glanced around. "True. Plenty folks here must have overheard our conversation."

Zane opened and closed his fists, trying to work the fresh soreness from his knuckles. "I noticed."

"If the land's on our side, that's not supposed to happen, is it?"

Zane smiled. "Hopefully all it means is that the lands want us on our toes. We should still go somewhere else, other than this bar, I mean. I ain't sure those folks who ran out won't send reinforcements."

"Can we finish our drinks first?"

"Why not?"

THREE

They sat huddled in the lobby of the border town's train station. The town's shrinking power grid didn't reach this far, so they'd built a fire in the shallow pit Zane had hammered out of the concrete floor after they ripped up the carpets. There was already a big rotted-out hole in the roof, so the smoke got out just fine. The remnants of dinner hung on the spit they'd built. They knew the dog had once belonged to someone, because it had still worn a collar when it attacked them. They'd only noticed the collar after hauling the corpse back to their hideout.

Sheldon watched Zane skin and spit the carcass. "What's wrong, man?"

Zane wiped his hands on his coat and went back to turning the spit above the fire. "Ah, just thinking...poor little guy. He was someone's buddy, y'know."

Sheldon leaned forward, taken aback by this big, brutal, ancient man's mournful, almost childlike sullenness. "Yeah, sure. Didn't stop him from trying to rip our throats out."

"That's right." Zane stoked the fire. "He never wanted to be *that guy*, though. Whoever ran off and left him, they were the folks he trusted, bonded with, thought of them like his family. In the end, though, they just didn't feel the same way."

"That, or they're dead. So what, you feel bad, about how he's gonna fill our bellies?"

"Nah. I'm just saying it's a shame it worked out that way for him. Plus, well, I always liked dogs, is all."

"So do I," said Sheldon. The roasting meat tickled his nostrils. "I like getting to eat better, though."

"Yeah," said Zane. "So did this good boy here. If he'd managed to tear our throats out, he'd have gotten to, too. You got him, though, with one of those shiny blades of yours, so now we do." He reached over and tore a barely-cooked chunk from the roasting dog. He chewed, swallowed, and said, "Mmmmmm…Yeah, I figure this is cooked good enough by now for your lil' glowstick stomach to handle."

Sheldon tore himself off a chunk of meat. "So I've told you why I'm chasing the High Natural. Why are you after him?"

"Huh?"

"Why did you abandon your brother for that asshole Rob Coscan, like I've abandoned my girlfriend and my sister, right when they could have used our help most?"

Not for the first time, Zane wanted to brain the cocky little prick. Instead, he said, "Because there probably wouldn't *be* a High Natural right now, if it weren't for the one damn time I didn't listen to the voices of the lands, the voices of the blood in my veins, more than I did the voices of all the assholes around me, telling me what to do."

"Huh?"

"I'll spin the setup for you quick, kid. Rob's parents were about the most badass Crimbone couple I ever saw, scarier than me or Jesse combined. You should have seen some of the crazy shit they pulled off."

"I know," said Sheldon. "I heard horror stories about them growing up."

"No shit! Yeah, that makes sense. Anyway, they had a kid between 'em, before she got herself killed. I believe you've met their offspring. After his mom died, though, his dad made the choice between raising his son in the world that had gotten the love of his life killed, or withdrawing into that quieter, more sheltered Earth-line world, on the fringes of things, so his son might grow up, have what the Earth-line folks call a *normal life*. Then there was some business in Richmond, Virginia, violent business that needed some Crimbone action to deal with it, and the Cabinets said, *You know who should go deal with that shit, Jesse and Zane? You two, and your ol' buddy Metaiew.* By then, though, Metaiew had retreated as far out into the neutral territory boonies as he could get, along with his son. Married some total stuck-up cunt of an Earth-line woman, too, liked to keep a bear-trap clamped on his nutsack. To this day, I couldn't tell you what he saw in her, unless it was to punish himself for something. All the while, Metaiew's kid was damn near the age to become a castoff fledgling, except Metaiew wasn't about to let that happen. We all wondered, though, what *might* happen, if the kid got just a little exposure, at just the right time, to what his life might have been…

"All the while, my blood told me, *If that's how ol' Metaiew feels, that's his business. Let him go his way, along with his brat.* The Cabinet and my fellow Crimbone all cheered me on to go fetch Metaiew, though. I let 'em get me all worked up, so I took the job. My whole drive down there, there were violent storms that kept trying to run my Jeep off the road. Like the lands were telling me to turn back. Funniest thing was, whenever I'd stop for gas or a bite to eat, or just pull over for a break, the storm would ease up. The wind would die off and the rain would taper off into a little sprinkle. Just like that. Every damn time. It was like…the lands were giving me a chance to turn back, like it'd be all nice and easy like that, the whole way home. Whenever I got back on the road, the storm kicked back up, nasty as before, and I still didn't listen. When I got to the farm, who should greet me first but lil' eleven-year-old Rob Coscan, looking up at me all starstruck, like I was some superhero out of one of his Saturday morning cartoons come to life. Then I saw Metaiew, and all the years fell away, between who we used to be and who we were by then.

"I told him why I was there…the official business, anyway. I didn't tell him what else the Cabinet hoped might happen. Looking back, I think he saw right through that shit. He told me, *The boy can't hear or see any of that. It might wake him up so he follows us into that kinda life.* But by then, I'd already looked into the kid's eyes, and I knew it was too late. Metaiew's suppressing that kid, letting him endure the abuse he'd already known from his stepmom and the little shits he went to school with, keeping him low…Beneath all that childish innocence, there was something *ugly*, already growing in that child's eyes. I knew right then what had to be done. As soon as the boy was out of earshot, I told Metaiew so. In that moment, I saw him turn into a wild animal. He'd have killed me right then and there, if his son hadn't been watching. If I'd pressed the issue, I think he would have done it anyway. Maybe I should have stuck to my guns, killed the boy or had Metaiew kill me, doing my damnedest to take him with me. Instead, I backed down. I told Metaiew he could keep his secrets from his son, so long as he did this one last run with his fellow Crimbone. For the rest of my visit, I met that boy's eyes, with his own Crimbone nature, every chance I got."

"You're saying you had a chance to kill Rob Coscan, to end all this before it started."

"That's right."

"Hang on, I thought we were headed to *team up with* Rob, not kill him."

"That's the thing. By now, it wouldn't do any good. It's all tied to this shit happening around us, the way this world's falling apart and putting itself back together in ways it wasn't made to fit together. It doesn't matter anymore whether his own intentions or actions are directly responsible for it or not. He's the one it's all leaking out of, and the rest of it's all pressurized within him, ready to burst. Hell, Jesse was right. *The High Natural doesn't belong in this world.* Killing Rob, while he's here in this world, it'd probably just make it worse, without him here to anchor it. Hearing your side of it, what Puttergong told you, that just makes it all fall that much more into place. Sounds to me, you're the one who needs to take him *out of this world*, to where he needs to go, so the rest of us can hopefully get on with cleaning up the mess…not that it's ever gonna go back to how it was by now. Either way, it's a mess I *let* happen, what I should have clipped at the bud a long time ago."

"I don't know, man," said Sheldon. "Sounds like maybe you're giving yourself too much credit, like your little decisions ever had so much power over anything."

"That's pretty rich, coming from a little glowstick cracker punk who thinks he's gonna go *stab the gods*. Hell, maybe you're right. I'll tell you what I *really* should have done when I had the chance. When I first met Rob as a grownass young man, I should'a kicked the shit out of his little bitch ass, taught him some humility."

Sheldon sputtered laughter. "I ain't gonna disagree with you there!"

"Here's the thing, though. Part of why the world's so fucked up is that too many people *don't* stop to think about how all their little choices affect the *big fuckin' picture*. It's *never* just about you. Hell, it ain't even ever just about *you and yours*. All I know is this: that trip I made to see Metaiew and his boy, that was the one time in my life when the lands and my blood told me to do one thing, and I did what other people told me to do instead. I gotta live with that. So does everyone else. That's why I'm following the voices of the lands and the voices in my blood now, even though I'd rather have stuck by my brother's side. That's why I'm with you now, while we go to find the High Natural."

They sat and ate in silence after that. Then Sheldon got up and walked to the window. He looked back and forth across the platform. Two giant shards of yellow light cut through the snowy haze outside. The light spread like ripping cloth 'til it converged on the snowy exterior. An ear-splitting whistle blew. A giant missile of metallic blackness plowed by, spraying more snow up onto the walkway as it slowed down.

Sheldon looked back at Zane. "Am I going nuts, or is that a train going by?"

"Neither." Zane stood up. "You're already nuts, and that's a train pulling to a stop."

They trudged outside cautiously. The train settled in front of them. Through a glowing doorway, there stepped a tall, broad, ice-pale, square-faced man in an old-fashioned conductor's uniform, complete with one of those funny, stiff, round hats. "Anyone getting on here?"

"Maybe," said Zane. "Where's this rig headed?"

"Brattleboro, Vermont. *Everyone's* going to Brattleboro these days. Anyone who's anyone, that is. That's the word on the rails. Ain't you heard, boy? Where you been?"

Zane resisted the urge to knock the dude's head off for calling him *boy*. Hell, it must have been a good fifty years since anyone threw that one at him. Then again, this guy was dressed like a train-conductor from at least fifty years ago. Zane and Sheldon looked at each other then back at the conductor.

"This track goes straight to Vermont?" Sheldon asked.

"Not this one," said the spectral conductor. "You'll have to switch trains a couple times, but don't worry.

Anywhere we stop, there will only be one other train running. That will be yours."

"Great," said Zane. He grabbed up both his and Sheldon's travel sacks. "Let's go."

Sheldon planted his feet. "Hold on a second. We're still waiting for someone."

"This train leaves in five minutes," said the specter in the funny clothes and cap.

Zane glanced at Sheldon. "Seriously, little dude? You wanted to learn to listen to the voice of the lands? Times like this…well…it don't get much clearer."

Sheldon leaned in, pointed, and hissed. "That's not *the lands*. That's a fucking walking corpse inviting us onto a ghost train."

"And you can see it and hear it, right? Ghosts live on in the lands. Sometimes the lands speak to us through 'em. I just got through telling you what happens when we don't listen. I'm listening now. Are you?"

"Yeah, but—"

"So grab your shit and let's get on board."

Sheldon shook his head. "We have to wait for Puttergong. I told you, we—"

Zane sent a straight gunshot punch into the center of Sheldon's forehead. Sheldon stared at him for a second, then bobbled like something on a coiled spring. His wide eyes rolled up towards the purple imprint Zane's knuckles had just made, then he fell forward. Zane caught him by the armpits.

The conductor watched impassively. "The kid your son?"

"Sure," said Zane. "Never could stop the boy from playing in the bleach."

"You have tickets?"

Zane pushed back his duster and tapped the swinging hammer on his belt. "This do?"

"That'll do. Best go find some good seats. There are plenty to choose from, but there won't be for long."

GREAT BALTHAZAR'S

LITTLE BUDDY

ONE

It was too cold in the prison bus to sleep…Too cold, too noisy, too smelly, just too uncomfortable, especially when they were moving, with the rusty, studded metal seats rattling under his ass. Or so Fishhook had sworn during the first week.

That was the thing about conditions where it was *impossible to sleep*; if you were stuck with them long enough, you slept anyway. Fishhook had first learned that lesson on the road. He'd learned it all over again as an *Earth-liner*. That's what they called him and the others they kept alive. He guessed that's what they called the ones they killed, too, any normal people, people who weren't one kind of Deschembine or other.

How long had it been? Just a few months, though it felt like years. He only knew otherwise because it had been early fall when Norm and Fran had picked him up and driven him into Rock Spring…the first day of his new life. Now it was winter, and he hadn't seen spring or summer. He'd have remembered that much, he told himself.

Half the time, he could barely tell the difference between dreams and awake. What was left to dream about, other than more of this endless cycle? Sometimes stuffed into one jail cell or another, in whatever town Balthazar had occupied this time, or worse, freezing outside in some yard surrounded by wire fences. Or out doing whatever manual labor they had for the Earth-liners this week. Or on the road, in the back of an old prison bus, like now. They fed him better than the others, gave him a longer, thicker coat to wear. They wanted him to last longer, partly because he was young, strong, rugged from the road life, hence better for the heavier labor. That wasn't the only reason, though. Whenever Balthazar showed up…

Hey!

Sometimes he dreamed of drowning in the waste of the *food-prep duty*. Or of being one of those bodies in the middle of the heap, while someone else pushed him and the other corpses to the *prep station.*

Hey! You! Are you fucking deaf?

Right now, he was a severed head, on top of a pile of bones in a wheelbarrow. His brain must be the only internal organ that hadn't been torn away from the bones and thrown in some other cart…the muscles and organs to feed Balthazar's troops, or be ground up into the chum they fed Fishhook and the other prisoners, the skins to be tanned and stitched together as the troops' clothes…their *uniforms*, Fishhook guessed.

Are you retarded? What the hell's wrong with you?

Somewhere in this wheelbarrow were the rest of his bones. He knew this, because they somehow still had nerve-endings, so he felt the cool, congealing blood all over them.

Just…just…say something. C'mon, anything, just talk to me, pleeeeeeeaaaase!

Whoever kept shouting, he wanted to tell them to shut up. But how could he? He was just a rotting brain inside a skinned skull, on top of a pile of wet, rattling bones…

The smell of shit flooded Fishhook's nose, fresh out of someone's diseased bowels. His eyes snapped open, ripping at the thick crust that had gathered around the lids. He almost fell off his seat. They didn't keep you shackled to these benches. The closest to a safety measure was the wire mesh between the prisoner space and the driver up front. He sucked in a deep, gasping breath, which just pulled the shit stench in deeper. He doubled forward and belched a splash of bile onto the center aisle.

"Aw God, that is *so gross*," shrieked the bitch across from him, in the same voice that had been invading his dreams a second ago. "Thanks a lot, asshole! That's cute! That's real fucking cute! You nasty motherfucker!"

It was weird, how she shouted her insults in the same sobbing tone as someone pleading for his help. She was a petite, pasty-pale blonde, maybe either twenty or fifty, missing all her upper teeth. He couldn't tell if that was because Balthazar's Deschembines had knocked them all out, or if she'd already been busted like that when they caught her. She wore only her panties and an oversized blue button-up shirt, which hung open, showing the edges of small, withered tits above jutting ribs. Brown water spread out around her ass. He didn't spot any red stains around her thighs, so they must not have passed her around yet. Whenever they decided to, with a mouth like that on her, maybe she'd annoy them enough so they just snapped her neck. For her sake, he hoped so.

Fishhook hacked and spat out more bile. A few stringy chunks floated in it, from the last time they'd fed him.

"Oh god, you are so gross!"

Hey, bitch, you're the one who just shit yourself. His mouth opened to say so. Oh, right. He couldn't do that anymore.

"Why won't you talk to me? Just tell me what's going on! Someone, please, tell me what's going on! Speak to me, damn you! *Speak!*"

Fishhook opened his mouth wide, showing off his swollen, infected gums where half his teeth had fallen out. He pushed out a series of hacking grunts.

"*Ew! Why are you so gross? What the hell is wrong with you?*"

"Hey, shut up," someone yelled from the other end of the bus.

"Hey, fuck you," the woman screeched back. "Fucking prick. *Oh God, what's going on?*"

Fishhook looked around. The man who'd shouted was completely naked, smeared in his own crusted shit and puke. Fishhook vaguely remembered him first coming onboard. Back then, Fishhook had guessed the stocky, muscular guy to be only a few years older than himself, with a ruggedly tangled mane of rich black hair. By now, he'd dropped at least twenty pounds. His belly sagged in his lap like a shiny, hairy pustule sack, and his hair had gone stringy and thin. Only his arms and legs still looked hard. Those were the bits that lasted the longest, thanks to the heavy work, 'til your back gave out, at which point you were tomorrow's dinner. He sneered at the woman, then hung his head against his chest again.

There were less than half a dozen people in here now. There'd been more when Fishhook had nodded off. The others must have died while he was asleep, which meant they were now piled into the meat truck that drove behind the prison bus. He'd see them later, whenever this caravan stopped. He'd be ushered onto the makeshift disassembly line, handed a skinning knife, and left to separate the bones, organs, skin, and muscles from each other, then toss the bits into big wooden wheelbarrows. Recently, they'd gotten fancy new metal tables, instead of the old long wooden ones, like from medical labs or something. The new ones had raised edges and holes in the corners, so the blood drained out to be collected in receptacles. They'd only recently started collecting the blood.

"Why do you keep doing that?" the woman shouted. "God, you're gross! Stop doing that, please! *Why won't you speak?*"

He noticed he was still leaning towards her with his mouth open. If she hadn't noticed by now that *he didn't have a fucking tongue*, she never would. He sat back and tried to catch another wink of sleep or two. It wasn't happening.

Before long, the caravan pulled to a stop. The rear door shrieked open. Balthazar's overseer jumped up inside, tall and lean with long black hair like the prisoner in the back used to have, with mottled gray skin and bad teeth, wearing a coat and jeans of patchwork leather, of numerous shades. How many parts of those clothes used to sit in here next to Fishhook? The overseer clapped his hands, rubbed his palms together as his grinning face scanned everyone, and shouted, "Okay, rise and shine, Earth-liners! Time for another hard day's work!"

A couple more Deschembines jumped up into the van, wearing the same patchwork leather outfits. None of them wore any kind of military insignia, like medals or buttons or whatever. Was that what all the fresh ritual scars were for, on their faces, necks and chests, to tell rank and shit? Most of these dudes had a lot of scars anyway, but you could tell the ritualized, self-inflicted ones apart, all in straight lines, sometimes crisscrossing together to make weird symbols, always left unstitched and weeping, often with bright red infections that they didn't seem to mind. At least these weren't the *really* messed-up guys, the ones who'd been taken apart and put back together or some shit. Fishhook guessed those guys had more important duties than watching prisoners. These ones passed the overseer, filed out into the aisle, and hauled the prisoners to their feet.

The man hauling up the woman across from Fishhook went "*Ow!* You little bitch!"

A thunderclap echoed through the metallic space. The woman landed with a clang across the floor.

"Shesh, you asshole," shouted the overseer. "You've been warned about knocking them around too much. They break easy, remember?"

"The little bitch bit me!"

"I don't care! Just get her up and moving."

"Shit. I…think I busted her neck."

The overseer sighed. He didn't sound angry, just disappointed. "Great. Just great. Okay, leave her for now and look to the live ones first. Try not to break any more of 'em, huh? Just for that, you're on peeling duty with the Earth-liners for the first half of today."

"But I didn't mean to—"

"They break easy, and they don't last as long now that it's cold. Plus, they're getting better at running and hiding since more of 'em hear about us in advance, so we've been catching fewer of 'em. We start running out of Earth-liners for shit-work, who do you think the higher-ups are gonna start shafting with that duty? Think it over today while you get a taste of it. Now shut up and get back to work."

The one called Shesh sighed, then turned to Fishhook. "Okay, boy, on your feet."

"Careful with that one," barked the overseer. "That one's Great Balthazar's favorite pet. Great Balthazar's gonna be mighty disappointed if you damage his favorite pet."

Shesh rose slowly. His face ran pale. "Great Balthazar's…coming?"

"He's already here. He's made this stop ready for us. He's mighty eager to see his *little buddy*."

Fishhook's eyes widened. Not so long ago, the prospect would have made him shit his bowels out worse than the dead lady on the floor. Now he let out a heavy sigh, of relief.

TWO

On that day in Rock Spring, Fishhook had thought for a hot minute that he might make it out of there. Even with his broken arm, his head light from blood loss from all the broken glass stuck in him, he'd made it unnoticed to the back edges of town. If he'd had any idea what he'd meant to do after that, he couldn't recall.

He'd run huffing and puffing, constantly falling and getting back up, the end of the deserted street getting closer and closer. Beyond that, the Tennessee wilderness awaited him. Then out from around the last two buildings, there'd come more of those *things*. For a brief, frenzied moment, it had occurred to him, this must be what ragamuffin crusties like him and his friends looked like to normal folks, with their filthy bodies, wild hair, and bloodstained clothes made from some strange kind of leather. They'd kicked his legs out from under him, laughed while he squirmed around, then lifted and carried him back to the center of the nightmare.

He'd cussed a blue streak the whole time, even when they slit off his clothes and tossed him on top of the pile with the other writhing bodies. They'd been about to slit his flesh open next, then out of nowhere, there was their leader—*Great Balthazar*—standing between Fishhook and the others, his wings still spread, those black horns sticking out from his heels and hands, a strutting King of Nightmares, next to whom all his subjects looked like merely gross little bad dreams.

"Hol' up, boys and girls, I like this one's spunk. Go on, get him cleaned up, reset and bandage that arm, then stow him with the other keeper-Earth-liners for now. I's lookin' forward to this'n showin' me direct-like what he is."

Fishhook had assumed that meant Balthazar wanted a fresh victim to sodomize at his leisure. No, it turned out, Balthazar sometimes plucked Earth-liners from the harvest for that, but they were usually women and girls, and they never survived. Fishhook knew this because Balthazar sometimes made him watch. Afterwards, Balthazar would eat what was left. At first, Fishhook would refuse when Balthazar offered him some.

"Ain't gonna eat what you're offered, Ronny, I reckon that means you're fine goin' without."

Fishhook couldn't figure out how Balthazar knew his given name. Eventually, he found out that when they'd caught and stripped him, they'd gone through his shredded clothes and found his wallet with his expired learner's permit.

So Fishhook was sent back to the cells with the other Earth-liners, *like a child sent to bed without his supper.* Come the next feeding time, the guards separated him from the others. They gave him just enough water to keep him alive. He lost count of the days without food, before Balthazar sent for him again. The guards led him to a clearing in the nearby woods where they'd settled that week. He got there in time to see Balthazar finishing off his latest *girlfriend.*

Balthazar went and sat on a stump, had the guards sit Fishhook down across from him, then sent the guards away, leaving the two of them alone with the sobbing, shuddering, broken body lying in the dirt a couple yards away. Once the last traces of life rattled out of the body, Balthazar got up, dragged it over, tore the first ragged, dripping gob of meat off the bones, and sat there eating in front of Fishhook.

Finally, he tore off another gob of meat, held it out, waved it around under Fishhook's nose, and said, "Ready to eat what you're offered this time, Ronny?"

By then, Fishhook's belly was screaming so loud for food that he was on that chunk of raw meat before he knew it. While he gobbled at it, he heard Balthazar cackling with mocking congratulations. Balthazar laughed even louder when Fishhook puked it all up the first few times. He kept eating, though, 'til he learned to keep it down.

For the longest time, that was the worst thing Balthazar ever did to him physically, except for smacking him around those few times he'd tried to run or fight back. Over time, though, something happened to Fishhook's current fix, something that'll happen to any situation that lasts long enough, no matter how shitty: it became the new normal.

After that, it all made sense: Balthazar just wanted someone to hang out with, whenever he spent time in his conquered towns. For whatever reason, he'd sensed the perfect candidate in Fishhook; someone to talk to, to eat and drink with during his leisure moments, to make believe he was just a normal guy, spending time after work with a buddy. Because that's all any of this was to Balthazar, *a game of make-believe*. This was the creature at whose whims the whole world was burning, some kind of superpowered mutant with a head full of military tactical and strategic genius, yet somehow, at the same time…just a child playing a game of make-believe.

Fishhook remembered being a little kid playing in the woods by the creek, catching frogs, thinking in his dumbass little kid mind that he was making friends with the critters, not turning their whole day into a traumatic nightmare. That's what he was to Balthazar: the creature's pet frog.

Something snapped in him at the realization, so he started laughing and couldn't stop. When Balthazar asked what the fuck was so funny, he just laughed louder. He watched Balthazar fume with rising rage, telling him to shut up, and he couldn't stop.

Here it comes, he remembered thinking, driving his deranged, cackling glee even higher. *Any second now, he's gonna fly off the handle and finally kill me, and I'm still gonna laugh 'til I croak…Hahah,* croak, *like a frog!*

Balthazar hadn't killed him, though, just removed his tongue.

Shesh and the overseer now hauled Fishhook out of the back of the bus. He looked around blearily in the frosty morning light. The caravan had pulled into what used to be a high school football field. Beyond the wire fence, the bleachers still stood. Amidst the pervasive stench of blood and rot, he briefly felt like a gladiator being escorted out into the colosseum. He was sure as shit no gladiator, and they weren't using the area as an arena of sportsmanship.

Yards off, the metal tables had been set up, with a string of Earth-liners lined up around them. A pickup truck with a bed full of naked corpses drove through the gate. It rattled over the untended field and parked at one end of the tables. Other troops hauled out the remaining living prisoners from Fishhook's bus and two others and marched them over to the tables. As they escorted him out of the playing field, he noticed wheelbarrows full of buckets of blood, being herded in the same direction as him.

What state was he in by now, anyway? Indiana? Ohio? Pennsylvania? It was somewhere further north, he knew, because of how cold it kept getting.

Alongside the slaves pushing carts of blood-buckets, he noticed other carts full of stripped bones. Up ahead, across a frosty field, a dugout pit awaited them. The pushers of the wheelbarrows spilled their contents into the pit, then turned around swiftly and went back for more. Shesh and the overseer stopped a few yards away, then shoved Fishhook forward. He hobbled to the edge of the pit. The smell hit him before he saw it. To either side of him, the other Earth-liners hauled their buckets to the edge. There was about a fifteen-foot drop, to the surface of the crimson-black lake. He couldn't tell how deep it was, just that it got a little higher with every bucket they emptied into it. Amidst all the bobbing, gleaming bones, a pink-slick shape paddled and kicked languidly, turning over, dipping under and back up, then backstroking its way to the steep shoreline.

Fishhook stood and stared. A deep gulp rolled through him as the naked figure clawed its way out of the blood and bones and climbed the hillside. Knotted, stocky muscles rolled and flexed beneath the dripping skin. Balthazar reached the top, grinned joyously, then shook himself like a wet dog, raining crimson mist all over Fishhook and the two soldiers who'd escorted him here.

"Ronny!" Balthazar hooted, grabbing him into a bearhug that felt like it would crush his ribs, leaving the whole front of him sopping and stinky. "I've missed you, little buddy! Gets so lonely, you got no idea, carryin' on the Daddy's good work like this. What're y'all lookin' at me like that for?"

"Nothing, Great Balthazar," said Shesh.

"Oh, quit blowin' sunshine up my ass! I get it. There's some things changin' around here. It's okay if you're confused. Over the next couple weeks, you're gonna notice plenty more things changin'."

"Of course, sir. Oh, some of those scouts you sent out came back. They wanted me to tell you—"

"You can tell me later. Get gone and take the rest of these yahoos with you." Bathazar flung his arms about, indicating the folks with wheelbarrows.

"But Great Balthazar, trust me, you're gonna wanna know—"

"*I said git gone!*" Balthazar's grin split wider. He cast one eye over his shoulder, back towards the lake of blood and bones behind him. "I been…doin' some scoutin' of my own, you might say. You'll hear all about it soon enough. Right now, I just want some time on my own. Just me an' my little buddy Ronny." He draped a heavy arm around Fishhook's shoulders. Fishhook no longer even shrank from the touch. The extra warmth was a relief.

The overseer walked away, clapped loudly, and shouted, "Okay, you all heard the man! Get lost! Don't worry, we've got plenty else for you to do around here. Great Balthazar wants some privacy."

Once they were all gone, Balthazar said, "Oh Ronny, stop starin' at me like that! You're gonna make me bashful! What is it, little buddy?"

Fishhook let out a wet, grunting sigh, lifting a shaky hand to point.

He could tell something was different about Balthazar—other than that the guy was naked and soaked in blood—but at first, he couldn't put his finger on what. Now that most of the blood had run off Balthazar's body and pooled at his feet, Fishhook's eyes started processing it. Balthazar's skin had taken on a yellowish tinge, with engorged, blackish veins standing out all over his muscular arms, chest and neck, like he'd caught some kind of infection by swimming around in all those human remains.

Then Fishhook spotted the black, puckered gash in Balthazar's side…same spot as the spear wound on Jesus in all the pictures, he couldn't help noticing. The cut had mostly healed shut, but all the dark trails seemed to spread from the spot. Not all the blood was from the pit, either. On either side of his forehead, a pair of curved horns now stuck out. The skin at their base was raw and tortured, weeping red from where the horns had split through the skin.

Fishhook now noticed a small bundle of bones clutched in Balthazar's left fist. His eyes went back and forth, from the bones to Balthazar's forehead, and it hit him: *those horns aren't growing out of his skull.*

"Oh, huh, right, this." Balthazar chuckled, walked over to where he'd left his pants, and hopped back into them. "C'mon, little buddy, lets take a walk. We got us a lot of catching up to do."

They walked to the cracked, weed-strewn edge of an old parking lot. Balthazar sat down on a bench, set his little collection of bones to one side, then patted the space on the other for Fishhook to sit. As Fishhook sat down, Balthazar drew and opened a pocketknife from his trousers. He pulled a toothless jawbone from the pile, and started whittling at it like a twig.

"Man, Ronny, I can't wait for you to be able to meet my new girlfriend! Huh? Aw, no, I don't mean like one of *those.* No, I mean my *real* girlfriend…the same one who was talkin' to the Daddy for all those years, who's now talkin' to me." He waved a hand around his new horns, as though tracing a halo in the air. "That' s what this here makeover's all about. It's a work in progress, sure, but…oh boy, by the time she's ready to come through, I'm gonna look gorgeous for her! So you'd best hang in there, Ronny, 'cause if you're still alive by the time she gets here, you're gonna be the first to see us together, side by side, proud and victorious, ready to usher in the new world. She was just tellin' me all about it, how it's gonna look…

"That's right, I was just down there talkin' to her, in my new swimmin' pool, when you came up to say hi! I used to think I had to fly aaaaaaaaaalll the way home to the swamp where I grew up, if I wanted to talk to her. Then it all fell into place, see, so I'm like… what's that the Crimbone always say? *Listen to the lands and listen to the blood?* That's when it hit me, so I started makin' my little swimming pools, wherever I stop for a while. And hey, what do you know, I was right! See, when you got that much blood, soakin' into that much land…she can speak to me loud and clear, anywhere! She's been tellin' me so many wonderful stories, of what's been happenin' all over this great country of ours. Whatever those scouts who just got back have to say, it won't hold a candle to what she was just tellin' me. Things are about to heat up in a big way, Ronny ol' buddy, gonna get a lot more interesting, real quick. *Real* quick.

"She's dead, Ronny." Balthazar sniffled a little. "No, not *my* girlfriend. Hell, she's only just startin' to get to live, like she ain't done in a long time. No, I mean the High Natural's girlfriend. *My* girlfriend just got through tellin' me all about it. My real daddy's dead, too. Between you and me, I's actually sadder about that first death than the second. Maybe it ought'a be the other way around, but…I d'know, hearin' about the High Natural's girlfriend bein' dead, it's like one more piece of *the* Daddy gone forever, like I really am all that's left of him." Balthazar let out a louder, gurgling sniffle. A tear ran down one of his leathery, malformed cheeks. "Shit, Ronny…Now you've seen me cry!" Balthazar threw an arm around Fishhook's shoulder, this time squeezing tight enough that it got harder and harder to breath. "I hope you know, Ronny, how much that means you mean to me, how long it's been since I let anyone see me cry! You ain't gonna tell anyone, are you? Hehheh, no, I don't reckon you will. Before long, we ought'a be about due for our reunion with that dirty little High Natural. Once that fight's out of the way, there won't be nothin' left, Ronny, between us and the beautiful new world comin' together, just like the Daddy always envisioned."

Balthazar let go and went back to whittling. Fishhook caught his breath and glanced at the bone Balthazar was working on. It looked more and more like one of the new horns on Balthazar's forehead.

"From what my girlfriend tells me," Balthazar went on, "anyone who's anyone on this big ol' chessboard is all findin' their way towards Vermont...towards a little place called Bratt-o-borrow. She says that's where she'll finally be able to step forward, into the flesh, where everyone'll finally get to meet her. She's been talkin' to all of 'em, y'know. I's just the only one she's let know who I's really hearin'. 'Cause she loves me, 'cause I's the one she's waited all this time for. I reckon that's where the High Natural means to show up, so that's where our little band's gonna head next. In a few minutes, I'm gonna go gather up everyone, share the big news. After that, I'm gonna have to take off, get the word out to the rest of my whole big gang that I've been growin' all over the place, tell 'em it's time for us all to get together, so we can surround that place, sweep on in, put the big ol' finishing touches on the Daddy's good work. But I wanted you to hear it first, little buddy. Damn, it's been so nice, havin' you around to talk to. Old Lords, this is gonna be so damn sweet!"

BRATTLEBORO

ONE

Sheldon felt all kinds of fucked up. At the moment, he could only identify two kinds specifically. First, he'd been unconscious for a while, so his brain still felt plastered to the back of his skull, because a giant black Crimbone had punched him in the forehead. Secondly, his abdomen was on fire.

He bolted upright. Heavy blankets tumbled away from him. He'd been sweating like a whore beneath them, so he went straight from burning to freezing in a few seconds, within the chilly room. He toppled sideways and landed on a hardwood floor. Rooms away, people moved around and talked. Their every whisper and shift vibrated through the boards. Whatever touched the floors of this building seemed to cut him from a thousand directions. It would have nauseated him except there was no longer room in his stomach for anything but the sharp, centralized pain, shaking him to pieces, soaking him in more sweat. He had on the same clothes he'd worn in the train station, minus his coat and blades—*the blades!*

Sheldon grabbed the edge of the mattress, pulled himself up to his knees and clawed at his shirt. It would suffocate him if he didn't get it off. When he swayed back, his eyes rolled everywhere. The room was sparsely furnished, with the bed, nightstand, and dresser. There was a couch parked at the other end. Posters for Earth-line Goth and Punk bands decorated the walls, along with black construction paper cutouts of bats and skulls and such. The one window in here looked so ghostly ashen that there might as well be a bleached sheet hanging over it outside. He couldn't focus on anything. He *needed* to focus, needed to find his knives…

…Because he heard and felt the people responding to his loud awakening. The blazing trail through his gut told him who one of them was.

He couldn't get himself together, though. The beast's presence overpowered him like a drug overdose.

So what? You know how to deal with bad drugs. Hell, you were forced to snort your way to a cocaine overdose when you were nine. This feels a little like that. Work through this, like you were trained to work through that.

His lower legs were numb. He fought through it. By the time he stood up, the pain hadn't lessened. The worst vibrations were headed towards his door. He wanted to grab something for support. His hands flailed for the bedposts but couldn't find them.

The knob turned and the door swung inward. In stepped Zane. His raised fist clutched a belt that sagged with two long knives in their scabbards. He looked like he might extend it as an offering, except he wasn't sure if he should yet. Behind Zane, there stood the High Natural. Sheldon barely recognized him. Hell, it had been six years. Fresh scars and bulk could never mask some figures, though. Behind the High Natural, there stood a Crimbone woman Sheldon didn't recognize. She was really tan, maybe half-white, half-Hispanic. Her maroon eyes looked strikingly out of place among her other features, like some beautiful demon wearing a humanoid face it had peeled off of someone else. It didn't matter which Earth-line ethnicities her ancestors had mingled with. She was pure Crimbone, beautiful in that lean, hard, cruel kind of way. There was a weird tenderness in her otherworldly eyes, in the way her hand clutched and rubbed the High Natural's shoulder.

Everyone looked unpleasantly surprised to see Sheldon up and about. Considering how he felt, he'd probably feel the same way if he looked in a mirror.

"Damn, Zane," said the Crimbone woman. "I thought all you did was punch him in the head."

"Don't look at me," said Zane.

"I ain't," she said. "I'm looking at him, wondering how long it'll take him to drop, or vomit his guts out."

Sheldon swayed, bracing his legs as best he could. "*Beasts*," he spat.

Zane lowered the belt and knives and stepped closer. "Sheldon, buddy. C'mon, man, chill out. Don't make me hit you again."

Sheldon pulled himself into a shaky fighting stance. "Bullshit! You brought me to *them* so they could kill me."

"C'mon, man, you're the one wanted to find 'em so bad."

"Not like this. I never should've hooked up with you…I told you, we needed to…"

"If you hadn't, you'd be likelier to end up going toe to toe with 'em…*if* you ever managed to find 'em. 'Cause, kid, it looks like your other plan didn't pan out."

Sheldon simmered down some. He kept his eyes on Zane. "How long have I been out?"

"Define *out*. What's the last thing you remember?"

"The train station."

"Which one?"

"What do you think? That fucking weirdass ghost-train you were telling me to get on, back in the border-town."

"Wait, you mean...*Shit*, kid! I knew you were in and out of it the whole time, but *damn*."

"Where the hell exactly are we now?"

"Greenfield. Massachusetts," said Zane. "Least that's what the place used to be called. Damn town's deader than where we caught that spookyass train from. You're seriously telling me you don't—"

"*Yes, I'm seriously telling you, I don't remember shit!* What the fuck are we doing in Massachusetts? I thought we were going to Brattleboro."

"We did. That's where the last train dropped us off. Rob wasn't there yet. I hotwired a truck and followed the land's voices here—and hey, look who the fuck we ran into." Zane cocked his head sideways at Rob Coscan.

"Whose house is this?" said Sheldon.

"How the fuck should I know?" said Zane. "Someone who used to live in Greenfield, before everyone cut and ran."

"Let me guess," said Sheldon. "Brattleboro's deserted, too."

"Nah, a fair chunk of the Earth-line population's still hiding out there. A few hundred or so, I'd say. Some freakyass, gangly, hairy little fucker stepped up as their leader. He's been holding everyone together. They're calling him the *new mayor*. Some of their police department's held out, too. Not that their jurisdictional authority counts for shit anymore, but they ain't been completely useless, either."

"Who else was on that weirdass train?"

"Mostly Crimbone, plus a few civilian Schomites and even some Earth-line people. Most of the civilians hung back in Brattleboro. Look, do me a favor and get your shit together before you make me explain anything else. I don't wanna have to keep repeating myself every five fucking minutes."

Sheldon tried to shake more of the floating sensation from his head. The blazing agony in his gut hadn't subsided, but he was managing it better. He looked past Zane, at the High Natural, then back at Zane. "You've filled him in?"

"I've filled him in on what you told me, *about the Familiar.*" Zane leaned forward a little, some urgent implication in his tone.

Sheldon looked again at the Crimbone woman's hand on the High Natural's shoulder…something about the just so-way her palm and fingers worked to calm him.

The High Natural doesn't know Sally's dead, does he?

Why hasn't Zane told him?

Either way, he sure hasn't wasted time getting his wife—my sister—out of his system, since he abandoned her. Will he even care when he finds out? Fuck this guy.

"What else, Zane?" the High Natural grunted.

"About what?" said Zane.

"What else has happened?"

"Lots of shit. I'll tell you later."

"Where's Sally?" Deadly urgency electrified the words…more than deadly. Rob Coscan wasn't just physically changed. Those eyes burned with more than the brain behind them was built to hold, powered by a soul that didn't know how to stop asking for more.

"*I said later,*" Zane barked. "You and this kid need to talk. A lot of folks went through a lot of shit to put you two face to face, so you better start getting really fucking well acquainted. Better act like adults about it, too, for once in either of your dumbass lives."

Rob shrugged off the woman and shoved past Zane. He moved towards Sheldon. The man wore his blades in plain view. The closer he drew, the hotter Sheldon's gut pulsed. The last time they'd seen each other, on that long-ago night on Marlboro Mountain, Sheldon had been half as tall as his assailant. Now he was almost as tall, yet he couldn't shake the feeling of looking up into the eyes of an enraged giant. Back then, those eyes had been an out-of-control inferno. Now they glowed with more of a slow burn. Before Sheldon knew it, he forgot to feel anything but…what was it…fascination?

"I hear we're on the same page," said Rob Coscan.

"Are we?"

"Yeah," said Rob Coscan. "I'm headed for the Old World, to end all this. Zane tells me you mean to do the same." He sounded like he was inviting Sheldon along on a road trip to shake down some asshole who owed them money.

"Depends what you mean by *end all this*," said Sheldon.

The High Natural didn't seem the least bit impatient. Somehow, that felt like the most chillingly inhuman thing about him. "To stab the source, to cut us all free from the Spirah Gods, so we can clean up this mess they've made."

"Okay," said Sheldon. "I'm with you so far. I'm told I'll need you to get us *through* the old world once you're there."

Rob Coscan stared through Sheldon's open shirt, at the black scar on the solar plexus. "It makes sense," he sighed. "I don't know why I didn't figure it out sooner."

"Figure what out?"

"We're brothers, Sheldon Wildfire. Like it or not, there's no other word for this connection between us…not in any language either of us know. From here on out, we fight side by side as brothers."

Something in the voice caressed Sheldon's brain, from the inside. He squirmed against it, but he couldn't make it stop. Rob's mouth moved, forming the words, yet the voice seemed to speak from within Sheldon's own mind, like his own thoughts. Each thought seemed to form a fraction of a second before hearing the words. Sheldon's whole frame quivered against it. He wanted to shout, *Get out of my head, you genocidal asshole!*

Before he could stop himself, though, he heard himself say, "I see your point. Hell, I guess you don't like it any better than I do."

The High Natural smiled. "Actually, I like it fine."

"Sounds like you've really thought about this."

"I only pieced it together just now. What don't you like about it?"

Sheldon let out a bark of bitter laughter. "You're the guy *who fucking murdered my parents and my sister*, and you're asking me why I don't like having to accept you as a brother?"

Rob shrugged. "They started it. You're the guy who tried to murder my girlfriend—your other sister—in front of me. If I can get over it, you've got no excuse not to."

"Like you say, it's something to work with."

Sheldon extended his hand. The High Natural caught him, not by the palm, but by the wrists. Before Sheldon knew it, the burning in his gut subsided to a gentle throb. It wasn't just the immediate physical agony that abated. It was like some weight he'd carried all these years had suddenly lifted, something so constant, he'd forgotten it was there.

Once they let go of each other, Sheldon looked back to Zane. "What about the rest—those other Crimbone, the ones on that train?"

"They followed us here," said Zane. "They're outside, along with the ones these two picked up on their way from Texas." He jacked his thumb over his shoulder, at Rob Coscan and the Crimbone woman.

"What are they doing out there?"

"Waiting for you. For a guy who spent the whole trip out of it, you got 'em pretty taken with you. Must have

286 ~ MATT SPENCER

something to do with that weird urge they all felt, to *not* slaughter all those other Spirelights who also caught that train. Right now, everyone's just waiting for you boys to kiss and make up, so we can get moving."

Sheldon looked at Rob, looked at the woman in the doorway, then back at Zane. He took a deep breath. "Okay. Let's go."

"Your coat and backpack are out in the kitchen," said Zane. "You'll want a fresh shirt. Actually, probably two or three more. 'Cause *baby, it's cold outside.*"

"It's cold in *here*," said Sheldon.

"You'll get warm once you're moving."

Sheldon peered at Rob. "Once we get to Brattleboro, do we have any idea what to do...about how to find this gateway back to Deschemb we're supposed to look for?"

Zane looked at Rob and Sheldon. "Hey, you two assholes are supposed to figure that out between you, right?"

Sheldon shrugged and nodded. Zane grimaced and tossed him the belt with the knives. Sheldon caught it, threaded it on, and followed everyone through the apartment.

Out in the kitchen, he started layering up, then said, "I gotta piss like a racehorse."

Zane pointed down the hallway. Sheldon found it and did his business. When he came out, he still expected to find everyone ready to spring a trap on him. Instead, they all waited impatiently.

"Can y'all hold up?" said the Crimbone woman. "I actually gotta go too." As she headed down the hall to the bathroom, she pointed at Sheldon and said, "Keep this one here. I don't wanna miss how this all goes down."

Once she returned, they all went out. The front door led into a narrow, winding hallway. Through a small window on a door at the end of the hall, a sea of shapes milled about…Crimbone shapes. Sheldon couldn't see any of their faces yet, because the ground rose up from the far end of the porch. He sure knew how to spot Crimbone, though, and the bastards were all around him.

The porch turned out to be a long suspended wooden walkway, leading to a short staircase up the hillside. The world looked like a fuzzy drawing that hadn't been shaded in, except in a few places. All the whiteness hurt Sheldon's eyes. He focused on the Crimbone as he climbed towards them. They were an incongruous crowd, that was for sure; some burly, leather-clad biker-types, some old cowboys who looked cut from the same cloth as Jesse and Zane, like they'd walked straight out of a wax museum, some lanky hippies and train-hopper kids, some renegade cops, in a collage of skin-shades. They all had three things in common. One, obviously, was the weapons of black metal strapped to their sides. They were all under-dressed for this weather and didn't seem to mind. Then there was the unified, timber-wolf steeliness in their eyes, which they all now directed towards Sheldon.

As he got closer, he realized something even spookier about their collective gaze: it mirrored Rob's eyes from moments ago, when he'd spoken in that uncanny, powerful voice that had seemed to echo from within Sheldon's head.

He's been leading them, commanding them all, in that same voice. Now he's in my head like he's in theirs. Is he in Zane's head, too? What have I gotten myself into?

Sheldon and Rob Coscan climbed the stairs side by side. Something about their new union—this so-called *brotherhood*—already felt oddly natural. Rob was the only one not wearing a coat. He must have put on quite a few layers of shirts. The guy didn't even shiver.

"So what now?" Sheldon asked him.

Rob stared forward, over the heads of the surrounding Crimbone. "We head back to Brattleboro. Once we get there…well…guess we'll have to find out together, won't we?"

"Great. Where's the caravan?"

"Right here," said the Crimbone woman.

"I meant—"

"Everyone here knows what the fuck you mean," she said. "The roads around here are all snowed over. There won't be any snowplows coming through. Best start leading the way, boys." She swept her hand in a mock-dramatic gesture.

"Sorry," Sheldon said as he passed her, "I…don't think I caught your name?"

She gave him a deadpan, almost pitying look, like she thought he was awkwardly trying to hit on her. "Remelea."

"Hey. I'm Sheldon." He didn't try to shake hands, which she didn't seem to mind.

"Yeah, I know. I'm almost as sick of hearing about you as this crazy fuck." She gave Rob's chest a swat.

The crowd parted. Sheldon's legs had gotten used to deep snow over the last few months. He knew Rob had spent plenty of winters in Vermont. Zane and Remelea trudged behind them 'til they passed through the crowd, then they stopped among their people. Both Rob and Sheldon turned back, startled. Remelea gave Rob a look and Zane gave one to Sheldon. Rob and Sheldon looked at each other, shared a deep sigh and started walking. The others followed.

TWO

They trekked a few snowy miles along a lonely highway. Sometimes Sheldon almost forgot about the rag-tag band crunching along behind them. Such icy calm was almost soothing. Then he remembered that the guy next to him—his new *brother*—had led more Crimbone to slaughter more Spirelights than any leader in living memory.

Sheldon felt the need to break the silence. "What's on your mind?" he asked Rob.

"Puttergong. Hell of a thing about that critter, sticking around like it did."

"Zane didn't tell you why?" Again, Sheldon thought of everything else Zane obviously hadn't told Rob.

"Puttergong gave you one answer, you told it to Zane, and Zane told me. I want to hear you say it."

Sheldon tapped the pommels at his sides. "These blades I wear were made to stab the gods."

"So were mine," said Rob.

"Sure, but first, we need to get to the Old World. Somehow, you being the High Natural is supposed to make it so we can find our way *to* the gods through the Old World. Something tells me it's gonna take both your blades and mine to reach them."

"Huh," Rob muttered.

"You aren't sure you believe it?"

"I ain't sure of anything anymore." Right now, Rob almost sounded like just a dude, someone you might kick back with over a few beers. "I'd sure like to know where that critter got off to, though. So I hear you've been back to Brattleboro, since the old days."

"*The old days.*" Sheldon shook his head. "That's one way to put it."

"Look, really, I'm glad to let all that shit go if you are."

Sheldon thought, *Easy for you to say, asshole. You're not the one who came downstairs at eleven years old and found your whole family butchered.*

Then, *Yeah, and I'm not the one who was just living a ho-hum Earth-line life one minute, then met a great girl who I fell in love with, and the next thing I knew, had to deal with a carload of joy-riding lunatics rolling into my town, killing my friends, trying to kill me, while they hunted her down.*

Sheldon cast an eye back at their entourage. "Doesn't look like we have much of a choice."

"If you got a better idea, I'm all ears."

"Y'know, you're smarter than I expected. Anyway, yeah, I've been back to Brattleboro."

"So how is the ol' place?"

"About the same. Some of the stores are different…well, were."

Rob winced. "Right. So what did you find there?"

"What do you want to hear about?"

"Any clue as to what we're supposed to do there…? Oh hell, I *know* what we're supposed to do. It's just…"

"I know what you mean, but…shouldn't you be the one telling me?"

"What, 'cause I'm the High Natural? Seems like everyone's got their own ideas about what that even means."

"What do *you* think the High Natural is?"

"Something that doesn't have a place in this world. That's all I know anymore." Rob looked around, as if for a better answer. He shivered. "This world's so damn *cold.* Why'd it get so cold all of a sudden? I can't smell anything in this cold, still air. It doesn't feel real, like I'm a ghost drifting through it. I can't tell whether it's wrong or I'm wrong for it."

Sheldon peered over curiously. Right when he'd almost gotten used to Rob, the guy's voice had changed again...like some truly otherworldly consciousness, waking up in a strange shell, struggling to make a human mouth pronounce its alien thoughts. Before Sheldon knew it, he reached out and put a hand on the guy's shoulder. "Hang on, man. It won't be much longer."

"Yeah." Rob smiled at something only he could see. "We're going home, Sheldon. We're headed back to the real world, where we can taste and touch and smell everything again, where we'll be able to hear the real voices."

Sheldon peered off ahead. "Say, you ever know a guy in Brattleboro called Lou?"

"Oh, Louis? Aw, fuck yeah, we go way back! Shit, when was the last time I hung out with that motherfucker, anyway...? You telling me you've met him?"

"I have."

"Shit, man, how's he been?"

"You mean the Schomite guy, right? I mean...the one with the long, dark hair, the one who...?"

Rob's face lit up boyishly. A new spring entered his step. "Oh yeah, that's the man!"

"He told me he was of Crimbone descent, yeah. 'Cept he didn't choose to make...what do you guys call it? The *Call*? Anyway, yeah, he says he pretty much just...never left Brattleboro."

"Figures. No one ever leaves Brattleboro. That's what they say, you know? Everyone comes back eventually. I heard a story once, about an ancient Native American curse, created a vortex. Abenaki, I believe. Sure looks like someone called that one right, huh? *In the end*, you know? That vortex, anyone who matters to the lands of that town, it sucks 'em all back there eventually. Hey, man, I can't wait to catch up with Louis! It's been too damn long, man, you know?"

"Yeah," Sheldon sighed. "I do."

~

The pack descended off an overpass, onto a lonely back road. Far ahead, headlights bloomed through mist and glistened towards the pack. Zane sensed the source before he saw the faded red paint behind the lights and gleaming plow blade. He wanted to trudge past Rob and Sheldon, be the first to meet the glare as it ground to a halt. All around, he sensed hands edging towards weapons.

"Ease up, boys and girls," Rob called back, "I'll do the talking. Or the fighting. Me and Sheldon here." He clapped the kid on the shoulder.

Everyone but Rob had stopped. He approached the oncoming van like any casual pedestrian. Sheldon followed, but kept back. Zane watched both them and the approaching phantasmic vehicle. He glanced at Remelea. She stared forward with him. The van's engine cut off, the headlights stayed on, and the driver climbed out.

The driver and the leader of the pack approached each other. Maybe it was the way the light caught their silhouettes, but right then, Rob and Jesse seemed to have matching height and breadth. Zane was the same size as Jesse. He was used to looking down at Rob by at least two or three inches. Jesse's coat fluttered open. The hilt of his knife gleamed.

"Finally decided to follow your pal's good example, huh, Jesse Fuckin' Karn?" Rob swaggered, arms swinging at his sides. He sounded wild, delirious.

"What example's that, Rob?" said Jesse. "Good to see you too, by the way."

"To join the winning side, you mean."

Jesse looked around. "There's a winning side? In all this crap?"

"Sure there is, right here."

Jesse leaned sideways and said past Rob, "Oh, hey, there you are, Zane. You hear what the High Natural just said? He says this here is the *winning side*. Is that what you think we got here, brother?"

"What the fuck are you asking him for?" Rob growled low, close to Jesse's face. "*This is* my *pack*. Zane's in it. I'm the one looking you in the eye."

"Rob," said Jesse, "why are you trying to pick a fight?"

"Ain't that why you're here? Wanna strap me down to another operating table and leave me to rot in another basement?"

"I don't know. Is that what I need to do, to keep the people I'm responsible for alive and safe?"

"Oh, yeah, sure." Rob splayed his arms and roared, *"Just look around at what a great job all you old fuckers have done, keeping everyone safe!* That's the only reason anyone puts up with your shit, you know that? 'Cause you keep 'em low and convinced they need you, *to keep them safe*. See all these folks back there? You can't twist their heads around like that anymore. Because *their blood tells them to follow me*."

Jesse looked around at the pack following Rob, the one that included Zane and Remelea and Sheldon. He met Rob's glaring eyes again. "You know what I think? I don't think any of these people know what the fuck they're following. Just like you still don't have the first fucking clue what you're letting work through you, what you're about to unleash on us all with your crazy, stupid fucking—"

A wet thunderclap echoed as Rob clocked Jesse square in the jaw. Jesse spun, stumbled, and caught himself against the front of the van. Rob loomed in on him. "Didn't I just tell you? Can't you smell it? I ain't a fledgling anymore. *You don't get to boss me around anymore, you sonofabitch!*" Rob's palms settled on the pommels of his knives.

Jesse's eyes darkened. *"Fucking out of control whelp!"*

Jesse's blade sang free. So did both of Rob's. Something heavy and metallic banged the flat of Jesse's knife, sending it wild. Something almost as hard slammed into Rob's gut. Both men staggered. They righted themselves and stared at the one guy who could have gotten between them like that and stayed in one piece.

"Quit fucking around, both of you," Zane growled. He brandished his hammer, took another look in both their eyes, then clipped it back to his belt.

Rob blinked at Zane. "What the hell's gotten into you? Thought you said you'd picked a side."

"I'm on both your sides, you idiots," said Zane. "Rob, from the minute we heard you were on the move, I knew once you and Jesse came face to face, you'd act like a couple junior-league thugs on a playground."

"Hang on a second," said Jesse. "You're telling me *that's* why you ran out on me, for him, this whole time?"

"I got my own reasons," said Zane. "But yeah, I thought this might happen."

Jesse cast an eye at Rob and Sheldon, side by side, apparently cool with each other. "Guess I'm behind on a lot of things."

"Yeah. You've got no idea."

Jesse met Rob's eyes and pointed at him. "Don't think you're off the hook. You've still got plenty to answer for, more than you—"

"I just said there's more than *you* know, Jess," said Zane. "Rob and Sheldon have this crazy idea hatched between 'em, and…well, if there's anything to it, they're both about to become *not-our-problem-anymore*, pretty damn soon." Zane rattled off the short of it, to the best of his understanding. He looked back at Rob and Sheldon. "That about right, boys?"

Rob and Sheldon looked at each other and both said, "Yeah."

Jesse looked over all three of them, then at the poised pack at their back. For the first time, he spotted Remelea. She stood at the fore, smirking humorlessly. His hand drifted towards his blade. Zane's hand, in turn, drifted towards his hammer. *You stupid motherfucker, don't do it.*

Jesse's hand slipped into his coat pocket instead, squeezing around something that crinkled and crackled. "Okay. That explains a lot."

"What do you mean?"

"The lands seem to just keep finding one way or another to push anyone who's anyone to Brattleboro."

Rob elbowed Sheldon. "What I tell you? The fuckin' vortex, man."

"And Rob, Sheldon," Jesse went on, "wherever you two wind up from there, you *ain't* gonna be *not our problem.* Pretty much the opposite, from how it sounds to me. Just, looks like we're gonna have nothing to do but try to hold out 'til you guys get done what you need to get done. Fuck…"

"You're telling us," said Sheldon. "So who'd you bring with you?"

"The United Deschembines. And Sam and Anya."

"In Brattleboro? How the hell did you get all of 'em there?"

"Having Sam and Anya's help made it possible to pull the caravan together, fast as we did. Anyway, they're back there now, squaring things up with that Liam guy."

"Wait, hold up," Rob cut in. "You mean Liam *Cameron?*"

"Oh, you know him," said Jesse. "That figures."

"Yeah," said Rob. "We use to fence and do martial arts together. That was before either of us ever thought we'd actually have to use swords and shit in a real fight."

"Yeah, I met that guy too." Zane smirked. "So he the one told you which way Sheldon and I went?"

"Yeah," said Jesse. "Makes more and more sense why the lands chose Brattleboro for where everything ends and begins, huh? They sure have room for a good mechanic, though."

"Is Sally with them?" Rob said.

Everything fell into an awkward silence. Jesse looked at Sheldon and Zane. "Neither of you told him?"

"Told me what?" Rob looked around frantically, like a little kid lost in the woods. *"Told me what?"*

"Rob," said Jesse. "Sally's dead."

~

Rob didn't react at first, like he was still waiting for the answer. He turned slowly and seemed to stare right through the whole pack. His lips quivered fiercer and fiercer. His eyes glazed over and drifted to Sheldon. As he moved towards the kid, he noticed the handles of his own knives, pressed to the bone against the palms of his frozen hands. It was the strongest sensation in his body, aside from the shaking sickness that wafted from his gut. When had he drawn his blades? Had he even sheathed them after pulling them on Jesse? No wonder Sheldon stood so tense, ready to draw.

Rob didn't sheath his blades, but he turned the points away from Sheldon. His legs went out and his knees hit the ground. Snow seeped through his jeans against his knees and lower legs. He kept staring up at Sheldon. Jesse, Zane, and Remelea kept shouting his name for some reason. Jesse almost rushed in, but Zane grabbed him and held him back. Rob looked down and saw the tip of one black knife pointed at his neck, extended from his own fist. His whole upper body sank towards it.

"*Rob, quit it*," Sheldon yelled.

Rob felt the razor tip prick the soft spot under his chin. He gave a hushed gasp and drew it away. The world kept floating for another moment. He blinked, and it was cold, still, quiet and real again. Sally wasn't in it anymore. He fought to wrap his head around that last part, at the same time fighting futilely to deny it.

"How," he finally rasped. "*Why?*"

Zane placed a hand on his shoulder. "She died a hero, man. That's all you gotta know. She went out like a champ from what I hear, like she—"

Rob twisted, shrugging Zane off violently. "*Shut the fuck up with that bullshit!*" He said in a low tremble, "All I really wanted was for her to be safe. That's all. The rest was all just crap I let the rest of you assholes fill my head with. But now I'm still here, when she—she—I don't…" The flats of his blades settled in the snow at his sides. "I just don't…I just don't…*Ah, fuck! Fuck!*"

Remelea knelt and squeezed Rob's shoulders. He almost swatted her away, but he didn't. *Hell, this must be the best news she's heard all day.* No. That wasn't what her hands told his shoulders. Whatever else they were to each other, whatever she'd wanted from him, whatever he had or hadn't been able to give her of himself, she had to be the most stupidly loyal friend in history. Right now, Remelea was the only reason Rob didn't lose it. He let go of one of his blades so he could reach back and squeeze one of her hands. Eventually, he eased her away, took hold of the knife again, and forced himself to his feet. He sheathed both knives and met Sheldon's gaze. "This shit needs to quit happening to people. Please, Sheldon, just help me stop this from happening."

THREE

A Vermont winter's nightfall was on its way in when they saw the streets of Brattleboro. The rest of the pack hung back and made camp on the outskirts, for now. Rob had given the order, following Jesse's strong advice. Rob, Remelea, and Sheldon rode in the back of the Big Red Beast.

The van wound down off an exit ramp from Ninety-One, onto upper Canal Street, next to the ruins of an Outlet Center strip-mall. They didn't need the plow from here, it turned out. Apparently, Liam had kept folks busy. They passed the remains of a Burger King, a Price Chopper, and an Econo Lodge motel. Jesse remembered that last spot well. So would Rob and Zane. What a reunion spot that place could have made, had they stopped there. All they were missing was Sally.

"You knew she was dead by the time you found Rob," Jesse said to Zane.

Zane rode shotgun. "Yeah."

"So why'd neither of you tell him?" Jesse glanced at both Zane and Sheldon.

In the back, Rob was so far away, he might as well be in the Old World already.

"I decided it would be better to keep him rational long enough to get other shit taken care of first," said Zane. "So what do you think the deal is with Brattleboro, other than whatever business Rob and Sheldon have here?"

"I don't know yet," said Jesse.

Sheldon asked, "Is Janie okay?"

"She's still with the United Deschembines," said Jesse.

"Where are they?"

"Well out of our way, for right now. Don't worry, she's safe."

"Sally wasn't safe with the United Deschembines," Rob muttered. Everyone in the van jolted a little, now that he finally spoke.

Jesse spotted Rob glaring through the rear-view mirror. "What would you have done if you'd found her alive with us, Rob?"

"I was gonna take her with me."

Remelea sat in the opposite back corner from Rob. She huddled up, as far from everyone else as she could get. Back at the Renaissance Kingdom, Jesse had told her of his decision to keep Rob chained beneath ground, and why. He'd watched her reactions close enough, and he'd still shown her to where Rob was. He should have known she'd do what she'd done, setting Rob loose and going with him. As he spied on her through the mirror, he figured he knew the real reason she'd done it.

The Big Red Beast reached Harmony Parking Lot. No one was out and about. Jesse took the same spot he'd picked last time he was here, six years ago in the dead of night, listening to a CB, watching the red brick building to the left. He'd acted alone that night, without Cabinet permission. When enough time passed without anything happening, he'd gotten out and decided he needed a drink. Since those days, a new bar had opened right in front of the same old parking space, with a wooden fenced-in area of sidewalk and a stained oak bear sculpture standing guard by the door. Of course the place was closed now. On that long ago night, Jesse had found a couple other bars back up Elliot Street. The scene there hadn't appealed to him, so he'd found his way back down to Main Street. That's where he'd run into an addled, banged-up girl named Sally Wildfire, searching desperately for the boy she loved...a wild, restless kid named Rob Coscan.

"Okay," Jesse said now, "let's have a look around." Once everyone was out of the van, he drew near Rob. "Your head clear enough to do what you gotta go do?"

"Sure," said Rob. "Is yours?"

Before Jesse could answer, some smell on the cold, still air paralyzed him.

"Jesse?" It was Zane, right behind him.

"Quiet, everyone," said Jesse, in a tone not even the High Natural was about to argue with.

The whole town suddenly felt like a dream. Jesse followed the smell of the dream out of Harmony Parking Lot, out onto Elliot Street. The others followed. Up the street on the left were the same two old bars...actually, no, one of them had a different name and looked swankier. Swankier, sure, except that the front door swung open and shut in the wind, on a broken lock. A short young man stepped out of the place. He wore black clothes that were faded to gray in places, with matching long hair. Jesse used to have long, black hair just like that, back before he took to keeping his head shaved. He also used to be just as skinny. He hadn't been that short, though. The kid had gotten that from his mother.

Jesse approached the young man. "What are you up to in this town, son?"

"Same thing as everyone. Just doing my part."

Jesse smiled. "No doubt. What part's that?"

A shout broke the reverie: "Louis!" Rob barreled past Jesse and grabbed the black-haired young man in a bear hug. "How you been, motherfucker?"

"Good as anyone, Rob. How 'bout you?"

"Pretty shitty, honestly." Rob's eyes and voice were still thick with tears.

Jesse stepped in and shoved them apart. He grabbed the kid by the skinny shoulders and looked him in the eye. "Louis, it's me! Your dad!"

"I know. I guess Sheldon gave you that drawing like I told him to."

"Yeah! How'd you know that little punk was gonna run into me? Ah, fuck it, never mind. I'm sorry I didn't figure it out earlier. I'd have been here sooner."

"No, you wouldn't."

"But I—"

"Dad. It's okay. Really. You were where you needed to be, and I'm proud of you."

"*Proud of me*...Louis, I'm so fucking proud of *you!*"

"Thanks, Dad. That means a lot."

"You've become a great Crimbone."

"I'm not Crimbone, Dad."

Jesse blinked rapidly, drawing back slightly. "Sure you are. Sure you are." The air up and down the street suddenly grew more still and quiet.

"Can we get out of this damn cold?" Remelea stepped past everyone to the door Louis had walked out of. It had swung shut behind him. She tugged the handle and found it locked. "The fuck?"

Louis glanced at Remelea. "Sorry, ma'am. The place hasn't been open in weeks."

Zane smiled. His fingers twitched towards the hammer on his belt. "Who wants me to fix that door situation?"

"We don't have time." Louis looked over the rest of the group. "Hey, Sheldon. Thanks for getting the drawing to Dad."

"Wait, what...Oh, right."

Rob perked up. "What drawing?"

Jesse reached into his coat pocket and brought out the folded, crumpled sheet of paper. "This one."

Rob snatched the sheet from Jesse and unfolded it. He looked it over, then stared at Jesse. "Where did you get this?"

"I drew it, remember?" said Louis.

"Yeah," said Rob, "but...you gave it to *me*..."

"That's right," said Louis. "Then you went and left it behind."

"Where?"

"In your old place, up on South Main Street."

"Oh shit, I never got to show you that place, did I, huh, Lou?"

"Don't worry, man, it's all good."

"Damn, man, and here I thought I lost this on the road somewhere. I never forgave myself for that, you know...I mean...Look, after you...left...this was the last thing I had of you, you know?"

"Obviously not, brother. 'Cause look, here we are."

"Still, man, I'm so sorry. Look, you always knew how I loved this drawing. Right? Remember?"

"Of course. I'm the guy who remembers everything. That's my job now."

Rob clutched the paper tighter, stared at it again, then looked back up. "Why'd you leave, man? You took off right before shit got interesting."

"Nah. You're the one who *took off*."

"Yeah, that's right," said Rob. "It's all coming back to me now. You convinced everyone you were dead. You even fooled *me* for a while, you sneaky little bastard. So...uh...why the act?"

"I never pulled an act," said Louis.

Rob stared past Louis, at the locked door Remelea had just tried to open. His face quivered as the real memories flooded back, so he blurted, "*Goddamnit, you asshole, why?*"

"It doesn't matter," said Lou.

"It fucking *does* matter, though. Everything matters. Goddamnit, Lou, I'm still so fucking sick of all your glum fucking *I-don't-matter-to-anyone* bullshit! So you figured out how to stick around afterwards, huh? Great. Good for you. Happen to drop in at your own memorial service up at the college? See your ex-girlfriend up on the dining hall stage, talking about how much you mattered to *her?* She had the whole damn place bawling with what she had to say about you. I've never seen anyone so broken. So yeah, go ahead, give me the old *nothing matters* pile of—"

"So what do you wanna do about it, kick my ass?" Rob didn't have a ready comeback, so Louis sighed and looked around. "So. How was Gwen anyway, last you heard from her...before all this? You kept up with her any?"

"Not really," said Rob. "She never much liked me. I was always kinda, y'know, *that* friend, remember?"

"Oh, right!" Louis busted out laughing. So did Rob. For a long time, neither of them could stop. Then Louis's face settled gently, in that unmistakable old Louis way. "Look, I'm here now. So are you."

"Yeah? For what?"

"So I can show you and Sheldon to what you've come looking for. We both know damn well what that is, but you have to say it out loud. Look, man, I don't make these rules."

Sheldon started forward. "It's—"

Louis splayed a palm out to the side. "Rob has to say it."

Rob looked again at the drawing of Magur Sevi, then back at Louis. "You're here to take us to the Old World."

"I'm here to lead you to the door to the harbor, so I can open it for you. Either of you could've found it if you'd thought hard enough, but I'm the only one here who can open it for you now. That's why I couldn't leave. And believe me, I tried...because of something I'd figured out."

"About what?"

"About you, Rob. Where I'm about to lead you. I still don't like it, and neither will you, but...let's just say, it's about as inevitable as anything gets. Because here we all are. I really can't say any more about it than that...any more than I could prevent it."

Rob stared down again, at Louis's old drawing of Magur Sevi, like he expected to find clearer answers there.

Jesse shook. "Louis...son...Will there be more time?"

"No, not in the—No, Dad. I'm sorry."

Jesse pulled his son into a long hug. "You've done great, Louis. You're *doing* great."

Louis let his dad hold him for a while, then slipped free like a wisp of mist. "It was great to see you again, Dad. I love you. Time to show Rob and Sheldon off in style, though." He looked them both over. "You both brought your backpacks along. Good. It's time for the trail to split again."

The words and their meaning sank in for everyone separately. Rob shared rough hugs with Jesse and Zane. He grabbed Jesse's big, rough hand and pressed Louis's drawing back into the open palm. "Hey, Jesse? Sorry I almost butchered you back there."

"Just make sure, when the time comes, you put all your pent-up shit where it belongs."

Rob grinned. "Oh, don't worry about that. So you're a believer now, huh?"

Jesse smiled sidelong at his son. "I just got all the confirmation I'll ever need."

Louis looked Remelea over slowly, head to toe...not with the mix of lust and dread her presence typically elicited from men and women alike, but with a whole new kind of wonder, like he saw something in her only a ghost could appreciate. His face lit up with genuine surprise "Knew for a while we'd meet face to face, Remelea. Didn't exactly expect it to be like this. Do me a favor and take care of yourself, 'til next time."

"Uh…thanks." She peered at Rob. "So what are the rest of us supposed to do, now that you boys are off to kill some gods?"

Louis looked at the three Crimbone he and Rob and Sheldon were about to leave behind. "Well, when Dad first stopped here a few days ago, he did some great work with that Liam kid, establishing order in the streets. Dad, how 'bout you show Zane and Remelea around the checkpoints?"

Sheldon said to Jesse, Zane, and Remelea, "Keep Janie safe."

"We will, long as we can keep anyone safe," said Zane. "Right, Jess?"

"Nice to know we're back to thinking on the same page," said Jesse.

"Hey, little dude." Zane grinned at Sheldon. "It's been great on the trail with you, man."

Sheldon grinned back. "I don't think my forehead's ever gonna let me forget it, you old bastard." He slapped backs with the two old Crimbone. He and Remelea shook hands.

"Yeah, it was…good to meet you," Remelea said blankly to Sheldon.

~

Remelea turned away from Sheldon, almost in time to hide how her face broke out quivering with barely contained sobs. Her eyes met Rob's. That's when she broke down, like someone losing their dinner after chugging a bottle of whiskey then spinning in circles. She tried to turn away before anyone saw it. Goddamnit, she already felt all their eyes on her, though. Fuck this! The world had gone to shit, and she'd probably be dead soon, along with everyone else. For now, for once, just let the world leave her the hell alone!

"You'll find what you need," she said to Rob. "I know it."

Rob stepped close. His eyes blazed into hers. "Thank you."

That was all he had to say? Fuck him! "For what?"

"Because when I hear you say it...*you, Remelea, your voice*..." He squeezed her hands. "I hear you say it, and I know it's true."

"You're the one with the *magic voice* that makes folks believe and follow shit that ain't true. For whatever it's worth, it was never about that for me." She pulled free, turned and hurried to catch up with Jesse and Zane, who were already headed back towards Harmony Lot.

Rob shouted after her, "Remelea!" She froze, turned back, and looked at him, tears streaming down her face. She shook her head, made to turn away again. He strode up to her first, though. "I love you, too." He leaned in for a goodbye kiss. When their lips touched, her arms shot up and locked around him, yanking him in hard and close. They melted against each other and grew warm together against all the icy air.

When he let go, she looked like she might run. She arched her shoulders back, so her duster coat slid off. "You're fucking freezing. Take this."

"Remelea, don't. You—"

"Just fucking take it! I won't send you off to the Old World without it."

"You need it more than me."

"Take it!" She thrust the coat forward. Once he accepted it, she turned and ran to catch up with Jesse and Zane.

~

"You're shaking like a spastic," Jesse said to Remelea when she caught up. "Here." He shrugged off his own coat and held it to the side for her.

She shoved him away. "Stop trying to be nice. I don't need to be cheered up right now. I need to get it out of my system, so I can get back to my duty, whatever the fuck that is anymore."

Jesse stumbled from her shove and bumped into Zane. Old Lords, the little lady was strong, even for a Crimbone woman! Jesse tried to think of a worse moment to get turned on. "I'm trying to be chivalrous," he said. "Don't make me slug you."

She shrugged and yanked the coat out of his hand, threw it over her shoulders without putting her arms through the sleeves. "Fine. Thanks."

They walked on. Jesse glanced at Zane.

Zane said, "So…off to see your *checkpoints*, huh?"

"Sounds like the plan."

"So what kind'a work you been doing so far with this Liam kid, you ain't told me about yet?"

"Just he had his hands full, you know, keeping order since everything fell into chaos around here."

Zane nodded thoughtfully. "What kind of trouble we talking about?"

"Some trouble with rape-gangs, you might say. So I put the word out, any rapists in this town get caught in the act, they get skull-fucked with their own severed cock. That's the new law."

"Oh yeah? How's that working out?"

"Well, a few days before I left to catch up with you, some of my boys caught some punks with a thirteen-year-old girl behind a dumpster. Get me? So yeah, we dragged then out into the middle of Harmony, called up as big a crowd as we could gather, and made everyone watch how literally we meant that. Since then, gang-rape's turned into a lot less of a problem, last I checked."

"Yeah, no shit," said Zane. "Damn, man, the beer folks buy you around here these days must be worse than that possum-piss in Louisiana."

"Nah, Brattleboro brew's good as ever. Let's find what's left of it later, once we check in around town."

"Sounds good." Zane looked at how Jesse was shivering. "I'm not giving you my coat, man."

FOUR

Rob, Sheldon and Louis got to High Street via Main Street, then trudged uphill. The sidewalks were all piled high with snowdrifts, but the road was mostly clear. There was a lot of black ice, but their boots had good tread.

"Hey," Rob hissed sideways at Sheldon. "You hear that?"

"What?"

"No cars coming, up or down. We don't have to worry about traffic. Listen to the winter air through the trees, through the hills. It's like the lands have finally been let out of jail."

Sheldon shrugged. "I kinda miss the traffic."

Rob punched him in the shoulder. "Dude, you've got issues."

"The pot has duly noted the kettle's observation."

Louis glanced back at them. "I'm with Sheldon on this one."

"Yeah, well, you're a ghost," said Rob. "You're allowed to miss whatever the fuck you want."

"Damn straight," said Louis without breaking stride. He turned right, leading them up Chestnut Hill. The street sign didn't exist anymore. From there, they climbed between an even steeper, more winding cluster of houses, dipping and rising.

Rob's nostrils flared. "There's Spirelights 'round here, by the plenty."

"Hold it together, man," said Louis.

"It's not that. These ones feel…different. Their *glow's* like…like…" Rob kept staring at the larger houses.

"Yeah." Louis nodded. "Like the United Deschembines."

Sheldon perked up. "Then that means—"

"Keep moving, guys," said Louis. "Time to leave this world's regrets in this world."

That sounded good to Rob. He was tired. He felt ready—truly ready—to close his eyes on all this and open them on something else. He knew damn well what Sheldon was thinking, though…figuring his Earth-line girl was in one of those houses, wanting to go bang on every door looking for her, or hoping she'd spot him through a window, cussing her head off at him for leaving her behind up in Canada, before they melted into each other's arms for one last goodbye. Wouldn't it be nice if both Janie and Sally ran outside together. Considering the man in the lead right now, that wouldn't have surprised him.

They passed a big, crumbling, empty stone reservoir. Not far ahead, between a few more big houses, the forest awaited, split down the center in a jagged trail just for them. Once they passed into the woods, there was no more doubt, where they were headed. The trail was treacherous, but Rob knew it well enough, even in winter. He fell right back into its rises and dips. Glancing over, he could tell that Sheldon did, too, though the kid was less used to the thick snow through which their boots crunched. Ahead, there rose a stone edifice belonging to another time, one that was old for this world.

"The Bloody Tower," breathed Sheldon.

Down the hill, just outside the woods, there waited a mental institution. In the late nineteenth century—or was it the early twentieth century?—the doctors had decided it would be good for the patients to have manual labor. So they'd brought them into the hills, had them build this local landmark. Apparently, the tower made a fine lookout point over the whole town. It was also a great suicide method for patients who snuck out late at night. So the heads of the institution had padlocked the door.

Louis dug through his pockets and produced a key. "The Earth-line people could give you keys to this tower, if any of its custodians were still around. If you opened this door with their key, it would lead up to where you could look out over all this land, see all its beauty. This key unlocks the same door, but it'll open on another set of stairs."

He crouched and fitted the key into the padlock. The iron door swung inward. Rob and Sheldon peered in. At first, all they saw was inky blackness. Then something hissed and sparked, first to the left, then to the right. On either wall, ancient, massive torches flared to life, hanging high on sandstone walls, in braziers of black iron. At first, there were only the two, then more flames spouted to roaring life, in a winding line that stretched far back across the walls. The interior ran back farther and wider than the tower's outer walls. Thick old dust and cobwebs coated the walls, then it all broke and floated free, pulled spectrally into the newly awoken flames, which pulsed higher and thicker. The spectral orange lit up the foyer, so you'd never guess that it had lain dark and dead in limbo, for all these countless ages, until just this moment. The light illuminated deeply chiseled wall-carvings that were so detailed and numerous, they seemed to move like images on a screen when the eyes scanned them. Sheldon stepped through and stared.

Rob looked on, mesmerized, but he didn't yet step inside. He tore his eyes from the unreal sight and faced Louis. "It could've been you, Louis." He felt his voice choking up. "Going off together on this journey with me, discovering our homeland together."

Louis chuckled. "Here you are, beholding a long-forgotten wonder, the very presence of which defies this world's laws of physics, and you're still sad about what could have been." His gaze dropped. "If things had gone that way, you know, we probably wouldn't have *missed* the Wildfire boy that night. Look what the little shit and his sister—the love of your life—accomplished together."

"Yeah. Still, though…you'd've gone through it all with me, right?"

"Rob…of course I would."

When they hugged, it didn't feel like hugging a ghost. Rob let go and walked through the doorway. When he looked back, Louis no longer stood out there in the snowy landscape. Rob still took one last look at the forest. Then the heavy metal door swung shut by itself. Sheldon already stood before the staircase at the back of the foyer. At first, they could only stare mutely at each other, the air congealing in the pits of their guts. As far as anything they'd ever known was concerned, they'd just died…had ceased to exist in the world on the other side of that door.

They started down the steep stairs. The way ahead was ever pitch-black and icy cold, yet with each bend of the staircase, more torches sprang to life above them, drinking the gloom and warming the narrow way. After what must have been two mountains' worth of stairs, the stone ran forward in a straight, short hallway. A soft, silent wind whispered in through the archway.

They stepped out onto a long, wide dock, made of the same sandstone as everything else here. More torches hung from the walls on either side of the door. At the end of the dock, two more torches stood, held at either corner in high posts of black iron. The torches cast bright orange across the dock, reflecting off the black water…a long way of pure black nothing, between this world, the Old World, and many others. The walk down had left their legs sore and stiff, though it hadn't been allowed to sink in 'til they paused. Their knees gave out, and they sank back against the wall.

They opened their eyes to the soft splash of an oar in water. They got up and walked out across the dock, towards a long narrow craft of solid shimmering gray. At its head, there stood a tall, thin man in ragged clothes, his features beaten hard and sharp. His chillingly ancient pale eyes caught the torchlight.

"I thought it would end here." The voice was roughened gold, raspy but vital. "No, that's right, I remember now…Yeah. I'm supposed to take you boys across, aren't I? Yeah, that's right. You'll see the land of Deschemb, and you'll start to discover…"

"What'll we discover?"

"How it happened there, why our ancestors crossed these same waters."

"So what's left back there?" asked Sheldon. "What survives of the Old World? I mean, after all this time, it must have recovered from those days, when everything…?"

"How should I know?" said the ferryman.

"Come on, Sheldon." Rob climbed down into the boat.

"That's the spirit, Rob." The ferryman smiled. "Then again, who's to say what you're really bound for? The missing pages are stacked high, after all."

The ferryman shouldn't have known Rob by name, yet somehow, it didn't strike him as odd. The familiarity in the tone was a little much, though. He settled shakily into place and looked back up at Sheldon.

"So you know who we are." Sheldon climbed down into the boat. "I guess you know what we're headed to do, too."

"Sheldon Wildfire, the Spirelight who isn't a Spirelight anymore. Rob Coscan, the High Natural. You're headed to kill the gods."

The boat rocked slightly as the ferryman shoved off. They glided off across the black, still water in a straight line, through an emptiness that lay outside of time and space and war. The torchlight faded behind them, giving them up to that emptiness.

PART TWO:

WHAT'S LEFT OF

THE OLD WORLD

THE SHORES OF

DESCHEMB

ONE

Sometimes the air was cold. Mostly, all they felt were their asses and boot heels pressing the hard, icy seats and floor. Wind howled high above. Its chill touched them, sometimes sent water misting up across their faces, yet somehow it never shoved the long, narrow craft off course. The boatman kept silent, a tall, statuesque figure that stayed ever fixed forward. Only his arms moved, to guide the oar, which sent tiny waves splashing against the sides.

The pitch-blackness swirled in a thousand shades. It told them stories, of themselves, of everything they'd heard of, everything they'd never dreamed. The journey was long enough for one to learn many things, to forget them and remember later, without realizing that you'd ever lived without the knowledge. More than once, Rob forgot he'd been Rob Coscan, or that the world Rob Coscan had lived in was anything but the setting for stories he'd read in books or seen in movies about someone else's life. He remembered the trail he'd left behind. How had he gotten stuck there for so long? How many years had he spent in this little boat?

It had started outside something called a boarding house, on a street called South Main, in a town called Brattleboro, in a state called Vermont. His Familiar had appeared in the front yard and told him of his Crimbone heritage, and he'd followed his Familiar onto his trail like any other fledgling. Along the way, he'd met a girl named Sally. She'd needed his help because the Spirelights were after her. So he'd followed the trail across a river, up a mountain to the house where the Spirelights waited. There he'd taken up the twin black blades of Magur Sevi and drank deep of the glow. After that, he and Sally had traveled all over the American countryside, because more Spirelights were after them. They'd gone to New Orleans, where an evil man named Talino told him what he needed to do. So he'd killed Talino, and followed the trail further with Sally, seeking the edge of the black ocean. Then in frozen Canada, he'd found his Familiar again, and the Familiar had sent him back to Brattleboro. He'd wanted to take Sally, his queen, with him across the black ocean. Louis told him he couldn't do that, though.

…Louis, the ghost who'd opened the harbor gates…

Light faded towards them, from above, like spreading fog through the darkness.

"It's not the shores of Deschemb," said the boatman without looking back.

"But it is," sighed Rob. "It has to be. Look! It's the first great tree on the shores of our homeland, rising so high…so high…I can't even see the bottom of it…"

"That tree touches no ground you'll ever see, nor any shore we'll ever set foot on," said the boatman.

It loomed close overhead, yet always far away, like a rainbow with its phantom promise of a pot of gold. Pale air shimmered and rippled around it like waves…an impossibly thick, petrified trunk running up forever, with millions of gnarled forking branches spreading out. Thousands of bulbous, twittering bat-like shapes perched there like crows. They hopped and scuttled left and right. Some glided from branch to branch, peering down curiously at the three figures in the boat.

"We've passed into the ephemeral realms themselves," said Sheldon.

Rob looked through the spilling crystal-blue light. He remembered who Sheldon was and why the guy was here with him. Sheldon looked much older than he had moments ago—ages ago—back on the dock. More than that, he *sounded* older…Wait a second, though, was Rob looking at Sheldon or the boatman?

"You passed into the ephemeral realms when you set off across the black ocean." The boatman had just said that. Rob shifted and lurched in a moment's confusion. For a second, he'd been sure that had been Sheldon. These waters kept sending funny sensations through his brain as they reshaped it. The boatman continued, "That's what the black ocean's part of; an area where higher ideas of matter and those you're used to line up, so our bodies and minds can pass through them, just as those of our ancestors did. What you see now is the great eternal tree, home to the creatures you call Familiars. Within these realms also is the pantheon of the Spirah gods."

"We set off on this voyage to kill the gods, right?" said Rob. "So bring them on!"

"Don't say that so loud, unless you've thought long and hard about what it means. When you reach the shores you seek, the gods will only lift their hands against you through their agents of flesh and blood…and on stretches of land that have been remapped in their image."

"That sounds a lot like the world we just left," said Rob.

"The gods are closer to the world you approach, in ways you've not yet met...but yes, Rob, you're right. They're still more...distant there, in ways you're used to. On these waters, you're as vulnerable to them as to any enemy with a blade. Your own blades would be useless against them, as they will be everywhere...except at the appointed destination. The gods have sensed you passing through their realm. They sense your intent. They'd have drawn our course beneath their pantheon by now, shoved us all under to drown, but other forces told the Familiars of your passing. Apparently, the Familiars approve of your intent. Congratulations, boys. They've drawn our course beneath the branches of their tree, so we might pass in safety."

Rob craned up at the many shapes hopping and gliding overhead. Their true voices floated down around him, melodic and ancient and wise, little enough like the speech they adopted for mortals in the purely physical realms. "Is Puttergong up there?"

"No," said the boatman.

"Where's Puttergong?" said Rob. "On its way back here? Did it make it out of the other world okay?"

The boatman shrugged and kept rowing. Rob kept staring upward. They were directly beneath the branches now. Yet when his eyes trailed down the great trunk, it still seemed impossibly far away, fading out miles above and ahead, shimmering through the wavy, crystalline air. Rob's gaze got caught in the shimmers and floated through them. Finally, his vision blurred and his brain lulled. He reclined as far back as he could, his elbows on the rims of the boat. The great tree's light blurred, 'til it might be any other bright open sky, the soft waves of any other ocean lapping around the boat. The waves thickened and tossed them here and there, so he worried they were about to capsize.

The water settled around them, and they coasted smoother than ever. The bottom of the boat scraped and plowed through something…

…Sand…The shore.

Rob's eyes snapped into focus. Overhead, there shown a bright, clear blue sky like any other…No, not quite. This was a different shade of blue. Not brighter, not bleaker, just *different*, tinged with hues from another spectrum entirely, from a different reality…*the reality of dreams…the only one that's ever mattered.*

Rob sat up, blinking. He didn't see that sun itself anywhere. Maybe it was behind those massive trees rising from the other side of the beach. Never before had he seen anything quite like this—the sky, the sand, the trees, the smaller plant life, all colored *just slightly differently* from any shade he recognized…yet none of it registered as unfamiliar. Wherever he looked, he felt like he'd already known exactly what he'd see. The salt in the air was familiar, sort of, though it carried unfamiliar scents, from an ocean with unknown things swimming and churning, growing and festering within its depths.

The boatman had already climbed out into the surf. He hauled the boat effortlessly onto the shore with Rob and Sheldon still in it. Either of them would have jumped out to help, but it all happened while they were still collecting themselves. They climbed out now and took hold of the sides.

Sheldon stared in stupefied awe at the same things that felt so strangely familiar to Rob. Rob felt almost like there'd been no journey, or like he'd slept through it. A moment ago, the boat had shoved off from the subterranean dock. Then it had come ashore here…on the shores of Deschemb, *in the bright light of day in Deschemb.*

Yep, nice to be back here. Rob drew breath after deep, revitalizing breath of true Deschembine air. It felt wonderfully warm and cool at the same time, both on his face and within his lungs. Something splashed against him, so he braced up. The lapping surf rolled back, his long coat and all, like it was giving slow, loose, watery birth to him. Something thrashed to his left. Sheldon had also climbed out but wasn't having such an easy time of it. Rob pulled him up. For now, Sheldon let himself be led. They slogged out of the surf together, onto the sand. The sun felt great on their faces and hands, yet they were still too comfortable in their long coats to think about taking them off.

Sheldon said, "Is this…?"

Rob smiled. "It's the birthplace of both our races. Welcome home, little brother."

"Home…that boat…the black ocean…How long were we…?"

"I still can't tell. It's weird. Like I remember everything before the journey fine, but…"

Except did he? He half-remembered sensations from the trip, of his consciousness, his memories, his identity, all washing away like a sandcastle in the tide, then flowing back together and falling apart again, each time differently…in different *shapes*, as Puttergong would say.

Different shapes…Puttergong hadn't even said that. No, wait, yeah, Puttergong *had* said it to someone, not Rob, except now he remembered it all the same.

This is no time to go to pieces with a stupid fucking identity crisis. Of course you feel right at home in the Old World. You need to keep it together. Sheldon needs you to keep it together, 'til he catches on.

Sheldon clapped his hands in front of Rob's face. "*Rob!*"

"Huh? Yeah, what?"

"The boatman. Do you remember what the boatman said to us?"

"Some of it, yeah, I think…"

"Holy shit, the boat!" Sheldon spun back towards the shore. Rob looked with him.

The boat was already back in the water, gliding away, over the point where the clear lapping surf faded into the black ocean. Above it, the blue sky gave way to the blackness of the ephemeral realms.

Sheldon ran towards the water. "Hey, man, hold up! You haven't told us—"

Rob followed and put a hand on Sheldon's shoulder. "He's off to wherever the next stage of his journey will take him."

Sheldon turned back. "Great. So where does that leave us?"

"Right here. This is where we start. Sheldon, please. Calm down. Let yourself take it all in. Take a deep breath and savor it. It's the air of our homeland. We're the first of anyone we've ever known to breathe it. It's glorious."

After a moment, Sheldon smiled. "Home…Wow, Rob, look around!"

Rob smiled back. "I've *been* looking. And listening. And feeling."

"I guess all those stories were wrong," Sheldon sighed. "Deschemb *hasn't* been destroyed, or even crippled…Hell, fuck *crippled*, it's not even polluted! Rob, *this is what air tastes like without Earth-line fossil-fuel polluting it!*" He took another deep breath. "You're right, it *is* glorious!"

They crashed against each other in a fierce embrace. *Here we are in Deschemb together!* Rob pulled free and stared out across the sea. He didn't see the boat anymore.

"Rob," Sheldon shouted. "Man, I know it's amazing and all, but can we keep our minds on the matter at hand?"

Rob turned back, then looked around. "The matter at hand, yeah." His eyes changed. "We haven't been off this beach yet. What we've come to find, I can feel it here, somewhere."

"So what's *here?* We're on a whole other planet, in a whole other damn *reality.*"

"Yeah. A reality that already feels more real to me than the other one ever did."

"It still doesn't feel quite real to me."

At that, they sat down side by side and laughed their asses off together. Rob wasn't even sure why they were laughing, but it felt good. It felt right. They kept laughing 'til they were both out of breath.

"So what do we do," said Sheldon, "walk along the beach 'til we find a road to civilization or something?"

"No. Remember what the boatman said? Any roads we find are probably Spirelight-made. That puts us on the gods' radar." Rob looked around, then pointed off along the beach. "That way, through the forest."

"Why that way?"

"The air just smells…clearer through there. I don't know, it's like I can…see the shapes, in the textures in the air, of the different smells around me."

"Could you…do that, back where we came from?"

"A little, I think, but not like this! Now I don't even have to close my eyes to see it clearly."

As they neared the giant trees, the sand gave way to soft brush—Deschembine brush, Deschembine foliage.

"Look at all this," sighed Sheldon. "I just remembered, back in the other world, when I was with the United Deschembines, we'd get word sometimes, of plant life like this, things no Earth-line botanists could explain. I never saw any of it myself. By then, we were already making our way north. Apparently it was all happening further south, where it was warmer…"

"Yeah, I know," said Rob. "I saw some of it in Louisiana, like…hybrids of the native plant life there, and this. Just think, in a few years, everywhere will be like that in that other world!"

"What?"

"Huh?"

"Rob, you just said..."

"Why are we talking about that other world anyway? Just look at how it all grows here. Man, it flourishes so peacefully."

That much was true. The grass—if grass was what you'd call it—sprouted in corkscrews, greener than any Earth-line grass, edged in gold. The trees didn't have trunks of bark, but giant green stalks like sunflowers, except smooth and shimmering, seeming to carry down the sunlight through the branches above like the tubes of pitcher plants, radiating softly outward beneath the canopy. Around the bases of the massive stalks, there slithered sleepy things Rob and Sheldon at first took for thousands of snakes. Then Rob saw that they were vines, like the ones he and Remelea had faced in Talino's church.

These vines had never known Talino's corrupting sorcery, though. The smaller ones milled and squirmed languidly over the ground, routing through the soil, plucking nourishment with tiny hair-like feelers, sending it up to the larger vines, which wound midway up the tree trunks, where they reached out and entwined with each other, forming a crisscrossing network. From that network, swelling green pods dangled. Once night fell, they would bloom into lightpears. Their radiance would shower the forest.

Flying beasts with blurry wings like hummingbirds darted around the lightpears, maybe eating bits of them or performing some alien pollination ritual. They were too high for Rob or Sheldon to see in detail, larger than condors, not quite birds, not quite bees, not quite butterflies. Every rock and stone seemed to shine like a smooth, precious jewel.

This tranquility wouldn't hold as they ventured further, Rob knew. His eyes dampened, still wishing he could have shown it to Sally and Remelea. To Jesse and Zane, too, even to Sheldon's Earth-line girl, and all Sheldon's friends among the United Deschembines.

They'll all see it, he reminded himself, *once your work is done.*

As the forest closed around them, he looked and saw similar feelings on Sheldon's face. Would Earth-liners be able to breathe the air here? Some of them, no doubt, sure, hopefully.

Right now, though, the sensation that overwhelmed both Rob and Sheldon—what they'd never expected to feel again—was joy.

TWO

"Oh, shit," Shelton blurted.

Rob spun to face him. "What?"

"Our bags."

"Huh?"

"Our fucking backpacks. We left them in the boat. I can't believe I didn't notice 'til now. And that fucking boatman, he just…left without a word to us."

"Oh. Shit, you're right." Rob gaped at the realization, then busted out laughing.

"Sure," said Sheldon, "fucking hilarious!"

"Dude, relax. What did you have in there that was so important anyway?"

"A couple changes of clothes, for one thing. Plus all my wilderness survival supplies, and some MREs Zane gave me."

"We've got all the tools we need right here." Rob slapped one of his knife pommels. "What, did you think all these things were good for was stabbing motherfuckers?"

"Okay, Daniel Fucking Boone, what are we gonna do for food now?"

Without breaking stride, Rob glanced around for edible foliage and recognized at least five on-hand snack options...from memories in his blood, real memories he'd once tried to dismiss as dreams. He could even remember how some of them tasted. "Why, you hungry yet?"

Sheldon took a deep breath and calmed down some. "No, actually. It's weird. I feel like this whole place is nourishing me. Like it fills me with every breath, soaks into me through my feet with every step."

"Yeah. Same here. Like I'll never need to eat or drink again."

"You expect that to last forever?"

"No. Matter of fact, I figure we'll be working ourselves up an appetite before long."

They'd run through the forest off and on for miles, and they still weren't tired. They could never run for long, though. There was just too much to look at, to take in.

Sheldon broke back into a run. Rob ran to catch up. The foliage broke, and they entered a stony clearing. More gold-rimmed corkscrew grass spread out for a stretch, then gave way to a smooth, horizontal, steadily downward-sloping outcropping of rock that dropped off into a series of steep cliffs leading down to a vast lake. They cleared half the smooth rock slope. Sheldon paused and looked back. Rob stood tall and regal upon the outcropping. He gazed off with sublime melancholy across the lake far below.

"What is it, man?"

Rob whispered, "The Old World...I've heard of it and I've dreamed of it. I've dreamed about its giant lakes that were miles deep, yet so clear. You could dive from the immense cliffs, and the air between the peaks and the water's surface was different somehow from the air anywhere else. If you leapt into that air, you could just glide down for miles, almost flying but not quite. When you splashed in the water, it was so clear you could look down through it and see the stone ruins of the ancestors far below, covered in glowing moss of every color. And the people of the Old World...they say some of them could actually hold their breath long enough to swim down through all those miles and through the ruins."

"You saying we can do that now?"

"Yeah," Rob went on, to the ghosts that had followed him across the black ocean, "and in the ruins, the walls...they told stories. Yes, Sally, the walls told stories!"

"*Rob!*"

Rob looked back at Sheldon.

"Sally's not here, Rob."

"I know. That's how it used to be. We're passing beyond the untouched reaches. The lands here feel the effects of the Schomite-Spirelight wars, and rebel against them." He smiled mirthlessly. "Ain't you noticed it? The animal life has been less and less happy to see us, less willing to let us see it."

"Right. Just how much of that animal life might try to eat us?"

Rob considered it and shrugged. "How should I know? You think I know *everything* about this place?" He looked around some more. "This world may have fallen to ruin and repaired itself a million times over, but the wars that ravaged it—drove our people away—still go strong here, somewhere." He inhaled fiercely. "Yeah…there's blood on the air now, humanoid blood, hot with the rage and fear in which it was spilled. Not all of them left for the other world. The descendants of the stragglers are still fighting, somewhere nearby."

"Just how *nearby* are we talking?"

"Close enough that we'd better make sure to find it before it finds us. This world falls apart against it, then realigns itself better than ever, like night and day. Right now, it's day. But I think…every time it shakes down the fighting like a dog shaking off fleas, it's…it's better for a while afterwards, then the madness comes back. It gets a little worse every time. It stays darker longer, so it's harder for anyone to keep going through it."

"So that's it, then. Just one more vicious cycle that'll never stop."

"Not while the gods still live here, it won't."

"How close is Spiralla, then? *Rob, are we close to the Great Temple of Spirah?*"

"I don't know." Rob's eyes went weird again. He spoke more in that ghostly whisper. "I walk the ancient halls, and there are others there, both Schomite and Spirelight. As I walk, I know that I'm Crimbone, and everyone around me knows too, but this doesn't matter as much, even among the Spirelights, because…I guess it's before the wars got so bad, before the blood-hate got so strong. But the walls are amazing! They tell the stories of all they've seen, not in paintings or carvings or even writing, but in the elemental swirl of the matter itself. I don't know, it's like…like if you look at it right, you'll see all of history in the stones of the old halls. In those sacred places, all time, all things can truly be one to you, if you know how to see it…I keep looking deeper and further back, and I keep thinking I'm about to see the beginning of everything, and then…" His eyes grew lucid and he looked around.

"So you wanna go to the edge, see if we can see down that far?"

"No. We have to be extra careful now."

"So what do we do?"

"Get back into the woods."

~

As they climbed the slope, Sheldon found himself considering their whole situation more clearly. Rob's alive-and-active blood-memories gave them a leg-up, that was for sure. And yeah, the guy belonged here, body and soul. They were both still essentially aliens to this realm, though. Of course they wanted to drink it all up…but Rob seemed to be drinking too fast, like he'd overdose on it if he wasn't careful. So here was Sheldon, stuck with him.

As the forest grew darker, Sheldon spotted the setting sun through the branches. They were in for their first Deschembine night. He hoped they weren't too late to stop the next *deep long night* of their people, as Rob put it. Overhead, the lightpears pulsed with their first evening glow. Around the bases of the trees, the night moved. Or rather the vines did. They weren't the only things moving, Sheldon noticed. Something else had already drawn in closer. His hands edged towards his knives.

"No," Rob growled, splaying a hand at him.

From all sides, the moving shapes shot at them—no, shot *past* them, crisscrossing each other, almost gliding. Rob and Sheldon spun back to back at the center of it. Their eyes darted to keep track of the blurred shapes hemming them in. The shapes settled, pointing weapons of the black metal in an inward circle. Rob kept motioning for Sheldon to stay cool, even though it looked like they were about to become the centerpiece of a Crimbone blade-bukaki. Sheldon peered harder 'til he made out all the glittering eyes. He couldn't even count them, for how they seemed to blur and melt into each other. It was like the low foliage had melted together into shapes that almost floated like bubbles, like big infinitely flexible leaves, out of which grew human heads and arms. The heads and hands and hair were a swirl of earthen shades.

"Told you we'd be working up an appetite soon enough," Rob muttered.

"Yeah, great, asshole," Sheldon whispered. "So what do we do now?"

"*We* don't do shit," Rob hissed. "*I* do, or rather I *talk* shit. So shut up and let me talk some shit."

One barely visible shape talked some shit Sheldon recognized as the ancient Schomite language, in a dialect probably not even Rob understood. Sheldon glanced at Rob's face and couldn't tell. Rob stepped forward. The speaker stiffened. The leafy bubble settled some around this one. Sheldon caught more of an impression of a full human shape.

Rob spoke in growling gutturals Sheldon hadn't thought a human mouth could make. All the figures but the leader drew back sharply. Their plant-based garments settled around their frames, so their body-structures stood out, more clearly outlined, every one of them muscled like they were carved out of knotted wood, not bulky, but rather impossibly long-limbed and limber. On some of them, it looked like cloaks turning into long coats such as Rob and Sheldon wore. Others drew up completely around the figures, like loose-fitting bodysuits. At first, Sheldon had taken them for all male, though he now spotted distinctly feminine chests, hips, and facial structures among them. Male or female, there was a weird, feral, catlike sort of androgyny to how their eyes gleamed accusingly out of the darkness.

The leader stepped forward. He was shorter than the others, but with broader shoulders, with a higher, thinner forehead and sharper, thicker eyebrows that arched quizzically. He held his composure and spoke to Rob in the same strange language…the *Crimbone* language. When Rob used that strange tongue, the forest seemed to speak it with him in the air and night noises, through every rustling branch and whispering blade of grass, sending shivers through everyone. It almost seemed like the sound didn't come from him at all, or that he was only one of its many channels.

The figures stared, first at Rob, then at Sheldon. When Rob spoke again, the Crimbone looked confused. The leader questioned Rob again. For a moment, Rob's frame relaxed glumly. He eyed the guy bemusedly, like you do when someone asks a question so stupid that you just don't know what to say. Then he roared and drew both knives.

Great, thought Sheldon, *here we go.*

Rob thrust the blades skyward for all to see. The Crimbone drank up the sight and settled. They were his. Satisfied, he nodded and sheathed the weapons.

Okay, Sheldon surmised, Rob was obviously telling these folks that he was the High Natural, *heir to Magur Sevi, come to free them from the Spirelight menace*, all that shit. So what was he telling them about Sheldon? Sheldon felt the weight of his own knives on his hips, so he had to restrain his hands.

Rob's not gonna fuck you over. You're the only one who can wield your *blades, and they're the ones that need to be plunged through the heart of the gods. Puttergong made that explicit. Rob understands that. Right?*

The leader turned and spoke to Sheldon in common Deschembine. The dialect was strange, as expected, evolved from a different path than where he came from.

Still, with a little brain-straining, he got the gist of it: "You are the High Natural's brother in arms."

"Yeah," Sheldon said in his own dialect. He nodded, just to be on the safe side.

"The High Natural calls you *the man with no race.* Your trail is bound to our new would-be chief in what he must do."

"In what *I*…" Sheldon spotted dangerous concern in the leader's eyes. "…What he and I *both* must do."

The leader nodded. "Your trails are bound as one."

"Right. So now he's…your new chief?"

"More or less."

"So you were the chief 'til now."

"Our former chief is newly dead. I was his second-in-command. I have guided my pack until the lands showed us a new chief. Now our chief has shown us himself, as only he can, for he is the High Natural…or so his evidence would have us believe. He speaks a name of another High Natural, one we know not."

"Magur Sevi."

"That is the name he spoke. We must discuss that and much more, back at our camp, some distance from here."

No wonder Rob was so confused. The former leader gestured to the other Crimbone, who fell in behind him. Sheldon now counted fifteen of them. Before he realized it, they were all off and running. He had to sprint to catch up.

THREE

Rob and Sheldon bustled along as the former leader showed the way. At their heels, the other Crimbone followed. The woods no longer showed any clear path, yet the brush cleared and curved in all the right places, so they wound and darted along like lemurs alongside the pack.

Sheldon had to admit, all this running and jumping was getting to him. Before these guys had come out of the woodwork, he'd felt on top of the world, nearly as manic as Rob, like setting foot in Deschemb had given both of them superpowers, like all the self-abuse they'd put their bodies through throughout their brutal lives in that other world had been magically washed away. Rob glided along like he still felt the same way. Meanwhile, Sheldon's limbs and chest started to burn like any other guy who'd just run a marathon.

He caught up with Rob and asked in Earth-line, "What's going on…*chief?*"

Rob grinned sideways, without breaking stride. "We're already on our way! The temple we're looking for…Kashen knows where it is, and he'll take us straight to it."

"Kashen?"

Rob nodded towards the man leading the charge.

"Oh," Sheldon managed between deep breaths. "So…that easy, huh?"

"I guess so." Even while running so fast, Rob said it as though they were seated around a campfire together. "Wow…"

"What…?"

"Something's…*off*. How could the wars have destroyed so much of their history, their *heritage?*"

"Fucked if I know," Sheldon huffed.

"We'll end it soon, Sheldon. We can end it forever. Across two worlds."

"So they'll take us straight there?" Sheldon kept spitting his words out like machine-gun fire, through frothing lips.

"Breathe slower and steadier," said Rob. "Can't have you burning yourself out."

"So where's this pack leading us?"

"To their nearest camp, where there's food and a place to sleep. Wow. Think of it, Sheldon, our first taste of Deschembine food. We'll sleep our first night beneath Deschembine stars!"

Night had fallen completely, but the moon showed the way clear as day, glistening off the crystalline rocks and blade-like leaves. It was strange to look up and not see the same old splotches and crags of the Milky Way, that rotted-skull jack-o-lantern face of *the Man in the Moon*. This world's moon had a strange color…a florescent mixture of red and blue, but not purple, was the closest way to describe it.

They passed into an open, rocky space. The land of Deschemb was still unimaginably gorgeous, but it no longer looked or felt *perfect*. These rocks were sharp and jumbled, like rocks were supposed to be. All around was the dusty wear and tear of harsh nature, one they recognized and understood. As the terrain changed, so did the dress and skin and hair of these native Crimbone, like chameleon hides. These Old World Crimbone were truly of these lands, like no refugee Deschembine had ever imagined. It even let them mold their clothes like silk from its plant life. However these people worked such wonders, it must feel simple as sewing to them.

"They keep staring at us," Rob said. He suddenly didn't sound so cocksure.

"What'd you expect?" Sheldon panted. He glanced around. "You're the High Natural, remember?"

"It's more than that. We're both alien to them, but they don't stare at you as much because they already have you in perspective."

"Huh?" Sheldon panted. "How?"

"They see how our skin and weird clothes don't fade with the landscape like theirs do. They accept that easier. You're the *man with no race*. That's weird, sure, but they can go with it, figure it out later as they need to. They know I'm Crimbone, but in their eyes, I'm so *unlike* what a Crimbone's fundamentally supposed to be."

From the next set of trees, a lone figure leapt and darted silently across the rocks. The long leaf garment became a cloak, or a coat, or a cape, or a bodysuit as it needed to, allowing the wearer to catch the wind and glide or sprint along without snagging itself.

The figure stopped in front of the pack. Kashen lifted a hand. Everyone halted behind him. Sheldon saw that it was a man, panting and snarling from rage and exertion. Kashen stepped up and exchanged some quick, increasingly heated Schomite words.

Kashen turned back to Rob and Sheldon. He spoke common Deschembine. Sheldon was still getting the hang of the dialect, but he got the gist of it fine: "We have to get to the camp, quickly."

Without so much as a nod, the messenger turned and ran back the way he'd come. Everyone else followed over the rocks, then through the trees.

As they ran, Kashen looked over his shoulder. "There's a Spirelight encampment town far to the east. It's the farthest Spiralla has pushed our way. 'Til seven moons ago, the town was a neutral civilian dwelling. Civilian Spirelights lived there in peace among other races, even a few Schomites if you can believe it. Apparently, there were spies there mingling, making way for Spiralla. The Spirelight police came, and…" Kashen's voice choked up into a snarl. "Now only Spirelights live there, except a few slaves who used to be citizens. Earlier this week, a little girl wandered too far from our camp and disappeared. We thought *they* might have taken her, to be sent back as a slave to Spiralla. Cragor here tells me her father went to investigate and found her still in the town. But the Spirelights had already worked their... *experimental magic*, probably to learn what labor she'd prove best for. Apparently not much, because she died in his arms. He retreated, but snuck back out later. He called on the *death rage*."

A shudder of understanding rippled through the running pack. Rob and Sheldon felt it without having to look back.

"Did that guy just say... *death rage?*" Sheldon whispered to Rob in Earth-line.

"Nastiest bit of Old World Crimbone battle magic I ever read about or remembered. This guy Kashen's talking about made a murder-suicide run, on a whole town. He turned his whole body and soul into a WMD."

The longer Sheldon spent listening to this dialect, though, the less he needed Rob's translations, he realized.

"Someone must have sensed the attack in advance and gotten out in time," Kashen went on. "A platoon of the Spirelight police has reached the ruins. We have to reach our camp and hide the children before we meet them."

Ruins? Sheldon thought. *What ruins? For that matter, what camp?*

The pack sped up too much for anyone to talk. Sheldon struggled to keep up. Rob didn't look like it bothered him. In fact, he looked ready to outrun everyone. He shook with battle lust...a Crimbone's battle lust. Sheldon felt it spread through the pack around him, driving them insane for it...the essence of their enemies, an essence he'd once possessed that would have drawn them to destroy him...the Spirelight glow. If he slipped up even a little, he felt sure his new companions would trample him without noticing.

Battle as it's fought in the Old World…Guess I'm about to see what that's like.

'Til now, it had never occurred to Sheldon how ferocious the danger might be here, compared to anything he'd known back home. Hell, he'd never stopped to think it could *get* worse. The air seemed to turn to soup around his head. The rocky terrain bit at his feet through boot heels that weren't made for it. His fingers edged towards his weapons. His limbs burned and throbbed. Once those weapons were out, he'd burn ten times worse.

Ahead, the trees broke again, this time into a sprawling field covered in tall corkscrew grass. At the center, a cluster of smaller trees was on fire. The blaze licked across the field into the forest, pulling the pack faster towards it. Sheldon couldn't see or feel this fire, but he felt its effect on those around him.

"They've reached the camp," Kashen exclaimed.

"I know," said Rob. "The fighting there's almost over."

"But there's still so many glows, so how…" Kashen cut himself off, as the obvious answer to the question set in. His face sank.

Rob took the lead. "So let's fix that."

"Wait!" Kashen grabbed at Rob's shoulder. "Their archers will be in the trees by now."

"So be ready for arrows."

For a second, Sheldon thought Rob had truly snapped. Then he remembered why the Secret Police back home rarely bothered with firearms. *But I'm not Crimbone. Dodging projectiles by letting the land guide me out of their path wasn't exactly in my training. Does Rob expect me to go out into that hail?* Plus, shooting from cover at a bunch of guys coming at you across an open field would be ideal against most enemies, but it was about the *most* useless way to take on the Crimbone. So why wouldn't these Spirelights know that…unless it didn't quite work like that here in Deschemb?

Sheldon watched how Rob peered out, glanced back and around at everyone else, then signaled them into place one at a time with the tiniest gestures and looks. *He knows this is nuts. So do they. Still, here he is, calling all the shots, and everyone falls right in line with his judgment, on the spot, ready to see what happens.*

How the hell did Rob have the first idea how to call *any* shots in this world? He'd said something back in the other world about dreams of Deschemb so vivid that he'd woken with memories of spending years in the place, throughout many eras of its history. He'd sounded convinced that those hadn't been just dreams, like on some level he really had lived all those lifetimes here, had done this sort of thing a million times. He'd seemed delusional, 'til now.

"Kashen, Cragor, you seven closest, come with me. We'll take them head on through the field, but not just yet. The rest of you, fan out, look to the trees that face out onto the field, quietly and invisibly as you can."

Someone started in Schomite, "But the Spirelight glow—"

"…Is all around us, already. It flares at that center, blinding you to those other pockets. They know we see it, how we thirst for it. That's how they planned this." Rob clapped Sheldon on the shoulder. "Follow this one."

"But he stands out! Look at him, he's not even—"

"He knows how not to be seen. *Follow his lead.*" Rob addressed them all in Crimbone, "Obey the man with no race as you obey me, as you obey the lands…no matter how weird the little bastard gets." He turned to Sheldon and said in Earth-line speak, "I just put you in charge."

"I…put that much together," Sheldon said. He turned to his half of the pack. "You four, go that way around." He pointed right. "Everyone else, come with me. Start close together 'til we take the first of them then spread out slowly. If you lose sight of me, just stick to the plan and fight for the best."

Rob added, "Keep your eyes on the field through the brush. We won't break for the camp immediately. 'Til we do, concentrate on taking as many of the ones farthest from the camp. Take your time and do it right. Once you see us running in through the field, though, move fast and kill fast. Once you've dealt with the ones hiding in these trees, come join the fight in the camp."

Kashen said to Rob, "How do we know when to break for it?"

Rob looked around at everyone champing at the bit. He sniffed the air. "Wait for my signal."

~

Sheldon trailed quietly through the brush, his Crimbone braves close at his back. Hopefully they'd scent out the closer glows, over the overwhelming central blaze.

He knew how to move about unseen on turf he was used to, sure…but in a world he'd just arrived in hours ago? This was just a forest, he told himself. How much different could it be from any of those he'd seen in the other world? The obvious answer was *a lot*. Oh well, he seemed to be doing okay so far, in that he wasn't already dead.

I've traveled from one world to the next. Soon I'll see the first of my original people, as they live in our homeland. And I'll kill them.

The Crimbone behind him tensed and snarled. No life stirred around them, not even crawling vines. The nearest Crimbone darted past him. Sheldon looked up. A yard and a half above, a figure stood with its feet crossed in the crotch of the tree, legs and back straight against the trunk. It was a woman with long, silky golden hair braided down her back. She wore high black boots, silky black trousers, and a black leather utility vest over a light gray tunic. Her skin shimmered like porcelain with a slight purple tint. Her cold eyes were reddish gold, peering patiently across the field.

How tall was she? Surely not as tall as she looked from where Sheldon stood. Strapped to her thigh was a quiver of short arrows. In her hand was a chiseled plank of what looked like dried green wood. Sheldon couldn't tell how arrows could be fixed and fired from such a weapon. Whereas these Old World Crimbone felt so one with their native forests that it was hard to tell them from the brush and vines unless you knew how to look, this Old World Spirelight stood out as the very essence of otherworldly godliness. Her consummate, gleaming *otherness* seemed to scorn the thicket around her.

Sheldon remembered how Earth-line people used to look at him, unable to figure out what was weird about him, just knowing something was off. His grandfather used to tell him and his sister, *It's the kiss of the Spirah gods they see on your pretty foreheads, even those too lowly to comprehend it.* For the first time, he saw how he must have looked to all those people, to the Schomites, too, even the Crimbone. Lowly or not, though, he comprehended it just fine. Then she blinked.

Sheldon ran quickly and silently. He wouldn't let the Crimbone reach the Spirelight woman in the tree. She was his, damnit. He sprang and grabbed a low branch with one hand, dug his boot heels into the trunk, and pulled himself up. She turned and looked down. In the same blurred, passionless motion, she plucked an arrow from her quiver and nocked it to the beam of green wood.

Sheldon ripped one of his blades from the scabbard. It seemed to absorb all the moon's light and blaze it out in a white-hot razor-edged beam. Its edge flashed as the arrow pointed at him.

FOUR

Captain Vesha Sting strode across the upper knotted regions of the tree-woven enclosure. Until a few minutes ago, this had been a Crimbone camp. Even striding across the unnaturally shaped walkway made his feet feel filthy, through his boots. Smoke still rose from within the grove below. Vesha gazed down at his troops while they finished off the last of the adult Crimbone. Soon it would be just a matter of whatever children his agents hadn't chopped aside on the way in. Some of the little brats had run roaring from hiding, punching, kicking and biting, like they thought they could aid their dying parents. Obviously, those parents hadn't taught them about what happened when the Blades of Bathshire showed up.

Vesha smiled. It just went to show what ignorant little beasts all these Schomites and Crimbone were. Ever since he'd been recruited into the Blades, he'd wondered increasingly what all the fuss was about. To think, these Crimbone had been stupid enough to believe the lands of Valaka so valuable that they held out and kept fighting this close to the capital, to the true home of the gods.

Vesha had led his division into these hills, naturally assuming that the enemy expected action from the Blades of Bathshire. From what he'd seen so far, he'd overestimated these vermin. He turned from the pathetic massacre below and climbed into one of the trees facing the direction the rest of the Crimbone would come from. According to the scouts, a small pack had just cleared Scheshca's Rocks. That was odd. The gods hadn't solidly planted their hooks there, yet the Crimbone typically avoided the area. For the last few hundred years, they'd thought it was unfriendly land or something…as though they sensed the captive limbs and digits of the gods within the soil, already clawing their way towards freedom, to dominion. So what the hell drew these Crimbone back through the region now? Oh well, those upstarts would make their move soon, from the obvious direction.

All it usually took to put down these uprisings was some halfway-competent outskirts unit. So what had gotten the Tribunal's attention so they'd called on the Blades of Bathshire? Vesha watched soft air whisper through the field and trees beyond. He fought off some unease as he looked for the right position.

The tree Vesha climbed was dead, along with all the plant life that had formed the camp's natural defense. In Spiralla, under the scientists' instruction, the Schomite magician-slaves had fashioned two drugs to be used in conjunction with each other, one to be given to a small trained animal in its food over a period of time, the other to be injected right before the moment of use. The animal was then sent scuttling into enemy quarters while a fatal gastric reaction overtook its bowels. Once in with the enemy, the gas would burn and expand so violently that it split the animal's body open and dispersed into the air. The smell would be undetectable to all animal senses, but it killed the surrounding plant life—particularly the dangerous plant life, such as the Schomites had sewn through the soil—within minutes. The plants wilted so subtly yet swiftly that most Crimbone wouldn't realize they'd been left vulnerable 'til the Blades of Bathshire were on them.

Tonight marked the weapon's first use. Vesha liked the results. Death had weakened this tree's structure, but it still held the weight of his long, lithe body. He glanced back, caught the eyes of some troops who were expert caster-shots, and signaled them to join him up here. Their hands and feet whispered as they joined him throughout the woven branches.

The scientists had offered Vesha another animal, one fed on a variant drug that would kill off the Crimbone in the camp directly. Vesha had declined. He preferred to at least give his enemies the honor of a fight to the death. It was a polite gesture, as he saw it. Next time, he might try that alternative. When more Crimbone emerged, there'd be no hand-to-hand fighting. Bolt-casters were usually useless against Crimbone, but Vesha had arranged it so they'd only be ready for the bolts coming from this grove. Between these troops and those in the surrounding trees, there was no way the Crimbone would evade the barrage. Vesha smiled and waited patiently against the dead trunk. All around, dead plant matter smelled like wet pungent char, mingling with spilt Crimbone blood and guts soaking into the ground below.

Steady and silent, Vesha thumbed out his bolt-caster…one of the simplest death-dealing devices ever created, but only for those with the genetic musculature to wield it…the fastest and most accurate, too, but only in trained Spirelight police hands. Along the top, stopping just before the curve of the grip, a smooth cleft was carved where the arrow fit. At the front was just enough space for the back end of the bolt to slide into place, before half an inch of cord strung across the cleft. The cord was hard woven metal, but once nocked, it stretched to the back of the cleft before launching the shaft. Skilled hands could empty a quiver in seconds.

At the other end of the high grass, the Crimbone pack burst from the surrounding trees in a dark swarming mass. Their shades shifted to match the grass, but Vesha still saw them just fine. One hand aimed his bolt-caster while the other dipped to his belt for the first bolt. As he nocked, he drew a breath and held it as his arms tightened. He almost loosed the shot, then paused. The man in the lead was different than the others. Neither his body nor his clothes were colored like a Crimbone's. He didn't even fade to blend in. He was one of them, though, no doubt about it. Something about him seemed...more Crimbone than Crimbone, his movements somehow crueler, swifter, more purposeful than the rest.

By experimenting on prisoners, scientists of Spiralla had determined that a Crimbone's power was inextricably tied to how its existence defied the laws of its environment, like a moth building the strength for the world beyond by breaking out of its cocoon. Wherever this new one had come from, his environment had tried very hard somehow to stamp out his abominable existence before it began, so he ravened with all the more despicable delight, once loosed wild and free upon the world.

Part of Vesha regretted missing the privilege of meeting the man blade to blade. Then his hands did their trick, and every bolt in his quiver joined those of his fellows in the barrage. The bolts swarmed like a cloud of bees across the gloomy field, onto their targets. Those targets darted uselessly, then lurched and spilled into the grass. That strange leader of theirs went down first, from one of Vesha's own bolts if he wasn't mistaken.

Vesha started to smile, then his eyes widened. He spun and leapt from his perch. Dead, sopping earth crunched under his boots as he landed. The others descended more leisurely.

"Hey now," said someone, "that was...insultingly easy."

"It was all wrong," barked Vesha, voice quickening. Sweat broke out all over him. In a single motion, he clipped his bolt-caster back to his belt and reached for his blade.

"What do you mean? You see how they went down?"

"Of course, you idiot. That's what they *wanted* us to see. Anyone else happen to notice what we *didn't* see?"

It dawned on one face, then another. All the bolts had come from them, none from the surrounding forest where they'd positioned the real surprise attack.

Everyone shifted. Before they'd fully turned, the dead brush exploded inward, filling the air with ash. Through it sang many blades of black metal. In the close dark space of the dead camp, the air crackled with the crunch of severed bones, gurgling with spilling bowels and the spray of blood. Most of the Crimbone blended so perfectly with their surroundings that only their blades could be seen, so black that the surrounding nighttime space looked bright in contrast. Only one stood out fully visible. His long dark coat billowed like monstrous wings as he closed in on Vesha, his scarred face a twisted mask of clear, bright hatred. From it, there blazed all the distilled elemental fury of two worlds and beyond. Vesha dug in his heels and raised his sword. Some troops tried to swarm the demon from either side. His eyes never left Vesha's as he closed in. He moved like a freshet of mist across water at dawn. His twin blades licked left and right, almost absentmindedly. The converging agents went to pieces and spilled their guts.

Vesha swung his sword in a perfect downward arc at the onrusher's skull. The twin black blades scissored the sword at the hilt, shattering it. The twin strokes continued seamlessly from there and caught Vesha across the chest. Vesha's ribcage split and he saw his own blood splatter his enemy's face. He toppled as his chest folded inward, bone-edges grinding and scraping.

Vesha's gaze rolled everywhere. In the delirium before death, he saw the strangest thing. Where his troops died, where the soil drank their blood, the ashen death of the grove seemed to recede, as though where blood spilled, the dead ground came back to life. Then his knees struck the ground. The monster crouched over him, snarling.

~

Rob had observed the physical difference between these Spirelights and those in some other world. It made no difference to him…except that the glow already tasted sweeter and purer than ever. Never had he felt so weightless as when he drew his black blades on it in this world. He sheathed the blades and grabbed the Spirelight commander, holding eye-contact. The commander let out a fading squeal. Sliced ribs stuck out of the yawning mouth in his chest like crooked teeth.

"*Look at me!*" He jerked the commander up nose-to-nose. "*Look your death in the eye, motherfucker…the death of everything you've polluted these lands with. It all starts here, with you.*"

The commander sucked in his final gulp of air and breathed it out as "Blasphemous beasts…never be the death of us…You move through the lands…We walk in the light of the gods…"

Rob recognized the Spirelight language. He growled in it, "Exactly. *Those* gods. *That tells me everything I'll ever need to know about any of you.* I'm your god now, your *last* god. *Look into the eyes of your god of death.*"

Rob's hand plunged through the commander's yawning ribcage. His fist closed around the heart and yanked. All the connected tubing strained and popped. He held eye-contact with his enemy. The eyes went dead in the same instant he bit into the heart. He drank deep of the commander's glow while he sucked the heart dry.

Now his pack swarmed into the grove. More of the glow flared around him as they cut it loose. The glow sure screamed a lot when you did that. Rob drank it up 'til he overflowed with it. He felt the lands beneath his feet overflow, too, blazing with him.

FIVE

Sheldon ran through the field, side by side with the Crimbone who'd helped him take the surrounding tree line. They'd be eager to tell their brethren what they'd seen him do, of the strange weapons he'd wielded…weapons that seemed to have been forged from the essence of the same enemies it killed. They must be more confused than ever. He hadn't liked some of the looks he'd gotten from them. Yeah, he probably owed Rob an extra thank-you or two, for instructing them in advance not to kill him and all that.

He and his companions trotted to a stop outside the dead fort. Bloody shapes staggered out to meet them. At first, in the moonlight, Sheldon couldn't tell if they were friend or foe. The Crimbone seemed to know instantly. Of course they did. If those had been Spirelights coming out to meet them, the Crimbone would have tasted the glow.

A Crimbone woman shot frantically past Sheldon. "My kids…"

"Don't go in there, Reila," Cragor shuddered.

Reila clenched her jaw and had to dig in her heels to stay on her feet.

Rob strode out last. Once he appeared, everyone around him looked a few inches shorter. He sniffed the air and growled, "More Spirelights are on the way…more than we just faced."

"Then let's go to meet the fuckers," Reila snarled through quaking sobs.

"No," declared Kashen.

"But they—"

"Our duty is to the High Natural and the man with no race. We have to get them where they need to go. We—"

"Damn right it is." Rob strode over and locked eyes with Kashen. "So why the fuck are you talking like one who makes the calls here?"

"My chief, we can't—we shouldn't risk more unnecessary losses."

Rob looked at Sheldon. "What do you say, Little Brave?"

Sheldon looked around. He hadn't seen what the Spirelight Police had done in the grove. He already knew he didn't want to. "I like Reila's idea best. But it's not the smartest move right now. Later, we'll take vengeance. Kashen, you say you know how to get us where we need to go?"

"That's right."

Rob and Sheldon exchanged heavy looks. "So lead the way," Rob told Kashen.

Kashen nodded, then sprinted past the ruined camp. He made for the trees at the opposite end of the field from which they'd come. Everyone followed him. The forest this way was full of rocky, brambly slopes, gullies, and hills. Ahead, there sounded the rush of water. From behind them, the ground rumbled with what sounded and felt like hundreds of feet. The pack crashed through some brush, down a final sandy slope, to the edge of a roaring river. Behind them, their pursuers thundered ever nearer.

"Can we swim this?" Sheldon asked, mostly to himself, staring out across what looked like half a mile or more of roaring water.

"Sure," said Rob. "Can't have those assholes at our backs make the same call, though." He looked at Reila. "Well, lady, looks like you'll get your wish after all."

"Yeah," she rumbled. Something in her had changed, so even Rob stepped back cautiously. "Get into the water," she growled, "all of you."

Winds rose, howling maliciously through the branches, seemingly centered on Reila, battering her, lifting her hair and clothes, so it seemed she might be carried into the air or swept away like a leaf. She stood strong at its center. Her face twisted into something unrecognizable.

Kashen's eyes bulged at her, in dawning comprehension. "Do what she says, now, all of you!"

Sheldon waded in. He glanced back at Reila. She stalked back the way they'd come, drawing her blade with that chilling singing hiss only the Crimbone metal made. On a distant hill, the first Spirelights broke through the trees.

"What's she doing?" Sheldon asked Rob or Kashen, whoever would or could answer through all the roaring water lapping up around them.

"She's called on the *death rage*," Rob said.

Kashen nodded and waded quicker 'til the riverbed dropped off beneath him and he fell forward into a swift, powerful swim.

Sheldon almost paused but kept swimming harder. "Shouldn't we—"

"*No*," Kashen barked. "If we tried to help her now, she'd just as likely kill us as them."

"So how many you think she'll kill?"

Rob spat water out of his mouth long enough to answer, "A lot. With a little luck, all of them."

Sheldon remembered the numbers he'd glimpsed. Was that possible? Before he could ask more, though, the riverbed dropped away under him. The current almost swept him away. He fought it as it filled his coat and tugged him downward, almost irresistibly. Staying afloat wasn't the problem. It was staying on a straight course, on *any* course but that of the river's choosing. It only got stronger the further out he swam. His pumping arms felt feebler against it by the instant. The shore he fought for still looked well over halfway off. His coat sleeves felt like lead on his arms. If he'd really been thinking on his feet, he'd have ditched the coat before wading in. He would have shrugged it off now, except he couldn't afford to break his paddling. Yeah, this really sucked.

Through the water splashing his face, he tried to see how Rob or anyone fared. There wasn't much he could tell. Near the shores behind them, he fancied he could hear the roar of slaughter surrounding Reila. It was inconceivable that only one woman was at the center of it, that she'd stay up no matter what they did to her, until they were all dead or there was nothing left of her to fight. The *glow* must be exploding like a supernova back there. Sheldon wondered if it did these Crimbone around him any good while they battled the current. All he could do was swim on furiously and blindly.

Eventually, Sheldon's feet and palms kicked and pressed through the mud and rocks of the shallow. He lumbered through it, hunched forward. Slimy water poured out of his clothes and hair. He wiped at his face. At first, his slimy arms and hands only blinded him further. He blinked his eyes clear and looked around. The Crimbone were trudging onto land, not much better off from their swim.

Sheldon scanned for Rob. "Everyone still with us?"

Kashen sputtered water from his mouth. "Reila…She's dead…The lands just told me. They carried the message to me through the water just before I reached the shallow."

"Then she killed them all?" someone asked hopefully.

"No." Kashen squeezed his eyes shut and shuddered.

"Will they cross after us?"

"Not here. They might search down river for a better crossing point. We won't have to worry about them now. She weakened their ranks—killed enough, wounded most of the rest—that they won't make a go for us now."

Rob slogged towards Kashen and clamped a steadying hand on his shoulder. "You two were close, huh?"

"She was my wife."

"Then those kids of hers who died back there—"

Kashen shook his head. "Their father died some years back. He was a good friend. So were those kids. They were growing to be fine fighters." He shoved his grief aside with one deadly, clench-tooth growl. "Let's keep going. We need to find another pack, another camp. With the lands on our side, we'll find one before dawn."

Before anyone could move to obey, a high-pitched shriek split the air. Everyone spun back towards the river, many nearly losing their footing in the mud. A long reptilian head sprouted from the muddy surf. Its fanged, frothing jaws clamped on the midsection of the nearest Crimbone. With failing strength, he hacked futilely, chopping out one of the creature's eyes, but the jaws only tightened, sounding off the wet splinter of bones. The shrieks grew louder, ever more hopeless and agonized. The pack came in a running slide, Rob and Sheldon in the lead. One of the younger ones made it past them and reached the beast first, swinging his black axe down on the base of the long neck. The edge turned on tough scales. A sinewy reptilian arm swung whip-like from beneath the muck. The man's skull shattered. It sounded like soggy cabbage smacking around inside a fractured clay pot. He fell limp and slid beneath the muddy water.

The man in the creature's jaws kept screaming. Sheldon ripped both knives loose and swung. The doomed Crimbone's head spun free and splashed somewhere. Sheldon hacked and slashed at the monster with both blades. Rob was at his side, doing the same. The water around their knees turned to bloody soup. The creature's great, serpentine bulk shifted irritably. It swam away beneath the muck, taking the headless Crimbone with it.

~

The pack's first shared impulse was to harry the creature as it fled, but they found themselves settling with weary relief.

"Damn," Kashen panted glumly, "guess ol' Nagga there's the one gets dinner tonight."

Even as he said it, one of the creature's clawed hind legs made one final defiant, fleeing kick from beneath the muddy waves. Rob shrieked as two of those claws impaled his leg beneath the knee and dragged him under. The riverbed scraped his back then dropped away. The water monster dragged him deeper and further out, faster and faster. If his companions had run in after him, he'd been carried away too quickly to know. His fists still clutched his knives. He'd have hacked off the creature's leg, kicked for the surface with its claw still embedded in him, but the rush pulled his arms straight back above his head.

Water filled Rob's mouth, nose, and lungs. The current wrenched one of the black blades of Magur Sevi from his grip, then the other. Soon afterwards, he lost consciousness.

WAITING FOR THE

MIRACLE

ONE

Jesse led Zane and Remelea to the great, gray Stone Church on the upper end of Main Street. There were a lot of big, fancy old churches on this block, with looming spires stabbing the sky…architecture crafted with love, from a time before utility replaced reverence and artistry. There were also lots of banks, most of them big, sterile, and box-shaped. No one had much use for the banks lately. In times like this, though, people loved churches, even though whatever old Earth-line faiths such buildings had Once celebrated scarcely mattered anymore. The Stone Church hadn't been used as a place of worship for decades, yet it now stood out with grim portent from all the rest.

Warm, red light spilled through the great archway-shrouded doors of the looming gray edifice. At the top of the front steps, Sam and Anya stood talking with a tall, rail-thin Earth-line man in a rain-slicker and high rubber boots. Even from here, his limbs and neck looked impossibly long and thin. The narrow beard on his pointy chin curled downward, almost as long as the shaggy hair that spilled past his shoulders, from beneath a wide slouch hat. He spotted Jesse, Zane and Remelea, and descended slowly towards them. Sam and Anya hung back on the porch, all steely.

"Hello, Jesse. Zane." The guy's big eyes darted with cartoonish nervousness to Remelea, the newest Crimbone in town. It wasn't hard for Earth-line folks to learn how to spot Deschembines, once they knew what to look for. "We...wondered where you'd disappeared to."

"*You* wondered." Sam's deep, resonant, deadpan voice sounded from up on the porch. He caught Jesse's gaze. "The rest of us had a few ideas."

Jesse stepped aside. "Liam, meet Remelea. Remelea, meet Liam. What have we missed?"

"Shouldn't we be asking Sam and Anya about that?" said Zane.

"We'll ask them later." Jesse gave Liam a hard *Yes, son, this is a test* glare.

"We've got the whole downtown area pretty well covered. Everything's mostly secured, from Vernon Road to the far end of Putney Road, then up to the edge of West Bratt. Everything from the upper end of Canal Street's such a shitshow, I don't even wanna think about that just yet if I can help it. Upper Elliot Street's still a nightmare. It's...y'know, not in the middle of things, but it's too close for my comfort."

"You mean because you're used to it always being a big shit-den full of junkies," said Zane. "A...what do you modern white Earth-liners like to call places where mostly black folks live? *A bad neighborhood?*"

"Well, it's mostly white, but otherwise, yeah."

"Yeah, well, the whole damn world—past what we can reasonably secure —is a *bad neighborhood* now."

"You're telling me! I had to move my wife and toddler in here from Dummerston, 'cause it ain't even livable out there, even that far out! One minute, those hills are filling up with all the escaped nut-jobs, like rats leaving a sinking ship, then there were all those mutated freaks swarming in. Man, the way they came at us…I had to start killing actual people. I mean…I practiced for it my whole life, but now I've been…shit…*I've actually felt men die at the end of my arm when I stuck a blade in 'em…actually seeing their brains leaking out of the back of their shattered skulls when I got 'em with a shotgun…*I…I…"

"Suck it up and bitch about it on your own time," said Sam from up on the porch. "That shit ain't in the job-description."

"Kid, shut the fuck up," Zane told Sam. He stepped up to Jesse's side and peered at Liam. "Got a headcount yet on how much of the population's stuck around?"

"I'd say five, maybe six hundred on the outside? It's hard to know how many are still holed up tight indoors." Liam rubbed his high forehead. "Some of the Main Street restaurants have their work staff and some of their families camped out in 'em. The Fireworks crew has that place locked down like a fortress. I'm…impressed."

"Fireworks?" said Jesse.

"Yeah, the fancy…the place that used to be a sorta fancy restaurant, back a ways down Main Street."

"Sounds like, by *impressed*, you mean *worried*," said Zane.

"Yeah, my little brother took this big pizza-cutter knife to the face when we tried to jimmy our way in there. We thought it was deserted. Holy shit, I didn't think they kept weapons like that in there, you know, in restaurant kitchens. Apparently, they actually call that thing the Pizza Sword."

"Your little brother still alive?"

"Yeah, with a face full of stitches. He might keep his left eye. He's in good spirits about it, at least. Keeps saying how now he'll have a badass scar to show once this is all over."

Ah, kids. Jesse smiled. "How'd it shake out with those guys?"

"Ah, well, not too bad, actually. Their main dishwasher—this guy everyone calls *the Bird*—it turns out he's one of my old Kung Fu students. Him and their head chef have been keeping 'em pulled together in there. Those two guys are…well…they're kind of couple of raving lunatics, actually."

Zane nodded. "Good."

Jesse leaned in on Liam. "So you've gotten around to all the local restaurants, huh? How much food inventory they have left?"

"From what hasn't rotted since the power went out? Well, they've been making it last, rationing it among their own."

"I meant the restaurant scene in general. We can break down the specifics later."

Liam sighed and splayed his palms. "Everyone's been making do best they can."

"You say one of those raving lunatics is one of your martial arts students," said Jesse. "What kind of a fighter is he?"

"Oh, he's…a brawler, that's for sure. Almost had to ban him from class a couple times, when he almost killed some bigger guys while sparring."

"He got a brain in his head, not just some thug?"

"Oh, yeah. Like I said, him and that Jack guy are holding those folks at Fireworks together pretty well. Nah, he's smart, that's for sure. He used to be, like, some kind of freelance journalist, when he wasn't working in restaurants."

"Right. What about the other guy? Jack?"

"Oh, you know, jacked like a Navy Seal, talks and moves a mile a minute like Ricochet Rabbit. I, um, get the vibe he's, like…the kind of guy who, y'know, never sleeps. I met him a few times before all this started. Back then, I just assumed he did a lot of coke, but now…well…there's not a lot of coke around, because there are no more dealers to traffic it into town, so…well, I guess he's just *like that.*"

"Perfect," said Jesse. "We need to figure out what's what with the rest of the old restaurant spaces, get everyone's stock accounted for, factor that into keeping the rest of the town fed. Get them all coordinated with the local trained hunters and gatherers. You set to handle that?"

"Sure," said Liam. "Wanna take a little walk and talk it over with the Fireworks folks?"

"Later," said Zane. "Right now, it's Elliot Street I'm worried about."

"Guys," said Liam, "I really think we ought'a—"

"Zane's right," said Jesse. "That stretch cuts straight down the center of what we need locked down. You guys have been pussyfooting around it long enough. Let's go for a walk up Elliot Street. Zane, Remelea, you guys come with us."

"I was thinking I'd hang back," said Zane, "touch base with Sam and Anya, find out what the deal is with how we're using all these churches on this block." He sounded almost like a little kid going, *Aw, but I wanted to stay and play with the cool kids in the old spooky stone church.*

"Liam can fill us in on all that on the way," said Jesse. "C'mon, ol' buddy, I might want you along on this."

Remelea sauntered easily into step between Jesse and Zane as they took the lead, so only Liam had to scuttle to keep up.

"Okay, kid," said Zane to Liam, "fill me in on that situation."

"Uh, yeah, ah, we've, like, taken the Stone Church as...I guess you'd call it the stronghold. For the local leaders and our families, whose own homes have become unlivable. We've made the other churches on the street...ah...livable as we can, y'know, for whoever wants to shack up there. First come, first serve, though, y'know?"

They walked through the center of the street. Their boots crunched through a bed of snow that hadn't been plowed in a day or so. The sidewalks were all covered in snowdrifts five feet high or more. You could tell which buildings had people living in them, some from short shoveled-out pathways, others from semi-fresh, deep-sunk foot-tracks over the drifts, leading up to the front doors.

Liam went on, "A lot of the people in the rest of those churches are, y'know, whoever's left who used to go to those churches. It's where they seem calmest, so they don't, y'know, freak out and make trouble. I don't wanna sound, y'know, prejudiced against religious people and shit, but..."

"Nah, it's cool," said Zane. "We don't trust folks who worship gods, either."

"The Stone Church hasn't been used like a *church-*church in years. It's really more of a community-owned event-space, for music shows and dance parties, and...well, I mean, before it was like that, but now..."

Jesse spotted Liam shivering harder, from something other than the biting cold. He gave the guy a hard slap on the shoulder. "Hey, man. How's that wife and kid of yours holding up?"

"Oh, they're...Yeah, pretty well. Little Emil, he's a tough little trooper." Liam smiled through the shivers with wistful, bittersweet pride. "So's Aurora. I gotta say, in there, she's the one who's really pulled all those fuckers together, keeps 'em from rioting. She's no joke. I love her. Just...she gets really sad, you know? She used to teach dance classes in that church. Now it's like some refugee camp in there. She goes around, talking to everyone who's not holding up so well, keeping their spirits up. There are only a few other little kids in there. I wish there were more kids around Emil's age for him to play with. Mostly, when things started going bad, it was the families with small kids who split town first, looking for somewhere safer."

"Yeah," said Remelea, "I've seen a lot of folks over the last few months, taking to the roads, looking for *somewhere safer*, in whatever direction they think they're gonna find that. Now wherever you go, it's like you can't take a piss without squirting on some half-starved, whiney, runaway wanker who thought he'd be Mad Max or some shit when all this hit the fan."

"Uh, yeah," said Liam. "Can't argue with you there...Remelea, right?"

"Anyway," said Zane, "there's also some strings of houses in the neighborhoods up off High Street where we've gathered people into communal housing. That's where most of those United Deschembines you brought are staying."

"You mean next to the woods that lead to the ski jump?" said Jesse.

"Uh, yeah, around there."

"Fuck. That's gonna take some work."

"For what?"

"Moving them out of there and shacking 'em up someplace safer. Right now, though, that's the absolute worst place to stash a bunch of civilians."

"Yeah, but it's like...as far as we could get 'em, in town, from the worst of the danger."

"*Within town*, sure."

Zane shot Jesse a grim look. Jesse looked at Remelea, hoping to catch a bead on what she was thinking. She kept her mouth set in a hard line, peering forward.

Elliot Street came into sight, jutting off to the right, just before where Main Street dropped into a steep ramp. All Jesse's straight-ahead focus was on that road, then he glanced again at Remelea. Her eyes flickered at his, then darted downhill to the left. Jesse's gaze followed hers. The first thing he spotted was the swinging, snow-crusted red-and-black sign of Fireworks Restaurant. Two figures skulked in the deep-set archway. A third ambled before them in the street. It was Remelea who first steered subtly towards the trio. Jesse shifted into her lead. Their two companions followed accordingly.

The figures in the doorway were too heavily bundled to tell much about them physically, though they both held themselves stalwart and vigilant, like men ready to back up whatever stance they took in the face of anything. The shorter one gripped a long metal rod with a broad flattened end in both hands. He held it like a bow-staff, like someone who knew how to use one, so he could probably split someone's skull with the paddle-end. His eyes were wide and crazy, peering from beneath a knitted hat that would look goofy on most people. His companion leaned on the corner of the archway. His gaze was hard-set, somber and cruel, his face shadowed by a large green hood. A gleaming, curved bar of sharpened metal hung easily at his side from one hand. That, Jesse gathered, must be the fabled Pizza Sword. Neither had shaved in weeks, which did nothing to hide their chiseled faces.

A granite-faced, leather-jacket-clad man talked to them from the narrow shoveled outer walkway. He swung loose and easy, with an absurdly happy-go-lucky air about him. He was younger than either of them, built bulkier, taller than the crazy-eyed one, not as tall as the cruel-eyed one. He might have stood taller than either, except for a life of brutal injuries from which he hadn't healed right, leaving him bent into the wrong shapes in all sorts of places. His upper back jutted out in a Quasimodo-hunch. All his deformities would have crippled a man of Earth-line bone-structure. He wasn't Earth-line, though. A forked prong of black metal hung from his belt.

Most of this Crimbone's injuries were five months old or less. Jesse knew this, partly because he'd been looking at such injuries since before the kid was born, partly because he'd seen him before. The guy had been a lot greener five months ago.

Before Jesse could address him, Remelea stormed forward. "Joel," she shouted, "what the fuck are you doing here?"

The ruffian spun. His granite face lit up obscenely. "What the...Is that Remelea, or am I having an acid flashback?"

"Yeah, this is Remelea. The rest of that's your business."

"Well, fuck me!"

"Not right now, baby." She and the hunchbacked punk crashed into each other for a hard hug. "*What's going on, you fuckin' prick?*"

"What, you mean other than you showing up out of nowhere, you dirty cunt?" His tone and eyes went a shade grimmer. "Other than that, sort of a lot."

Jesse stepped up, a little too sharply. "So what *is* new?"

"Hey, Jesse Karn," said Joel. "So you're part of the wave moving everyone into Brattleboro. Yeah, that makes sense."

Zane leaned in and whispered to Jesse, "Ain't this motherfucker supposed to be dead?"

"Look," said Joel, "I know what you're thinking. Don't worry. I'm not...one of them. Believe me, you'd know if I was."

"Wait, wait," said the guy with the long metal paddle, "you mean there's more of *them* weirdos crawling around out there than you guys?"

"Oh yeah," said his companion in the green hoodie, the one brandishing the pizza sword. "Lots more." He smirked mirthlessly beneath the shadow of the hood, then leaned out of the archway. "Hey, Liam. Hey, Jesse."

"Bird, how do you keep knowing this shit?" said his shorter companion. "*You're freakin' me out, Bird!*"

Jesse thought of what he'd seen on Sally's operating table. He asked Joel, "How would we know?"

"Ha! I don't need to tell you, do I? Look, I talked with Sam and Anya before we all split, okay? Back in Virginia, I mean. We *all* got an idea, what was coming. From Balthazar, I mean. Hell, I deserted not long after them, for the...same reasons. Funny shit. My blood told me to run like a little bitch from Balthazar, and I...*Old Lords, all I did was follow my blood!*" Joel's eyes squeezed tight. His big open palm crashed against his own face. "Ain't that what we're all supposed to do? I just...followed the voice of the fucking lands here, through all this frozen shit, like a Crimbone's supposed to. To this place called Brattleboro. Lot of good it's gonna do us all now, right? He's still on the way."

"Balthazar?" said Jesse.

"Who else?"

Remelea got right in Joel's face. "You gonna help us or not, you little bitch?"

Joel drew up straight and proud as his bent back let him. He nodded. "I did some scouting on the way. Balthazar's guys are filling up the surrounding areas, taking over in small groups, one at a time."

"What do you mean, *surrounding* areas?"

"Keene, what's left of Boston, you name it. Anywhere like Montpelier, Burlington, all those places…They're gone, man, forget about it. I scouted around, first in my truck, then on foot and hitching rides to be more discreet, picking up whatever I could. Look, I don't know what those assholes are planning, but whatever it is, it's big."

Jesse grabbed Joel by both shoulders. "Is anyone holding out, anywhere?"

"I don't know, okay? I heard something about 'em having trouble with Meredith Falls…"

"What's up in Meredith Falls?" asked Bird, like he was worried about someone he loved there.

Joel shot him a dismissive look. "Bunch of pinches and some other weird assholes from some other boats off the black oceans, from some worlds I don't know much about. That town's always been a haven for those freaks. Why?"

"Hey, wait," said Liam, "just how many *other worlds* do we got people from—"

"Bro, shut up," said Bird. He said to Joel, "You say they're doing a better job holding out?"

"Maybe. I heard the pinch population there doubled, like the little bastards flooded in from Canada or some shit. Lots of good that's gonna do. You think those little tricksters give a shit about what happens to anyone in this physical realm?"

Bird shrugged and smirked, like he knew something no one else did.

"Sounds like Balthazar's insurgents are staking their turf quietly," said Jesse. "When they hit us, it'll start as a slow trickle. They won't all swarm at once. First it'll be small packs that we'll be able to deal with easy, so it'll seem like isolated incidents. Not everyone who comes will be fighting. Someone'll be watching, to get a sense of how we're operating. When those strikes come, we can't let any of 'em retreat alive. We might get two or three of those before the full strike hits."

Zane whistled. "Talk about overkill!"

"That's probably what Balthazar's going for," said Jesse. "Joel, don't think for a second you made it here undetected."

"You make it sound like we're all fucked already."

"Maybe we are," said Zane. "Outer defense strategizing ain't gonna count for shit, once the full brunt of it starts, so we'll keep our ranks concentrated as much as possible in the close quarters surrounding the town. We'll be the ones with our backs to the wall. That's a good thing. I figure we'll get a lot of our number waiting to meet them in the streets, and a lot more inside the buildings, ready to spring when the time's right. The more of them who swarm in, the more they'll crowd each other. From there, it'll be all about endurance."

"Oh, sure," said Bird. "That makes me and mine feel a lot better."

"This town's got its own weird layout," said Jesse, "with a lot of twists and mazes and hard-to-navigate back-ways, both naturally and in the local structure. I've been checking it out and figuring out how we can use that."

"You guys haven't seen this pack," said Joel. "There's enough of 'em to last weeks, months even. You expect to hold that long? You guys are insane."

Jesse and Zane looked at each other, then Zane said "Well…yeah."

"We'll *endure* 'til Rob and Sheldon get where they're going and do what they need to do," said Remelea.

"Hey, wait a second," said Joel. "Where *is* Rob? You mean Rob Coscan, right? Who the fuck is Sheldon?"

Zane glanced at Jesse. "You wanna bring him up to speed, or should I?"

"I wanna get back to business with locking down Elliot Street," said Jesse. "Joel, you come with us. Let's see what you got." He pointed at Bird and Jack. "You boys keep holding this spot down."

~

Things had always been more dilapidated past the commercial area on Elliot Street. Now that the whole town had gone to shit, the winding residential stretch that followed was even worse. It shrank, swelled and twisted beneath its snowy coating, like a rotting ghost-town.

Somewhere nearby, glass shattered. Someone shouted, from someplace downhill. Someone else screamed. There were at least three people screaming, echoing from within stone walls. One of the latter sounded like a small child.

Ahead, there rose a long shack with a church-marquee in the front yard and a Superman symbol hanging between the glass of the front windows and the curtains behind. Before, there'd been some kind of slogan about how Jesus was the real-life Superman. The marquee letters had been rearranged to say something about how the gangs ran this street now, how they'd rape Jesus or Superman if either got in the way. The building dropped off down the hillside, into a small gravelly parking lot in front of an old junk yard. The only vehicle left was a Winnebago spray-painted all over with hippie art. All the windows were smashed and the doors were torn off. Everyone outside downhill ignored it, either because they'd already raided it or because someone else had gotten all the good stuff first.

Jesse didn't smell any corpses in the Winnebago. He smelled all shades of fear from within the church-building's basement, which looked to have been converted into apartment space. He smelled wanton lust and abandon from the half-dozen guys clustered around a basement-apartment's deep-set entrance, like a pack of feral dogs barking at a stray cat they'd chased up a tree. They looked like they ranged from their mid-teens to mid-twenties.

"C'mon, Katie, jus' let us on in," shouted one of the punks, probably the ringleader. "We know you're in there." He turned back to exchange bestial, infantile giggles with his companions. "Look, wha' you all worried about in there? We the local law on this street, yeah, you can trust us. We hear you been holdin' out wit' de food in there. Can't have that now, y'know? It's share-and-share-alike 'round here these days, baby. Y'all jus' gotta get with the program, yo, ya hear? Look, all we wanna do is come on in, have a look around, make sure everything's square." The punks exchanged more ugly giggles.

The woman in there didn't sound convinced.

"Hey, you know we gonna come in there, one way or the other, right? This don't gotta be so bad for you, yo, you jus' open up now." The ringleader hammered thunderously on straining wood. Glass rattled. *"Lil' bitch, you open up this fuckin' door right now, or I'm'a fuck you in the ass. Yeah, then I'm'a let all my boys here fuck you in the ass, too. You an' your fuckin' screamin' brat an' whatever other bitchass motherfuckers you got in there!"*

Jesse, Zane, Remelea, Liam and Joel paused and looked down the hillside. Jesse smiled at Remelea. "Ladies first."

Remelea's hand didn't go anywhere near her hook. She brushed absently at her bangs. "Thought you'd never ask, handsome." With that, she strode down the driveway. "Excuse me, boys? I think there's been some mistake. Did I just hear you say you're the local law? Sorry to disappoint you, 'cause, see, that's who me and my friends here are."

The thugs all turned and gaped at her. "*Whoooooooweeee!*" one of them hooted, striding forward, swinging his arms around like they were in some glitzy, goofyass dance-off competition. "You boys hearin' this crazy bitch?" He tried harder and harder to give her the scary-eye, wasting too much energy on that stupid fucking clown-like swagger punks like this always thought looked so intimidating. "You want some a' this, baby? Who the fuck are you, huh, *Xena, the Warrior Princess* or some shit?"

Remelea just grinned. The punches and kicks started flying. Screams and snapping bones echoed up through the deep, still Vermont-Winter air. Jesse ignored everyone else, mostly just enjoyed watching Remelea have fun. There was one unbroken window in the abandoned Winnebago, he noticed absently. Remelea grabbed, twisted and threw someone. Okay, no, there wasn't anymore. Remelea grabbed the guy by the ankles, dragged him out of the window, tearing his face and neck to shreds along the way, right before she swung him around and hit two other guys with him.

A gun went off. The echoing crash vibrated through all the ice-crusted tree-branches. Remelea's back arched, evading the shot. Her open palm struck sideways, breaking the gun-hand at the wrist, before yanking the arm out of the socket. She drove her boot heel into some asshole's chin, so the man's head lashed backwards. The neck broke with an echoing pop. In the same instant, another pistol cocked, echoing as though in slow-motion, from yards away. Before the guy's finger could tighten on the trigger, Remelea snapped off a round from her own appropriated handgun. The punk's head lashed back, chasing after his flying brains, which splattered across the snow. Another three shots snapped from Remelea's fist, so a kneecap, a hip, and a set of testicles all exploded.

She sneered at the weapon in her hand, stripped it, tossed it aside in two directions, then walked to the door, not minding the spreading puddles of pulpy red sludge she stepped in. "It's okay," she called softly inside, before smoky cordite-stench cleared, "you can come out now."

"You didn't mention how many of these Elliot Street assholes still have loaded firearms," Jesse hissed in Liam's ear.

"You didn't ask," said Liam. "Thought you Crimbone bastards were supposed to be street-smart or some shit."

Joel stepped to Jesse's side. "I swear, I can't help it…Whenever I see that girl fight, it makes me wanna see her naked. Of course I've already seen her naked, but that's beside the point."

Jesse smirked and glanced down. "How'd you get all those scars on your hand, Joel?"

"You don't wanna know, trust me."

TWO

Janie hugged herself while she shambled down the back streets of Brattleboro in the middle of the night. *Backstreet's back, oh yeeeeeaaaaahh!* Yep, there came that phase of her musical taste as a kid. Wow, that was annoying to suddenly have stuck in her head, but hey, anything to distract her from the cold, right?

Not far from here, she'd once sat with Sheldon in the park on a chilly morning when they were both still kids. Some teenage goth-girl had hurried by in front of them, wearing a skimpy, lacy outfit, hugging her bulging boobs awkwardly against the chill.

Janie's caustic, judgmental, slut-shaming thirteen-year-old self had pointed her out, all "What is she even doin', dressing like that, if she doesn't wanna flaunt it? If you don't wanna show it off, cover it up, girl!"

At the time, Sheldon had been so much more innocent about stuff like that. He'd blushed so much, whenever she brought up a woman's form, what a woman's body went through, as though she hadn't caught him eyeing her budding tits more than once. Hell, when they'd shared their first kiss, did he think she *hadn't* noticed him *oh-so-accidentally* copping a feel through her T-shirt? Boys were stupid. Then he'd been gone, and she suddenly hadn't known what to do with herself. To this day, she couldn't figure out how that weirdo kid had managed to invade her life, then take up so much of it in such a short amount of time, that he'd left such a big hole in her when he up and disappeared.

Then he'd come back, suddenly so much the *real man*, pulsating with passion, purpose, burden, and mystery, so handsome and rugged…How could a girl *not* get infatuated with that bullshit, especially when she was the one he fell for so hard? The whole time, though, it was always the scared, sensitive, inquisitive little boy underneath all that, the one he hadn't managed to kill within himself no matter what the rest of the world put him through, who she'd truly *fallen in love with.*

Whatever. Sheldon was gone, off to that mythical fantasy-land of his ancestors, probably primed to fuck lots of slave-girls wearing chainmail bikinis or some shit, because it wasn't like he was ever gonna see her again, right? He'd realize in a week that he was better off without her, that she'd never been fit for his world anyway. She was the one still stuck here, wandering the cold, wet post-apocalypse ghost-town of what used to be her hometown, because of what violent men with swords, like him, had done to the world. That's right, *men and women with swords*, if men or women was what you'd call them. Whenever she stopped to think about crazy shit like that, she wondered how much difference was even left, between this world and the land of Sheldon's ancestors.

Why the fuck had she decided to go outside in this weather? Oh right, because she'd felt so cooped up inside that house they'd stashed her in, along with the rest of those *civilians* among the United Deschembines. Here she was, back in her hometown, on the cusp of the end of the world. Life was funny like that. The town wasn't even the same place anymore, yet while she strolled through it with no one else around, it still *felt* the same. Something about that was soothing. She should probably have felt more wary, of lurking dangers within all the night-black houses around her. It wasn't like she felt brave, just numb. Hey, if some vagrant jumped out of the shadows to rape and murder her, at least all this shit wouldn't be her problem anymore, right?

Ahead, near the bottom of Grove Street, Janie saw lights glowing through the windows of the old municipal building. Okay, that was weird. She drifted towards it and climbed the steps. When she reached for the knob, she found it busted. Someone had broken it to get in. She shrugged, pulled it open, and walked on down the hall. To her right was a glass display of antique firemen and policemen uniforms from a century ago. Emblems of the *bold heroes of days past*. Yeah, right, old dead white men with guns and batons, who used to beat up and kill her ancestors on Mom's side of the family.

A cold hiss shuddered out at Janie. A keen, metallic edge settled against her throat. She nearly spilled forward right onto it, which would have cut her whole head off. Instead, she sucked in a deep breath, drew backwards, and lifted her hands to the sky.

"Don't kill me," she squeaked.

"Sure," said the voice at the other end of the blade. "Don't sneak up on me again. Fair trade?"

"Fine, I didn't mean to! Sorry! Jesus!"

"Ain't you noticed, bitch? Jesus ain't here." The blade withdrew from Janie's neck. It was shaped like a pirate's hook, only bigger, made of that unearthly black metal...a Crimbone's weapon. The Crimbone on the other end of it was a woman. "Shit. Another townie. Figures."

Janie backed away, lifting her hands higher. "Okay, okay, I'll go! Sorry, sorry!"

The Crimbone woman relaxed, shrugged, and clipped the hook back on her belt. She didn't even seem to notice how close Janie was to pissing herself. "Nah, it's okay. It's cold out there. Stay for a while and warm up."

It wasn't much warmer in here, Janie might have mentioned. She still wanted to run, but she wasn't sure the Crimbone woman wouldn't take it as an insult, chase her down and gut her for it. "Uh, okay? What are you doing here?"

"I'm digging through a lot of old historical records on this town, because some people told me this was where the old historical society library was. Turns out some motherfuckers didn't lie for once. What are *you* doing here?"

"I...just got bored, decided to take a walk, and saw the lights on in here?"

The Crimbone woman looked Janie over, then casually reached out and felt up the scrawny, under-developed muscles of Janie's arms. Janie stood and took it. "Damn, girl, I guess you've got a death-wish on you or some shit," said the Crimbone woman.

"Maybe."

"Hey, I hear that. Don't we all?"

Mere moments ago, Janie recalled, right before she'd walked in here, she'd been all bitchy and moany like, *Yeah, life sucks now, so I don't care if some monster jumps out and kills me. I wish one would. Bring it on. Waaaaah!* Now that a monster stood before her, trying to make casual conversation in the same breath as threatening her, she realized, no, her self-preservation instincts were still alive and well.

"What's your name?" said the monster.

"Janie."

"Hi, Janie. I'm Remelea."

"Hi, Remelea."

Janie followed Remelea into the reading-room of the old Brattleboro Historical Society. The place looked like an old, posh Edwardian study, with walls lined in bookshelves full of musty old leather volumes. In the middle of the room, there stretched a big table, with a bunch of those books laying open, tossed about haphazardly, like someone had been searching through them furiously for answers. Old-fashioned oil lamps had been set about, on either end of the table, along with other surfaces around the room.

Remelea strode around the table and sat down. In surroundings like this, Janie would have expected to see some old proper English gentleman in a smoking jacket, not some dirty, wild-haired cowgirl, all the blood and guts and shit she'd spent her life wallowing in caked permanently into her skin, with that razor-edged meat-hook of murder hanging against her hip. To one side of her sat a half-empty bottle of whiskey she'd found God-knew-where. On the other, there sat a clear plastic bag full of white powder.

Remelea spotted Janie peering askance at the latter and said, "Yeah. Y'know, this town kept their *historical society* library in the same building as their police department? Hey, c'mon, have a seat."

Janie pulled out a chair and sat down across from her. "Of course I knew that. I grew up here."

"Yeah, turns out their contraband impound lockup hadn't been raided completely dry yet." Remelea doled out a smidge of white powder and chopped it into lines with someone's old credit card. "Why not, right? Want a hit?"

"No, uh, I'm good."

"Suit yourself." Remelea took a rolled-up dollar bill, snorted a fat caterpillar line, then stared across the table. "Hey, wait a second. Are you *that* Janie?"

"Which Janie?"

Remelea took a swig from the bottle. "The one Jesse Karn won't shut up about."

"Jesse's been talking about me?"

"Yeah, he keeps going on about how you're his first Earth-line friend in decades, h0w amazing it is that you've still got such a kind *heart to help* after all the hell you've seen, how you *give him hope for the future* or some bullshit."

"This…is all news to me."

"Hey, don't look at me! Jesse Karn's one of those old-school, delusional *man of honor* kinda guys. It's funny, how men like that always think they're *better* than the rest of those assholes, when they usually just end up making things worse."

"I'll drink to that," said Janie. "If you don't mind."

Remelea slid the bottle across the table. "Knock yourself out, girl. Hey, wait, right, you *do* know what I'm talking about, don't you?"

Janie took a swig. "What do you mean?"

"Sheldon was with you, right, before he left this world for the other with Rob?"

Oh right, Janie remembered, this was the woman who Sally's husband had cheated on her with. Not that any of that mattered now, she guessed. She still said, "Can we please not talk about that?"

"Sure. So what else do you wanna talk about?"

"I don't know, like…what do you want with this town's historical records?"

Remelea peered at the pages before her. "I'm looking for…why we're all here. In this town, specifically, I mean. Seems like, anyone who's anyone, from all over, keeps finding their own, completely separate reasons to all converge here, so it looks like this is where *Ragnarök* or some shit's about to go down. I guess I'd feel a lot better if I just had some idea of why…about what's so special about these lands." She looked up. "Rob mentioned something called the Brattleboro Vortex. You grew up here. What's that mean to you?"

"Well…it *is* the place where Rob and Sheldon found the doorway back to you guys' *Old World*."

"There's that. So what's this *Brattleboro Vortex?*"

Janie squirmed in her seat while she fished for the right words. "Everyone who comes here and leaves eventually comes back, no matter how far they go, or how much they told themselves they'd never come near this shithole again. So it's like a running joke among people who moved away and then came back. *The damn vortex sucked me back in to stay.* Y'know?"

"No," said Remelea. "I don't. Look, I know you're lying. Quit being bashful."

"I…don't know what you want me to say."

Remelea nudged the bottle. "Drink more whiskey. You'll figure it out."

"I really shouldn't."

"Neither should I, but hey, we're fellow sufferers. Drink, bitch."

Janie lifted the bottle for a small sip. She wound up sucking down a bigger one than she'd meant to. "Okay.

My mom was Abenaki. White historians like to claim that no Native Americans lived in Vermont before the European settlers, but that's bullshit. Anyway, Mom sometimes talked about how…this town was built on some place of power, some nexus-point within the lands. Like, at the bottom of downtown, where the rivers meet. There are urban legends about it, like, *we're all living on an ancient Indian burial ground! It's spooky! Wooooo!*" Janie lifted her hands and wiggled her fingers. "Mom always said, no, it ain't like that. Yeah, it's a center of power within the lands, but it ain't like it's *good* or *bad*. It just *is*."

"Sure, I get that," said Remelea. "Funny thing I've noticed, though, about when folks notice the power and will of the lands, when they get all spiritual about it and shit. They love to say *it ain't good or bad; it just is*…especially when it's good for them. Right up until it's bad for them."

"I guess I hear that." Janie stood up. "Anyway, look, Remelea, I'm getting tired. I should head…well, back to where I sleep."

Remelea looked nonplussed. "Yeah, sure. Good meeting you, Janie. Good talk. We should talk more sometime, about what you know, when you're better rested."

~

"Little Long-Face is a very fascinating girl, isn't she?"

The voice piped up a few seconds after Janie walked out, right when Remelea had settled back into having the reading room to herself. She looked up and saw a Lepod sitting on the table, wearing a long red coat and a black stovepipe hat.

"Christ," she said, "where the fuck did you come from?"

"The same place as you: these lands."

"Don't bullshit me. You know damn well I didn't come from these lands, and neither did you."

"You…how would you say it, Lost Queen? You *know what the fuck I mean.*"

"Ha! Right. No, really, what are you doing here?"

"I came along with the same caravan as Little Long-Face. So did many of my people."

"Huh. Jesse didn't mention that."

"That is because he didn't know we had stowed aboard his caravan. He will know, when the opportune moment comes. You are greatly privileged to learn of my presence now, Lost Queen."

"I hate to break it to you, guy, but I'm about as far as you can get from a *queen.*"

"Oh, but you are a queen, Lost Queen. That much has been made very clear to me. Now that I look at you face to face, it is confirmed."

"Dude, what the fuck are you talking about?"

The Lepod stood up, walked across the table, crouched, grabbed Remelea's rolled up dollar, and snorted up one of the lines of coke she'd carved up.

"It's polite to ask first," she said.

"From all that I have heard of you, Lost Queen, it is curious to hear you chide others about what is polite."

"Fair enough."

"Did you intend to snort this entire bag, here and now, all by yourself?"

"Probably not, but it's tempting. So tell me, little man, just who the fuck's been telling you so much about me?"

"Your king's pet."

"My *king*, huh? So who's that supposed to be?"

"The one who would not have had his crown without you…the one whose riches you should have shared in, except that he left you in this sad, cold place, while he went where you should have gone with him. His pet has told me much about you, Lost Queen."

Remelea's eyes widened. "Puttergong?"

"That is the creature's name, yes."

"What the hell's that little sonofabitch still doing in this realm?"

"Barely clinging to life, until very recently."

"Okay, never mind about Puttergong. Here." Remelea sprinkled out and carved out another line of coke. "Have another. Hell, hey, have a drink." She shoved the bottle forward. "What's all this about how I'm supposed to be a queen?"

The Lepod giggled. "Oh, there is no need to pander to me with vices, Lost Queen. I will tell you for the asking…how you may yet still have your crown."

Remelea took a swig of whiskey and peered at the creature. "I'm listening."

"The moment is not yet here for your taking, but you must be ready to act swiftly when the time comes, to…how you would say, *drop whatever the fuck else you are doing and move your ass quick*. There is another would-be *queen*, after a fashion, who will be coming for your crown at that same moment. But I can give you the key she lacks: Little Long-Face."

"Wait, what, you mean that whiney little Earth-line bitch who was just in here? What the hell's she got to do with me getting to be a queen?"

"I am quite fond of Little Long-Face, so I am sad to say, she will not enjoy how you should follow my advice. Neither will many others. Many who have called you friend may come to hate you…but you will deem it worthy in the end, I think, if you take what I offer. The choice will be yours, at the moment when your enemies see something other than what is there. If your wits are sharp, you will realize what is there, and you must make your choice quickly."

"So why are you offering it to me?"

"After much listening and much consideration, I have decided it is likeliest in my people's best interest that you be offered this crown…or whatever else you choose to take from the ritual hour. Funny enough, I couldn't help but overhear just now, you and little Long-Face were just discussing it, without even realizing it."

Remelea leaned forward. "Go on."

THREE

By now, Jesse had the winding, sloping maze of the town pretty well memorized, from the outlying roads and forest trails, to the back alleys, the abandoned parking lot and transit center beneath, the subterranean ant-farm-passages connecting various old buildings, even a whole new network of ways to get around discreetly, once you learned your way around some of the rooftops.

The outer borders comprised the broadest expanse, and those areas would count for the least, except to slow Balthazar's guys down, for a few minutes maybe. Then again, minutes could count for everything. When he thought back on his bad days of Earth-line warfare, all of this was a remarkably small battlefield. That was both a comfort and a problem.

Sam and Anya were Jesse's only hope for even knowing about the siege in time. Even that was still a shot-in-the-dark. When it happened, everyone had to stay sneaky within the close quarters of the town, to the last possible second. Discreet little bands patrolled various areas at all times. The patrollers knew anyone who was anyone, and where they were at any given time, whether their subjects were aware of it or not.

Jesse was now more grateful than ever for all his talks with Sally, taking mental notes on whatever she had to say about Spirelight Secret Police shadow-network tactics without electronic communication. It'd be even better if they'd had a living former Spirelight Secret Policewoman in town now.

Either way, Jesse, Zane and Remelea had trained their lieutenants to set off a silent butterfly-effect chain of signals, so word would reach everyone and they'd hustle into position when they needed to. The more of Balthazar's guys swarmed in, the more they'd crowd each other. From there, it'd all come down to raw endurance.

While first scouting, Jesse had expected the lingering townies to stay hidden in their homes. That scouting walk happened after he, Zane, Remelea, Joel, and Liam made a series of examples up and down Elliot Street, of whatever looters and rapists they caught in the act. There'd been time for word to spread, apparently.

Many locals sat out on their porches, more than Jesse had figured were still here. Smoke wafted from several chimneys. Some of those porch folks cleaned and loaded shotguns and rifles, but they didn't point them at Jesse or his companions. Sometimes old guys wearing veteran caps stood up and saluted the passing band. Jesse and Zane saluted them right back, even though that wasn't the protocol those old Earth-line soldiers were used to. A few folks even left their porches to come talk. Jesse spoke openly with everyone, answering questions candidly. He told the young and firm ones to report to their posts, then left everyone else to comprehend whatever they could.

No way around it, though, plenty of folks in this town were going to die on Jesse's watch. Most of them, probably. He thought of that old restaurant down the street, The Common Ground. Sally had told him how when she'd found Brattleboro, that's where she'd ended up first. That place hadn't had electricity at the time, either. From what she'd described, the young folks running it had practically thrived on the circumstances. Liam had been one of those kids. Working with Liam now, Jesse could believe it. Yeah, he'd picked as good a spot as any, for whatever was coming. By now, everyone out there was as ready as they'd ever be.

All week, more Crimbone had shown up. None of them had word of Balthazar, beyond whatever isolated trouble they'd fought their way through on the way here. Jesse, Zane and Remelea got a sense of them all, one at a time. Those who failed the test, they executed on the spot. Those who passed, they directed into their most useful places accordingly.

After a few days and nights of that, they managed to wind things so tight, there was actually some time to kill. Jesse found himself wandering through the cluster of refugees shacked up in the Stone Church. He caught up with Liam's wife, Aurora, while she played with her son. The toddler took one look at Jesse and burst out shrieking. Aurora gathered the kid up, patted and cooed to him, sparing apologetic glances at Jesse.

"No, no, ma'am," Jesse said, "it's…okay. I get it."

He'd crouched and relaxed his hulking frame, doing his damnedest to look non-threatening to the little one. He thought of Louis as a baby. He hadn't been much better at this kind of thing with his own son, now that he thought about it. How the hell was he supposed to navigate it with an Earth-line mother and child?

The kid kept staring at him, so he held the gaze, gently as he knew how. He bobbed up and down on his haunches, making goofier and goofier noises and faces. Eventually the kid cracked something resembling a smile. Jesse widened his eyes and made sillier sounds. Before he caught himself, some deep, rolling, growling noises escaped him, sounds only Crimbone vocal chords could make.

Great, now I've done it. Now the little bastard's gonna be really terrified!

Instead, the kid grinned, made a few weird noises of his own, and went into giggling fits. Jesse bobbed up and down and let out more Crimbone noises. The kid leaned towards him and tried to mimic the sounds.

Liam came in and swept his boy up into his arms. Jesse smiled sadly, watching the father and son play. He spotted Aurora smiling sadly at him.

"Do you have any kids?" she asked.

"Right now? Yeah, ma'am, everyone hanging out in this town, whether I like it or not."

"Aaaaaaaahhh…Yeah, 'cause you're *Jesse Ripper-Man Karn*, isn't that right?" Who the hell had let that get out around here? "Anyway, seriously, thank you."

Her eyes didn't match the sweet smile, though. She must be in her mid-twenties, maybe early thirties, but she kept reminding Jesse of girls no older than sixteen, the ones he'd found huddled with their babes, in the basements of blasted-out buildings during the Civil War. He looked around now, at the stolen moment of laughing joy between this family who called him a hero, treated him like one of their own. When he thought of all that ugliness touching them, he almost doubled over and puked.

Keep it together. The monsters coming for these folks are worse than you or Zane ever were back in the day.

"Hey, Jesse," said Liam, cutting in cheerfully, "we should throw a dance party in here tonight."

Jesse looked up. "Yeah? Here? In the Stone Church?"

"Hey, you're, like, the mastermind around here…about finding who's who for what jobs, right? So…like…go find us some musicians who still have some instruments tucked away, and…hey man, yeah, let's see if we can get a little shindig going in this place."

Jesse looked to Aurora. "What do you say, ma'am?"

"That sounds wonderful. I'd have to find someone to watch this little guy here for a while, though."

"Hey Liam, anyone put together any babysitting-detail divisions around here yet?"

"Ah…uh…No, I don't think so, now you mention it."

Jesse clapped Liam's narrow shoulder. "Well then, guess you better go jump on that, then. I'll go round up some musicians."

Within the next four hours, the lower floor of the Stone Church came alive with dance and song. Aurora held the main stage that used to be the pulpit, at the center of a few other belly-dancers. Off to the sides, several musicians on various instruments played and sang their own folksy stripe of every sort of song Jesse had ever listened to, and a few he hadn't.

Jesse sat atop the balcony, watching everyone downstairs party it up before the end. Longtime lovers crashed into each other and fell in love all over again.

Someone slipped up the narrow, secluded staircase towards the balcony, too stealthy for any but the most seasoned Crimbone ears to catch. Jesse looked over at the high, slim doorway. A tall, lithe shape drifted in from the landing, into the candlelight that spilled up over the railing.

"Mind some company?" said Remelea.

Jesse sighed. "I do in fact, but I'll make an exception for you."

It didn't hurt how easy on the eyes she was…or the nose, for that matter, no matter how long everyone around here had gone without a proper wash. She smelled like a Crimbone woman, still musky and high from blazing her way through life on the blade's edge. Her wild, dark hair shadowed her constantly crackling eyes just right. Her hips always swayed confidently when she walked, so all her enticing angles got a turn in the candlelight.

"Thank you so much, old dog." She flopped down a few feet from him, stretched and twisted to dig through her pockets, brought out a silvery flask, unscrewed the cap, and swigged. When she noticed him looking, she held it out. "Snort?"

He took the flask and sucked out a glug. "Thanks. This is some old damn bourbon. Where the hell'd you find this around here, anyway?"

"You kidding? I pinched this shit in New Orleans. Wondered what I was saving it for. This seems like as good an occasion as any." She shrugged, took the flask back, held it out and said, "To a bunch of fools dancing to the end of the world." She swigged and held it his way again.

Jesse took the flask. "I'll drink to that. Everything cool out there?"

"Cool's a polite word. Patrols are tight as a drum. They'll find us if they need us."

Jesse leaned forward, eyeing her hard. "That's good. I figured." His voice deepened a little. "You sure we want 'em to?"

"Huh?" She gave him a weird look.

Damnit! Being *on your game* sure as hell wasn't *like riding a bike*. Jesse had never learned to ride a bike, but that's how the Earth-liners put it. "Nah, don't mind me. Guess I'm just…still trying to remember how to relax."

"Yeah, me too." She shifted closer to him. "I just spotted a balcony up here. Looked like no one was using it. Just my luck, I find your big lummox ass already claimed it." She elbowed him in the ribs. "I think this must've been where they made black people sit, back in the day…must'a been about as long ago as whenever this place was actually a church. Speaking of which, where's Zane?" Her eyes bugged out as soon as she said it. "*Holy shit, sorry!*"

"Nah, it's cool," he said. "He'd just laugh if you said it to him, probably say something even worse. Anyway, nah, he just opted to keep up with patrols. You really are from Texas, aren't you?"

She punched him in the knee. "*Oh, fuck you!*"

They shared a laugh before Jesse said, "Nah, this just ain't really his kind of party."

She hunkered forward, put her elbows on the railing, and watched the celebrants below. "Or yours, I guess."

"Not tonight. How 'bout you?"

"Nah, just…That many people sometimes, in one cramped, tight space…It's hard to know what to do with it, y'know? Being in the middle of all that raging energy when it's not trying to kill you."

"And you can't remember how to just let go and have fun with it, huh?"

"Oh, honey." She swayed upright, prideful and defiant like a snake getting ready to strike. "You have no idea about how to *just let go and have fun with it* anymore, do you?"

Watching her move like that, he sure had a few notions. "Those folks down there look like they've got a pretty good idea. That's what's important tonight. Them, not us."

She rolled her eyes, snatched her flask back, and swigged. "Ohforfucksake, you really are one of *those* assholes."

"What kind now?"

"Still wants to be a true-blue old-school good guy."

"Like I said before, don't make me hit you while I'm trying to be chivalrous."

"Hope for you yet, boy."

From there, they fell into trading war stories, mostly about their fledgling days. The ones about him and Zane during the Civil War got a few chuckles from her. The actual memories were horrific, but he still had to downplay the whole thing of *Hey, baby, I fought in the Civil War, was there for Sherman's March, would'a seen the battle of New Orleans, if Zane and I hadn't met when we did, and…*

Fuck it, who was he kidding? He was more interested in hearing her stories, from after her Second Call. She'd spent a lot of time in Roanoke, Virginia, during the eighties and nineties, for reasons still mysterious to her.

"Roanoke ain't far from where Rob grew up, you know," Jesse threw in. By the look on her face, that was still the wrong thing to bring up.

"Yeah. Too bad I didn't find him and hook up with him back then, instead of that other dipshit fledgling boy I wound up falling for. That guy was still in the last phase of his cast-off days. He and some Earth-line friends were stopping for a few days, on a road trip or something. I got him *and* myself into all sorts of trouble with the Earth-line law."

Some things added up to him suddenly. "So I guess that was our pal Joel, right?"

She sighed. "I can see where you get your reputation as a detective."

"Didn't know I had one. Far as I've ever heard, all those crazy stories people tell about Zane and me, they just make us sound like…who's that guy with the big sword, wearing the loincloth and the bullhorn helmet? Arnie played him in the movies."

"I think you mean Conan the Barbarian."

"Right, that guy. So…you and Joel, huh?"

"You really are determined to *not get laid tonight*, aren't you?"

"Sorry?"

"Hey, I was a lot younger. Don't judge."

Jesse drew another sudden connection. "Roanoke, huh. And that was in…?"

"'89, I think."

"Holy shit, that was *you?*"

She blushed a little brighter. "I guess you read my headlines."

"Zane and I were in Virginia over some other business. The Cabinet came *this close* to sending us to take you down."

"We were *that* out of control?" She laughed and shook her head. "Old Lords…" Her eyes glimmered with old sentiments. "Eh, he thought he was such hot shit. Fuckin' fledglings, y'know? We were together for a while after that. You push that whole Autumn-Spring thing too long, though—I mean, before you're both past a certain age—yeah, you know what I mean. I think he was too jealous of my Familiar."

Jesse snorked. "*Jealous of your Familiar?* Okay, I already figured you for one perverse little bitch, but…"

"*No, not like that!* Just…I used to wake up with the thing curled up asleep on my crotch. Warmest spot on the body, you know."

"Those things sleep?"

"Mine did, or at least it pretended to, 'til whenever Joel reached over without realizing it was there."

Jesse remembered those scars on Joel's hand. He looked her up and down. He still liked what he saw…except, of course, for the tense, lingering uncertainty around the corners of her shoulders and jawline. She still had Rob Coscan on the brain. No matter where Jesse went these days, it seemed, he couldn't get away from younger women who'd been left all perpetually fucked-up by that little High Natural bastard. He curled forward and got lost again in the joy of the dancers and music-makers below.

Remelea's fingertips touched Jesse's face. "Hey, you know…all those people enjoying themselves down there…They only get to do that because of what we've done for them. So why ain't we taking what we want from this?"

"Maybe 'cause we just ain't in the mood for all their shit."

"Who said we had to go down there with them?" She grabbed him by the scruff of the neck. "Don't worry, big boy, there's no Familiar cock-blocking you right now." She yanked him forward and kissed him hard.

Jesse hadn't realized how much ugly, buzzing tension he'd let tighten him up, not 'til Remelea's kiss washed it all away. His mouth opened and closed slowly on hers. Whenever he sensed her hesitance, he eased off, giving her every chance to draw back. She didn't, so he kept kissing her. She let him slide the coat he'd given her off her shoulders. Right when he was about to try for her tank top, a set of boots tromped up the steps. Remelea shoved him away. Goddamnit…

Zane stepped through the narrow doorway. "Hey, guys. Was wondering where you two went."

"Yeah?" Jesse growled. "What for?"

"Just I came in, tried this scene out earlier."

Jesse was about to tell Zane straight-up to fuck off, but Remelea straightened her top and put her coat back on. "No, don't worry," she said. "We didn't either."

Jesse took a deep breath and said, "Got an alternative in mind?"

"Thought we might take a little stroll through the neighborhood, see what we could see."

"I was just about to try to talk Jesse into that very thing," said Remelea.

Could'a fooled me, Jesse thought. Also, *Fuck you, Zane.*

What did you expect? She's still busy half-missing Rob, half-hating his guts, probably all she can do most of the time to keep herself distracted by doing her damn job. So you caught her eye. You must have seemed like a good idea, 'til she had a second to think about it, realize that's a third can of worms to deal with.

He followed them downstairs. As they reached the lobby, the front door flew open and smacked the wall. The three of them braced for trouble, then stared at the shape that fluttered in and perched atop the nearest coatrack.

"*Damn*, you fellers ain't gonna believe the shit I got to tell! Okay, maybe you will. Anyhoot, sorry I been so scarce lately."

"No need to apologize for that," said Zane. "Really."

"Hey, didn't wanna disappoint my fans, but I's back now, so you can all relax. *Thank you, thank you, thank you, thank you…*" Puttergong crossed its claws over its bulbous gut and took four bows.

"What's up, Puttergong?" asked Jesse.

"Whelp, first off, Ripper-Man—oh, and hey, Thumpy-Bumpy, Foxy-Girl—you guys got no idea the kinda can o' shit that's about to get poured all over everyone."

"Yeah we do, actually," said Remelea.

"Okay, good. Might wanna be on your toes, though, for the word to git your asses movin' right quick…like a few days at the latest."

"What have you seen," said Remelea, "from up in the sky?"

"All'a Balthazar's boys an' girls, campin' out for miles around, like they's all just waitin' 'til the last of 'em roll in."

"What about Balthazar himself? Wherever he is, I sure hope he didn't see you—"

"He didn't see me, no…and I didn't see hide nor hair of him, neither."

"Shit," Remelea muttered under her breath. "This whole thing's just one giant Goddamn distraction."

"What's that?" said Jesse.

"Never mind," she said. "We're all just as fucked either way, if we ain't ready."

"So where's the boys, the biter and the cop, that is? Figured that second lil' shit wouldn't wait around like I told him to. Hope his lil' feelin's didn't get too hurt, thinkin' I stood him up or some such. Can't seem to find 'em now, though. Don't tell me they ain't here yet."

"Oh, they've been here," Remelea said. "You just missed 'em, by about a week."

The Familiar's eyes bugged out. Its snout sank, seeming to get longer. "*Missed 'em?* What in the Sam Hell Fuck are you talkin' 'bout, Foxy-Girl?"

"They're already off to the Old World. They found their way just fine, no thanks to you."

"*Fine*, my twinklin' asshole! Lemme guess, Ripper-Man. Biter-Boy didn't need to get filled in on as much as you reckoned, like he already heard it from someone else?"

"That's the idea I got."

"He already knew he had to go to the Old World," Remelea added, "and that he'd find the harbor gate here, if that's what you mean. We found all that out in New Orleans."

Puttergong's wings hunched up. "That's what I was fuckin' scared of. Bet you folks heard all about what I told Cop-Boy he's gotta do over there, too, huh? An' I'll bet you heard Biter-Boy mumblin' an' snarlin' all sorts of shit that seemed to line up with all that. How I doin' so far?"

Jesse and Zane both nodded. Remelea didn't move a muscle. Jesse glanced and caught something strange going on behind her eyes…something stranger than usual.

"…And you was all in such a big fuckin' hurry, you didn't notice their two dis-respective variations on the plan didn't all quite match up. Listen, I don't know how much you fuckers think you know 'bout this inner-die-mentionable travel shit, but take it from me, y'all don't know your asses from the dick fuckin' you in it. With where an' when them two's headed, if they don't stick to the fuckin' playbook, they's likely to fling shit all over *the big fuckin' picture* like a couple monkeys in a zoo."

"What *playbook?*" said Zane.

"The one I was *gonna* shove Biter-Boy's nose in 'fore he took off, if I hadn't gotten way-laid, and not in the fun spanky way, and you ain't sent him off without me gettin' to say goodbye. I made it damn fuckin' clear to Cop-Boy that it was *him* needed to shove his shiny blades up the gods' asses. All Biter-Boy's s'posed to do is make sure Cop-Boy can find his way around the Old World, so he can yank the gods' hold out'a *this* world, here. And that's *it!* I figure when Cop-Boy gets a feel for the magic energies in that temple, he'll know that, much as that sucks for good ol' Deschemb. If I know Biter-Boy, though, he ain't gonna be happy with stoppin' there, which is why I wanted the chance to hammer it into his skull, tough-love like."

"Fuck." Jesse started to get the idea. "So what happens if they get to that temple, and Rob does things his way?"

"It'll be so fucked that by the time he gets finished, if we're still here at all, we'll be worse than hammered shit that's been hammered twice. Our brains'll be too busy droolin' out our ears to tell us it was ever any different anyplace else."

Remelea swigged from her flask and met Puttergong's eyes. "Okay, birdie, so what are you waiting for? Ain't it time you were gone from this realm anyway?"

"That's what I done figured too, but apparently I ain't finished with whatever I was still here to do. Now that business ain't around for me to see to it, so…hey, you got me!"

"So can't you at least send a message through the ephemeral realms, back to wherever you come from, so they can—"

"Foxy-Girl, if I could do that, you think I'd be sittin' 'round here sweatin' over this bullshit? Nope, them fuckers back in the ephemeral realms has cut me off, seems like, so I'm set to take it in the ass with the rest of y'all."

"Great," said Remelea. "So what the hell do we do?"

Jesse took a deep breath. "Stick to our end of the plan, that's what."

"Remelea," said Zane, "I think it's safe to say, you know Rob better than anyone else here. Shut the fuck up, Puttergong. You don't count right now. So how 'bout it, girl? Wherever those boys are, what's the chance of Sheldon talking sense into Rob?"

She gazed out into the night. "If Sheldon makes the score clear to him…I think Rob will want to do what's right."

"Sounds about as good as anything right now, Foxy-Girl," said Puttergong, "which is to say abso-posi-lutely fucked."

GETTIN' READY FOR A BIG DATE

Down on Main Street…

Fishhook groaned and shifted against the soft leather seat, while the road rumbled along beneath him. As he swam towards consciousness, he tugged his coat tighter. Almost immediately, he loosened it back up, because it was sweltering in here. He'd just gotten used to waking up cold. If anything, it was *too* warm now, especially in his heavy coat. Otherwise, everything felt so…comfortable! How long had it been since he could say that?

He held onto half-sleep, while his dad's truck rumbled along beneath him, with Bob Seger singing about *all those lonely nights, down on Main Street*, out of a scratchy old cassette-tape deck. *I must have fallen asleep again, after another drive home with Dad, with one of his old classic rock tapes playing. What a nightmare I just had!*

Then the cauterized stump in his mouth moved against his back teeth. He jolted and his eyes snapped open. He was in a dusty old pickup truck, alright, with an old-fashioned tape deck playing Bob Seger. That wasn't Dad in the driver's seat, though. It was a big guy, in a long brown duster coat, with a big, floppy cowboy hat pulled low over his face. There was something…off, about how the coat and hat fit over the body and head, like an awkwardly stuffed scarecrow. A spikey-toothed, deformed snout stuck out from beneath the brim of the hat.

The last time he'd woken up, he'd been laying across a metal cot, in a jail cell. One of the other Earth-liners had awoken him with dying gurgles. He'd bolted upright through the gloom. Through the scant moonlight, he'd recognized Balthazar's bulk, curled forward over one of the bunks. The occupant thrashed weakly to a stop.

Balthazar had risen and turned to Fishhook. "Shhhhhh...Time to get up, Ronny. No, no, easy there, little buddy. You gotta be *real* quiet now. *Hey, hey,* take it easy! No need for that! Yeah, naw, you're still my little buddy. Today's the day you find out why I picked you. We're gonna go see her together. I just had to make sure your cellmates here didn't spoil the moment for us. Didn't wanna spoil the surprise for the rest of 'em, either."

Balthazar had led Fishhook outside to the old Chevy pickup truck. Something had thumped on the ground at his feet.

"Well, c'mon, little buddy. Time to get stripped down and suited back up. Can't have you goin' where we're goin', still wearin' them stinky, shit-stained old duds."

Even after all this time, Fishhook's body had still rebelled against the idea of getting naked out in the cold night air. It rebelled even stronger, though, against the idea of disobeying Balthazar, with the creature's shape looming in front of him. Once he got the new clothes on, though, even with his body still so filthy and achy beneath them, the sensation was so startlingly pleasant that his heart felt ready to burst from the shock: *I'm wearing fresh, clean warm clothes!*

The euphoria passed quickly, because there was Balthazar opening the passenger door, urging him to climb on in. "Yeah, I know. Ain't how I usually like to travel...but for the special occasion we got comin' up…well, it's just gonna be more convenient like this. My girlfriend wants you there for the big event, y'see. I'm lookin' forward to havin' you there for it, too."

Fishhook must have fallen asleep not long after they'd sped off into the night. Now he peered around through the windows. The first faint shimmers of dawn bled between tall, snow-caked pine trees, around a winding, rural highway, somewhere in…where were they by now? A lot further north, that was for sure. Pine trees and mountain ranges stood out against the brightening sky. There was also a big, dark smear on his side of the windshield.

"Oh. Right," said Balthazar. "Hitchhikers. Y'know, there's still a lot more of 'em around than you'd think. Especially since we crossed into Vermont, for some reason. Must be 'cause I've been leavin' these colder regions alone, for the most part. The look on that last one's face when I swerved to get him…*Pow!* Man, Ronny, I'm surprised that shit didn't wake you up, 'specially the way that sumbitch screamed when he went flyin'. Anyhow, mind if we switch up the music? This damn tape's played itself through like three or four times." Balthazar punched a button on the tape deck. He pulled the tape out, grabbed another one at random, and shoved it in. As a new song started, he sighed, "*Aaaaaaaaah, yeah,* I gotta admit, whatever old buzzard owned this ol' rig, before me an' my boys and girls got hold of it…I like his music. Never got to listen to tunes like this before. The *classical rock*. It's nice, y'know? Soothin'."

For once, Fishhook agreed. He tried to enjoy it while it lasted.

"*Somebody's gonna hurt someone, 'for tonight is through,*" sang the tape deck.

That was for sure, except by now, the morning was getting brighter and brighter. Still, without a doubt, there was in fact nothing Fishhook could do.

Balthazar pulled over, next to a twisted, rusty guardrail. "Okay, little buddy, time to get out."

Fishhook got out. The bracing cold hit him across his whole body. There was no wind, yet the icy power of it hit him so hard, all at once, that it might as well have been the gale of a hurricane, trying to shove him back into the truck. He pulled his coat shut against it.

Balthazar had already gotten out. He didn't seem to mind the cold at all. He came around the truck and stepped over the guardrail. "Okay. Well, c'mon, Ronny, what are you waitin' for? We're just goin' for a nice little hike in the woods."

Fishhook stepped over the guardrail and followed Balthazar down a short hill, to a frozen, marshy creek bed. His boots crunched deeper through it than the rest of the snow as he crossed it. *I'm wearing boots. When did I put on boots again?*

As Balthazar led him up a far steeper, taller hill, between the frosty pines, he noticed that the creature's clawed feet were as bare as ever. There was something very wrong with Balthazar's shape, beneath the duster coat. Fishhook hugged himself, glanced down, and noticed he was wearing a matching duster.

Halfway up the hill, Balthazar glanced back. "Aw, Ronny, quit laggin', buddy! C'mon, pump them legs, *pump 'em!* Yeah, that's right, that's right, you can do it, I believe in you...*Yeah, there ya go, you got it!* Yeah, like that. *Left...left...Left, right, left...*Aw, yeah, that's the spirit. C'mon, now."

They stepped onto a well-beaten, steady uphill trail. Even through the deep, crunching snow, that made the climb easier. Far ahead, something rustled and tore through the icy brush.

Balthazar cast a clawed hand back. "Okay, little buddy, that's your cue to take a breather. No, no, don't sit down and get your ass all wet. Just lean back against the nearest tree an' take it easy for a spell."

Fishhook didn't have to be told twice. Once he found a tree to rest against, though, his burning, wobbly legs tried harder than ever to give out beneath him. He leaned forward, gasping, and clutched at his knees. He pressed his ass as hard as he could against the tree, the better to keep from falling. When he looked up, he saw two blurry shapes descending the hillside towards them. By the time his eyes cleared, they were still far away, but he could already tell that they were Balthazar's guys.

They're already here? Wait, no, that can't be right. That's not how he—

No, he realized, those weren't Balthazar's, but they were definitely Crimbone. They looked every bit as lean, mean and gnarly as the ones Fishhook was used to looking at, but their clothes didn't look made of stitched-together patches of human flesh. They wore long brown duster coats, flapping open in the winter air, revealing lighter layers beneath...*dressed just like Balthazar's dressed...like he's got me all dressed up.*

Balthazar strode up towards them, his feet crunching louder than before through the frozen brush. The two Crimbone paused and perked up, like they'd just now spotted him. As they dashed forward, Fishhook spotted their otherworldly weapons flapping against their hips within the scabbards, beneath the fluttering coats. He kept expecting those weapons to disappear from the scabbards and magically reappear in their fists. At least that's how it had always looked to him, whenever he'd seen Crimbone draw their weapons. Instead, they slowed down in front of Balthazar.

"We just took in the road down along the bottom of the ridge," someone said. "It looks and smells all clear."

Fishhook blinked, bewildered. Who the hell had just said that? He could swear, neither of the two Crimbone's mouths had moved. In fact, they appeared to be exchanging looks, as though weighing the words.

"Oh yeah?" said one of them. "So what happened to your buddy back there?"

"Oh, we caught a couple of Balthazar's scouts a mile or so out. He took a bit of a gash. Just walking him back. He'll live."

"Oh yeah? Thought you just said it was clear down that way."

"Of course it is, thanks to us."

"Well, it won't be for long. Come on, it's time to fall back and get into position."

"What? You mean Balthazar's almost here?" said Balthazar. He faced away from Fishhook, which was why Fishhook had been so confused for at first…that, and he could hardly believe such a normal, human-sounding voice was coming out of the creature's mouth.

"That's what Jesse Karn says. C'mon, let's go!"

"What's the High Natural say?"

"The what?" said the second Crimbone.

"Rob Coscan. The High Natural. The Crimbone who's led us all to this—"

"Wait, hold up a second." The first Crimbone lifted a hand. "You must be from the outlying patrols, the ones from that pack who first showed up following Remelea."

"I don't think it was Remelea they were following at that point," said the second one. "It was that guy she came in with, the one who just up and vanished along with that weird Spirelight kid."

"Vanished?" Balthazar spat. "The High Natural's just *vanished?* As in, not in Brattboro no more?"

"That's what I said. Thought you'd all been brought up to speed. Look, there's no time to explain. Word's just come from the front. We've all gotta...*Oh, shit!*"

Balthazar lifted his head, so both Crimbone got their first good look at his ugly face beneath the big brim of his hat.

"What do you mean the High Natural ain't in Brat-o-burrow no more?"

Now those black metal weapons shrieked free into their hands. As they rushed in, Balthazar spun into the air like a top. One bare foot smacked the first Crimbone across the face in a crescent-kick so the man's whole bottom jaw ripped off and went flying away in a bloody shower. The other Crimbone's knife sailed straight at Balthazar's heart. Balthazar caught the arm and twisted 'til it let out an echoing pop. The black knife dropped, stuck in the frosty ground, and stood there bobbing. Balthazar's other big, corded hand fastened around the guy's throat and squeezed.

"How the fuck can the High Natural just up an' disappear?" Balthazar roared in the Crimbone's face. The guy didn't answer, because his face was bulging and turning purple. Bright blood streamed down his chest from where Balthazar's claws sank into his neck. Balthazar noticed that the body had already stopped shaking, so he tossed it away. "Fine, fuck you too, then."

Another Crimbone had appeared on the scene, Fishhook noticed, trying to sneak up on Balthazar from behind. No, it wasn't a new one. Fuck, now Fishhook really *had* seen it all. It was the first Crimbone, the one missing half his face, the entire front of his body sopping dark and wet. He was back on his feet, making a last, desperate, shambling lunge to stab Balthazar in the back.

The shock and blood loss caught up with him before he could get there, though. He dropped his knife and crashed to his knees.

Balthazar turned as though noticing the man for the first time. He plucked the dead one's blade from the snow as he approached the prostrate man. The jawless Crimbone swayed, shuddering and gurgling, eyes bulging with agony and fury, unable to speak while Balthazar loomed over him and grinned. Fishhook knew the feeling…except this bastard's eyes were going glassy, like he'd be dead in less than a minute. Some guys had all the luck.

Balthazar hooted, "Well I'll be fucked, look at you go! Shit, and you just a youngin', too, ain't you? Who says they don't make Crimbone like they used to? I'm a little sad now, 'cause if you ain't just the type I'd normally like to keep alive, put back together, and hammer you 'til you was good and whupped, so I could put you back together again, as one of *my* soldiers. I ain't got time for that shit no more, though. That's okay. I got enough. *More* than enough. Speakin' of such, you was right about one thing, buddy. All my pretty little soldiers, they *are* on the way, as we—Hey, boy, I'm talkin' to you! *Eyes up here*, as the ladies say. What are you…Oh, this." Balthazar looked at the dead Crimbone's weapon, bobbing in his fist like a child's toy. "Yeah, your buddy back there's deader'n dirt, which I guess means this black metal blade's gonna go crumble to dust any second now, just like yours will before long…" Balthazar eyed the knife. It didn't crumble. He put his free palm to his mouth in mock-surprise. "Wait, what's this? Well, hot-diggity damn! Oh, you never seen that before? Could it be that's one more trick I learned from the Daddy?"

The jawless Crimbone fell over sideways. A dark red halo spread out around the head through the white snow.

Balthazar picked up the guy's blade and weighed it against the one in his other fist. He strode back down the hill towards Fishhook.

"Well how 'bout this, Ronny! Now *I'm* the one with *twin black blades*. Reckoned I'd collected enough, but two more can't hurt, right? That make me the new *High Natural?* Nah, the High Natural don't matter so much now. 'Cept now we just know, that much more, that he never meant shit, and all them cocksuckers in that little valley is fucked. Hey, Ronny, man, what'cha starin' for? You look all nervous and timid...more than usual. I mean."

Somewhere in the scuffle, Balthazar's cowboy hat had fallen off. Where before, he'd fused two jagged, crooked, bone-carved horns with his forehead, a total of seven now stuck out of his skull. All around the swollen edges, that unhealthy yellowish tinge had bled through his flesh, except where the infected, purple-black veins stood out. His eyes gleamed almost paler than those of that jawless Crimbone in the moment before death, like shimmery cataracts had formed over them.

"Oh, this!" Balthazar plucked at the tips of the horns. "It's my new crown, Ronny! How you like it? Had to look my best, goin' to meet my queen in the flesh for the first time, and all. I'm a little sore we're gonna have to miss the big shit-fight about to happen, except...well, when you get right down to it, especially now that that dirty coward of a High Natural's done hightailed it, it's just one more shithole town to knock over. Hey, let the rest of them poor bastards have their fun with it, I say! There'll be plenty more towns, and plenty more fun to be had...except better'n ever after, today. Y'know why? All them stupid fuckin' Spirelights wanted to take over this world for their gods, while the Crimbone wanted to kill them gods. My queen an' me, we're gonna do 'em both one better. We're gonna make them gods *our bitches*, so we can make the gods take over the world for *us*. And you're the one who's gonna get to be there with us for it, Ronny, in a big way, oh yessiree."

As Balthazar closed in on him, Fishhook saw ever clearer how wrong the rest of Balthazar's body looked, beneath the coat. When Balthazar breathed, he swelled like a puffer fish that had swallowed a lot of jagged bits and pieces that now poked up from beneath the surface in all the wrong ways.

Balthazar threw an arm around Fishhook. "C'mon, little buddy, time to get goin'. We still got quite a hike ahead of us, and we don't wanna be late."

MANY TRAILS END

ONE

Jesse and Zane stowed the van under a snow-heavy cluster of trees, at the edge of the woods over the hill along Cedar Street, near the Harris Hill Ski Jump. Right on schedule, a large party of civilian Deschembines of both races showed up to meet them nearby, along with about a dozen Earth-line fighters.

Most of the Earth-line band weren't official military, exactly, except for the crazy AWOL Green-Mountain Boys who'd trained and organized them, hiding out in the back hills further north, convinced in their collective paranoid brains that a day like this was coming.

Okay, so maybe this wasn't quite what they'd had in mind. One of their former members was Crimbone, though, naturally. When this shit had hit the fan, he'd hunted them up and led them to Brattleboro. Along the way, he'd brought them more or less up to speed. It hadn't taken Jesse and Zane long to assert themselves as the new natural leaders. Around seventy of them had gathered, clogging this back road on the edge of the deep woods. They came from all over the state and beyond, carrying everything from pistols to fully automatic rifles, along with big hunting knives they looked ready to wield like full-length broadswords. As to how competent they'd all be with any of that weaponry, from what Jesse and Zane could assess…well, it was a mixed bag, to put it kindly, but it was what they had to work with. With the help of the best of the lot, they'd hopefully weeded out the worst by now.

Zane strutted back and forth in front of them, arms swinging loose at his sides, his deep voice booming at a sharp, no-bullshit clip. "Okay. When the bad guys show up, Jesse and I are gonna spring out to meet them first. You guys shoot over our heads, into the fighters that haven't reached us. Don't waste your ammo on the front lines, 'cause you won't hit shit, except maybe us, and we wouldn't like that. Once you run out of ammo, take to the trees and show us what you've got in close quarters. I understand, for those of you with Earth-line military training, a lot of what we're telling you to do goes against all your common sense. You'll see why, soon enough. Remember, you're about to see some freaky shit. I know you all think you've seen plenty of that over the last few months, but when you get your first look at what this enemy can do with their bodies, you're gonna think someone just dosed you with the brown acid. Just ignore it and keep doing your part."

They all nodded, cold eyes peering bloodthirstily from granite faces. They followed Jesse and Zane off the road, into the woods, across a low frozen brook, then uphill, towards the westernmost woodland point their scouts had determined Balthazar's foot soldiers would come from. They trekked up the cleared, bare expanse around the abandoned ski-jump, crested the hilltop, descended again, and settled behind a cluster of rocks. Behind them, Jesse and Zane heard a lot of guys still catching their breath from the hike. Hell, Zane was huffing and puffing a little himself. Maybe he was finally getting old. Or maybe there was something to all the shit

Jesse gave him, about a century and a half's worth of cigarettes. They faced a wide, long space, cut for a string of power lines that rolled uphill and down, for miles back.

It was Anya who'd found Jesse on the street, less than an hour ago. The haunted, distant look in her eyes told him what she was about to say before she said it: "Balthazar's here."

"You mean he's on the way?"

"I mean he's *here*. That's what the wind through the tree branches tells us. Just like back in Virginia, when we ran. Even under all the ice and snow, the rustling trees are making the same sounds, for miles around."

"That means his soldiers are on the way," said Zane.

"You gonna run this time?" Jesse asked Anya.

"Fuck that." Her lips drew back in a thirsty smile.

Jesse had looked around and spotted Bird, strolling up and down the other side of Main Street. Jesse caught the guy's eyes and gave an unmistakable signal. Without missing a beat, Bird stopped, took four quarter turns, making as many signals in as many directions. Whoever was there to see and pass it on, Jesse's butterfly-effect plan worked. The whole town came together, ready for action like a well-oiled machine, almost before anyone knew it. A sharp collective instinct ran through them like an electrical current, something most of these folks hadn't known was in them 'til recently, some as little as a few days ago.

By now, Sam and Anya would be at the easternmost woodland point. Back in the town, runners had been sent to gather people from houses and get them into position, to get those who couldn't fight into the underground corridors beneath the buildings downtown. The central defense was built mostly on folks hiding in wait, stretching from the end of Main Street to halfway up Putney Road, both covering the nearest bridges over the Connecticut River. Remelea and Joel would face the bridge near Main

Street. Crimbone Jesse and Zane didn't know faced the other bridge. The streets were full of as many Crimbone as possible, along with civilians turned fighters from both Deschembine races. The surrounding buildings were crammed like Great Depression tenements with more civilian Deschembines and as many Earth-line people as could fit. Earth-line folks with guns—gang-bangers, ex-military, survivalists, hunters, regular gun-owners with any real marksmanship to speak of, all side-by-side now— were placed on upper floors, near windows. The Earth-liners that thought they were up to the hand-to-hand fighting–those who claimed enough martial-arts, military, or street-fighting credibility—were placed nearest the exits, along with the Deschembines. They'd been given makeshift weapons, mostly machetes and sharp farm tools. Jesse heard some of them carried chainsaws. When they burst forth, he hoped they didn't buzz as many friends as enemies in half. He expected such fools to die quickest, so he'd positioned them where they had the best chance of at least slowing the enemy down.

The longer Jesse stopped to think about it, the more fucked it all felt. Still, granted, he hadn't realized how many fighters they had 'til the organization commenced. Most of them weren't United Deschembines. By now, there were even former Spirelight Secret Police who no longer thought twice about fighting side by side with the Crimbone. Better still, the feeling seemed mutual.

On his and Zane's way to the van, Jesse had noticed the rising rumble in the concrete under his boots. Had the roads and highways throughout this countryside been alive with normal steady traffic, he wouldn't have noticed the difference. It had been absent for months, though. Soon enough, everyone would feel it.

Jesse and Zane peered down the hilly power-line trail. The approaching rumble felt lighter than expected. The way was full of icy terrain and slick-jutting rocks, not at all convenient for an effective sprinting charge...except these sprinters didn't sound like they ran on human feet.

Zane looked back at fighters gathering behind them in the snowy brush, sneaking in close together. He put his eyes back on the power-line trail ahead and said to Jesse, "You know that old favorite wish of yours, ol' buddy?"

"Ha! Which one?"

"The not-so-relaxed one, the one that *doesn't* end with us kickin' back on some porch as a pair of old geezers."

"I...Fuck, Zane, I didn't think I ever told you about that!"

"You didn't need to, brother."

They clasped wrists. Through the misty wind ahead, dark shapes came over the farthest rise, first in sprinkles, then a rolling mass, like a swarm of rats. Jesse smelled many of his own kind, no matter how much their scent had been putrefied by whatever Balthazar had done to them. Byron's pack had smelled just as bad, but Jesse hadn't known what it meant at the time. *Should've greeted those fuckers like I'm about to greet these.* The thought fed his bloodlust as powerfully as the Spirelight glow that mingled with the stench. This approaching glow hadn't been softened by Sally's touch. For the first time in what felt like too long, Jesse's mouth watered for Spirelight death.

Neither the brutal terrain nor the deep snow slowed the enemy down. The swarm might as well have come running over smooth, soft grass. Those weren't even humanoid shapes coming. No, wait, they were...except the front lines ran on all fours...or in some cases, all sixes or eights.

"Crouch low 'til Jesse and I spring," Zane shouted, then slid down along the side of a rock in time with Jesse.

Jesse's hand edged towards his knife of the black metal. A pulsing rush fluttered through him, like he'd not known since his fledgling days. He didn't stiffen against it, just let it flow through him freely. The world was about to explode. During the Civil War, he'd faced battlefields at least five times as packed, and it had never done this to him. He felt almost lightheaded.

For the first time in his life, Jesse Karn clutched tight to the handle of his weapon before the instant of drawing. "Old Lords," he breathed. "Why you saw fit to guide our ancestors to these frail, beautiful shores of the Earth-line people, I'll never know. They say when you guys got here, you died and merged your spirits with these lands, so our people would have a chance. If that's right, I figure I've talked with you plenty over the years, while I talked with the lands. We never really had a direct conversation, though, have we? Seems these lands you've fused with are just sitting back to watch. I don't know if you're even fucking listening. One way or another, everything I've ever known is about to get hammered to dust. I'm glad I was here to know what we're about to lose. Most of all, I'm glad I shared it with the bastard sitting next to me. Whatever comes next, I ain't asking for a chance to see it. All I know is the side we've chosen. Here's all I'll ever ask of you, Old Lords: let every bit of strength I've ever possessed, in body and mind and spirit, in my blood and in my blade, any time in my life, be with me now, all at once. Share it with my brother here, with our friends back in the town, with all their loved ones still alive. Let us show you what we can *really* do with it, Old Lords!"

As he spoke, his free hand pressed harder and harder against the ground, palm splayed, defying the snow between his flesh and the frozen soil. An electric tingle spread from his fingertips. At first, it might have been his imagination...'til it reached his shoulder, then bloomed through his chest, neck and temples, then down through his other arm, all the way to his knife-hand...'til he glanced over and saw the same power surging through Zane.

The rock against his back shuddered as the horde of abominations closed in. He and Zane leapt onto and across the rocks then sprang into the air, towards a sea of scarred, bloodthirsty faces that stretched back forever.

Yeah, the front lines of the horde were definitely running on all fours, gliding and plowing through the treacherous terrain as though sliding over a smooth surface, thanks to the abominable surgery and magical alteration they'd endured. The alteration had also done its crazy work on their bare hands and feet, apparently. At first, only those touched by Jesse and Zane's sailing shadows reared up to meet them. Jesse's feet landed right on one of them, splintering a spine and some ribs. Zane crashed similarly into the fray nearby.

So here they were, surrounded by mutant-freak enemies who went into a panic like spooked cattle. The closest ones reared up on their hind legs, drawing nearly every kind of hand-to-hand weapon imaginable. Jesse twisted evasively. His knife sailed in a circle, gliding so his whole arm felt like a great, bloody, razor-edged wing. The blade dipped and rose, above and beneath enemy weapons. He cleaved throats and bellies, chopped through bone. He crouched and righted himself, never thinking to parry, just trusting his focus so his edge found his enemies before theirs found him, redoubling his speed with every cut. Severed heads and limbs bounced off his shoulders and chest. Blood soaked through his clothes to his skin and mingled with his sweat.

Nearby, Zane's hammer splattered its first skull before his boots hit the earth. Brains and bits of bone rained everywhere, briefly blinding the nearest attackers. Zane battered his way through the ranks, the head of his hammer bouncing from skulls to chests to arms to kneecaps to groins like a pinball, leaving shattered ruin wherever it touched. His body blurred like a ghost behind the sailing hammer. When weapons came at that ghost, those of normal metal shattered just like the bodies. Zane ignored the raining chips that cut his hands and face. When Crimbone weapons came at him, he bobbed under them to smash the fingers and wrists before finishing off the wielders with a smack to the skull or spine. Impact after impact rolled up his arm, burning his neck, chest and shoulder. He crouched as an axe swung overhead, and he brought his hammer's pointed cap up between the attacker's legs. The pelvis shattered, and the impact rolled up the spine, vertebrae by vertebrae, splitting the insides like a grape. Already, the snow was soaking up the first few enemy lines.

Overhead, gunfire barked and chattered. Chests and skulls exploded, igniting a panic that rippled further and further back. Many enemies not hit trampled each other. Those in front recoiled involuntarily, knocking into those behind them, sending back a destructive wave that caused more trampling. By now, Jesse and Zane hardly felt the bodies come apart around their weapons, just saw them fall away one after the other, in red spray after red spray. It reached a pitch that would have shamed the fiercest jungle beast in speed and grace. Friend and foe alike barely believed their eyes.

Through it all, the latest wave pressed in, a line of abominations who hit the snow in a synchronized barrel-roll…and stayed in that balled-up shape. They kept rolling and bouncing forward, smacking aside their own. Some of these ran into gunfire and splattered. Most of them, though, rolled in too fast to aim at. Jesse and Zane managed to whack a few, but it was mostly all they could do to hop and dodge and not get run over.

Jesse drove his blade through one, to the hilt, then jerked his hand back and shouted "*Shit!*"

"What?" Zane shouted back.

"Fucker just tore the shit out of my—*Zane, watch it!*" Jesse grabbed Zane by the collar and yanked him out of the way of one of the rollers.

"Man, your hand—"

"No shit!" Jesse passed his knife to his other fist. The edge of his dominant palm had been shredded to ground chuck. "*Fuck!* Those freaks are wrapped in razor-wire."

That explained the new flavor of shrieks echoing up where the rollers had gotten through. The rest of Balthazar's troops made way and drew back towards the trees. The front line of rollers skidded to a halt, yards from the lines of rocks that sheltered Jesse and Zane's followers. The settled rollers stretched their arms forward…and those arms kept stretching, and stretching, and stretching, on weaves of gooey cable. One of the gunmen screamed, then another, as unnaturally elongated arms plucked them from behind the rocks and flung them so they splattered against nearby tree trunks.

Other militiamen took to the trees, to head off what enemies had fled there. Jesse and Zane heard dying screams from both sides. The snow had all turned to deep red sludge. The gore sank through the frozen earth, thawing it to pungent mud. Jesse and Zane pulled their feet free and used the dead and dying like stepping-stones…or sometimes more like rafts or logs, as the bodies sank and slid.

Zane's hammer struck someone so hard in the gut that the flat head pulverized the spine and burst through the back. As he wrenched free, an enemy's blade gashed his back. He twisted with a grunt. One of his feet slipped and sank in the muck. He slid partially off balance, his hammer flailing wildly. It smashed the attacker in one ear, so brains squirted out the other. The skull shook limply like a sack full of broken glass. A red and white shape blurred by, yanked him sideways by the arm. Several shapes fell apart in its wake.

"*Let go*," Zane snarled. "I'm fine!"

"We can't keep up like this," said Jesse. "We're already down by a third."

"*What did you expect?*"

"Lead half of them that way." Jesse pointed to the trees to the left, then ran to the right, making eye contact with half the dwindling pack as he went, motioning them to follow.

Zane went the other way, doing the same. On Jesse's end, the enemies at the front saw what was happening and broke for the trees after them. The pack made it several yards in before those who'd followed met them, forced them to turn and engage. In the heat of the moment, it took those further back longer to catch on. When they did, the snow-covered brush slowed them up. Now their numbers truly started working against them.

Jesse sprang, grabbed a low tree limb, howled, and landed on his ass in the snow. The wailing, inhuman shapes were closing in all around him. He shambled to his feet just in time to sheath his blade and grab the branch with the hand that hadn't been mangled. He forced himself to ignore the pain in his hand, long enough to leap from branch to branch over the fight by his arms like a monkey, then flung himself back out onto the power line trail. Soon as he landed, his whirring blade created a new bloody shamble of confusion. Zane had done the same. Eventually, their swaths of carnage converged so they stood back to back. By now, though, both of them were bleeding, heavier and heavier. Jesse spared a glance at his mangled hand and saw bones gleaming through the meat of his palm. The horde pressed in heavier, hammering and hacking.

Something had changed in the air around them. It ran strongest through the trees, but also out here in the open. Jesse couldn't yet tell if it would do them any good, or even whose side it was on. Whatever this new presence meant to do, it had better do it fast! So where the hell were all those other fighters they'd brought to back them up? Probably dead by now.

All through the trees, far away yet all around, Jesse swore he heard *laughter*…high, giddy, ethereal, *childlike* laughter from a million tiny throats…

TWO

Remelea tore off the coat Jesse had given her. The damn thing was too thick, not tailored for swift, lithe movements like a proper Crimbone duster. How the hell had he put up with the damn thing? Soon as she cast it aside, the biting Vermont cold seeped through her. Fuck it. Before long, she'd be too active to stay cold.

At the edge of the bridge, she sprang atop a pickup truck that had turned on its side. Moaning metal sank beneath her boots as her hook dipped through the broken passenger window. Up came the Spirelight man within, caught on her hook through the chin. Remelea didn't have time to look over how he'd been surgically turned into something other than a Spirelight. She suckled the spilling glow quick as she could, then wrenched back. Half his face ripped loose from his skull, along with a spray of teeth. The body fell back through the smashed window.

Remelea sprang to the next overturned vehicle. Snarling like a lioness, she crouched and looked ahead with thirsty eyes. The pileup stretched back for almost the whole length of the bridge. Off to either side, cars and trucks and vans had smashed through the guard rails, into the frozen Connecticut River below. They bobbed amidst broken ice.

It had been Remelea's idea to spike Bridge Street at this end of the Brattleboro Road bridge, next to the Whetstone Station. She'd sent Joel to see to the other roads intersecting nearby, up Vernon Street. She'd sent along similar instructions to the farther off points, to the next bridge at the far end of Putney Road. With a little luck, some of those idiots Jesse and Zane had assigned to those stations were busy taking her advice.

At the other end of the bridge, Balthazar's troops left their vehicles and made their way over and around the wreckage. Remelea roared, brandished her hook skywards, and took off to meet them. Behind her, those she led ran to catch up. As her blood heated, she fought down an impulse to meet the enemy first, thin it out for everyone else as much as possible before she went down, selling her life at the highest price.

No, she reminded herself with every breath. *That ain't what I'm here for, that ain't what I'm here for…*

…Doesn't mean it won't happen if you slip up for so much as a second, though, does it?

Far behind, gunshots echoed through close quarters. That meant the enemy already pushed towards the center of town from the other direction, hopefully from High Street. If they'd pushed from Putney Road, it meant everyone past that bridge was already dead. Either way, those gunmen had *better* be shooting the right folks. She hadn't thought guns were a smart addition to start with, especially in Earth-line hands. As a Texan girl, she knew guns. They came in handy sometimes, but as a Crimbone, frankly, she felt a little annoyed at the Chinese for inventing gunpowder. Lots of Earth-line folks around here owned guns, though, so all the live ammo might as well be part of the plan, instead of something some morons brought into play unexpectedly.

After another few seconds, all she could concentrate on was the clusterfuck around her. Her pack was at her back. The enemy rose around them from the wreckage. Many were mangled and blindly clawing, like zombies digging themselves out of the earth. Remelea's hook whistled down left and right, ripping them open. A few seemed to crawl eagerly for the death she gave. Many more still scrambled to kill, no less deadly for their crushed limbs and shattered faces, some with the flesh already hanging in meaty flaps from their bones, eyes dangling down their cheeks. Her companions swarmed around her. Some killed those she missed. Many more died screaming.

Deep red streamed and welled over the concrete, around the vehicles, dripping off the bridge, splashing onto the ice below. The caravan had driven at a speed meant to pulverize anything in their path. When her trap had halted them, the effect had rippled back through them instead.

As she hopped from car to car, someone's half-skinned fingers shot up and closed on her ankle. She twisted and pivoted. Her hook's inner edge sheared the wrist. After several more bounding leaps, she noticed the dead severed hand still clinging to her. She shook herself 'til it fell off.

Ahead, the bridge crossed an island and veered right towards the next shore. Behind the island, the caravan had had more time to realize what was happening. They'd slowed to a stop, so fewer of them crashed into the pileup. Only the first few halted vehicles had some fender-benders. More fully able-bodied foes swarmed out of those vehicles, over the island. Remelea crossed onto the island and skidded to a halt. Her ankles stung when she landed on them. She motioned over her shoulder for those behind her to keep fighting, no matter what. Those swarming from the second half of the bridge came slower, filling the island thinner than the shore behind them. She hadn't been in time to see some of them swarm off into the trees on either side, but she sensed that's where more of them would be. Those meeting her directly would fight more feebly than they could, throwing away their lives 'til nearly all of her fighters were on the bridge or over it. Then the ones in the trees would spring out and surround them.

Falling back, she motioned for a cluster of fighters to follow her. She spotted a Spirelight woman at her side. She grabbed the Spirelight woman by the collar. "You used to be Secret Police?"

"I *am*—"

"So use your old skill!" She stood on tiptoe and scanned the crowd behind her, catching all the eyes the woman would need. "Follow her!" She growled low to the woman, "Into those trees." To the left, she marked a man for former Secret Police, and did the same. Then she ran to join her fighters on the bridge. She met them halfway across, engaged the decoy warriors and those behind them. "Hold them here!" she shouted.

After a moment of blurred, rampant slaughter, Balthazar's hidden troops rushed from the trees on either side...but in flight rather than attack, at less than half their original number. Remelea would have smiled, but she saw what now came to meet them from the other side. They choked the whole bridge, obscuring the halted vehicles as they rushed over and around everyone. The way these bodies moved, she swore for a second that she was looking at more of those vine-infested zombies she and

Rob had met in Talino's cellar. No, these abominations were very much alive.

She already bled from a dozen small wounds. Glancing back, she saw that she had half as many fighters with her as she'd thought. Many at the rear had probably been pulled off to help with Joel's defenses. If those defenses fell, the enemy would close in along this little bridge from both ends. Remelea spun back to the onslaught ahead. She braced her legs. Her arm shot out so a man ran neck-first onto her hook's outer edge. The headless corpse back-flipped like a Scotty dog, feet brushing her shins right before he landed. She leapt over him, down between two large vehicles. Her boots splashed into a soup of blood and entrails. Here, only three narrow ways faced her; behind, in front, and above. Eventually, either she'd run out of energy or the corpses would pile so high that they'd bear her above these metallic trenches.

All around, metal moaned and strained from pounding feet. The bridge shook as the two forces crashed into each other. Remelea stalked on in a low crouch, meeting and gutting them as they rounded corners. Her hook lashed up to cut the feet from the ones who came from above. Raining gore saturated her hair. When someone barreled into her from behind, she twisted in time to get a knife-gash in the upper side—five knives, actually, surgically fused where the fingernails used to be. She kicked the attacker so the blades slid out. The wounds didn't feel deep, but she was still locked too tight with the attacker to use her hook. Their feet slipped and slid together on the bloody pavement. She yanked the knife-arm down, snapping up her knee so the elbow crunched the wrong way. The attacker still barreled forward 'til Remelea's back slammed against the guardrail. She'd have pitched him over the side, but over his shoulder, she saw an ally and an enemy rushing each other. She put all her strength into one good kick. Her attacker shambled back so the onrushers smashed and skewered him between them. After slashing his throat, she hewed off the other enemy's arm. The one she'd helped was the former Secret Police woman she'd sent into the trees.

Remelea's pack looked thinner by a lot, but so did the enemy's. The latter was drawing off…but not in retreat. Half of them still fought on the bridge, while the others slipped away to regroup. Nothing but ice spread past the bank, yet it looked like Balthazar's troops meant to cross it. No matter how thick the ice was, no way could it hold all that weight. Stupid fuckers, it would break before the first of them were halfway across! Or would it? There'd be Crimbone among them who could sense such things and maneuver accordingly, all while guiding their fellows forward. Except why take this long to figure that out?

Because they see something other than what's there.

All at once, she knew what she was looking at, just like she'd been told to watch for. She'd also been told that would be her signal to make some choice. That part was bullshit, because she'd already made it.

Someone was shouting her name now, that Spirelight Secret Policewoman she'd rallied moments ago. She didn't wait to hear what the woman had to say. She was already making her way back through the mess, back between her own fighters across the bridge. Friend or foe, whoever was left of these motherfuckers better stay out of her way now.

THREE

On the other side of the river, a hulking dark Crimbone shape howled, turning the heads of his companions who hadn't already rushed onto the bridge.

That way had turned into a complete clusterfuck. Still, enough fighters were engaged there to occupy Remelea's forces.

The dark man couldn't see her from here, but he saw enough of how the fight was going to guess whose work he was looking at. Out of Pittsburgh, he'd followed her into enough skirmishes to recognize her wild strategy. Like guiding their pack into Rob Coscan's leadership, right after they'd all first met the little bastard sitting comfortably with the headless corpse of the local charge.

But all that was irrelevant now. Rob Coscan didn't exist. Neither did the trail down which he'd led the pack. The dark man hadn't figured this out 'til Balthazar brought the pain. The pain had consumed the dark man, burnt the whole world down to his own bones, all of which must have been broken and mended a thousand times over in a single instant that lasted forever…only to heal into so many wonderful, useful new shapes he never could have imagined. Finally, the pain had burned away his confusion. Balthazar had spoken to him through it. That's when the dark man realized Balthazar *wasn't* causing the pain. No, the pain had been his entire existence *before* Balthazar. That's how it was for anyone who followed the voices of blood, or blades, or lands, or gods, or coteries, or men who used names like Rob Coscan. Such followers were victims of the pain, but also its makers. They must be set free or put out of their misery, in the service of the great world unborn.

With that goal in sight, the dark man saw everything clearly, including the bright new advantage that had presented itself to him and his men…except he couldn't figure out how they'd missed it 'til now. He leapt from his perch, ran to the front of the ranks, and led their charge downhill to the river.

River...Hell, more like a deep gorge where a river used to flow, leaving a shallow frozen stream at the center. In a great body, the pack ran across the ice...No, not ice...the rocky, frosty riverbed. Why, for a moment, had his feet told him there was slick ice down there, starting to crack? It didn't matter. The other side was in sight, full of sources of pain. Soon they'd be set free, one way or the other.

The dark man only *imagined* the cracking ice giving out beneath him, the stab of a million icy fingernails as the water sucked him and the others under. Beneath the waves, he heard the echo of the ranks at his back, still running to join him as this imagined ice kept breaking underfoot. Then they were spilling in, crowding him, pushing him deeper through the icy water, through the pain...

FOUR

Sam and Anya ran side by side, first through the woods, then through the streets of Brattleboro. In the last few minutes—or had it been hours, days?—the universe had become an inferno of twisting, straining butchery, nothing to do but give their bodies and souls over to it. It seemed unbelievable that their strength hadn't run out yet. A moment of blades hacking them to pieces couldn't be much worse than pressing on through this heaving agony, every muscle boiling, threatening to rip from their bones.

They reached a thin scattering of houses, most of which were in flames. Cooking flesh went up their noses in the smoke. Whoever burned in there, they'd stopped screaming by now. At least all the fire was melting the snow. Water ran to the center of the nearest road and mixed with a river of gore. Corpses slid downhill through the shallow current.

Near the center of town, gunshots boomed from windows and rooftops, mostly on Main Street, adding corpse after corpse to the heap underfoot. Large clusters of enemies broke from the melee. With bare feet and webbed, elongated hands, they scaled up the sides of buildings like insects towards the shooters. Mainly the gunmen had ended up picking off whoever tried breaking into each other's buildings. That had worked for a while. Now they just blasted into the rising blankets of bodies surging towards them, up their own walls and windows, like an army of nightmare spiders. Halfway up, one climber smashed a window and swung inside. A dozen more followed in. A chorus of gurgling shrieks echoed out. Moments later, flames licked out of the first broken window.

Right as Sam and Anya were about to throw themselves into this new street fight, they spotted Joel running towards them, evading friendly fire, hacking enemies aside as he came like a berserker. When his eyes lit upon them, they braced themselves, half expecting him to attack them. Next thing they knew, he doubled forward, clutching Anya's shoulder, screaming at them in words they couldn't make out over the cacophony. Something hurtled towards them from the side, letting off a trail of skittering sparks. Before they had a chance to make out what it was, Joel's burly arms collared them both, dragging them sideways, into the alleyway next to the Hooker-Dunham building.

Halfway down the alleyway, Joel lurched and barked, "*Aw, motherfucker!*" right before they all took cover in the alcove by the building's side door. "Thought you guys were covering the trails in West Bratt," he shouted.

"I thought you were on the bridge out there," Sam barked back.

"Something *happened* to the enemy foot soldiers out there. I can't explain it. It was like…"

"Yeah, us too," said Anya. "Our whole pack was dead. Thought for sure, so were we. Then those freaks all just started…*dropping*, like invisible arrows were hitting 'em or something. Or they started attacking each other, like their eyes were suddenly seeing…more of *us*. Whatever it is, it's holding them there."

"Something like that happened at the river, only weirder," said Joel. "They're going into it, just…drowning themselves like lemmings. There were more trying to get through from Townsend, but it's like they're boxed in by invisible walls. Just crowding and crushing each other."

Sam crept to the edge of the alcove and peered out, up the alleyway to the street. "Well, enough of them have gotten through. Time we—*Ah, fuck!*"

A stray shot had just ricocheted into the alleyway and hit him in the chest. He shambled backwards, crashed through the glass, and landed across the floor of the Hooker-Dunham lobby.

"*Sam*," Anya screamed as she ran through the shattered frame to his side. He lay gasping, lurching, and failing as he tried to sit up.

Somewhere far away, a set of feet echoed into the alleyway towards them. Anya heard Joel run out howling to meet the intruder. She felt herself rising instinctively to join him. She saw him clash with the attacker, halfway back through the alleyway. She closed with them, saw and felt her hatchet crunch through the side of the attacker's neck. By then, Joel already leaned wearily against the alley wall, one scarred hand clamped to his ribs, blood streaming between his knotted fingers.

When Anya glanced out of the alleyway, she spotted a distant shape through the chaos, one that shot fresh clarity through her brain: a limber, wild-haired female shape running at cheetah-speed up Main Street, a goddess of the wild, an unmistakable black meat-hook carving out a path before her, indiscriminately as she bobbed and weaved through them.

"*Remelea*," Anya shrieked. "*Remelea, come on! It's Sam and Joel! C'mon, please, it's Sam and Joel! They're hurt bad! They're fuckin' dying over here! I could really use some…What the fuck, where the fuck are you going? Remelea, please, we—*"

Something landed hard against the side of her neck. A numbness spread swiftly from the point of impact, which turned quickly into blackness.

FIVE

From her high window in the Brooks House, Janie watched one of those powerful Crimbone warrior-women go down screaming, at the edge of the Hooker-Dunham alleyway, spraying blood everywhere, out of that gash in the side of her neck.

To this day, even after warming up to Jesse and finding out what a nice ol' fatherly teddy bear he actually was beneath the decades of murder and mayhem, Janie had still looked at all those Crimbone as such larger-than-life, unflappable fighting machines, like noble savages out of old Westerns on TV or some shit…not just *people* like herself, who could collapse into shrieking, useless gobs crying for their mothers, like Earth-line war-veterans she'd talked to or read about in history books, or watched interviewed on the news, or in documentaries. She turned numbly back to the room where they'd stashed her, high in the Brooks House. It wasn't like the carnage on the street below had stopped mattering to her. She'd just gotten tired of looking at it. It would reach her soon enough, either way. Her brain must have prepared her for the inevitable without her noticing.

It was kinda funny now. A few years back, half the Brooks building had been gutted by fire. After a lot of reconstruction that had choked up downtown forever, it had been reopened as a higher-rent space, doubling as a community-college tech-center, out of someone's snotty effort to gentrify downtown. *Joke's on them.* From what she could see, the Brooks House seemed like the one major building on Main Street that *wasn't* on fire.

How long would it take the flames to spread to where she was? How many of the little houses throughout the town were going up? How about her and Mom's old place? It didn't look like any of those freaky eugenics-mutant climbers had swarmed this building yet. Overhead, from the roof, gunmen still snapped off shot after shot.

Half a dozen Earth-line men and women sat about in the room, huddling up together, all too old to even think about fighting. No one was too young, apparently, no one who could hold a knife or a gun, anyway. Most Earth-line people with small children had skipped town well before this fight started. By now, they were probably dead too, from running into this rabble on the way. Everyone else in the room stood shivering with terror. Janie couldn't blame them. They hadn't been watching like she had. How much worse must that be, just *hearing* it?

The only Deschembine here was Lilly...not a Crimbone, just a tired-looking twenty-something woman with a Japanese sword strapped to her side. It looked like a costume piece on her, like she was on her way to a comic book convention or some shit. Janie couldn't exactly knock her; she felt just as silly, wearing the small machete on her belt, the one someone had scavenged from the old Brown and Roberts hardware store, which had probably also gone up in flames by now. What the hell were they supposed to be here, her and Lilly, some kind of *last line of defense*…for what?

"Not joining the fight?" Janie asked Lilly.

Lilly shook her head. "I'm staying right here with you."

"Why've you latched onto me so much, anyway? Don't say it's just 'cause I'm that cool. I'm Earth-line, not stupid."

Lilly sighed and lowered her eyes. "The day Sally died, Tiger and I left the base for some time to ourselves. That's it. We'd been messing around in that old car, like a couple of Earth-line teenagers at a lookout point, when those renegade Crimbone attacked. That's why you and Sally showed up for us when you did. She died saving us, because we—" She choked up for a moment. "Anyway, a lot of good that did Tiger. I was still out cold when he died. Everyone says it happened so fast. Like one minute he was pulling through fine, same ol' Tiger, then he just…died."

"Yeah," said Janie. "Like people do. They just die."

"Right. Someone told me you were with him at the end."

"I didn't…I mean, it's not like I was trying to…Look, anyone else in my position would have…"

"Sure, but no one else was there. Now everyone tells me you were. Is that true? *Is that true?*"

"Yes."

"I couldn't be with him at the end, but you could, and you were. Janie, you're…you're the first link the United Deschembines have made, in *uniting* with the Earth-line people…and you did that for him…for me. So now I wanna do this for you. Can you please just not argue with me about it?"

"Sure." They shared a long, tight embrace. Janie drew back, looked around, and asked, "Where's the bathroom around here?"

Lilly pointed. Janie didn't really have to go. She just wanted to be away from all these shaky, cowering faces. She shoved her way through the crowd. As she shut and locked the door, a big crash echoed from the lower floors below, like someone smashing the front door. Before any alarm could register, Janie jumped at the sight of the tiny figure seated atop the toilet tank.

"Little Long-Face, how'd your face get so much longer?"

"I guess 'cause all the friends I have left in this world are outside dying, and I figure I'll be dead soon too. Who wants it to end like this, y'know?"

"Many of them fighting and dying out there, for a start. I do not understand that desire any better than you do, but there you have it."

"Right. All that *go out in a blaze of glory* shit. So where'd you come from, anyway?"

"The same place as you."

"That's not what I meant. How long have you been hiding in this bathroom?"

"Not hiding. Waiting for you. I have watched you since before we both arrived in this town, Little Long-Face. My people have come from all around. Congratulations! Your friends' pet made his case well. So did you, Little Long Face, even though you didn't know you were making one. All you tall people, you've acted more unpredictably than we'd thought was in you. We've decided it's worth keeping you around, so we can watch what you do next."

"*What anyone does next.* You taken a look outside? I think that's about it."

"Perhaps, but you're not dead yet, are you? Had my kind not decided it was worth the trouble to make an appearance, to thwart these deformed invaders with our illusions and other trickery, you doubtless would be by now. So would all of your heroic friends out there, with no one to remember all their valorous efforts. There are still so many interesting new ways…anything might go. As we speak, my people bring yet more of our illusions, clearing the next way for you."

Before Janie could ask what he meant, everyone outside the bathroom started screaming as several sets of feet thundered in.

"Oh no you don't, you fuckers," Lilly shrieked. Through the walls, Janie heard that Samurai sword sing free. Two meaty crunches echoed, followed rapidly by two thuds. "Everyone else, back into the next room!" From the sound of things, she was no cosplayer after all!

Janie sprang up, towards the door. "Lilly! I'm here! I'm coming!"

"*No!* Janie, stay where you are! *They're* coming!"

More feet sounded up flight after flight of stairs, roaring as one in their hungry hatred. The screams of the dying rose around them. Janie sweated and shook, all that numbness gone. *No!* She'd be dead soon anyway, so she might as well draw her machete and go out swinging.

Janie reached for the doorknob…There was no doorknob. There wasn't even a door. She must be disoriented, clawing at the wrong wall like a blind fool. She looked around. There was no door out of here, *anywhere*.

"*You* did this!" she yelled at the little man.

He looked cheerful as ever. "Oh? But I've only made you safe in here, Little Long-Face."

Janie pounded the wall where the door should have been. "Lilly! Get me out of here! Let me *help you!*"

Everyone out in the room screamed as the marauders burst in among them. More wet chops sounded. Janie couldn't tell if any of them were still Lilly. There were fewer and fewer screams, so probably not. She looked again at the little man. Flashes of folklore rushed back to her from childhood bedtime stories Mom used to tell, of *the Little People*. That's what this little guy was, and he'd just cast one of their *illusions*...one big illusion. The *Little People* could do that. That meant the door was still here somewhere.

Janie's palms swept up and down the wall where the door should have been. The invisible knob had to be there somewhere.

"No! Leave them alone, you shits! Please!"

She had no idea how long she banged on the wall. By now, all the screaming and chopping sounded far away. The room out there had fallen silent.

An ugly voice said, "Hey, what the hell's that? I thought we cleared this room."

"Well, someone missed one. Hey, is that a Katana that dead bitch has got there? No shit, I always wanted one of these!"

"We can collect souvenirs off the dead after we're done. For now, keep—*Hey, where the fuck did you—?"*

The man's yelling turned into a sharp cry, then to a wet gurgle. In the same instant, his buddy let out a similar series of sounds. After that, the room was quiet, save for a single set of footsteps, padding much more quietly, closer and closer to Janie.

Janie froze and fell silent. Her hand slid down the wall, touched the doorknob and jerked away in surprise. She looked up and down. The door was back. The knob turned from the other side. Janie backed away as it swung open. Framed in the light beyond, a Crimbone woman loomed in over her, soaked in gore from head to toe, a dripping black hook at her side…the same hook that had pressed against her throat, nights ago, in the old municipal building. The woman's face wasn't friendly. Through the mess, Janie recognized her.

Wait a minute, what the fuck? I thought she was one of ours!

"You done yelling your head off?" said the Crimbone woman. "Better be ready to keep your mouth shut, or I'll shut it for you. It's time to go."

SIX

Fishhook's eyes lifted from Balthazar's unnaturally undulating back. They'd been walking for hours, uphill and down, even crossing another lonely backroad or two along the way. He stared through the trees atop the hill, and thought, *Is that…a fucking medieval tower?*

"She's on her way, Ronny," Balthazar sighed as they topped the ridge. "Hell, she's already here, just…well, she's still gettin' here, too. *One piece at a time*, like the feller said."

Fishhook blinked and wobbled. His throat tightened like he'd swallowed his phantom tongue. Balthazar had just spoken with such giddy, romantic joy, at the prospect of uniting with whatever demon lover he'd come here to summon, like he and Fishhook really were *buddies*, sitting in a coffee shop, or by the tracks, or down by the river during the summer with a couple of forties or cans of Four Loko, and Balthazar had spent all day gushing about how his old girlfriend or boyfriend was coming into town, and he had such high hopes for rekindling that old flame. For a moment, Fishhook almost got swept up in the fantasy.

Then the cold, his own withered, broken body, his missing tongue, the sight of the thing in front of him, it all reminded him just how fucked-up all this was. Except, why not, right? This was his *new normal*, after all.

After a while, it had been like, *Feel guilty about the rest of those poor bastards back there in the cells or on the disassembly lines that didn't share his privilege? Fuck that shit, man!*

Earlier, when those two Crimbone guys had shown up and attacked…the ones Fishhook guessed you'd call *the good-guy Crimbone*…Right before Balthazar had painted the peaceful white snow with their spraying red insides, had Fishhook thought, *Yes, please, kill him; here's the good guys, come to rescue me!* Or had he seen that second Crimbone's blade get so close to Balthazar's chest so he'd tried to shout, *Balthazar, buddy, watch out!*

He couldn't remember anymore. Even if those guys had killed Balthazar and rescued Fishhook, who'd want anything to do with him, as he was now, other than Balthazar? His tongue wasn't gonna grow back, and neither was anything else the bastard had taken away from him, a piece at a time. He just wished he could sit down and rest a while.

A big sob shook its way up through Fishhook's whole body, 'til it broke from his mouth in a series of rasping barks.

Balthazar turned back, suddenly looking more…what was the word; contrite?…than Fishhook had ever seen him. "Oh, I know, buddy, I know! Aw, *c'mere…*" Balthazar enfolded Fishhook into a bear-hug. One of those big, gnarly clawed hands stroked Fishhook's back soothingly. "Yeah, I know. This is a real emotional moment. I feel it too. *We're about to take the gods themselves as our slaves, man!* How 'bout that? There ain't no one—and I mean *no one*—who I'd want to share this moment with other than you."

Fishhook settled against Balthazar, melting comfortably into the old, familiar warm embrace.

"Just a little longer, Ronny. It'll all be over soon."

God, I sure hope so.

Fishhook followed Balthazar out around the tower, into the beaten, gravel-strewn clearing that faced the front of the looming, anachronistic structure. It was a majestic sight, Fishhook had to give it that. If he hadn't been stuck here with Balthazar, he might have imagined for a hot minute that he was in a *Lord of the Rings* movie or some shit.

Balthazar stepped out into the center of the rocky patch, facing the door to the tower. Fishhook followed him, 'til they faced it together. They stared at the old door together. It hung open on rusty hinges, showing just more bare earth beyond the archway, with the gray daylight spilling down through rotted boards onto the desolate, forgotten remains at the bottom. Fishhook expected Balthazar to throw a fit, like he'd come all this way for nothing. If that happened, Fishhook was ready to bust out laughing his ass off, not caring about what hacking laughter he could get out without a tongue, just like he had when Balthazar had ripped his tongue out. What was Balthazar gonna do now, rip his dick off? It wasn't like he'd ever get to use it again anyway. No, hopefully he'd just hock out barks of laughter 'til Balthazar flew off the handle and either beat him to death or just ripped his head clean off. Either way, it'd be Balthazar's problem after that, not Fishhook's.

Instead, Balthazar stared awestruck, at how the light spilled down between the rotted-out stairwell boards, falling across the frosty stones at the bottom. He flexed and slid out of the long duster coat, so it dropped into the snow around his feet. Fishhook gasped and stepped back. Balthazar stood naked from the waist up. The old metallic horns bobbed backwards from his wrists like a pair of giant, sharpened black dicks. Fishhook was used to that sight. What he wasn't used to was the smaller horns, sculpted from the same black metal, sticking out of Balthazar's back and shoulders, stapled into dozens of wounds of self-mutilation, all boiling and swelling with infection many times worse than the horns he'd implanted in his forehead, all weeping pus and blood down his back, pooling in clumps of half-congealed red-black and shiny green-yellow at the base of his jeans.

Balthazar stretched out his arms and turned in a circle several times like a fashion model, showing off his mutilated back, flexing his muscles so the wounds split and drooled down his back afresh. All those curving little horns of black metal quivered like porcupine quills. The blackened gash in his side looked more tortured than ever, the infected tendrils spooling throughout his flesh like the vines around Sleeping Beauty's castle. "How you like how I made myself pretty for her, huh, Ronny? *Ah, yes!* This is where it starts! Can't you feel it, man? It's about to start any second now. *That sonofagun's a comin'.*"

"No it ain't," said a woman's voice from behind them.

Fishhook and Balthazar both spun sharply at the same time. Through the trees came a tall, lean, wild-haired Crimbone woman…not like any of Balthazar's, but no, not like those two poor bastards they'd encountered downhill, either. Wet, pungent gore coated her from head to toe, her hair sopping with blood like she'd just stepped out of a shower of it. Except for the mad fire in her eyes, her facial expression looked almost lazy. So did the way she carried herself, neither idle nor excited, just…relaxed and poised at the same time. She looked Balthazar and Fishhook over, like she had no idea who they were, didn't much care, had yet to make up her mind about them.

"Well look who it is," said Balthazar. "Hell-Fox Bitch! What you doin' here, girl? Come for Round Two?"

"Not exactly. I've been studying up about you, Balthazar."

"Oh, you have, huh? And what are your sources, pray tell?"

"Closer to the true lands themselves, more reliable than any of the rest of these wankers around here, I can tell you that much. I hear you're a would-be king, in the market for a queen."

Balthazar threw his head back and let out booming laughter that sent snow-crusted tree-branches vibrating, so fresh mist sifted down over them. "Oh, you wanna be my queen? Was a time, I'd'a jumped at that offer, but *naaaaaahhh…*"

"No, I ain't here to be *your* queen. I'm here to become *my own* queen, just like you came here to finally, truly become your own king, with the queen you've come here looking for at your side."

Balthazar snorted. "Hate to break it to you, girlie, but once I get done with what I come here to do, ain't gonna be room for you and your plans in that equation."

She shrugged. "Yeah, well, we can burn that bridge when we get there. For now, I can tell you one thing for sure. You're never gonna see your queen without my help…not without the missing puzzle piece I've come here with."

She stepped sideways. Yards behind her, on the edge between another trail and this clearing, there stood a short, shivering, dark-skinned Earth-line girl, draped in someone else's oversized coat. It hung all the way to her feet like a cape, her arms tightened across her shivering chest. The way she hung back, helpless and petrified, the involuntary lackey to this crafty Crimbone woman who Balthazar called *Hell-Fox Bitch*, Fishhook saw a mirror of himself.

Almost instantly, he felt ashamed to even think it, to find that involuntary flood of relief. No one deserved to share this hell with him, let alone some poor, shivering little girl. He tried to meet her eyes, to somehow say *I'm sorry*. She didn't even seem to notice him.

"Who's that?" said Balthazar. "What the hell does that little bitch have to do with all this?"

"Oh, her? She's half of that *key* you need. I see you've already brought your half, to where we both wanna go." Hell-Fox Bitch cocked her head at Fishhook, met his eyes and winked.

"Let's say I don't believe a damn thing you gotta say," said Balthazar. "Let's say I just pop off and kill both of you bitches then get back to my own business."

"You could do that. But what if it turned out I was telling the truth? What if it turned out, after you killed me and this little Earth-line bitch, that we'd been the one final piece in your puzzle all along—the one your beloved queen, this celestial love of your life you've been chasing—had been trying to tell you, through the lands, through all the blood you've spilled, that you've been looking for this whole time? You'd be stuck wandering this dying world, forever cursed to try to fill that void by killing everyone else who could've otherwise been your faithful underlings sucking your dick, but now you can't and it's too late. Damn, it sounds like a Goddamn Wagnerian Opera! If that's what you're in the mood for, for all eternity, be my guest!" She splayed her arms.

Balthazar chuckled and wagged a gnarly, clawed finger at her. "Wow, Hell-Fox Bitch, you're good...a whole lot smarter than that so-called *High Natural* I last seen you around with. Whatever happened to his cowardly little ass, anyhow?"

She shrugged, snorted, and rolled her eyes. "Oh. Right. Him. Who knows? Who cares? Looking back, I can't believe I thought I was in love with that little asshole for so long. I mean, seriously! Okay, granted, he *did* somehow rally the most pathetic, scrounging, dirtbag pack of Crimbone I've ever hit the trail with, and somehow led them to drive the Spirelight Secret Police themselves to the point of extinction."

"Yeah, but *I'm* the one who finished their asses off!"

"That you did, baby, that you did. *Shhhhh…*Don't get ahead of me now. While we're on the subject, correct me if I'm wrong, but ain't *Rob Coscan* the only one who's ever defeated you in single combat?"

"*That weren't fair fight! He fought dirty!*"

She giggled. "You think a single one of all those other fuckers you beat into submission didn't? C'mon, Balthazar." She reached up and stroked his cheek. "*Ah, ah, ah*, not so fast, big boy!"

With every moment, Fishhook had less of an idea what he was watching here. He'd given up trying to make heads or tails of what rules these Deschembine people lived by, and yet…was this seriously a strong, competent, confident, gownass woman, offering her love, consensually, to Balthazar? Whatever it was, *it was fuckin' gross*.

"*If he weren't shit,*" moaned Balthazar, "*why'd you follow him for so long? Why him and not me?*"

"Well, I've been thinking a lot about that. See, before him, once I had my blade and was off and runnin' on the trail, all I ever thought about was being wild and free, like any Crimbone gal who was first forced to grow up through her fledgling years going through the same degradation the Earth-line girls go through. After that? You say the Cabinets or the lands want to call me in to kill some Spirelights? That's just gravy! Then one day, this guy shows up, talking about *purpose and changing things for the better?* And he leads us across a crazier trail than we've ever dreamed possible? It was fun! How could a gal like me not fall for that? Except then I notice, day by day, I'm doing worse and worse things in his name, to folks who don't even deserve it, so I'm like, *Is this me? How'd this guy talk me into committing these atrocities?* I think maybe it was *feeling that sense of purpose* that I really fell in love with." She snorted. "Fucker actually had the balls to tell me before the end that he *fell in love with me too.* Bullshit. He got off on having someone at his side who was just as big of a blood-thirsty, murdering piece of shit as him, who also happened to be a hot piece of ass, who he got to have violent sex with after a hard day's killing. Since he left me, I've been playing Deputy-Sheriff in this shitty little town, babysitting all these weakass Earth-line folks, thinking maybe I could find that *sense of purpose* again. Like maybe my calling lay here, to be a *true hero* after all. Let me tell you, the last few weeks of that bullshit cured me of that delusion pretty solidly. I—"

Balthazar threw up both clawed hands. "Okay, fine, I get it! Look, Hell-Fox Bitch, I done agreed to hear you make a deal, not be your fuckin' shrink."

"I just wanted to make sure we're on the same page."

"If you're so disillusioned, why you already covered in the blood of my soldiers?"

"I just wanted to see what they're made of, before getting down to business with you. And frankly? I'm not impressed. Rob Coscan, with his ragtag, piece-of-shit redneck Crimbone pack, managed to kick the asses of both the Spirelight Secret Police and *you.* Now here you are, with your army of superpowered mutant freaks at your wrist, it's been three hours since they launched their attack, *and they still haven't even managed to put down one shitty little backwater Vermont town!*"

"Fine, I get it. *Rob Coscan, Rob Coscan, Rob Coscan!* Fuck, when I get to stop hearin' that little asshole's name get pissed in my ear?"

"That's exactly my point, baby. Can't you see? We're fellow sufferers, stuck in *his* shadow, when it's *ours* everyone else should be cowering in. Ain't you figured it out yet, what he had all along that you've been missing?"

"No, but I reckon you're about to tell me."

"He had me."

Balthazar looked her over, then grinned. "Okay, Hell-Fox Bitch, so what's your next move?"

"Same one you already planned, am I right?" She walked up face-to-face with Fishhook. "Mind if I do the honors?"

"But I was gonna make it special for him, like…I mean, I just wanted to…" Something in Balthazar's voice hitched. He and Hell-Fox Bitch exchanged a look, then he gave her a nod. He looked back to Fishhook with tears in his eyes. "Ronny, you knew this was comin', right? Look, it's…been real, man."

Fishhook gulped. Honestly, he hadn't understood a Goddamn thing either of these two had just said.

Hell-Fox Bitch stroked Fishhook's cheek. Their eyes met. She whispered softly, "Look, man, I'm just doing what I gotta. But I'm doing it my own way now. Tell me, though, to a face of love…once this is over, do you still wanna be around, to find your own way out?"

It took Fishhook a minute to figure out what she meant. If he'd had a tongue, he'd have shouted, *You kidding? Fuck no! Just get it over with already!*

"Okay, then." She took Fishhook by the shoulders and gently turned him about. He'd almost forgotten what it was like to have someone touch him so gently. Before he knew it, he was like putty in her hands. "Just turn and stand at this angle. Good, good, just a little more…Okay, yeah, that's it, perfect! Stay just like that!" Her hook swung up. Its outer edge went through Fishhook's neck and spine like butter. His head popped off.

It was funny. Fishhook had heard people say how someone could get decapitated and still be conscious, for like twenty or thirty seconds afterwards. Apparently, that was true. Who knew, right? What a weird feeling, to still be stuck inside his own head while it bounced and rolled across the ground like a basketball. It didn't hurt half as bad as he'd—

SEVEN

The withered Earth-line man's body and head landed across the frosty gravel. Blood sprayed from both neck-stumps like two fire-hoses having an argument. The severed head floated backwards through the rising, spouting river, like it was losing the argument. Remelea picked the head up by the hair. She carried it quickly, across the ground to the open tower door, while there was still blood left to pour from it, leaving a perfect red trail. She stepped inside through the tower doorway and let the blood pour out of the neck 'til it reduced to a slow drip. She walked back out, cast the head aside, went back over to the body, crouched and dipped her palm into the deepest, darkest part of the pool around the stump. She rose, went over to Janie, spilled the palmful of blood over the poor gal's head, rubbed it around through her hair like shampoo, then looked her in the eyes.

"Janie? It's time. C'mon, girl, that's right, just follow my lead. Like we talked about. That's it, that's right." Remelea looped her arm through Janie's and walked her out onto the blood-trail, up to the tower door, like a maid of honor leading a blushing bride to the altar. Then she let go, stepped aside and said, "Go on in, Janie."

Janie walked into the tower and stood there at the hollowed-out center, her back facing the world beyond.

"Okay," said Balthazar, "I still ain't sure what you wanted to accomplish with that."

"Oh, but don't you feel it yet, baby?" said Remelea. "She's the key, your missing puzzle piece. Without her, you'd have come all this way and been left standing around with your dick in your hand, waiting for something to happen. Ain't you glad you didn't kill me in New Orleans?"

"I don't know. Depends on if anything happens while we try it your way."

"Oh, damn, it's *already* happening! Oh, yeah, I feel *her*, Balthazar, your queen, running to us from all directions, from the great beyond, through the land under our feet. Can't you feel it, too?"

Balthazar quivered all over. "Oh…yeah…I know, right? Yeah. I feel it happenin'. Ain't it amazin'?"

"It is," gasped Remelea. "It really is!" She walked slowly towards him. "*Oh, yeah, here she comes, here she comes!* Can you hear what she's telling me, Balthazar? She wants to flow up through *me*, for us to become one, so we can *both* be your queen, in flesh and blood." She stroked his cheek.

Balthazar's eyes lit up. A boyish smile spread across his long, ugly snout, like it was the first time in his life a woman had ever touched him like that willingly. Then his mouth dropped open in agonized befuddlement. His eyes bulged, because she'd just driven her whole hook inside his belly by the outer sharpened edge, in a single powerful heave. He gaped and stared like he wanted to ask *Why?*

"Feel that in you, Balthazar?" Remelea hissed. "*Deep inside you?*" She twisted the handle. He lurched, doubled forward, caught her by the shoulders, and clung on for dear life. "You wanted the *blood* to tell you what to do, right? Feel my hook, twisting all your intestines up around it right now? Yeah. That hook came here slathered in the blood of your underlings. Can't you feel them all, everything you turned them into, seeping out through your own insides?" She twisted again. He crashed to his knees. "*Mmmmmm, yeah, baby, give it to me, give it to me, like that!* Oh, yeah, you just get tighter and tighter inside, the more I *twist*." She twisted again, slower. She pressed her cheek against his and whispered, "So what's all that blood telling you now, sweetheart?"

Her feet shifted as she wrenched her arm backwards. Balthazar's intestines flew through the air, for a good twenty feet, then splashed across the snow. She watched him bleed and contort, then her hook completed its sweep in a rainbow arc that opened his neck, all the way back to his spine. A bloody jet struck her across the waist. The severed edges of his neck clapped wetly against each other. He looked around at all the black metal infused throughout his body, right before it all crumbled and flew away as dust in the wind. For a moment, as he stared up at her, he looked like nothing but a terrified, confused little boy, choking to death on his own blood. Then he collapsed onto his back. Remelea stood over him, heaving.

"Well done, Lost Queen," echoed a spectral voice from the surrounding trees.

Remelea looked around. She spotted the open tower doorway into which Janie had walked. "Oh, shit, girl, I'm sorry!" She entered the tower and found Janie lying on her side, unconscious, in the lake of blood Remelea had led her to. "Janie?" She shook her.

Janie rolled over and stared up at Remelea. Those eyes weren't hers. "Take me back to the Brooks House," she said.

"Janie…"

"*Take me back to the Brooks House.*" That voice *definitely* wasn't Janie's.

THE MAN WITH NO RACE

ONE

After Old Nagga took Rob away, the pack hurried deeper into the marshlands beyond. Sheldon stayed close to Kashen, like a child tagging along at the heels of a guardian. The sensation of naked helplessness infuriated him, so he sometimes clutched the knife handles 'til his battered knuckles popped. It hardly mattered anymore, how strong or capable he'd made himself by the measures of another world, or that his grim-eyed companions hadn't turned on him yet. With Rob gone, he had no idea how tenuous their acceptance of him was. They all stood at least half a head taller than him. Their eyes constantly flickered at each other, their lean, hard bodies shifting and twitching midstride, as though carrying on fully formed conversations through body-language and facial expression. How many of them were talking about him? Whenever any of them caught him looking, they shot him forbidding glares before fixing their eyes forward. Kashen barely seemed to notice him most of the time, focused instead on picking out the trail by which he led the pack.

The moon rose high over the treetops, an even stranger moon than Sheldon had previously realized, sending out shimmers through the sky like curved blades of light, in every hue of blue, gold, and purple, seeming to dance with the stars, igniting them with their own swirling splendors. Beneath that alien sky, he sometimes forgot if it was day or night. Did the others see it the same way, or did it just bombard his alien eyes, one more taunting reminder that he didn't belong here?

His limbs and lungs had settled from all the running and swimming earlier, yet the longer he walked, the dizzier he felt. More than once, he ambled sideways and bumped into someone, who snarled at him. His feet always felt like he was trekking uphill, even when his eyes showed him flat terrain, so patches of still water appeared to defy gravity. However bigger or smaller this planet was from Earth, its gravity and curvature played havoc with his equilibrium. How had he not noticed 'til now? Had his connection to Rob shielded him from it? When Puttergong told him he'd need Rob to survive here, this wasn't what he'd had in mind.

When the marshlands gave way to an open field, the transition was so abrupt that Sheldon wondered if he'd gone to sleep and woken up while still walking. One minute, he'd been surrounded by trees and bogs, and now he wasn't. When he looked back, the darksome forest was already far behind him. Amidst the expanse, he lost all sense of scale. It looked like just a small, hilly clearing, 'til he saw where it dropped off into endless mountain ranges. The others had fanned out, giving each other greater breadth. They ambled along at an easier clip. A given patch of ground might seem to be mere feet or yards away, 'til he saw another body striding across it, so he realized it was more like hundreds of feet. A thin smattering of trees speckled the plain ahead. The pack converged towards it. Sheldon looked back to Kashen, who he'd left far behind while distracted. Even as everyone tightened up together, Sheldon felt little more sense of everyone's physical proximity to each other.

The trees drew nearer. Little hut-like shapes rose amidst them. One of his boots splashed in running water. He jumped and looked down. A smooth, thin stream ran by his feet, over clusters of shimmering pebbles, as though from some uphill mountain spring. Someone tapped him on the shoulder. He jolted, spun, almost reached for his knives, then saw Kashen standing next to him.

"You shouldn't wander off alone, friend." When the Crimbone chief smiled, years seemed to melt from his hard, creased, stoic face.

"But I didn't—" Sheldon looked around.

Far away, the others had congregated between the trees. The stream ran thicker there. Sheldon still couldn't pinpoint where it was coming from. He saw the ancient, tiny, mud-sculpted huts much clearer now, though.

As they neared the others, Kashen clapped him across the shoulder. "You ought to pace yourself better, friend. The clip at which you've been going, you're like an infant beast that rages about, with no idea of either its own strength or the limits of such, likely to burn itself out before reaching its potential, having done more harm than good in the bargain."

At least that's what Sheldon loosely interpreted from the man's dialect. As they came within the campsite, he blinked and said, "What…is this place?"

"A good place," said Kashen. "Places where these mud huts still stand are always good places. They're marvels, really. Such crude little dwellings, yet where left undefiled, they've remained as they are for thousands of years. We don't know why, but the Spirelights always shun whatever ground on which they stand."

"So you don't think the Spirelights will find us up here?"

"They never do, not where we find these huts."

"Who built them?" Sheldon asked, though he was already pretty sure he knew.

Kashen stared off. "An ancient, mysterious vagabond race, long gone from the lands of Valaka. They once trod far and wide across this soil, wherever the eight winds pushed them. You can still find shards of their pottery, hunting tools, and other leavings scattered where they used to make camp. Then Spiralla rose and spewed forth the Spirelights, with the will of their gods. Whoever those people were, the Spirelights hunted them to extinction."

No, Sheldon thought as he surveyed the crumbling dwellings. *These are the artifacts of the vagabond race that* became *the Spirelights, before they found their way into those infernal ruins, where Bathshire would one day find the gods.* Of course, he couldn't say that out loud, because then Kashen would ask how he knew that.

"I don't see anyone here making use of those dwelling spaces," said Sheldon.

"Many ghosts still sleep in them," said Kashen. "When we camp near them, they leave us be, so long as we leave them be."

"What happens if we don't? Leave them be, I mean."

"Bad dreams. *Their* bad dreams. These lands are full of bad memories and bad dreams. Here, the ancient dead allow us to feel peaceful. Why intrude on their pain? Why take—" –He grunted a series of ugly, guttural sounds, from which Sheldon could decipher no translation— "—where there is no need for it?"

The other Crimbone had already set about making camp, drawing their weapons of black metal to dig out fire pits and chop kindling from low-hanging branches. They cut off large, palm-like leaves, twisted them into funnels with the bottoms pinched shut, scooped up water and drank. It was weird to witness the black metal used for something other than violence. How had Rob put it? *Did you think these things were just good for stabbing motherfuckers?*

Where the creek flowed widest, some of the Crimbone stripped naked to wash themselves or their clothes. Sheldon got caught up staring at their naked forms, splotchy and multi-hued all over like turtle shells, no longer constantly changing color in the chameleon-like way they'd done while on the warpath. Some of them laughed and splashed each other as they bathed, like the danger and loss from hours earlier had happened in another lifetime. A few fell into playful roughhousing which became something more sensual, unembarrassed, many of them without regard for gender-differences or lack thereof. Sheldon drew closer, letting his coat fall absently from his shoulders. Huge, jagged wounds covered some of them, so fresh and ghastly, it defied reason that they were still breathing, let alone so spry. As his hands moved to peel off his river-soiled shirt, he felt the black scar in the center of his torso…not with the onset of paralyzing agony, as used to happen when his connection to Rob flared up, just an acute awareness of the tight, tough scar tissue. He left his shirt on and didn't get too close to the bathing celebrants. Whenever any of them noticed him watching, they eyed him in a way that was…well, too preoccupied with each other to be *threatening*, exactly, but definitely *forbidding*.

He walked out across the field, away from the campfires, and sat down on a rocky spot where the hillside dropped off. The far-off mountain ranges jutted and twisted at alien angles that gravity and geological evolution should have forbidden.

As the night deepened, he grew chillier. He wished he could remember where he'd dropped his coat, somewhere off in the shadows of the trees. He looked back at the smattering of campfires across the hill, decided *fuck it*, then rose and walked back towards them. To his relief, he spotted Kashen at the nearest one.

"You guys mind if I join you?" At least he hoped that's what he'd just said. Apparently, he hadn't fucked the dialect up too badly, because no one jumped up and tried to stab him.

Before Kashen could speak, a mostly naked Crimbone woman rose and walked over to Sheldon. The firelight behind her blackened her shapely silhouette. Three men and two women watched. Despite her nudity, there was nothing sexual in her body-language, or at least he didn't think so at first, even when she draped an arm around him and guided him over to the fire. He sat down on a rock. She sat in his lap and leaned back against him, running her rough, narrow palm across his cheek than back through his hair. Her hipbones settled on him uncomfortably, so he took hold of her waist and shifted her into a position that felt nicer. She ran her hands up and down his thighs, laughing back and forth with her cohorts all the while, at a joke everyone but him seemed to be in on. Even Kashen chuckled and shook his head.

When he let his hands explore her, she laughed louder at his awkwardness. He suddenly remembered camping out in the common rooms of Earth-line college campuses during his years on the run from the Secret Police Tribunals, using his Secret Police hypnosis tricks to convince Earth-line college students to see one of their own carousing amongst them. He wished he could pull that same trick on these Crimbone, that he could calm and focus his mind even halfway well enough for such mind-tricks. That's how he'd lost his virginity, to the first of a few Earth-line college girls who'd never guessed they were fucking a vagabond boy who was criminally younger than themselves, by their own culture's laws and norms anyway. In the years since, he'd sometimes looked back on such deception and felt a little bad about it. When the monsters of your childhood might literally spring from any shadow to kill you at any moment, you took pleasure and relief where it was offered. The temptation was strong to fall back on that now. He guessed this Crimbone woman felt the same way, that all these people did, with their wantonly free love. He must be something quite unusual to her, as she was to him. She gurgled something at her cohorts, something that might have been, "*I wanna know what the man with no race has in his trousers.*" They laughed and howled louder than ever, as though cheering her on.

Somehow, her writhing, alienly proportioned body just felt…weird against him, like she might as well have been a dog or cat humping his leg. When she twisted around to kiss him, something in his whole being rebelled against this encounter. For one thing, she just wasn't Janie. He pushed her away as gently as possible. Before he knew it, she sprang away like a grasshopper, shouting at him too fast for him to understand, as though he'd just been the one to get too fresh. Everyone else rose and snarled, some of them reaching for weapons…everyone but Kashen. Yet again, he was the one to shout them all down.

He stepped between Sheldon and the woman and said, "Now would be a good time to give everyone the wind of you, my young, strange friend."

Sheldon nodded and headed quickly back towards the hillside. His nerves buzzed like they were trying to shake his consciousness out of his body. For a long time, he sat trying to fathom just what social transgression he'd committed. No one came to bother him, so he got lost staring off across the multicolored alien mountain ranges. The longer he sat alone, the darker and more self-destructive his thoughts got. As the night grew colder, he glanced back at the distant campfire and wondered if it was safe to return. Probably not.

450 ~ MATT SPENCER

Part of him regretted rejecting that crazy Crimbone bitch's advances, and not just because she'd reacted murderously to the rejection, and he knew exactly which part. Sexual frustration was the least of his worries right now, though. What the hell was he supposed to do, here in the Old World, surrounded by Crimbone, with no Rob as a mediator? Kashen was doing his best, but something cold in Sheldon's gut told him that the man's mediations would only last so long.

Sheldon inhaled deeply and let it out slowly. *Just work your way through the old breathing exercises. Think of all this like a bad drug trip, and deal with it that way.* Once his nerves settled some, he rose and drifted back uphill, though the trees. No one came to bother him. He found his way to the doorway of one of the ancient huts. The structure was absurdly small, like his ancestors must have been. He crouched, crept inside, and lay down on the bare dirt floor. All at once, exhaustion settled through him so his mind swam away through a deep slumber.

In his dreams, a silvery, serpentine voice rose and caressed him, through a sea of sweltering rot, whispering, *Just a little further, Sheldon.* That wasn't Janie's voice, or the Crimbone woman from back by the campfire. It wasn't even male or female, exactly. *I'm waiting for you, darling, back where we belong...back where the new world waits to be born.*

Two

Sheldon awoke to the sound of Kashen shouting, "Get up, boys and girls. The trail's waited long enough for our feet."

The night before, Kashen had sounded soft and rational when he'd stood between Sheldon and the others.

Now his barking words cut through the morning's haze with all the sharp, uncompromising ferocity Sheldon had come to expect from this race of beasts. Sheldon dragged himself out of the ancient hut. Through the trees ahead, atop the hill, bathed in the sunlight, the others converged towards their chief. So far, no one seemed to notice Sheldon. After how last night had gone, he preferred it that way.

"Don't forget," Kashen continued, "there are still more packs on their own trails, all over the place, still holding the outer wilderness of Valaka from the rule of Spiralla…our brothers and sisters, our mothers and fathers…our children. For a shining moment, we had a High Natural to lead us. We all heard his voice…*the voice of the lands*, speaking aloud in the ancient Crimbone tongue, from a Crimbone mouth. We all felt it liven us with a fresh strength, fresh savage thirst. You all know as well as I do, if it hadn't been for the power which the High Natural reminded us of within ourselves, we'd all be dead by now. That gift lives on within us still. We must survive, to carry it to those other packs."

"Great, so what about him?" shouted a gravelly, high-pitched voice. He turned and saw a Crimbone woman pointing at him. It was the same one whose advances he'd rejected last night. It had taken him a moment to recognize her in the daylight, with her clothes on. "That weird kid the High Natural brought along?"

"The *man with no race*, yes." Kashen met Sheldon's eyes and beckoned him forward.

Sheldon had spent so much of his life, relying on the ability to be seen only when he wanted to be. More than ever, he wished he could vanish from these Crimbone's sight, to cloud their minds so they forgot he existed. The last time he'd felt anywhere close to this awkward had been back at the Renaissance Kingdom, when Claudette and Deacon had called him and Sally up onto the stage. Sally wasn't with him now, and no one in this crowd looked on him with the stupid, blindly desperate reverence of the United Deschembines. He walked forward to Kashen's side.

Kashen placed a hand on Sheldon's shoulder. "This strange young creature came to us, with the High Natural, who gave him his blessing. He led some of you through battle, to victory, did he not? Here I see most of you who followed him still sitting here." He leaned towards Sheldon. "So what about it, *man with no race?* What do you have to say to Ghella over there?" He pointed at the Crimbone woman. "Now that we don't have our High Natural, what do we need you for?"

Sheldon looked around. Kashen was a fine speaker, but his voice was no High Natural's. Everywhere, Crimbone eyes shimmered in the dawn's pale light.

Sheldon's words locked in his throat several times before he managed to speak. "Yeah, I came here with Rob, and—" He stopped. He'd just spoken in Earth-line. Everyone grumbled with ominous uncertainty. He cleared his throat and spoke slowly, in common Old World Deschembine, pausing a lot to find his way around the strange tongue. "I came to these shores, side by side with your…with *our* High Natural, yes…as his equal, not his servant. I am not—was not—*his* man with no race. I am *my own* man with no race, and I swear to you, I will stand with you and help you kill the gods."

Louder growls rumbled back at him. The one called Ghella clutched the grip of her long knife and said through her teeth, "Kashen, I don't like this whelp." She met Sheldon's eyes. He gulped, collected himself, and stared back at her. Her lips twitched and she continued, "But he's too weird, too *interesting*, to just kill and eat quite yet." She turned back and howled at the others, "What do you say, boys and girls? Are we agreed? Do we keep our man with no race for a little while yet?" They all howled in agreement, followed by a chorus of mocking laughter. She strode up, got right in his face, and whispered, "Run with a Crimbone pack, boy, that makes you a servant of the lands. Against the gods. So go ahead, make your case. Then we'll decide whether or not to let you run with us, or stay in one piece for that matter."

"I thought I just did," Sheldon whispered back.

"Not by half. Keep talking."

Sheldon held her gaze but spoke loud enough for the rest of them to hear. "The High Natural did his duty by guiding me into harmony with the lands of our ancestors, so I might do my duty by all of us. I had hoped to do that duty side by side with him. I still mean to see it through…if I don't die first. Now he's no longer here to help me. I hope that you, his fellow Crimbone, still will."

"*Guided you here*, you say," said Ghella. "*Into harmony with the lands of your ancestors*. I have to ask, boy, where in all Deschemb *did* the two of you come from?"

Of all the lore of Old Deschemb on which Sheldon had been raised, he only now realized how little of its geography he'd learned. He remembered Janie bitching about that, while she'd tried to decipher the subtleties of Claudette's book. Had anyone in the Old World even made physical, drawn-out maps on parchment or paper, or had that been an Earth-line invention?

These Crimbone called this region—these lands— Valaka. In all of Sheldon's old schooling, Valaka was the fabled dwelling place of Spiralla, the Great Sacred Capital of the Spirelight Empire. Some legends also called it *the Land of Mist*.

All this time, he'd thought Kashen still had his back, following Rob's posthumous lead. Now he realized he was stuck on his own, amidst a pack of savages, whose norms and nuances of social decorum were completely beyond his comprehension. He suspected he'd really put his neck on the block last night, not simply by rejecting Ghella's advances, but in something about how he'd done so. This was a test, and his survival from one moment to the next depended entirely on his luck at winging it.

"It's true," he blurted. "Neither I nor the High Natural came from these shores. We sailed here together from…lands none of you have heard of. However, I repeat, we both came here, as allies…as brothers…for the same purpose. You recognized that purpose in him, right? Listen to the lands and let them show you that same purpose in me. I'm here to find where the Gods of the Spirah Pantheon dwell, the source of where their power flows out, enabling the oppression from the Spirelight Priest Kings, onto *all* races of Deschemb…The Schomites, the Gestru, the Lepods…the strange hybrid Wallution people of the far north…even the civilian Spirelights." That last part got a lot more malcontented growls. Maybe they'd finally noticed that he used to be a Spirelight. "I repeat, I'm here to sever the power of the gods from all Deschemb, at the source, once and for all. With or without the High Natural. I could sure use your help finding my way there, though."

Ghella grinned ruefully. "So let me get this straight…*man with no race*…You think just *little ol' you* is gonna go and, over night, just…Boy, you *are* crazy!"

Sheldon shouted in her face, "*So do you know the way to them or not, bitch?*"

Those who'd gathered behind her fumed up, ready to attack. She waved them back, a new kind of wonder kindling in her eyes. "I…finally see that you truly believe all that you say, through your entire bloodstream."

Throughout this ordeal, put on the spot by the rage of the beasts, Sheldon remembered everything he'd been taught growing up, about *why* creatures like these Crimbone needed to be eradicated, why the order of the Spirah Gods needed to be imposed on this and all worlds. Then he blinked, saw Janie's face behind his eyes, along with every good memory they'd ever shared, everything that had made his miserable life worth living, and how those gods didn't want such moments to exist. Whoever truly preferred the safe, sanitary, orderly existence the gods offered as an alternative, Sheldon figured they could all go to hell. If these beasts were the monstrosity needed to oppose such gods, he would stand with them.

He answered Ghella, "I do."

Kashen's grip tightened on Sheldon's shoulder. "You want to meet the gods? Fine, we'll take you to them. We'll see what you amount to." His eyes moved over the pack. "Unless of course the rest of you have something better to do."

The Crimbone let out an earth-shattering howl of agreement that echoed through the mountain ranges.

THREE

Sheldon closed his eyes to a starry Deschembine sky, lined in the tops of the relatively small Deschembine trees that rose around him, out across the hillside. He opened them to daylight. Where the trees had been, many glistening corkscrew towers now loomed on all sides. Near the tops of these edifices, more of those vaguely insectile dragonfly-like flying dinosaur creatures swooped to and fro. The sinewy figures up there didn't seem to mind, while they climbed around and went about their shaping. They jumped from one structure to the next, carrying detached vines, linking the structures together, darting back and forth to weave whole networks of bridges. At one point, a worker lost his grip and plummeted towards his death, so one of those creatures swooped in, caught him, carried him to the next perch, and set him down safely.

The whole perimeter had reshaped itself overnight. Sheldon bolted upright, looking around in confusion. When he looked past the strange plant-molded towers, he saw where the ground dropped off into a deep, narrow gully, where there had been none before. A thin stream had become a river that roared through the freshly dug moat. Beyond that, he saw the same vast, sloping hillside where he and the Crimbone had camped, overlooking the civilian Schomite village.

"What the hell's happening to these lands," he heard himself say.

"Nothing but the lands themselves," said Kashen. He stood over Sheldon with a sly smile. "The will of the lands, finally rejoined with the will of these Crimbone and our friends from the village. They've all been busy, taking your advice."

Sheldon stood up and worked the stiffness from his damp joints. He flexed his feet within his snug new Crimbone-made boots. His old Earth-line-woven boots had needed to go. The terrain around here had done them in. The rest of his clothes had also needed replacing. He'd washed them a few times in the same free, cool, unpolluted mountain streams in which he washed his body, but the threads had still frayed away quickly at the seams. These new boots hugged his feet softly, yet they were more durable than any shoes he'd known in that other world. The village blend-lady here had been kind enough to fit him with three nice, new sets of trousers and shirts, along with a new travel sack, no less, woven from the same leafy material. To be honest, he'd been a little disappointed not to get one of those form-shifting bodysuits the Crimbone wore on the trail. Those things were cool. They wouldn't have worked for him the same way, though, as everyone was still keen to remind him, because he wasn't a Crimbone.

"Uh, right," he now said to Kashen, "my advice. Look, I know I said you should work fast, but this all looks…pretty above and beyond." He was proud of himself for how quickly he'd grasped the Old World dialects.

"You complaining…man with no race?"

"Uh, no."

In the Old World, kingdoms rise and fall in a day. Apparently that old saying wasn't bullshit…or rather *lizardshit*, as his companions were fonder of putting it. He took a closer look at these new structures. It wasn't exactly a kingdom, but it sure had risen overnight. Hopefully it would last longer than a day.

Since his trial on the hillside days ago, Sheldon had settled into a comfortable equilibrium with this world surprisingly quickly, like the tenuous approval of a Crimbone pack had bought him the approval of these lands. Whatever had changed, he was glad for it. He still wished Rob was here. Damn, that was weird. It wasn't just because the guy would have made a handy go-between. Sheldon honestly missed him. How did you grieve for someone like that? Rob Coscan had shattered Sheldon's whole world at a young age, had committed worse atrocities since. In a way, though, they'd never been each other's enemies. The forces that had set them against each other had been their common enemy. The man Sheldon had started to know bore little resemblance to the monster he'd painted in his mind over the years.

Nights ago, the pack had emerged from the latest stretch of forest, before a bare vista. Far away, there rose a smooth, massive edifice, sectioned into circular shelves that looked like giant stairs. From the top shelf rose a gigantic dome, shimmering like a pearl in the moonlight. No distance could tame the structure's immensity. Giant winged serpentine shapes soared to and from it, high over the ranges and beyond. Around the base of the dome, and on the upper plateaus beneath it, lights shown from millions of dwellings. Not even those who lived there knew who'd originally built the structure…the great city-state of Spiralla, crowned in the temple where the gods dwelt…the birthplace of the Spirelight race, when the warrior-poet Bathshire had braved the bowels of the city-state, beneath where the Gods of the Dark Lands still dwelt, and forged his people's first union with the shining gods of redemption…redemption not just for the city-state, but for all Deschemb.

To Kashen and the rest of the pack, it was the source of the mighty, shining evil that beat them down daily and nightly. Sheldon now moved against it with them, yet he couldn't suppress a swell of sublime ancestral pride. All he was had originated there, through wonders worked by countless generations, no matter how far his ancestors had fled from it…no matter how much further he'd fled since. The Earth-line word for this feeling was *patriotic*, he guessed.

According to the lore on which Sheldon had been raised, only Magur Sevi and his armies had ever broken the great city's defenses and lain waste to it. Sheldon had grown up with rituals where the songs still paid solemn memorial to all who'd died in that long ago massacre. His grandfather had taught him to sing the songs with closed eyes, to not open them 'til the last echo of the last note faded, absorbed back into his body and soul. Thus he may truly feel his oneness with those lost, carry them on within himself along with the kiss of the gods, to feel the true depth of his people's cause. Just for good measure, the rituals had to be performed in the most cramped, sweltering conditions, while positioning one's body as uncomfortably as possible, all to bring one that much closer to the agony of the dead. Young Sheldon had never felt any closer to the Spirah gods afterwards, or to the Spirelight dead. When he'd voiced his doubts to his parents, they'd beaten him. His twin sister Sissy always used to hiss taunts at him for the rest of the day, how it was his fault for not listening to the gods, and how she'd told him so.

Judging by the winged serpents flying to and from the glistening light, Spiralla had recovered just fine since Magur Sevi's long ago siege, with or without the descendants' meditations.

"So that's where we're headed," Sheldon breathed, mostly to himself.

"No," said Kashen. "That temple exists for the Spirelights' continued communion with their corrupt gods, within the walls those gods have gifted them. You didn't actually think the gods would place their arrogant puppets so close to their true selves, did you?"

"Okay, so…where *are* we headed?"

Kashen flung out his arm towards the northwest. "To the great valley of mist, where the gods truly hide."

Later, they'd made camp and slept for several hours. They'd awoken to hunger, readied themselves for a hunt, then pressed on. Before long, a hulking animal came roaring through the trees. It had been not quite an ape or a bear, with a leathery hide of golden brown and glistening eyes that bulged with hunger that mirrored theirs. Whatever it was, it killed two of the pack before it was done, even after someone managed to slit its belly open so its guts spilled everywhere. Afterwards, they cut hearty portions of meat that they ate raw. They'd have consumed their own dead with it, but the beast gave enough to fill them several times over.

That's right, Sheldon now remembered, when hunting their own food, the Crimbone slew and ate no game that didn't make for a good fight. He remembered the dog he and Zane had killed and roasted in the border town. They'd gotten off easy with that half-starved beast. Either way, he gobbled ravenously, almost too quickly to appreciate the sweetest meat he'd ever tasted. Once they were full, they skinned the carcass and cut more meat from the bones. A woman in the pack knew some land magic, which she used to preserve the meat in a suspended state. Her companions cleaned and dried the animal's hide, which they used to bundle and carry the preserved rations.

The sun rose and set several more times, and no more beasts came. They slept for only short stints, whenever they noticed weariness slowing their senses, day or night. The sun was setting for the fourth time when they finally found a straggling civilian Schomite village, watched over by a smaller, bedraggled, threadbare Crimbone pack. The two packs greeted each other with rough, crudely familiar joy. Sheldon couldn't understand what they said, but he'd spent enough time around Jesse and Zane to pick up on a lot. Kashen explained what had happened, and more or less who Sheldon was.

Now, a civilian Schomite village, *there* was a new experience…except stranger still, not so much. For a surreal moment, Sheldon had felt like he was back in that other world, specifically in the Renaissance Kingdom grounds, among the United Deschembines as he'd first found them. They lived within earthen hut-like structures not unlike those he'd found on the hillside that first night, except dug out far deeper underground. Kashen introduced Sheldon to a family of old friends, who'd treated them both to a subterranean dinner. Everyone sat in a circle, on the floor, the raw ingredients of the meal set out before them, with everyone taking part in the preparation, not so much as nibbling a bite 'til each plate was full. They ate crispy bread with a flaky texture and bowls of a noodle-like substance, peeled from the rind of a melon-like plant, slathered in a sweet red sauce. Sheldon spoke little while he ate. The children clustered around Sheldon curiously, fascinated by his strange skin and accent, 'til their mother shooed them away. Kashen and the man of the house bantered like old friends, the latter making filthy jokes at which his wife rolled her eyes. Kashen talked of the pack's travels, while the husband brought him up to speed on news from other directions, from the world beyond. The village was on its last collective nerve. Throughout Valaka, word went, the Spirelight Police were hitting harder than ever, driven by rumors of the rise of some great new Crimbone threat, like nothing in living memory, spurring them to new bloodthirsty panic. The fighting hadn't reached the village, but the husband grimly pronounced the peace out here to be on borrowed time.

Later, Sheldon and Kashen had gone out and found the two Crimbone packs camped on the outskirts of the village. Around a campfire, everyone listened to Kashen relate the tale of how his pack had first encountered Rob and Sheldon. Sheldon stretched out silently, sipping from a wooden goblet of strong, sweet wine the Schomites brewed from tree-sap.

"So I guess you're still our chief after all, Kashen," said a young man seated close by, one who looked a few years younger than Sheldon.

Kashen sighed. "I am, more's the pity."

The young man leaned back against Kashen's knee. "Hey, that's enough of that! We haven't been wiped out, so obviously you haven't done such a bad job."

"I suppose you're right, but…" Kashen shook his head. "That man, though, the one we lost in the river…He claimed to be a High Natural. I was starting to believe him. There was something unreal about him, and yet…the results to which he led us were *very* real."

The young man glanced at Sheldon. "What about this freak you found tagging along with him?"

"You mean *the man with no race?* All I can say is…he's good to have at your side in a fight. When there's no fighting, he's good company. He has a heart that sees and feels beyond his own…a man anyone, of any race, should want as a friend." Kashen met Sheldon's eyes across the fire and lifted his wooden mug. Sheldon felt all eyes at the campfire turning towards him.

"Oh, so where did either of them come from?"

"The High Natural never had a chance to tell me," said Kashen. "The man with no race chooses to say little more, for now."

"Have you tried asking him the hard way?"

"I've thought about it, but that might deprive us of his usefulness."

The young man rose and strode around the blaze, his eyes locked on Sheldon. "So what about it, little *man with no race?* You obviously knew this *High Natural* better than any of us."

"That's debatable," Sheldon muttered, lowering his eyes.

"*What was that?*"

"Nothing. What's your point, kid?"

The young man slapped the cup out of Sheldon's hand. "*You haven't earned the right to speak such flippancy at me!* Get on your feet and earn it!"

The rest of the Crimbone gazed on intently. Sheldon looked to Kashen but found no backup there this time. Fuck, Sheldon realized, this was another test, wasn't it? No matter how far he got here, he was still a man cast adrift in a world he had no business inhabiting, surrounded by people who called him *friend*, yet they were obviously more than willing to cut him to ribbons, over provocations he still hadn't learned to interpret. No matter how well he grasped their dialect, he had no way to predict how his next word or gesture might violate some random custom, or how their sudden explosions of wrath might be completely reasonable within a frame of reference he lacked. He hadn't felt this out of his depth since his family had been slaughtered and he'd made the youthful, foolhardy choice to go it alone without contacting the nearest homestead.

The closest thing to a *homestead* was this world's Spirelights. If he got stuck with them, he'd be even more fucked.

He stood up and looked the young man in the eyes. His blades felt heavier than ever against his hips, as though begging to be drawn, to taste his aggressor's blood. "Fine, asshole," he spat. "How do you want me to earn it?"

Kashen interjected, "The lad made a good point...*Schell-Doh*." These folks still had a hard time pronouncing his name in the old Deschembine tongue. "You knew *Robber-Costigan* better than any of us. What would he have to say, at a time like this?"

Sheldon stooped sideways and picked up the wooden cup. "Before I answer, could someone get me another drink?"

Someone pried the cup from Sheldon's hand. He turned quickly and saw Ghella grinning at him. "I believe the correct wording you were looking for, *Schell-Doh*," she said, "is *You want answers, get me another fucking drink first, you cunts!*"

Sheldon steeled his nerves and said, "Fine. *You want answers, get me another fucking drink first, you cunt!*"

She howled with laughter and shouted, "You all hear that? The little whelp's learning after all!" Kashen's laughter joined hers. One by one, so did that of the others.

As Ghella headed off to refill the cup, Kashen hissed in Sheldon's ear, "Don't tell them anything until you take a good, long sup, and let them see how tasty you find it."

Ghella returned with the freshly filled cup of sap-wine. Sheldon took it and sucked down half of it, too fast. He looked around and took a deep breath. "First of all, I think *Rob Coscan* would have told you, you have to *become* the great threat the Spirelights see you as."

"Will you listen to this?" growled the young man. "The strange whelp's finally gone crazy. Thinks he can tell Crimbone our own business, like he thinks he's the—"

Kashen clamped a hand on the lad's shoulder. "Shut up." He looked on encouragingly, or at least curious enough about where Sheldon was going with this.

"Rob Coscan would say, you have to turn what your enemies have done to you *back upon their heads*. They've unwittingly given you some blessings in disguise. Kashen tells me how your children are taken as slaves to Spiralla, forced to pervert the connection with the land you've instilled in them, blending their magic with that of the Spirelights' gods, to fortify your enemies while bathing them in decadent luxury. By doing that to you, haven't they showed you how much more *you're* capable of? The Spirelights fortify themselves by defiling the land. Fortify yourselves in harmony with it. I've seen how you use that harmony to shape your dwellings and strongholds. So why don't you use your magic to mold whole cities out of rock and tree and bush, like your ancestors did?"

"What do you know about our ancestors?" said Ghella.

"Look, I'm just going by what the High Natural told me."

"So what's that?"

"Build your own cities, with your own magic, *from* the land, *with* the land. According to the High Natural, that used to be your thing. In the other…In the lands from which the High Natural and I sailed, there were legends about the kind of cities a properly equipped Schomite blend-lady might shape, just with her mind and the energy that flowed from her hands, practically overnight. Look, whatever you're gonna do, do it fast. Whatever Spirelight forces might be on our trail, pressing this way, they're not gonna wait politely. Neither can we." He hurried back to Kashen without looking at any of the others. "Think they'll listen?"

Kashen smiled. "I think a little of the High Natural's voice lives and speaks yet, through you…almost as though he somehow passed along something of himself into you once, into your very bloodstream, something that comes out of your mouth now."

Sheldon felt the old black scar in his midsection ripple. "That's…something I was always afraid of."

"That's the last thing I'd be *afraid of* now, if I were you. In fact, it's the greatest of all reasons you're still alive."

"So what do you think of it?"

"My own blood tells me to wait and see."

After that, Sheldon sat alone, drank more sap-wine, and slipped into a deep, dreamless sleep. Now that he awoke, he and Kashen looked together on the first results of his suggestions.

"Guess we'll see how much good it does when the Spirelight Police come against it," Sheldon said.

"We might hear about it, but we won't see it," said Kashen. "It's time to go."

FOUR

Kashen led Sheldon for another day through the wilderness, accompanied by a replenished pack. They brought along some of the meat from the ape-like animal. As they passed the distant ranges of Spiralla, the land grew colder and darker, as though ruled by spirits who grudgingly tolerated as little corporeal life as possible. In the distance, the mountains of Valaka gave way to grassy hills and deep gullies, shrouded in thicker mist than Sheldon had ever imagined. As they drew closer, Sheldon saw that it wasn't a series of gullies, but a single giant valley, with hilltops rising from the mists like tiny islands.

"Somewhere in those hills lives Havard," said Kashen, "or at least he used to."

"Havard?"

Kashen looked surprised that Sheldon didn't know the name. "The great mad warrior-poet of the Crimbone. He was never the best of the fighters among us, but...the way he could spin a yarn, I tell you...He stuck such a thorn in Spiralla's side, the way his tales could liven the Crimbone blood, that for a while we thought *he* was the High Natural."

"Figures," said Sheldon. "The actual High Natural was a pretty good storyteller himself."

"If you meet Havard out there, tell him your story of the High Natural."

"So tell me more about this Havard guy."

"The greatest visionary and tactician I've had the privilege to see at work. He learned the location of the temple we seek...where the gods *really* live. He led his pack through the valley and over those hills towards it. He followed legends of an ancient book hidden there, full of secrets that might have turned the tide of war irrevocably.

The Spirelights learned where he was heading, so while he and his pack camped on one of the highest hills, they made their slaves cast a spell over that valley. The fog descended and spawned the monsters that dwell there. They're mindless things, those monsters, less than animal. Occasionally someone comes back alive from that valley. They don't typically bring much sanity back with them. So on one of those hills, somewhere, Havard still sits trapped with his pack. On another hill stands the temple."

The valley and its mist still lay several miles off. Sheldon said, "So how do we find it?"

"Best I can think is, we stand on the edge of the valley and look out across the hills 'til we spot its glow. From there, all we can do is point ourselves in the right direction and go straight ahead." Kashen paused. "Sheldon Wildfire...The man with no race began life as a Spirelight. Didn't you?"

Sheldon's hands eased towards his knives.

"No need for that," said Kashen. "You're no longer one with the Spirah gods, after all...because you chose not to be."

Sheldon's fingertips absently brushed the scar beneath his shirt. "Actually, I *didn't* have much of a—"

"Sure you did. A man's connection to his gods isn't something anyone of flesh and blood can *take* from him...short of striking down the gods themselves, maybe."

THE NINE PRIEST KINGS OF THE EIGHT WINDS

ONE

At the peak of Spirah, in the great Devotional Temple, High Priest King Nireves emerged from a hidden passageway, at the other end of which a great staircase led down for miles, through the center of the city-state, behind every level of dwellings on the immense rock rise from which it was carved. Many such passages honeycombed the temple, leading to places known only to the Priest Kings and the most sacredly tested of their holy warriors, a jealously guarded secret, passed down within the sacred bloodlines. Fewer still knew of this stairway. Nireves caught his breath from the great climb before ringing for his servants. It wouldn't do for them to see him so undignified, for rumors spread to the wrong ears…not when he'd come this close.

Finally, he pulled the braided cord that sounded the bell. His eight personal retainers spilled into the room in a matter of seconds, like a swarm of bleach-white, silk-clad mice. They stripped him of his robes and guided him to the bath. Their smooth hands bathed him reverently, 'til no trace remained of his secret, subterranean work. They no longer gasped at the fetid, cavernous stench that clung to his robes, though they didn't bother to hide their nervous looks at the other lingering smells…ever stranger, more noxious chemical residue from the most deeply hidden sacred laboratory…chemicals laced with the stench of scorched humanoid flesh…*Spirelight* flesh. At least such worries made them likelier to keep their mouths shut. The disappearance of a servant who'd displeased a Priest King was nothing unusual. If they feared becoming an experiment subject themselves, so much the better. In the last month alone, the staff had seen many young faces replace the old. By now, only one remained from the beginning of the month. That one, at least, Nireves expected to last as long as his own High Priest Kingship.

To think, he'd once thought attaining the station of High Priest King would mean being answerable to none but the gods themselves. If anything, it had only allowed those fools from the satellite city-states to drive a deeper wedge, between him and true communion with the divine.

Just a little longer, he reminded himself.

Once the servants dried him and dressed him in his brighter robes—of the sanctioned shades for serene meditation—he bid them leave him be. He poured two glasses of Cherakt, one for himself, the other of which he set at the opposite end of the small, ovular crystal table. For a while, he sat alone without touching his glass, paying little attention to the light through the small, high windows.

The door behind him opened and closed silently. The single returning servant's footsteps moved more quietly still. He stopped halfway across the room behind his gilded, high-backed chair, and waited until his High Priest King lifted a hand. The servant circled the table, stood next to the smaller chair, and waited to sit until Nireves made another, subtler gesture. They lifted their glasses and sipped in unison.

"I hear you've been a handful around the house, Diroje," said Nireves.

The servant froze in his seat, the glass an inch from his lips. "Y-y-your Grace, I promise you, your cousin and her children are afforded every—"

"Of course they are, my friend. She's cousin to the reigning High Priest King of Spiralla, married to her King's most trusted servant...one of his closest confidants, no less, not that she's any inkling of that little detail, I trust."

"Of course, not your Grace. Thank you, as always."

The houses that lined the base of the temple on the top tier were reserved for families who traced their bloodlines to common sources with their rulers. One such wife and mother was first cousin to High Priest King Nireves. She'd met her husband at a market on the next lower tier. He'd loved her enough to endure hours of prodding and torturous purification from the Priest Kings—chiefly her cousin—to be sure he wasn't marrying for political status. Since hiring his cousin's husband onto his most elite staff of personal retainers, Nireves had discovered the young man to be uniquely useful. Many men in Diroje's position would go mad from the holy men's perpetual heavy hand in their private family lives. Diroje embraced it as a burden of pride.

"I hear, though, that when you go home at night of late, you brood and storm throughout your great luxurious home, to your family's growing unease. Even your own household's servants lower their eyes further than usual, so they go about their duties more quietly and awkwardly. I am troubled, my friend, that your work here may have left you...unbalanced, that this may compromise your other duties, what I have set you to watch and listen for, throughout the rest of this city-state."

"It has not, your Grace, I promise you, it has *not*…"

"What has you so distracted, then, my friend?"

"It's just…I observe you every day, your Grace. I see your comings and goings, and I…see your heavy heart, over whatever wickedness brews deep beneath this temple, something even your wisdom struggles to analyze and contain. My heart, in turn, grows heavy for yours."

Nireves sat back in astonishment. Humble ignorance and natural intelligence could be a fascinating combination. Perhaps marrying his cousin off to this lowborn bootlicker had been a shrewder move than he'd realized. A cheeky blackmailer might have stated the truth less plainly than this awkward innocent. Nireves might just have to make a closer study of Diroje's bloodline, of the lad's untapped usefulness. That would have to wait, though. For now, the High Priest King of Spiralla had greater demands at hand…like elevating his own status to more than a figurehead to the rulers of the Eight Winds…how he'd found the key to it. The next few days would make or break his dreams.

"What about that highborn artist upstart?" he asked Diroje.

"Oh, him. From what I've gathered…no one can find the boy."

"*How the hell can anyone not find him?* My apologies for shouting, my friend. It's just—"

"Don't apologize to one such as me, your Grace. The student was last seen climbing aboard a dragon vessel, from the third tier down. That's where he comes for studies. My contacts tell me, that's where he's also formed…certain contacts of his own. The police are looking into it. They think he's on his way to meet his beloved, that girl from the markets…"

"The same market district where you grew up?"

"No, your Grace, to the west of that. They haven't been able to find her, either."

The young artist's family home lay somewhere on the tiers in between, half as large and luxurious as those directly around the temple, though still enviable to anyone who dwelt beneath. Half the young student's studies were in art, the other in anthropological examination of other Deschembine races and cultures, the people the Priest Kings and the Spirelight Police would unite beneath the wisdom and harmony of the gods. His eventual career would combine such expertise, gaining insight into the lesser races by studying their art, thus advising the priests and military on subtler diplomacy. He was something of an artist himself, a practitioner of Spirelight carving and painting, the only art in the land that could reflect divine beauty and grace. You could find his work here and there throughout the marketplaces and some public gathering halls. It had brought him praise…and more recently, suspicion.

A few critics had pointed out the influences of the lesser forms he'd studied, how impressionable eyes seeking divine solace in gazing upon art that was supposed to reflect divinity, might be exposed to the profane, against their will. No one had outright accused him, but anyone close to him would suffer were he ever found guilty. Rumors went that the young man had gotten jittery under such scrutiny, so as soon as he heard his High Priest King wanted a word, he'd started making clandestine travel arrangements. In truth, Nireves didn't want the young man or his beloved apprehended, but rather shadowed and observed. Likely the young artist and his betrothed wished to reach some far-off land, one still safe beneath Spirelight rule, but where such standards were less rigidly enforced.

"No need to look so defensive, Diroji," said Nireves. "You've been a wonderful friend, and an even finer informant. Here, why don't you finish off that bottle of wine on your own. After that, take the rest of the day off, go home, and be nice to those wife and children of yours. And be sure to treat your household's servants as well as I've treated you here today."

He would, too. Poor little Diroji lived between two worlds…that of the common citizens of Spiralla, and that that of the sacred mandates of the Priest Kings. His willful naivete on the matter, Nireves had come to realize, made him a uniquely useful tool on gathering such information. Normally, Nireves wouldn't have worried so much about the art student, but at a time like this, he couldn't appear soft on potential blasphemers…to anyone. Not with ancient Priest King Kalesha arriving later today, from the Northwestern Octosphere city-state of Trescha.

Two

No outer stairway led down from the top tier. Residents with friends or business below had to catch the dragons that provided the city's public transportation. Day and night, the dragons circled the city-state in crisscrossing, descending, ascending arcs. The creatures had been weirdly altered by magic, both that of the gods' gifts and appropriations extracted from enslaved Schomites…shaping them not just into beasts of burden, but into giant living vehicles. Their bone structure had been altered so a smooth space stretched along their backs, with stilt-like horns suspending a second spine with a flat spread of ribs, beneath which passengers sat, encased by railings of bone. The flesh covering this shelter was thin and vein-streaked but strong, like the wings. The passenger space covered the inner third of the creatures' backs and could seat three hundred bodies at a time. More dragons circled the barren, rocky stretch that bordered the city-state, above the entrances to the secret passages by which the Spirelight Police came and went. These dragons were trained to scent any life form other than Spirelight that tried to enter those passages—other than prisoners, of course—and swoop down and rip them to shreds.

Off across the black ocean, in the world to which the Refugee Deschembines at some point fled, you wouldn't search the headlights of a city bus, for signs of thoughts or feelings. Thus few Spirelights ever looked too closely at the eyes of the mighty dragons, so they didn't see the dulled yet unquenchable embers of defiled pride and ageless rage.

The first, second, and third tiers down had stairs between them, so those residents only had to use the dragons when leaving the city, or when they had some business above with the Priest Kings, or just wanted to save themselves the climb. The dragon that settled on the edge of the great platform at the top of the city-state, however, was no common transport vessel.

High Priest King Nireves strode out across the plateau, between two lines of Sacred Spirelight Policemen and Soldiers, all in their ceremonial dress-uniforms. Niveres held himself at attention, the proper figurehead who the rest of these assholes saw as the one who pulled their strings. He watched his own true master hobble on a cane, off the mighty dragon and down the gangplank, followed by her own retainers. As she approached, he sensed their audience clenching their sphincters. Who could blame them? She was the oldest of the Spirelight Priest Kings, after all…some said by five-thousand years, others by a mere six hundred. No one knew for sure how she'd stayed alive so long. Her most fervent supporters claimed it as proof of her divinity in the eyes of the Spirah Pantheon, while skeptics whispered in bitter secrecy how she'd struck foul deals with the loathed Gods of the Dark Lands. Either way, she'd been around for far longer than the Crimbone, holding her seat in Trescha the entire time.

Her greatest asset in holding onto her station, some said, was the simple fact that she'd outlived any historians who might have disputed her supporters' version of events.

"Your Grace," said High Priest King Nireves, as he greeted her arrival with the customary bow.

"High Priest King of Spiralla," she responded. She leaned a little closer and hissed, "For fuck's sake, stand up straight. None of your little ass-lickers here need to see their High Priest King grovel."

He rose to his full height and offered the ancient woman his arm. When she accepted it, he felt her old flesh crumple like the cloth of her robe around her old bones. As they walked back towards the temple together, he forced himself not to gag on her repulsive old smell.

After what felt like an awkward march through eternity, they stepped inside the temple. His retainers and hers followed them through the gleaming, angel-lapis halls, to the door of his private sanctum. He bid his servants leave them be. She waited a moment before bidding her own to see her luggage to her quarters.

Once they were alone, she grabbed him by the collar, with startling strength for her shrunken, ancient shape. "What the fuck have you been doing here?"

"Exactly what you told me to do."

"Is that so? Do not insult my intelligence, my dear boy. Do you think I've not my means to learn, what goes on in that basement of yours? Do you think the others are so blind?"

"If they know so much, why aren't I dead already?"

"Because lucky for you, they don't know half as much as they think they do. And because of me. Need I remind you who put you where you are in the first place?"

"No, my mistress, you do not."

"Good. Because the rest of them will be here soon. *All* of them."

"All of them?"

"Yes, the rest of the Priest Kings, from all the great city-states of all eight octospheres. They'll all want to see what you've been up to, down in the secret laboratories. They already call it blasphemy. They don't know that you and I seek the same goals…but either way, it will be my voice that determines the verdict they deliver. So whatever you have to show them, show me first. Oh, don't look so bashful, dear boy. I have spent my years playing a *very* long game, and the time has come for you to prove the worth of my investment with you. Show me what you have, down in your dungeon."

A sly, resigned smile crossed Nireves' face. "Fine, *Mom*. Come have a look at what I've got in the basement…in that laboratory you gave me to play with." He lifted his hands to snap his fingers.

"Don't bother," she declared.

"But our sacred refinery…"

"…Has always been a hollow, anachronistic ritual of theatricality, for which the gods themselves, I assure you, give not a shit. The better to keep spectators in line. I see no spectators here. Do you, dear boy?"

As he helped her along through the temple, towards the secret stairwell, he added, "You know, it's a long climb down those stairs. Shall I fetch my most trusted servant to carry you down?"

"No, thank you. You'd be surprised by what strength remains in these old bones yet…and at a great many other things, I don't wonder. Since you're being so kind, though, might we stop for a while in your private quarters, so I might rest a while first? There, you can *fetch* me a glass of your finest Cherakt, if you like. That should lighten my head, so it might be easier to endure your sole company for such a time."

THREE

The fourth tier down of the city-state was populated entirely by the Spirelight Police. No stairs led up from there. Tiny grooves etched the rock face, which only military men and women could scale, bred selectively with the right tendons and muscle-structure for such climbs. Police families were provided with everything necessary to live in basic comfort while at home, but were afforded no luxuries that might dull their hardness for battle and espionage. Beneath this tier was a steep drop of thousands of feet, notched in the same shallow grooves. Primitive, comfortless slave huts littered the bottom of the gorge, populated by both Schomites and the lowliest born of the Spirelight bloodlines. At the start and finish of every long workday, dragons flew the slaves to and from their masters above, though not the same dragons that provided citizens with transportation or guarded the secret entrances.

Sparse food and clothing shops formed the business section of the slave quarters. If word came down that a slave had performed unsatisfactorily, the shops would shun their entire family, until the slave either made amends or starved to death. The soldiers descended partly to keep the slaves in line, but also to reach the secret caverns leading to the worlds above. Other, more secluded passageways existed at the bottom of this gorge, camouflaged by mind-clouding spells of ancient Spirelight magic, through which High Priest King Nireves' specially selected, tongueless slaves came and went, to assist him in his subterranean work. Nireves' and Kalesha's descent sent air whistling through a network of smaller tunnels, alerting these servants, so four of them awaited the two Priest Kings at the bottom of the stairs.

At the end of the descent, Nireves took twice as long as usual to catch his breath, thanks to assisting a decrepit old woman the whole time. He expected her to take even longer to recover, but her breathing didn't even sound belabored.

Kalesha's watery old eyes squinted through loose, wrinkly lids as she scanned the servants. "I should hope that your assistants aren't always so…skittish."

"It's been more difficult keeping them all *chop-chop* of late, I confess. Out there, of course, the soldiers don't speak to them except to give instructions, but they…sense the unrest, as it spreads amongst the slaves. Save your chastisement. I've done all I can to limit it, and I like the results even less than you might imagine."

"As well you might, my dear boy. I understand the Crimbone of Valaka have grown more…spirited of late. Who'd have thought such vermin would prove such a fuss for the Blades of Bathshire themselves, hm? How is your little errand boy Vesha Sting, by the way?"

"You haven't heard? Killed in action."

"Well…that happens to the best of them, doesn't it?"

"His entire squad died, in that debacle near the Qalisade River. More's the pity. I'd so looked forward to his bringing me home fresh…specimens. He had such a gifted nose for them."

"An entire division of the Blades of Bathshire, wiped out in one swoop by a mangy Crimbone pack, and you say *more's the pity*, because their leader didn't live to bring you home fresh toys to play with." She shook her head. "Perhaps you are as mad as they say, after all."

"*They?*"

"Don't play dumb, dear boy. Still, I confess, our colleges give you too little credit. *To have corrupted a zealot such as a Captain of the Blades to your cause…*"

"*Corrupted*, or awakened him to *vision?* Of endless possibilities, of a new, deeper, closer connection to the gods themselves?" Nireves squinted. "Why are you looking at me like that?"

"Simply…for a moment, you reminded me of someone else, from long ago. I've never born children, you know, despite what the slanderous fables say. I'm too old now by far to ever hope to do so. Thank you for reminding me to be glad for that. Now, about those specimens…"

"Yes, about them…and this recently escalated Crimbone trouble. It just so happens, I think I've stumbled upon the explanation…though it raises so many more fascinating questions of its own. Would you like to see?"

"My dear boy, I thought you'd never ask." She waved to the servants. "Leave us be. See to other duties. I'm sure you have them." As they dispersed, she once again looped her papery arm through Nireves'. "Well, go on. Lead the way."

He led her through the caverns, where churned the true political machine of the Spirelight Empire. They walked down a hallway full of ovular glass enclosures of glowing liquid, full of writhing, silently screaming flesh-sculptures, some of whom had once been Schomite—Crimbone or otherwise—others Spirelights who'd been reported as "mysteriously escaped" from the jail cells of the city-state's various precinct houses. At the end of the hallway, there awaited an iron-barred, dirt-floored cell. No one had bothered locking the door, because the naked prisoner within hung from the walls by heavy manacles around either corded wrist.

Kalesha slipped her arm out of Nireves' and drifted towards the prisoner, her mouth hanging open. She no longer even leaned on her cane.

"What is that?" she whispered.

Nireves leaned in through the cell-door archway. "A Crimbone prisoner."

"Don't be coy, dear boy. How long has he been here?"

"Three weeks. He was part of the pack that slaughtered Vesha Sting's outpost, then fled across the Qalisade River."

"Oh, *part of* that pack, you say…"

"No, that probability hasn't been lost on me, either. I warn you, though, don't get too close."

"He's a starved, beaten wreck of a man, chained to the wall. Why the hell shouldn't I *get too close?*"

"Because I'm truly fond of you, Kalesha, and would rather not see you come to some unfortunate mishap by underestimating this one…and not just because you're the only other Priest King still at my side, not looking for a chance to usurp my place as High Priest King these days, which at bottom, makes you my one true friend in the world."

She looked back at him sharply. "If you want that to remain the case, you'd best explain all this to my satisfaction."

"I have every intention of doing so." Nireves scanned the Crimbone man head to toe. Before he knew it, he found himself caught up, staring in fascination right along with her, all over again. "Some scouts chanced upon him, after sorting through the mess of the skirmish. He'd washed up on the riverbank, nearly dead, next to the corpse of a water monster that had snatched him. By the look of it, they say, he put up quite a fight. At first, the scouts assumed the water monster had died of wounds our boy here inflicted. No matter how far or wide they dragged the river, though, they couldn't find the weapons he'd used."

Kalesha smirked strangely. "The better for them, I'd imagine. Those Crimbone weapons aren't just weapons. They're blasphemy incarnate, something no one should ever want to touch."

"True. All the same...I can't help wishing I'd been able to study his."

"Oh? And why is that?"

Nireves stared in deadly earnestness. "Didn't you notice anything unusual I just said? I said weapon*s*. He wore *two* scabbards on his belt. Have you ever seen that before, among the Crimbone?"

"My dear boy, don't lecture me about the Crimbone. I was a Priest King before they were even a rumor. I know full well what you imply, and believe me, the potential gravity of this matter has not escaped me. So forgive me if I'm *not losing my mind* over this sudden development. What have you learned from blood samples?"

"For one thing, the autopsy confirmed that the water monster died because it swallowed some of his blood, which proved toxic to its system."

"What have your scientists determined from his blood samples?"

"They're all still baffled...still just as much by the water monster. According to all our best anthropological and zoological research, water monsters like that have only been known to attack Crimbone when starving. In some areas, my troops have facilitated this by hunting to extinction the natural prey of beasts that otherwise lived harmoniously with Schomites."

"And had any operation like that taken place in that region?"

"No."

"I didn't think so. Either way, look at this man! Clearly, he lost a lot of blood in that river. Was the surrounding aquatic life at all affected?"

"Not so far as we've determined. That's another funny thing."

"I assume he didn't just wash up on the shores, naked as a babe like this."

"Excuse me?"

"Must I...? Fine then. *Bare-ass with his dick hanging out.* You didn't find him that way, did you?"

"No."

"So have you been sensible enough to keep his clothes around?"

"I was getting to that."

"Of course you were, my dear boy."

"Would you like to see what he had on him when we brought him in? Then right this way, m'lady."

She followed him out of the cell and down a narrower hallway to the right. At the end, there waited another candlelit room with a metal table stretching out in the center, with the prisoner's odd clothing flattened out across it. She observed the trousers first, stiffened with filthy, dried-out river water. The pockets were located in strange places, sewn too tight to be very useful. The weird foreign objects they'd contained had been set out to the side. Kalesha leaned closer and squinted as she went through them one by one.

"What practical function could any of this possibly serve?"

"We...still haven't figured that out?"

"You didn't ask him, while he was awake and you interrogated him?"

"I…we…didn't think to. We had other, more pressing concerns on our minds."

"Idiots," Kalesha muttered, shaking her head. "I work with idiots." She handled the moldered trousers again, examined the pockets woven onto either ass-cheek, then lifted a flap of woven leather. "This thing…Why, it's like a detachable pocket sewn to fit *within* a pocket."

"Take a look at what we extracted from it."

Kalesha examined several rectangular leaves of cheap parchment, stamped in base alien symbols and crude likenesses of strange men. Some of those men had Schomite features, some Spirelight, always with a ghastly Lepod taint, with even stranger hairstyles.

"Have you consulted diplomatic cultural researchers over these images?" said Kalesha.

"Of course I have, and they haven't a clue. Just my luck, the bastards recommended a prominent field student who'd excelled, even made a few breakthroughs in global iconography history, and it turns out he's some bastard artist suspected of promoting blasphemy. To make matters worse, he's proven elusive. I assure you, we'll have him in custody before…" He trailed off when he saw that she wasn't listening.

Kalesha picked up the smaller rectangular card, over which some sort of plasticine gel had melted and smoothed and hardened, probably to preserve the scrawlings. Next to those scrawlings was a marvelously painted picture of a young man even more racially ambiguous than those on the parchment. His features were Crimbone, yet his skin was like a Wallution Lepod's.

"I want to have another look at that strange Crimbone prisoner you have back there," said Kalesha.

"What…why…I mean…"

"Just escort me back there...at your leisure, of course, your Grace."

They returned to the cell. Nireves looked over Kalesha's shoulder at the strange, naked Crimbone man dangling from the wall. She looked back and forth, between the clean-cut visage on the card and the captive creature before her, with his shaggy hair, corded neck, and heavily scarred face and body. Both had the same alien skin-tone.

As though reading her mind, Nireves said, "Are you suggesting...that this monster and that little bitch-boy depicted on the upper left corner of the card are...one and the same?"

"You haven't realized that already?" Her withered hands reached up and stroked the prisoner's long, iron-hard limbs. "Dear Gods. How is this...*horrifically beautiful* creature not dead yet?"

"Your guess is as good as mine."

"Now is hardly the time to rely on guesswork, don't you think?"

"Of course. Only...why, just look at him, where the infection from his wounds has scarred him! I kept expecting him to die. But no, the infection just keeps boiling through him, and he just seems to keep...getting stronger from it. More and more, whenever I touch his flesh, it nearly scalds my fingertips, like I just stuck my hand in boiling water. The gods alone know what such a fever must be doing to his brain. And just look at his muscles! He was in no rude shape in the first place when we found him, either. Physically, he rejuvenates from anything I do to him at an alarming rate, even for a Crimbone."

"What of the chemical experiments you've done on his blood-samples?"

"It's the same way there. No matter what poison I feed it…those cells seem to attack the toxins, to absorb them, so they grow even stronger. The more I experiment on his body, the more pain I inflict on him, the longer I deprive him of sustenance…his muscle definition just accelerates, tightening and hardening, like it's literally drawing nourishment *from* the abuse…as though something within his bloodstream feeds on malice and cruelty…and it just makes him thirsty for more of it."

While Nireves spoke, Kalesha knelt and ran her palm over the prisoner's sinewy arms, legs and chest. To the old woman's credit, she only paused for a moment to fondle his cock and balls. "It's the gods he's feeding on. The gods within *us*, within this whole place. That's what the Crimbone do, except somehow, this one has taken it to a whole new—"

The creature's eyes snapped open. He jolted forward so his chains rattled and went taut. Dust sifted from the dank ceiling, as his strength threatened to rip the chains loose. Kalesha let out a croaking cry. She fell backwards onto her ass, suddenly no longer the proud Priest King, just a terrified old woman, shrinking into the protective arms of the young man who'd led her here.

The bloodshot eyes studied them thirstily. "Yeah," the creature growled through a dry throat, in common Deschembine, "I see it all so clearly now."

Nireves slipped free of Kalesha, rose slowly and peered back at the creature, still making sure to keep his distance.

"Yes." Both Priest Kings jolted afresh, for the Crimbone now spoke in a language it shouldn't possibly have known. "I see exactly what you are, what *all of you are*. You fat, spoiled weaklings can't even look me in the eye without cowering like scared little rabbits, even with these chains, and you *still* think yourselves fit to rule anyone…to tear down everyone else's world and rebuild it as…what? Something less intimidating to your delicate fucking sensibilities? You can't stand the thought of having to measure up to the will of the true lands. The best gods you can find as an alternative are just as big a bunch of pussies as you. If those gods really want to redesign a world in their image, what do they even need you for, unless they're just weak? Wouldn't you much rather just be spirits floating lazily through the ephemeral realms, sucking out nourishment from physical worlds as you please, dipping your fingers in the affairs of people who still *do* tough it out, as it amused you? Isn't that what gods do? Too bad, the spirits who truly run the ephemeral realms won't have you. You still fall for it, still twist and contort through every silly dance move, *and they're laughing their sick fucking asses off!* Go on, enjoy this divine Empire you've built, while you have it. It just breaks your hearts, doesn't it, that everyone else isn't stupid enough to want the same thing. It's the worst atrocity you can imagine when they don't all line up to kiss your asses. You don't know what atrocity is, yet. I'll show you."

For a long moment, all Nireves or Kalesha could do was stare. Then she shuddered and hissed, "Get me away from this abomination."

"Yes," said Nireves, trembling. "I believe you're right."

They reached the other end of the hallway and stood there shivering, hugging themselves for a long time.

"It…never did that before," he said, as much to himself as to her.

She kept rubbing her arms. "How…does a creature's voice…feel so much like…like he was just beating me, physically, both my body *and* my soul?" Without waiting for an answer, she looked at Nireves. "It spoke to us in our language, *our sacred, secret language.* How…?"

"I've no idea."

She stabbed a bony finger down the hallway. "*That* is your grand discovery, your key to bring us all closer to the gods. You have brought it here among us, into the walls of our oldest, most sacred city, to the very heart of who we all are as a people."

"But…but…whatever power sustains that ferocity…I tell you, it's the key to what sustains *all* of them! I'm so close to unlocking it! Just think how we could turn that power against them, what it could do for our medicine, our—"

"Don't speak to me. Get me out of here, back up to the surface. I need to breathe unpolluted air. After that, go someplace, where I don't have to look at you. I suggest you spend the following hours contemplating your life as you know it, enjoying it in whatever way pleases you. Because one way or the other, dear boy, that life is about to come to an end. The other Priest Kings will arrive soon. *They* will see this, then we shall all hold a special meeting, to decide your fate…perhaps the fate of our entire Empire."

FOUR

He never told them his name, but he remembered just fine, even if it was less useful than ever. He was Rob Coscan.

His enemies hadn't thought he was conscious when they found him. Through the slits of his delirious eyes, he'd seen the great rise of the city-state from afar, with its glistening lights and circling dragons. He'd seen the underground passages leading to it, then the slave quarters.

Shackled in this dungeon, his mind cleared. For the first time, he was truly free. All his friends and lovers were dead, or so cut off from him that they might as well be. He'd shared common goals with them, or so he'd told himself. Their thinking had been too clouded, too compromised, infecting his own for too long. This deep beneath the city, beneath the mountains, he scarcely even heard the voice of the lands anymore. Then he remembered, the rocks of mountains were *part* of the lands. That didn't change, no matter what the Spirelights had done to sap them of their living connection to the rest of Deschemb. The lands didn't shun him. They cradled him, 'til he was ready. For now, though, all existence boiled down to himself and his enemies. For the first time, he saw them clearly. Their torture was welcome, purging him of everything that confused him and held him back.

A long time ago, he'd liked to tell *stories*, to conjure things that had happened to him or other people, even those he'd only heard about…to feel them so powerfully in his mind that they might as well have been happening all over again. Then he'd discovered, when he let it out in words, people around him felt it with him. The power of what they'd felt had flowed back to him so he could drink it up like the glow, making him stronger, surely as any physical exercise. It was the same power that had let him wrangle the wills of those he'd led. Now he listened to what the lands told him, here in their deepest core. He told himself their stories in his mind, as though he were relating them aloud to an audience. He would lead again. When the time came, the power of the stories he learned down here would fill his words, so he would command all who heard him.

Now he'd seen all the Priest Kings, not just the old crone his chief torturer had introduced him to. He hadn't attacked the lot of them as he had those two. He had to save something for just the right moment, after all. Still, he'd felt the fear radiating off all of them. It had tasted sweet…sweeter even than his attack on the first two. Their *glow* flared through the darkness, tugging and teasing, whetting his thirst for the strength he'd soon take from it.

The Priest Kings were all utterly bald. He had an odd sense that they kept themselves shaved smooth as babes all over their bodies. They all looked so *little*, so jittery and pathetic in this rank, gloomy place. Did the warriors and scientists ever take a real, honest look at their masters? If they did, how long would their whole hierarchy last?

Before the others had arrived, the first of the Priest Kings had sometimes questioned him. Didn't he see that his people's aggression brought only strife to the lands they claimed to love? Only the gods could grant the lands harmony, to be achieved through the Spirelight people. By persecuting the Spirelights, the Crimbone only angered the lands, for the only life-giving spirits were the Spirah gods.

Now he'd given them a taste of what they had coming, by speaking to them in their own sacred language. Where had he learned that language? He didn't remember. He might search for the answer, *could try telling it to himself as a story.* Except what the hell could that possibly matter?

It would only take a little longer, for the pain and isolation to finish purifying him for the work ahead. *He'd told them their own story, pitch-perfect, planting a seed that already shredded them from the inside, sharp as the blades he'd once wielded.*

By basking so long in their false paradise, they'd made those they'd beaten down stronger than ever, while they grew weak within their security. All they could do in desperation was tighten their feeble grip, worshipping their petty finery as they worshipped themselves and their gods. Here, at the center of their realm, the land had found them anyway. Rob Coscan *was* the land. These were the people whose gluttony and decadence had thrown Deschemb out of its natural balance, forcing so many of its inhabitants to flee to another world that had since likewise fallen beneath even worse Spirelight corruption. That other world had sent him home, to be the embodiment of Deschemb's purest vengeance.

When his captors left him alone, Rob Coscan muttered aloud to himself in the Crimbone tongue. He spoke names in a language he no longer remembered otherwise, names of people for whom he used to fight.

"Remelea...Louis...Sally..."

That last name made all of this feel wrong. Everything he'd said to the Priest Kings, it no longer quite rang true. Yet whenever he looked around, he knew it *was* true. Hard physical evidence proved it. Those old names were trying to confuse him again...especially that last one. They'd forced that dullness on him all his life, *raised* him to be like them, and he'd still cast it off! When next he led the hunt as chief, he'd make sure to purge that weakness from his pack.

FIVE

Far throughout the dungeon, the slaves who'd been forbidden contact with the prisoner still heard him speak. They didn't understand his words. Even if there was Crimbone blood in them, even if they might once have made the Calls, their captors had stomped the knowledge from their minds...but not from their blood. So the spirit of the land's vengeance—*the spirit of the High Natural's story*—flowed through them all. They brought it out of the dungeon, among their fellow slaves. No matter how closely the local law-enforcement watched, it spread.

When the dragons carried them to their duties above, they carried what the High Natural had awoken throughout Spiralla. Even the dragons felt it, spreading the word in their own tongue to their fellows who transported Spirelight citizens.

SIX

Rob opened his eyes. It was bright in here now, though he saw no light source. The walls of his cell were shaped the same as before, except they'd gone from putrid dripping rock to glistening sandstone. The bars of his cell had vanished…not that it did much good, for the chains still stretched his arms at his sides. Before him, there stood a tall, hawk-featured Schomite man in a long green robe. Rob Coscan remembered that face. He jolted forward like a chained tiger. The manacles on his wrists jerked at his shoulders.

"You son of a bitch," he snarled. "What is this?" Sweat dripped in his eyes. When he blinked it away, the man in the green robe was still there. "I already killed you! Get the fuck away from me!"

"I beg your pardon, High Natural, but the last time I remember passing from a corporeal existence, I did so pleasantly of old age."

Rob shook his head, squeezing his eyes shut then reopening them. Yes, the features were the same, but their expression was soft and compassionate. "I…I'm sorry. I thought you were someone else."

"So I gathered. An evil man, I take it?"

"Yeah."

"What was his name?"

"Talino."

"I've never heard that name. Perhaps I should remember it. Personally, I don't tend to bother with names, except when I undertake occasional phases of corporeal existence. When I do, this is how I usually look at the height of life. I've sired many bloodlines during those phases. Perhaps one of them issued an evil man it fell to you to kill. *Had* anyone killed me—in the incarnation you'll hopefully have heard of—you probably wouldn't exist."

Rob's eyes widened. "You were a Schomite sorcerer...*the* Schomite sorcerer, the one the brave met in the wilderness. You gave him—"

"The teeth and claws of the Crimbone, yes."

"Yeah, and I was given those *same* teeth and claws, the blades of Magur Sevi."

The sorcerer looked perplexed, then shrugged. "I already knew you bore those blades, for you are the High Natural."

"Sure, but...how did you get in here, past all the—?"

The sorcerer chuckled. "No Spirelight mysticism or military force could keep me from coming as I pleased...not when the will of a High Natural called me here. I can see plainly that you're the one who called me. Just as you called the beast that took you from your companions, so you found yourself here. There could be no finer way to bring yourself to the heart of the enemy's lair, from which you must strike."

"I...Great Sorcerer, forgive me! I didn't know I drew that thing in the water."

"Oh, but the voice of your blood knows better."

"But...when it took me, I lost the blades. How am I supposed to strike without—"

"My dear boy, you've lost nothing. You removed yourself from much, for a while, to be distilled to the purest essence, worthy of working the land's will. Now go and play the strange role for which the lands have shaped you. If anything within you still longs for another trail you once imagined, you have my humblest apology. The lands will never apologize. Now neither can you, ever again."

"But how am I supposed to...Didn't you hear me? *I lost my teeth and claws!*"

The sorcerer smiled and receded into shadows that hadn't been behind him a moment ago. "Oh...have you really?"

Before Rob could speak, his vision went foggy again. He blinked and shook himself. Everything was dark and dank suddenly, like it usually was around here. His head hurt, along with the rest of the aches and pains throughout his body that had been so much easier to ignore within the dream.

The only light rose from a candle in the hand of someone who came silently down the hallway. The cell door creaked open. The black-robed figure entered. The candle flame bathed a pale, ancient face. As his eyes adjusted, he recognized the old lady Priest King who the High Priest King had first introduced him to.

"So you're my custodian now, huh?" Rob growled through a gummy throat. His face twisted into a malicious grin. "What in all the lands did you do, for the rest of them to decide that you deserve me?"

"They made no such decision, High Natural," she said. "They don't even know I'm here. As we speak, they gather above, no doubt wondering what's taking me so long to show up for their little meeting, where they mean to decide your fate, along with that of our mutual friend, the disgraced High Priest King Nireves."

Rob chuckled. "Oh, so you wanted to spend some time alone with me? Brave girl."

"If you're thinking of assaulting me with the power of your voice again, I'd advise against it...*especially* if you think to use the sacred language again. For one thing, doing so would evoke the attention of the gods themselves. Neither of us want that right now, believe me."

"Fine. What the fuck *do* you want?"

"When you asked what I've done to deserve you, you were closer to the mark than you realized. I'm here on my own volition, High Natural. Long ago, I realized that we *all* deserve you...the entire Spirelight Empire, the other Priest Kings, and most importantly, the gods themselves."

"You know the gods?"

"Know them? My dear boy, I became a Priest King long before the others were born. I was old before the first Crimbone rampaged through these lands. None of them can even figure how I've lasted this long. If I didn't know the gods better than anyone else by now...well...the one who groomed me for this position would have made quite the grievous error."

"*Groomed* you?"

She chuckled. "Yes, looking back, it's as grotesque as it sounds, I suppose. He was a warrior, but also a scientist and philosopher. He was a rare kind of genius...*a man of vision*. He'd also been in love with me since we were children. Part of me, I suppose, reciprocated his love. What I failed to see, until it was too late, was that he'd always loved his greater goals, and how I fit into them, more than he ever loved me, or anyone else unfortunate enough to love him back. He saw things within me that I did not see in myself, so saw fit to orchestrate my rise to power, whether I liked it or not. So before I knew it, there I was, a Priest King, reigning from on high, in charge of the lives of countless others. What could I do, but seek to live up to the burden placed upon me?"

"Sounds like maybe he was onto something after all," said Rob.

"Hah!" The old woman's gaze drifted through the ancient, crumbling halls of her memories. "He hadn't the first idea. He envisioned a better world, and he saw in me the ruler who could make that happen. It is through his discoveries in medicine that I have lived this long. In all that time, I have come to my own conclusions."

As she spoke, Rob watched the years—the centuries—melt from her eyes, from her face. He saw the naïve, passionate, beautiful young woman she'd once been, swept up into the tide of the tale she told, the tale she'd lived. For a moment, he felt all of it in his blood, as she'd felt it, as her dark, Machiavellian lover must have felt it. *Damn*, he thought, *so that's how it feels*. That wasn't the tale the two of them were living out right now, though.

"Yeah?" he said. "What are those *conclusions?*"

"There can never be peace, between the will of the gods and the will of the lands. The former haven't the right to impose their will upon the latter, and they will sooner extinguish all life on Deschemb than abandon their efforts for dominion. It is time for this Empire to fall, along with its gods. We deserve you, High Natural. Many a time, the position of High Priest King was mine for the taking. I saw fit instead to see Nireves instated into the title. He has served me better than he will ever know. He has brought me you."

"I'd love to help you, but…I've lost my teeth and claws."

"Oh, you mean *these* teeth and claws?" She opened her robe and brought out the twin blades of Magur Sevi, now encased in fresh scabbards, dangling from a freshly braided belt.

"Where the fuck did you get those?"

"I told you, Nireves' whole career as High Priest King has been by my design. *Of course* I had my own spies, among the field agents who fished you out of the river. Those same agents had been instructed to drag the river, until they found what you had lost. I've come to give you back what is rightfully yours. By the way, yes, I also remembered to steal the key to your manacles." With her free hand, she drew a jangling keyring from within her robes and dangled it in front of him.

While she spoke, the glow pulsed out of her, more powerfully and invigoratingly than he'd ever felt, from any Spirelight, with one long-ago exception. He salivated lasciviously. "You know, if you unlock these manacles and hand me back those blades, I'm still going to kill you and drink your glow, right?"

She rolled her eyes. "*Of course* you are, my dear boy! After all this time, can you imagine anything I'd consider a greater relief? Still, I hope once I unlock you, that you'll be able to restrain yourself for a few minutes. I'd very much like the chance to show you to some things I'm sure you'll want, for the rest of your journey."

She set the blades aside, then reached up and fitted a key into one manacle, then the other. All this time, Rob had been champing at the bit to break free, telling himself glorious stories of the lovely mayhem he'd unleash once he did. Once his arms were free, though, he crashed to his knees. His limbs felt wobbly, like his bones had turned to rubber. When he tried to push himself up, he just fell right back down. His head swam like he'd just chugged two bottles of whiskey. He pawed at the rancid soil, fighting and failing to will his atrophied motor-functions back to life. It didn't help that his ass felt chapped as hell, from shitting into a rotation of buckets for the last few weeks. Now was the most humiliating, disappointing time possible, for his body to remind him that he was just a man after all. His brain flashed back to a long-ago night, back in Brattleboro, when he'd stepped outside for a daydreaming smoke, when he'd first glimpsed Puttergong scuttling through the grass. Everything he'd made of himself between now and then vanished, so this was the broken, inept creature he was left with.

"Will this help?" The old lady dangled the blades in front of his face.

His shaky fingers reached up and tightened around the belt from which the scabbards dangled. The moment he touched them, his body and brain both remembered who he really was. The High Natural took the blades in hand and staggered to his feet.

Rob followed Priest King Kalesha out of the cell, down a narrow hallway. The room they reached smelled of sulfur and other, stranger chemicals. It also smelled like scorched flesh, though that scent was older. Within, a Spirelight scientist stood over a table, surrounded by bottled chemicals and hanging parcels of alien herbs.

"Where *are they?*" the scientist bellowed to what he still thought was an empty room. "I was just examining them. They were just lying here, the—"

The slave at his side looked sideways and noticed Rob and Kalesha enter the room "Sir…"

The scientist turned and struck the slave across the face, knocking him on his ass. "You! You've taken them, haven't you? Tell me what you're—"

The scientist froze and paled when he spotted Rob, as folks tend to do when they come face to face with a naked, enraged Crimbone. Rob neither howled nor roared. His snarling breath was barely audible. He moved forward as leisurely as he'd followed Kalesha. His mouth watered for the scientist's glow, but he didn't hurry. The scientist's hand crept sideways along the table behind him, probably for a weapon. One of Rob's knives sang free and cleaved the man's chest, splitting his heart in half. The corpse crashed backwards over the table. Glass shattered around him across the floor. Spilt chemicals flowed together with the pooling blood.

Watching from the floor, the slave hadn't seen Rob draw the knife, nor had he seen the knife go back into its scabbard. The blade had simply *appeared* for an instant in Rob's grip, then disappeared. To all eyes except Kalesha's, Rob couldn't possibly have enjoyed a drop of the glow before the instantaneous death. He'd absorbed all of it, though, the moment the blade split flesh and bone. That moment had felt long enough to savor, as deeply as he pleased. It inflamed his limbs and left him thirsty for more…*much* more.

Across the table lay his clothes, dried and shrunken and soiled from the river. He didn't bother with the shirt, but pulled on the pants so he could loop on the belt holding the knives. He slid back into his Crimbone duster. It was caked and stiff, but he flexed and twisted his arms, pivoted his body 'til it moved perfectly with him, settling over his muscles like a leathery second skin. On the table lay his boots. After pulling them on, he offered his hand to the slave on the floor. The slave scuttled away, whimpering.

"It's okay," said Rob. "Are there other Crimbone held prisoner here?"

The slave nodded.

"Go set them free. Send word to your fellow slaves to get out of the city above, fast as they can. Tell them not to worry about their masters. They need to get down the walls, in any way possible. You'll find Crimbone here among your friends and family—Schomite slaves who didn't know they were Crimbone 'til now or were forced to forget. Tell them to return to the wilderness and to spread word that the High Natural has arrived. *All*

Crimbone must gather, to full strength, then charge howling on the great rising storm, along the trails of the eight winds of Deschemb. Wherever they go, the will of our lands shall make itself known, decimating our oppressors and whoever stands with them. The Crimbone need only flow through that storm and finish them off. Tell them to circle the globe 'til it is done, 'til their trails lead 'round, back to the ruins of Spiralla."

The slave nodded, turned and vanished into the gloom of the dungeon. Rob turned and saw Priest King Kalesha watching him, a serene smile on her face. "There's only one thing left for you to do down here, High Natural, before you get on with the rest of your business." She splayed her arms and tilted her head back, baring her throat. "Come on. That's what you said you were going to do, wasn't it?"

Yeah, Rob recalled, that's what he'd promised her.

"So what are you waiting for, you filthy beast? Do it! Please! Let me out of this hell he *locked me in. Oh, what, are you some kind of soft-hearted cunt after all, just one more—"*

One of the blades sang free and slashed sideways. Priest King Kalesha's head parted from her neck with a jet of blood that splattered across the ceiling and rained down on Rob like a baptism. Her body toppled one way, while her head bounced off the table and rolled off into a corner somewhere. The room went silent. Thank fuck! Old Lords, he'd been starting to think she'd never shut up.

SEVEN

Rob found his way to the staircase, as though he'd walked these catacombs a million times. Where there was no light, his sense of smell guided him. Leisurely, he climbed the great spiraling staircase, up through the guts of the city-state. It was a long trek, certainly giving more than enough time for the slave to get outside and set the word spreading. The higher Rob climbed, the harder grew the pull of the great collective Spirelight glow. The urge to charge panting for it was gone. Instead, he let it tickle and tease. By the time he reached the top, his thirst had reached an overflowing boil.

He exited the stairwell, into Priest King Nireves' private chambers. He stopped to take a piss all over the old bastard's fancy sitting area.

From there, he walked out into the great hall. A blue crystal floor caught the light of the temple's smooth spherical dome above. The floor spread for a mile in every direction. Curtains of red and purple and gold draped the lower half of the walls, all the way to the floor. Before him, there rose an immense sculpture of a powerful Spirelight warrior of old...Bathshire, the fabled liberator of Spiralla. Beneath Bathshire's feet were the slain demons of the Dark Lands, who'd once ruled this city. In one hand, Bathshire held the crumbling tomes with which the gods had told him how to defeat the demons. In the other, he held one of the dripping blades with which he'd slain the dark gods. The other blade hung in its scabbard. Rob recognized those Spirelight blades. He'd seen them recently, in the hands of a man who'd fought side by side with him. That man's face had looked remarkably like the one stamped on the statue. No surprise there, really. It was amazing how all these Spirelights looked alike. All that divinely ordained racial superiority must have left them big on inbreeding, after all. By now, none of them exactly measured up to Bathshire. On the upper contours of the statue, there burned the millions of candles that lit the temple.

The Crimbone High Natural grinned up at the great warrior king of the Spirelights. "Silly bastard. Those aren't *real* demons under your feet. All you did was cut your own gods out of their Halloween costumes." A wild laugh escaped him. "You never freed your people from shit. They're all still slaves to the same demons who took their ancestors when they got here. They tricked you into making better puppets of yourselves. Don't worry, I'll cut your strings…all of you…for real this time."

The statue didn't answer, just kept staring coldly out over the temple. Rob shrugged. Words never worked on puppets. He knew just fine what did work. Behind him were more stairs. He turned and climbed them to an egg-shaped room, suspended only by crystal shafts spiking out of the walls in eight directions. Over the shafts ran walkways, leading to a balcony that ringed the wall, from which the curtains hung.

EIGHT

Within the egg-shaped room, the Spirelight Priest Kings had all come together, from their own satellite city-states in all eight Octospheres of Deschemb, around their great, egg-shaped council table. They were all clad in their holy robes of soft fabric, threaded with some distillation of the shimmering crystal that formed the temple. The table's shape and central position completed the room's perfect symmetry, conducting the light and power and wisdom of the gods with the utmost luminescence, through their highest of conduits. None but these men and women could have even beheld this inner sanctum without their brains exploding.

The High Priest King of Spiralla presided at the head of the table, in the last customary observance of ritual he had left in his favor. Officially, for now, they all still pretended he remained in charge, answerable only to the gods themselves...but he knew better. This wasn't his assembly. It was his sentencing hearing. Only one chair remained empty. No one in this room would speak until its designated occupant arrived. Those were the rules. No one ever set foot within this sacred chamber but the Priest Kings, and no Priest King within it ever uttered a word without all their brethren present.

Where the hell is she? For once, Nireves' thoughts probably mirrored that of the others. It wasn't like Kalesha to be late. Some of them were no doubt taking the extra time to meditate on their own bids for his title.

Fine, let them enjoy their little fantasies for now. Nireves had no illusions about the diriment of his predicament. He'd no intention of resigning himself to his fate without a fight, either. He'd made a mistake, yes, revealing his exquisite specimen to Kalesha too soon, before gaining a better understanding of its volatile capabilities...but in her rattled state, after feeling the brunt of those capabilities along with him, perhaps it was she who had finally overplayed her hand this time. Everyone in this room operated with the silent understanding that Kalesha of Trescha—not Nireves of Spiralla—was the true great power behind the Spirelight Empire...but not everyone liked it that way. Over time, her uncanny longevity had combined with her expertise at political maneuvering, so an aura of invulnerability had come to surround her. Age and arrogance could catch up with anyone sooner or later, though. If he played his hand right, it would catch up with her today.

Half of the people in this room already regarded her as a far more dangerous heretic than Nireves could ever aspire to be. In bringing them all together, here, to prosecute him on charges of blasphemy, she may well have snared herself in a trap of her own making. He scanned his fellow Priest Kings, up and down the table. Some of them owed their titles to Kalesha's string-pulling, but they might have just as much reason as he did for feeling she'd outlived her usefulness. He'd gain no sense of that 'til she arrived, and everyone started talking.

To his right, there sat Priest King Celest of Pilanche to the southwest, closest to the Dragon Coasts at the Southern Crown of the world. In those fiery lands, it seemed, no civilian Schomites even grew, just the mad, seafaring beasts, seemingly born with the blades of black metal in their hands. It fell on Pilanche's shoulders to hold back the worst of that threat from the rest of the Spirelight Empire, hence the rest of the Priest Kings afforded Celest some of their highest deference. She sat stiff-backed and stony-faced. Even in her glistening robes, she resembled more the hardened military commander than the stateswoman.

Nireves' first supposition was to think, *Right, don't count on any help there*, 'til he looked over the one directly to Celest's right: Priest King Naisace of Vischan to the Northeast. Vischan was the youngest of the city-states. At the moment, it happened to have the youngest of the Priest Kings seated in its temple. In that part of the world, the winters were harshest and the summers sweetest, with little if any spring or fall to speak of. Naisace's predecessor had all but driven the Schomites of those lands to extinction. In recent years, he'd come to face a growing Crimbone incursion upon his shores from the west. He'd been known to insinuate, but diplomatically avoided outright stating, that his kingdom's growing strife was the fault of Priest King Kalesha's blasphemously consorting with the enemy.

Of everyone here, Nireves calculated, those first two faced the greatest enemy threat. His case hung upon the plea that his own so-called blasphemy could turn the tide, by finally analyzing and harnessing the source of the enemy's might, to appropriate it in the name of the gods and turn it back against that enemy. Naisace's lack of love for Kalesha, and the far more egregious allegations against her, could surely come in handy on that front.

Then there were Priest Kings Menca and Merca, of Glanka directly to the South, and Tersa to the Eest. Everyone there pretended not to know how those two Priest Kings had been secret lovers for years…of how their bastard progeny had both been disowned and arranged to become officers among the Blades of Bathshire. Rumors persisted how they planned to arrange for said progeny to become incestuous lovers and create yet more bastard children, with the ultimate long-game in mind to create genetically perfected offspring with whom to elevate their joined families higher within the sacred hierarchy. More damning rumors went that Kalesha knew of their treachery, pretending to back them in their endeavors, in exchange for their loyalty to her own demands. That would make gaining leverage over them next to impossible…unless he managed to sway Celest and Naisace onto his side quickly enough. With their help, he might stir up enough of an atmosphere of sentiment against Kalesha, that Menca and Merca might no longer feel so secure under her wing of protection. The more Nireves thought about it, the more he realized his greatest advantage lay not in Kalesha's approval of him, but in how well he could stoke everyone else's disapproval of her, here today.

That left Alira of Egast, Arish of Sterlem, and Elose of Herngla. Those first two were the staunchest, most incorruptible true zealots of the gods. Once Nireves turned up the heat in here, it would all come down to who they judged to be the lesser blasphemer, him or Kalesha…unless one or both of them had their own bids in mind for the station of High Priest King. Elose, meanwhile, presided over the one city-state the Spirelights had reared in the Ghestru continents. It had held for centuries by allowing the Ghestruland nations to hold their own rule, at least officially, while eroding such power-structures slowly but surely from within, through clandestine trade deals struck with the region's merchant class, who'd always been the true rulers there. Herngla had always faced the least threat from the Crimbone, allowing its ruler to grow decadent. That fuck Elose would back whoever he thought would keep him richest in jewels, coins and dancing girls, shipped from all corners of the world.

As Nireves mulled all this over, a set of footsteps echoed up the staircase outside. *Oh, here she comes, at long last…just not to the meeting she expects. I'll make sure of that.*

Except it wasn't Kalesha who walked through that door.

NINE

They all jolted to their feet and stared at him, first in surprise, then in dull wonder, like they still couldn't comprehend that they were no longer safe, here in their natural habitat, decked out in their full glory. *Because how could the gods possibly have allowed him to reach this room?* He approached casually, sliding his blades free slowly so they all heard the echoing musical hiss.

The High Priest King placed his palms ceremonially upon the table, followed by the rest of them, in perfect synchronism. The glow of the table went from a gentle shimmer to a white-hot blinding glare. So did the floor and walls. "We cast you out," the High Priest King shouted. "You have no business in this sacred place, any more than your kind have business in the gods' lands."

For such a soft, cloistered ruler, this one sure did think on his feet. Rob felt the pure blast of the gods' light wash over him. It pulsed through him, hotter and hotter, trying to blast him senseless, to destroy him. All it did was feed him. "The gods' lands?" He smiled. "Not anymore, friend. *My* lands!"

With a sharp kick, he sent the whole massive table skidding with a screech across the floor like a small stool. It smacked the High Priest King in the gut so he folded over it. It crashed into the wall, crushed his back and pressed a jet of blood from his mouth that splashed across the immaculate tabletop. Within the walls, the white-hot glare receded and winked out. The other Priest Kings stepped away in a disbelieving trance. They didn't even try to run when Rob strode in among them, at least 'til he cut the first two down. After that, the others shrieked and scurried. His calm exploded into a spinning blur of black metal, weaving among the panicked shapes, getting the feel of it back.

He thirsted for true opponents, not all this scuttling practice. Oh well, he'd have the real thing soon enough. Dying screams echoed from the chamber and bloomed into a cacophony throughout the vast temple.

The last Priest King tripped over one of the corpses and scrambled for the door, slipping and sliding across the bloodstained floor. Rob didn't chase the man down, so much as walk past him and slice off his head along the way. The head rolled through the doorway and bounced down the stairs next to Rob's feet as he descended, like a puppy hopping along at his heels. He paused for another look at the edifice of Bathshire, then sprang onto the base of the statue and hacked once into the ankle. Angel-lapis chips flew past his face. He jumped down and moved towards the archway leading outside. Behind him, the statue shivered and shook, as though in poisoned agony, sending out a rumble beneath his feet. He didn't look back, but heard cracks spider-web up through the leg, 'til the whole statue groaned and teetered. By the time it fell, he was nearly to the archway. Right behind him, the ancient stone head shattered, shaking the floor so fiercely that he stumbled and swayed. He righted himself, though the floor still quivered.

The candles should have gone out as they spilled from the shattered edifice, for there was nothing in the floor's matter to burn. Yet the fire spread wide and fast 'til it reached the curtains.

Somewhere in his head, Rob imagined a voice from what felt like the distant past. *Whooooooooooooo-weeeeeeeeeeeeee, Biter-Boy! What I tell ye? Fuckin' High Natural, all the way, most badass High Natural there ever was! Didn't I say you'd get there, you stuck with me?*

Except I didn't get here with you, Puttergong. You're long gone. So is everyone else who wanted me for their own little agendas. This new agenda's all mine.

Outside, a stone courtyard spread forward, twice the length of the temple. As Rob reached the head of the stairs, flames exploded through the archway behind him. The blaze still didn't touch him, yet he seemed born of it to all who came outside to see. Blades lowered, he looked out over Spiralla. Inhabitants of the top shelf spilled from their houses, crowding and trampling each other like panicked beasts. Everywhere, on every level, they made for the dragon ports. Some of those dragons sat waiting, apparently unmoved by the pandemonium. Others circled the skies.

"Dragons of Deschemb," Rob howled out in Crimbone. "*Take back the skies!*"

Those dragons carrying passengers soared high above the city. Those at rest sat and let people bustle aboard, filling the seating areas to capacity. Finally, they all spread their wings and shot skyward to meet their fellows. Spirelight passengers screamed and tumbled against each other. The dragons flexed and arched their backs, shaking Spirelights off like bugs. Hundreds of wailing bodies plummeted in the starlight. Some struck rooftops and streets. Others vanished into the chasm bellow. At the bottom of the chasm, newly liberated slaves danced and howled as their former captors splattered like raindrops around them. Slaves with forgotten Crimbone blood tasted the glow as it exploded from the striking bodies, and became truly alive for the first time in their lives.

Behind Rob, the temple dome swirled incandescently from the rising blaze within. A dragon circled, drew a deep breath, and did something denied it for far too long: it opened its great fanged mouth and exhaled a long, sustained blast of fire. Several other dragons saw, remembered that joy, and swooped low to join in. The blasts obliterated the dome and eclipsed the flames within. Black smoke rose even higher than the dragons flew, blotting out the moon. The first dragon circled, loosing more fiery breath onto the surrounding streets and houses. It paused only to leave Rob a path to the edge of the plateau. That way was empty, save for a few Spirelights scurrying like cockroaches. Those caught in the blast were instantly atomized. Their collective glow burst from the fire in twin waves onto Rob, consuming him as the flames consumed them. No, *he* consumed *the glow*, swelling and blazing 'til he was sure he'd burst. He felt immense, like he'd expanded outward and consumed the entire city and surrounding ranges.

One Spirelight ran past him, more purposeful and lucid than the others, but still frantic. "Please, the temple! I have to get in there! My *brother-in-law*, he's—"

By now, Rob felt close to a state of pure energy. The world around him felt less like matter, more like a roaring endless sea of that energy, through which the shouting man moved like a hazy blot. Rob was mildly aware as his right blade licked backward and skewered the guy. He walked on, tasting the kill like a single sweet drop mingling with thousands. The dragon that had set the streets ablaze soared high then flew downwards, back towards the edge of the plateau. Rob was close to the edge.

Something about another set of running feet caught his attention. A young man and woman, barely out of their teens, stared up at the approaching dragon as they ran. The young man had a long coat with bulging pockets. His woman had a tightly stuffed bag slung over her shoulder. The little idiots, still looking to the beast as a means of escape! Hadn't they been paying attention?

"The dragon," shouted the young man, "there's one more dragon coming! Quick, we have to get to it!"

Rob's eyes bore into the onrushing couple, transfixed. Somehow, they seemed the most solid things in this roaring sea of energy. They saw him and skidded to a halt.

"We have to get out of this city," the young woman pleaded. "They'll say it was us. We have to get out, far away!"

Rob kept staring. Whoever they were, he gathered the city had become a hostile place to them well *before* this outbreak. Did they honestly think a lesser hell awaited them anywhere else?

"Please," the young man panted. "If we can just get out of here, they'll never hear from us again. Otherwise they'll say it was because of my—"

With a stroke from each blade, Rob dealt the only two acts of mercy he'd perform tonight. He turned back to the edge, thrust one blade skyward and outward, and roared so his voice echoed down into the gorge: *"Fellow Schomites, fellow Crimbone! The land has opened to devour the gods of our enemies. Now go and devour those enemies, wherever you find them!"*

The dragon settled at the end of the plateau, met Rob's eyes, and cocked its head in invitation. He nodded back, stepped forward, sheathed his dripping blades and climbed on, straddling the mighty neck. The dragon reared up and roared. Rob roared with it.

Pressed against the animal's head, he whispered, "Take me to the dwelling place of the infernal gods themselves."

THE TEMPLE IN THE LAND OF MISTS

ONE

Sheldon glanced back. Everything they'd left behind looked muddled in the mist that floated from the valley they approached. Out here, the world bled stark as a chessboard. Then out of nowhere, Spiralla went up in a booming puff of flame that cut the mist in half. It had been a day at least since he'd looked back that way. From here, the ancient city-state looked small as a dime. All the same, the whole pack halted and stared back at the billowing smoke and flames.

They'd been on the move so long and ceaselessly that even their Crimbone limbs throbbed wearily. Sheldon's limbs were sore and hot, stiffening further in the cool mist. Wet air bathed his lungs, soothing him just enough that he wanted to lie down for a while on the thinning grass.

"It's what we always said would happen with the coming of a High Natural." Kashen smiled…then frowned.

"You mean like the legends say happened before," said Sheldon. "With Magur Sevi."

"Nothing like this has ever happened before," said Kashen. "This…Magur Sevi. You keep saying that name, but I've never heard of him."

Sheldon's guts churned. "Let's keep moving. We're almost to the valley."

They almost ran on, then someone at the rear of the pack shouted, "Friends a-comin'!"

Sheldon and Kashen darted back down the earthen hillside. Far across the rocky field, hundreds of feet thundered over the thin grass. Sheldon hurried with the small pack to meet this larger one that approached. At first, he could barely make out the latter, with the way their skin and clothes constantly shifted shades, to blend with their surroundings. The desolate terrain seemed to boil and ripple, 'til they drew close enough for him to make out individual shapes. The closer they got, the more of them materialized. He kept thinking he could see them all, but they just kept coming in an ever thicker wave.

That's no pack, he thought. *It's a fucking army.*

The eyes of nearest ones bulged whitely. The woman in the lead halted and signaled the others to a stop. She looked younger than Sheldon, though her face was a hundred times more battle-hardened. "Kashen! That you?"

"Of course it's me." He sounded tired and bemused, as though greeting uninvited party guests. "How've you been, Cassella?"

Her eyes narrowed and her smile broadened playfully. "Better than you, if you're still with that little…What's the bitch's name, again?"

"Reila. She's dead."

Cassella had eyes like someone with venomous things crawling around in her brain. Behind her, across the soft field, there blazed hundreds of eyes just like hers.

"Oh." She forced the smirk from her lips. "She was a good fighter. She'd've enjoyed this new trail."

"What new trail?"

"Your guess is as good as mine. It's only now unfolding before us." She squeezed and caressed his shoulders ecstatically. "A new chief has risen to lead us...*a chief made of fire.* Just look over there!" She thrust out her upturned palm, at the distant billow of smoke and flame. "That's Spiralla, going up in *his* blaze. *Spiralla itself. Let that sink in!* Every Crimbone in central Valaka felt it. He drank *all* their glows as they burned. It was like he filled all of us, for miles around, like we'd never thought we could hold that much...but I'm still brimming with it, and...*Kashen, just wait 'til you taste it!* I've been running all night, picking up every pack I can find for the new trail, and I still don't even feel tired. Now it's you, the best I've found yet! Do you *know* how many of the central, highest Priest Kings were in there when it all went up? *All eight of them!*

"Without their great city and their Priest Kings, the Spirelights are *nothing.* Everywhere, storms are erupting, taking their harbor-cities into the seas, splitting the ground and swallowing their outposts. Whichever ones haven't died in all that are running scared. All we have to do now is run them down. With the power this new chief gives us, we'll be unstoppable! I can't *wait* to see the faces of their supporters, all over the world, when they realize all that security the Spirelights sold in exchange for hounding us isn't worth the scummy runoff of their servants mopping their blood from their streets. Hey, maybe we should keep some of them alive, as *our* servants, so they *know* they're living in the Crimbone's lands again."

Sheldon stepped up. "The lands don't belong to anyone. Not the gods, not Spirelights, not Crimbone, not civilian Schomites. *We* all belong to the lands."

514 ~ Matt Spencer

"Who the fuck is this?" Cassella looked Sheldon over. "For that matter…w*hat* the fuck are you?"

"He's our new chief," Kashen said. "He leads us to a place where all the wars can end. If he can do what he says he can, we can be free of the Spirelights without anyone else needing to die."

"Says who?"

"Look, it's a long story. I'll explain on the way."

"The way where?"

"To the deadly, misty valley."

"Seriously? You're about to follow this weird little runt off into that bottomless deathtrap, over some bedtime song, right when all this starts happening…*when it's real, ours for the taking?*"

"If this new power you've been feasting on is as strong as you say, and our packs fell in together, we could—"

"Did you let your skull get cracked one too many times? Look at him, he's not even Crimbone! I'm telling you, whatever you're looking for there, there's no more point even bothering with that forsaken place. All Crimbone stand united behind our one great Blazing Chief." Cassella's pack roared exultantly behind her.

"Not all Crimbone," said Kashen. "Not my pack."

"Think about that before you say it again," Cassella said through her teeth. "You don't get it yet. I understand, really. The cold hard truth is, though, as things stand now, if you're not in the Blazing Chief's pack, you're no more Crimbone than your false chief there." She stabbed a finger at Sheldon.

Kashen and Sheldon looked at each other, then back at their tiny pack. Those with them crouched and snarled, ready to draw knives on their fellows, who hopelessly outnumbered them. Sheldon's fingers twitched to pull his blades. If he ran for it now, he could make it into the valley alone.

He stepped between Kashen and Cassella, acting calmer than he felt. He spoke first to Kashen. "Fall in with Cassella's pack. Follow this new trail with her."

"*What?*"

"You heard." Sheldon turned to Cassella, who looked even more confused. "This *Blazing Chief* of yours, whoever he is. Do you follow only his word now, or do you still follow the voices of the land and your blood?"

"You don't get it," said Cassella. "They're one and the same now." She looked a hair-split away from attacking. "What could you know about it, anyway?"

"More than I ever expected to."

She peered incredulously. "How much has Kashen told you about what you're walking into?"

"Not the worst of it, I'm sure. Look, if you're so sure I'm about to walk into hell, why are we still even talking about this? You go do your thing and I'll do mine. As Crimbone, you only know your blade's true purpose when you stand before your duty with it drawn. Before you act, listen to *your* blood, and listen to *your* blades, and listen to the land. Your black blade will only fail you if you use it against the will of your true self."

Cassella threw up her hands and turned away. "Fine. You want to walk into hell alone? That's your business. The rest of you, you coming?"

"I won't abandon you to face that place alone," Kashen said to Sheldon.

Sheldon slapped Kashen's shoulder hard…a Crimbone's slap of friendship. "You haven't. You've seen me as far as the lands wanted you to."

TWO

The lower Sheldon climbed, the steeper and rockier the hillside grew. The mist thickened ever deeper around him, 'til he could see no further than five feet ahead. He made the last of the descent in a blind dash over the loose, sliding shale. After that, the ground was smooth in some places. In others, it felt so jagged that that even the tough, supple soles of these Crimbone-made boots threatened to give out, leaving his feet to be shredded to the bone on this razor terrain. Before descending into the valley, he'd spotted a faintly shimmering knob in the distance that might be the temple. He pointed himself at it and stuck to that direction. It was the straightest line he could manage, with nothing resembling a path to follow.

Nothing grew in this valley. The land down here was dead. All around, he saw hazy, rotted, petrified evidence that life had once flourished. There was still *some* kind of life around him, though. It scurried and clicked curiously, edging closer through the mist. The hopping, clicking things were very close now, on all sides of him. His sharp ears traced the approach of the stalking monsters. The first of them sprang into view. Sheldon's blades lashed free.

The creature was shaped like a man, but it hopped and scuttled somewhere between upright and on all fours like a monkey. Its body was covered in a tight black segmented shell like a beetle. Its claws and eyes and drooling teeth were a sickly yellow. The distilled Spirah glow radiated from Sheldon's blades, bathing the creature in their light. It drew back with a squealing hiss, shielding its eyes with crooked arms. The light cut through the mist for yards around, revealing hundreds of the beetle-monkey devils, speckling the rocks like maggots on a corpse. They hissed and retreated, shaking their claws scornfully. Whatever they'd once been, his knives glowed with the same power that had brought them so low. Down in this misty hell, at least, it hadn't bothered them directly 'til he showed up. With whatever rudimentary consciousness they had left, they recognized it, and feared it.

Sheldon held the blades out on either side, lighting his way. Everywhere in the newly illuminated terrain, black petrified trees twisted upward like the skeletons of shipwrecked men who'd drowned while clawing for the surface. More than ever, Sheldon was aware that his glowing blades were forged from the same evil that had drowned this land. Now that he'd drawn them, though, his feet straightened, so he walked fleeter and steadier. The blades seemed to guide him, pulling him towards their source. Obviously, that source didn't sense what he meant to do with them once he got there. Or maybe it did. Maybe it welcomed the challenge.

He reached the edge of a high, steep hill and started upwards. As he climbed, the mist thinned. The rocky ground softened. Up here, the land came back to life, covered in vibrant grass that glimmered greenly in the dewy sunlight. At the summit, a massive dome shimmered in the rising red sun. Sheldon's heart locked in his throat. He kept climbing. Atop the ridge, the ground sloped down again into the small gully that surrounded the temple. The earth down there was even deader than the valley. At the bottom of the slope, a giant, steepled archway jutted out, open to a passageway into the temple. As he started down towards the entrance, its poison shimmer beckoned from the corridor. From here, he saw how the glistening chamber floated with spectral irreality…something that existed outside of time and space, like the black ocean.

As Sheldon neared the door, the shriek of a huge beast split the air. He darted back up the ridge, expecting to see some reptilian monster rising from the valley, like the one that had risen from the river to carry Rob away. Instead, it came from above, beating the mist into swirls with the untellable span of its wings. It landed on the edge of the hill, dwarfing all before it. Something so massive should have shaken the ground when it touched down, causing him to fall flat on his ass. Instead, it settled with such supple grace that he barely felt the ripple underfoot. It didn't seem to notice him. At least he hoped it didn't.

It took Sheldon a moment to process the sight as plain, physical fact. Here perched a dragon, straight from every medieval legend of the other world, its golden-red scales glittering through the misty morning gloom, long like a serpent but with powerfully muscled limbs and razor claws to plant in the rocky earth. As its wings folded around its sides, Sheldon noticed something horribly wrong with its back. A long rectangle of flesh puffed up like a sloppy, infected skin-graft, crusted with dried bloody spatter around the edges. The dragon didn't seem debilitated by it.

The creature reared up and roared once more, exultantly, then lowered its long neck flat across the dead, brittle sward. A man climbed down from the top of the neck, clad in the war garb of the Crimbone of the other world. He reached up to stroke the dragon's mighty brow. The creature grinned and shifted to the touch like a purring kitty-cat. The man stood on tiptoe to whisper something into one of the ear-slits beneath the great twisting horns. The dragon huffed, grunted and shifted some more, apparently liking what it heard. The man stepped respectfully away. The dragon reared up again. Its great wings spread and beat the air. The wind-rush sent Sheldon staggering, so he nearly tipped and tumbled backwards downhill. He regained his balance as the dragon rose back into the sky. The man who'd dismounted strode towards the temple. His coattails fanned out behind him against the vista, like his own set of dragon wings.

Sheldon had to say this much for the guy: he looked cool. His shaggy dark mane flowed back to show every deep-etched scar on his face. His duster billowed, revealing more scars than ever on the torturously tight sinew of his bare chest. As more of him came into focus, there didn't seem to be much left of him *but* scars…scars, and a pair of murderously blazing eyes. He was halfway up the hill when he spotted Sheldon and quickened his pace.

Sheldon glanced back, at the temple door, then looked forward again at the approaching madman. He walked down the slope.

"Brother!" Rob broke into a joyous bound. "You didn't think you could go through with this without me, did you?"

"Kinda, yeah, actually. For one thing, I figured you were dead."

"Nah, I wouldn't leave you hanging like that, man. I mean, *c'mon!* Check it out. The lands won't *let* me die! They need me too much. You *all* need me. The lands have finally shown me how to satisfy your need."

"Oh, so it's the lands that have shown you what the rest of us all need, huh? Okay, brother, tell me what these lands have shown you."

"*The way*, that's what…to everything I've been looking for all along. Here it is. I've finally found it. So what, did you…somehow *not* pick up on that?"

"I think I must have missed something." Sheldon looked over Rob's shoulder, at the distant billowing flames. "You've been to Spiralla, I guess."

520 ~ MATT SPENCER

"Huh?" Rob glanced back, at the fire and smoke still belching from the mountains, leagues upon leagues away. "Oh. Yeah, that was me."

"Burning a *whole fucking city-state?*"

"Hey, it ain't like I set the fire. I just took the power from the Priest Kings, gave it back to where it belongs, and let everything else just happen like it wanted to. Trust me, man, the place needed to go."

"Guess that makes you the Crimbone's *blazing chief* everyone's talking about."

"That's what they're calling me? Huh. I like it. I'm surprised you didn't lead 'em here to see this."

"They had other things to do…for some reason."

"Ah, hey, fuck 'em, whatever. I saw some of your work from the air, by the way. Those organic Crimbone cities growing all over the place in the forests…*I knew something was missing*…Sheldon, I saw it, and I *knew* it was you! Only a brother of mine! The Crimbone used to have lots of those kinds of cities, but they've forgotten." Rob turned and splayed his arms for the lands out past the valley. "They've forgotten so much. Not just the Crimbone. All of them. We'll remind them of it, you and me, man! First, we just have to purge all traces of what's trampled them down, so both worlds can grow back up with a clean slate." He spun back and stabbed a finger at the temple. "Through those doors right there are the gates…not just to the Spirah Pantheon, but to *everything!*"

"Everything?"

"You remember the stories, how the Earth-line people were on their way to building the ultimate civilization, under Schomite guidance, before the Spirelights came and wrecked it all, like they wrecked this world? Once the gods and *all* their minions are gone, we can realize that dream, in *both* worlds. Once we've burned the gods' pantheon, we can open a direct gate between the worlds. The Crimbone packs will unite under our guidance to pave the way."

Rob's impassioned voice cut through the misty air around him like waves of heat. As before, it swam through Sheldon's brain as though born there. This time, though, he took a deep gulp and gripped his own knives tighter. "Slow down, Rob. What about everyone we both still love back home, huh? Janie? Remelea? Jesse? Zane? Think about *what's right* for them, will you?"

"Don't you get it yet? *They* were the ones confusing us all along. We let them fill our heads with a bunch of bass-ackwards half-measures, mixed messages and riddles. They did it to us both, from Day One, brainwashing us so we'd never rise above them, to our true potential. I once told you I didn't know what it meant, to be the High Natural. Now I know. I'm living it. So are all the Crimbone throughout Valaka, through all Deschemb, who've answered to *my* New Call. This is what I've *always* meant, don't you get it?"

"So what if everyone else gets a full good look, and they still don't like it?"

Rob let out a crazy laugh, without malice, like they'd been sitting around over beers and Sheldon had just told a raunchy joke. "They can't *decide not to.* They'll feel the power I enfold them in, they'll see it clearly like I do, and we'll all be one, rolling out in a great big wave of the land's wrath. You ought'a know, better than anyone. The Spirelights won't stop, even without their gods. Neither can we, not 'til they're all dead."

"I stopped. So I started something else. You just said it yourself. You're the one who freed me from the gods, remember?"

Rob looked down, then his eyes shot back up, lit afresh. "Did I? *So why are you still standing between me and your gods, holding blades they forged against my kind?*"

Sheldon almost protested, almost tried to explain otherwise. It already tasted like a lie in his mouth. When he didn't answer, he expected Rob to attack.

Instead, Rob turned away. "I don't want it like this." For a moment, the overwhelming power of the High Natural's voice receded within Rob Coscan. He paced and shuffled on shaky knees, like he'd honestly forgotten what it was like to face someone it didn't work on, and he no longer knew what to do. "Look, all I have to do is walk into that temple and finish it. *Please, Sheldon, don't put yourself in my way.*"

"So think of another way."

"I can't!" Rob spun and stared into Sheldon's eyes, with a strange new desperation. "Just look, will you? I've been carved away by the lands and its enemies a piece at a time. *This is all that's left.* The lands have filled it with their will. Now my will and theirs are the same. I couldn't stop it if I wanted to. Neither can you."

"I believe you." Sheldon heard himself speak with strange calm. "This is where you've been drawn, because *this* world is where the energy you're made of belongs. What you're talking about...for that other world *and* this one...It'll throw everything into chaos, worse than ever. I'm not talking about war and politics, either. What we do when we walk in there, it will effect all time and space."

"You think I don't know that? You don't know what you're talking about. You can't *feel* it, the rage in the lands, across both worlds, over what the Spirelights have done to them."

"Just the Spirelights, huh?"

"I swear, if you try to fuck this up, with those blades full of the power of Spirah...then you're still as much of a Spirelight as the day you were born, and I should have finished you off back on Marlboro Mountain."

Once more, the thunder in Rob's voice felt like a physical wave, like he'd already beset Sheldon with blows. Sheldon gripped his knives hard and said, "I guess I'll have to find out for myself."

For a long moment, they stared each other down like twin statues. Sheldon's jaw clenched, nerves buzzing like never before. Something changed in the knives he held. Through their shimmer stood Rob Coscan, etched against the misty valley. Rob shot forward with a roar.

Sheldon's weapons went up as Rob's sang free. All four blades clanged deafeningly in a shower of sparks. That first reverberation was great enough to send both their feet grinding backwards through the grass. Sheldon skidded down one ridge, towards the temple, while Rob skidded towards the valley. When they charged each other again, Rob went into a faster spin attack than ever. His arms and blades became a single blur around his pivoting body, like hummingbird wings. Sheldon reacted with a faster counterattack than he'd thought was in him. His blades whistled towards Rob's vitals as Rob's whistled towards his. When Sheldon voided and struck, Rob countered and pressed him sideways. They circled each other, blades striking hard enough to shatter any weapons but those they held.

The fusion exploded back through their bodies, threatening to shatter their bones. Their feet slipped and slid in the damp ground, tripped and faltered on rocks. They panted and sweated faster while their lungs tried to catch up with their weapons. They saw one another's feet faltering at the same instant, and each tried to trip the other up. Their knees and shins buffeted each other while their blades flailed wilder. The teeth on one of Rob's blades cut off a piece of Sheldon's left ear, just as one of Sheldon's edges scraped the bone of Rob's right shoulder. Rob's kick glanced off Sheldon's rising knee. The blow stung almost enough to stop Sheldon from hooking Rob's calf and yanking forward. Rob spilled back and crashed on his ass.

Sheldon came in for the kill. He ducked a wild swipe at his neck and went off balance, so he almost fell right onto Rob's other knife. He knocked the thrust aside. They crashed into each other again. They went over together, rolled and twisted in the dirt, blades locked, legs grappling, the rocks scraping them. Finally, their legs disentangled and they kicked each other away, rolling in opposite directions.

Sheldon spilled off a low rise and rolled down the hill. The mist swallowed him. He kept bouncing down the steep jutting rocks, while all kinds of sharp debris scraped at him. The fallen carcass of a black petrified tree smacked his shoulder. Gasping, he stabbed the trunk and pushed himself up on a knife handle. In the tangle of branches to his left, several of the beetle-monkeys hopped and chirped and hissed, staring with fearful hatred. Why didn't they draw away from him like before?

There wasn't much time to think about it, because here came Rob, running silently down towards him, skipping effortlessly over the rocks, either not noticing or not caring about the beetle-monkeys that hissed and clawed around him. Sheldon yanked his blade free of the petrified trunk, deflecting Rob's barrage with the other. He hopped up onto the trunk and danced backward across it. Rob followed. Sheldon's rear foot broke through the cluster of branches and crushed something that squealed as it died. Other squealing things bit and clawed at his ankle.

Rob was about to pounce, then his eyes bulged at something overhead. The parents of the baby beetle-monkeys ran nimbly over the branches on all fours at Rob and Sheldon, forgetting their earlier primal fear of the two superior monsters. So did some of their friends. Rob waited 'til the first one sprang. With a single swipe, he chopped it in two in midair. Oily guts streamed out of both halves, smacking and smearing him.

Sheldon scrambled out of the nest. He and Rob darted backwards side by side, exchanging glances of silent understanding as the black monsters swarmed over the trunk. For this fleeting moment, clumsy chance made them brothers-in-arms, one last time. Rob hacked and stabbed with his black fire, Sheldon with his unholy light, cutting open shell after shell of putrid guts, splashing the hillside in sickly purple blood. The further they drew from the nest, the less the monsters bothered with them. Rob's foot slipped. He spilled backwards and vanished into a narrow cloudy fissure.

As the last of the beetle-monkeys slunk away, Sheldon ran back up the hillside. He cleared the valley and saw the side of the temple. Over the ridge was the peak of the archway, now much farther to his left. He made for it on achy, weakening legs that he couldn't let slow down. Behind him, footsteps bounded over the rise. He spun as Rob closed in.

"Leave me to die, huh?" Rob growled. "That's cheating! That's why your kind never had a chance, you fucking cowards!"

As they clashed again, their bones and nerves jangled closer to the breaking point, driving them to madder extremes. Down in the mist, those things might be waiting more vigilantly, in case their young were threatened again. Maybe Sheldon could back Rob right into them. If so, he wouldn't make the mistake of lending a hand this time. Maybe Rob sensed his plan and got the same notion. He circled Sheldon and drove harder. Sheldon planted his feet, voided, parried and riposted. Every time one of them thought of something new, the other seemed to think of it at the same moment, 'til they both felt like they were beating themselves senseless against unbreakable mirrors.

Sheldon's arm pistoned at Rob's head, over both black blades. It wasn't Sheldon's blade that struck, though, but his fist. The punch tore flesh and scar tissue on Rob's cheek. The bone beneath scraped Sheldon's knuckles, right as Rob's uppercut drove into Sheldon's solar plexus, right onto the old scar beneath his shirt, hard enough to lift his feet off the ground. Sheldon's head went light as the air left him, doubling up his midsection. Distantly, he saw and felt his blade drag across Rob's cheek as he carried the punch through. Rob's head turned and moved with the slice, so it didn't go through the bone and sever his brain from the rest of his head. In the same instant, the teeth of Rob's knife dug into Sheldon's side and came a hair-split from slitting him wide open. Sheldon's feet hit the ground and he stumbled away. Rob came roaring and chopping. Blood pumped from his mangled face. Sheldon went in low and stabbed at Rob's crotch. Rob kicked him in the chin, rattling his jaw and snapping his teeth together. Sheldon rolled back across a rocky patch in a triple-somersault.

"*It should've been Louis!*" Rob closed in, blades turned downward. "*Louis* wouldn't be such a fucking pussy. He'd've gone with me to the end."

The black blades plunged towards Sheldon's neck and chest. He brought up his own knives and kicked both of Rob's feet out from under him. As Rob pitched away, Sheldon slashed him deep across the thigh. Rob landed and scrambled right back up. Blood gushed from the leg-wound, but Sheldon had just missed the femoral artery, so Rob didn't bleed straight out. It still slowed him down long enough for Sheldon to think, *Maybe you're right, Rob. You loved Louis as much as you loved Sally. Maybe they could've talked some sense into you, between them.*

Each man attacked more fiercely, even as they bled harder. All strategy had dissolved into blind drive. The temple and the valley were gone. They might have fought in Deschemb, or in the other world, or in the waters of the black ocean, or on the fields of some even farther unknown land. Sheldon might have wielded the black blades of Magur Sevi, as Rob might have wielded the shining blades of Bathshire. There was Rob and there was Sheldon, everything they had or might have been to each other, roaring to its finish here. *The big fuckin' picture* could sit and wait its turn.

Sheldon rolled in the dirt and strutted painfully to his feet, then simply limped out of the way. Rob's twin slashes clanged on something. Sheldon turned and looked dully, just before he stumbled back into the same surface. They'd both backed into the side of the temple itself. So where was the door? Rob steadied himself against the building while Sheldon bobbed left and right, forwards and backwards.

"Stop fighting, Sheldon," Rob pleaded. "This is fucking pointless, and you know it."

"Yeah…Yeah, it is." Which *way* had they taken around the temple?

Rob shrugged and shoved himself forward. Apparently, he meant to just walk by, almost like he'd forgotten Sheldon was there. Sheldon's face tightened. He waited 'til Rob was nearly past him, then he lashed his blade up for Rob to walk into. Rob deflected it, almost absently, then spun away languidly and swept at Sheldon's gut. Sheldon batted it away without looking down. The knives slid weakly out of the engagement, scraping musically. The men circled drunkenly, edging up and out along the hillside. They half crept, half slid down, away from the temple. The ground slanted under their feet towards a deep rocky drop-off.

Damnit, why isn't one of us dead yet?

Because neither of us will let that happen, even though part of both of us wants it. One of us would have to let the other win. The land won't let us settle for that, though. Because we both absolutely know, *in our heart of hearts, that we're right and the other guy is wrong.*

Sheldon's swollen eyes rolled past Rob. Far away, along the curve of the dome…yeah, there was the top of the archway again. He inched sideways. Once he had as much wind of Rob as possible, he broke for it in a shambling run. Rob shot sideways. His arm swung up, collided with Sheldon's neck and pushed, while the crook of his knee hooked Sheldon's and pulled. As Sheldon flipped backwards, several things in his leg moved in ways they weren't supposed to. The explosion of ripping agony hurt worse than his back when it smacked the stony earth. He howled and brought the ruined knee to his chest. Rob kicked him in the ribs, stomped his stomach, stomped his crotch. Sheldon twisted and contorted, his whole body curling and uncurling helplessly. He still gripped his knives, but his arms felt useless. The toe of Rob's boot struck Sheldon square in the forehead, snapping his neck sideways. Rob danced away and looked down panting at the broken heap he'd left. Sheldon lay fighting for strength, through multiple explosions of agony, distantly wondering how many of his bones were busted.

"Get up, Sheldon. *Get up!*"

Sheldon rolled on his side. He spat out blood and some tooth-chips. "Why?"

"I won't let you off that easy. C'mon, man, get up and die on your feet!"

No. This ain't about me, is it, Rob? It's about you. You won't kill me while I'm helpless, not someone you've called brother, because in spite of everything else you've turned into, that's not who you are.
"Fuck. You."

Rob looked more confused, closer to panic. Finally, he snarled scornfully and ran for the temple's entrance.

Sheldon pressed himself up. The world rocked crazily. When he lurched to his feet, his ruined knee let out a pulsing shock like his entire nervous system had been caught in a bear-trap. He fell on his side, then shakily forced himself to stand on his good leg. As he shambled forward, he dropped his knives. He reached down, but he didn't pick them up. Instead he grabbed a rock and chucked it as hard as he could. It bounced off the back of Rob's head. Rob went sprawling forward.

~

By the time Rob lifted his head, Sheldon had already shuffled by, limping towards his destination like an arthritic old man. He'd retrieved his knives, but they were back in their scabbards. Rob snatched up his own blades and shambled to his feet in drunken disbelief. His thick hair sopped with blood, and his eyes blurred. He could rush and attack again, even now. Something about the sight of Sheldon's movements halted him.

"Sheldon! What the hell are you doing?"

Sheldon shouted back in a slurred voice, "What's it look like? Gonna walk right on into that temple, like I came here to do…like Puttergong told me to do, like you were supposed to get me here to do."

"Wait…what?"

"What, did you miss that part, or just ignore it? *It's the blades forged by the gods that have to kill the gods.* I just couldn't have gotten 'em here, through the Old World, without the High Natural's help."

"Fucking lying asshole!"

"Nah, Rob, I'm just a guy doing what Puttergong told me to do. Just like you've always been. That's all either of us have ever been, since we met. You're the dumb fuck who just assumed that the *big fuckin' picture* was all about

530 ~ Matt Spencer

you. I'm just gonna go do my part now. That, or you're gonna come up behind me and kill me 'fore I get there…"

"No I *won't!* Not like that. You're gonna turn and fight me. *That's* how you're gonna die, like you *deserve*, like you *owe yourself, facing me!*"

"Like I *owe myself?* Huh. That's real thoughtful, Rob, but sorry, no."

"So what do you expect me to do? Race you there?"

Sheldon shrugged. "Why not? Whoever gets there second can still go in. I got a chance to look in there, remember? You didn't. It's like that black ocean we crossed together, *outside of time and space* and all that shit. If you follow me in, it'll be like we both went in at the same time anyway. 'Cept it won't be neutral in there like it is out here. 'Cause that's the gods' turf. You're a Crimbone and I'm a Spirelight, remember?"

"I won't let you go in there. I'll kill you first."

Sheldon reached the top of the ridge. "So c'mon, go ahead. I'm gettin' closer. Sounds to me like you're jus' standin' there…"

Rob clenched his teeth and shook his searing head. This was *wrong!* It couldn't be like this. Sheldon was gonna *make* him do it, though, damn the little bastard. After three shambling bounds, Rob lifted his blades…those ancient black blades, perfectly weighted to his hands. Suddenly they felt heavier than ever, like lead weights. *Even my blades don't want to let me kill you like this, Sheldon. So why are you making me do it?*

He still forced his arms to lift them and strike.

~

Sheldon heard Rob coming, but he didn't draw. Even the defensive reflex was gone. Rob closed in. The tip of one black blade touched the base of Sheldon's spine through his torn shirt, barely breaking skin. That's when Sheldon's body moved completely independently from his mind or will. In a single lightning movement, he voided the thrust, spun and drew one blade. Rob's knife glided past Sheldon's side. Sheldon stuck out his blade so Rob ran right onto it. Rob's mouth dropped open as he transfixed his own guts. The blade sank to the hilt into his bubbling abdomen. He didn't let go of the black blades, but they dangled harmlessly at his sides, his fists frozen on the handles.

Sheldon's ruined knee kept threatening to buckle, but he clenched his teeth and pressed forward. He walked Rob backwards down the ridge. "Guess it just *wasn't really in you* to stab a brother in the back like that, *was it, Rob?*"

Rob snarled and twitched, weaker and weaker. His feet dragged and kicked futilely. Rocks skittered and bounced around their boots, 'til they stood against a rocky drop into the mist below. Rob's feet slipped and slid at the edge, kicking stones and dirt out into the misty air. Sheldon stared into fading eyes that were still so bright, so defiant. *Quit prolonging it! Spill his guts. Draw your other blade and slice his head off.*

Rob sucked and spat out gurgling breaths on mouthful after mouthful of blood. When Sheldon's eyes went to the hilt of his knife in the solar plexus, something cold fluttered through his own body. Absently, his free hand touched the sore spot where Rob had gut-punched him...right in the old wound.

Sheldon's brain swam surreally, like his whole essence was being pulled through his arm, into his hand, into his outstretched blade. Rob's mouth twisted in a bloody grin. Sheldon recognized the beast that had raged at him through the Vermont forest...a beast defending its mate, along with everything the future might hold for them. Then the last of *that* Rob Coscan seeped redly through his teeth, down his chin. With a shuddering cry, Sheldon lurched backwards. His blade slid free.

Rob Coscan spilled backwards into the mist, the black blades still dangling in his hands.

THREE

Sheldon somehow made it back up the hillside. With every step, he felt things moving around inside his right leg, in ways they weren't supposed to. The pain was manageable if he moved cautiously, most of the time. On this terrain, though, it was always only a matter of time before he set a foot wrong, so it felt all over again like someone had twisted the leg three hundred and sixty degrees at the joint, so he clenched his jaw, bracing himself through thickening sweat, sure he was about to tumble back down the hill, back into the mist, probably landing right on Rob's corpse with his luck. Somehow, he eventually crested the ridge. He spotted the temple's entrance and descended towards it. He'd expected going down to be easier than going up, but if anything, it was worse. Halfway down, he stepped on a bulging rock, so his knee exploded with fresh pain. He spilled forward and managed to go into just good enough of a roll-fall that he didn't completely shatter himself. He made the rest of the descent in a tumble, like a Jack with no Jill.

For the next few minutes, he floundered around, like a drunk on ice, trying to get his palms and good leg beneath him just right so he could push himself up. The side of the temple was too many yards away to be any help. For a hot minute, he was convinced he'd die like this, so close to his goal, crippled by the enemy he'd just killed— the friend, the brother—in pursuit of this finish line. That sounded like a slow, uncomfortable way to go, but he had to admit, there *was* something hilarious about it. Finally, though, he made it to his feet. His knee felt worse than ever, like one big raw nerve, like all the cartilage had torn free and turned to liquid fire. He hobbled gingerly towards the entrance, his shaky arms outstretched to either side like a tightrope walker. With a gasp, he reached the entrance and caught the side of the archway. He could still see the strange, swimming way all matter changed beyond the threshold, yet it no longer looked quite as surreal. The way his vision blurred and swam, it could hardly seem weirder than his surroundings out here.

Once he stepped into the temple, only his own physical form felt real. All the screaming, full-body agony was all still there, but it felt far away. It wasn't that he could deal with it better, more like he no longer needed to. His body and soul were both one with this place. At some point, he noticed that he was no longer limping. It was like he'd stepped into an abstract oil painting, the only living, flesh-and-blood image here, drifting down the corridor, out into the main amphitheater. Everything rippled, like a dreaming reflection on clear water. He kept expecting to just float away through it. Even the knives on his belt felt like part of this glowing, thirsty mirage, reflecting the greedy light of the gods.

The gods welcomed him, of course. He wore the blades of his proudest ancestor, after all, with which he'd just slain the king of their greatest enemies. The love of the gods enveloped him. Their warm, celebratory laughter drew him in. He descended a long flight of stairs and crossed the vast floor towards a rising stone altar. Here, the gods would forgive him for all his transgressions, all his debased activity among the Schomites and United Descembines and Earth-line people. An immense peace flooded him. His bashed, strained muscles relaxed. Soon he would again be one with the light of Spirah. He would bear Bathshire's blades through both worlds, restoring the glory of the Spirelights.

Before the altar, there rose a podium, on which sat a massive, ancient book. Sheldon passed it by, not bothering to open it. His gods would fill him with far greater wisdom and power than written words ever could.

Draw your blades, said the gods as he stood over the altar.

Sheldon drew the blades of Bathshire and lifted them overhead.

Touch your blades to our altar, where they were forged, and receive the blessing of our power, as no Spirelight before you has ever known it.

Sheldon turned the knives downward and stabbed with all his might. For the first time since entering this temple, his body felt whole and alive, a true machine of flesh, blood and muscle. In the instant the blades touched the stone, he felt the latter's defiance of his effort, the absurdity of his arrogance, to think blades could pierce such a hard, ancient surface. Nonetheless, he put every fiber of strength in his shoulders behind the thrust. The metal drove through the stone with a shriek. All around him, the mirages flashed and swirled, with many stories, through many worlds and ages. Pain flashed up through his shoulders. He wanted to shriek but couldn't. The gods shrieked for him, as the temple melted away. So did the altar and the blades. Sheldon felt himself dissolve into the ether. In their burning pantheon, the gods writhed and bled. In his panic, he almost yanked the blades free. No, the gods would die, but their power, their essence would echo onward and outward through Deschemb like any spell, 'til it ran its course, ages from now.

Here and now, though, that power was Sheldon's to command…and *here and now* was wherever and whenever he chose in time and space. He already knew exactly where to go. His consciousness swam towards another world…the world of his birth. It rushed towards him, like a light at the end of the tunnel.

How is it this easy? I can already feel it, taste it, smell it…the lands…the scent of home. Why, it's where I first left that world for this, and what do you know, there's—

Yes, sweet boy, of course this is the tunnel through which you've found your way back.

"Who are you?"

I am your god, Sheldon, the only one who has ever mattered. It was I who followed your ancestors across the great black ocean, I who kept the glow of Spirah alive in them, as I guided them through the centuries, through wilderness and war over Schomite-defiled lands. When a Crimbone stabbed you so the other gods abandoned you, it was I who never lost sight of you, for I saw how you'd one day prove more useful than any of the others. It was I who spoke, first to Talino, then to Balthazar, so that they could bring me here, to this place of the sacred vortex, where I have waited for you…you, and the one other creature of flesh and blood whom you've ever truly loved.

"Janie?"

You feel her close by, don't you? You think her presence here wasn't always by my design? Do you think any Spirelight in this little, diminished world, ever fought for any god of that decadent, defeated pantheon? Of course they haven't. Because not a single one of them has ever had the rest of those gods on their side…because it was you *who killed them, worlds and ages before any of them were born. And now, at long last, my child, you have come home to me. Now rise the rest of the way through the ether. That's it, that's it, just a little higher. Meet your love anew, and make her your bride, so that you may both go forth, to forge a new world in my image, as Balthazar, Rob Coscan, and Talino before you never could.*

Whatever this thing was, Sheldon realized, it was offering to let him be with Janie again. As its serpentine energy slithered and caressed him, he felt her above, also in its grip. He couldn't exactly hear or see anything, because he no longer had eyes or ears, yet it was like being a drowning man, staring up through the murky depths as he kicked towards the surface, clawing for her…while she clawed to get free of this entity, the same one that caressed and eased him towards its demands.

He made himself relax, heard himself say, "No."

No? No, what?

"No, you can't have me, and you can't have Janie. Not for what you have in mind. While you've been stuck back there in that world, I guess you haven't been paying attention to me. I just clawed and fought my way, over months, through the lands of my ancestors, to do one thing: to free not just my people, but all people, from gods like you…from all gods. And I just stabbed the altar of the gods. You know as well as I know, even all the way from that other world, all that's keeping you from sharing their fate is whether I say yes or no to your bullshit offer. Well guess what, bitch? I say *no*."

There's a word for what you're acting like, boy…a word for a filthy, bloodthirsty, rebellious beast that refuses to learn its place within the divine serenity of the world unborn, forever futilely, arrogantly striving, to hack out its own existence, hacking away at all that would subdue it, stupidly committed to remain itself, no matter what the divine offers…a word for the very same abomination that stole everything from you, back when you walked the narrow road of righteousness. That word is Crimbone. *Are you telling me, Sheldon Wildfire, that that's what you are? A Crimbone?*

"I guess so, you piece of shit."

Then die with the rest of your kind, Crimbone.

Sheldon felt himself become physical again, partially…just enough to feel the stone beneath his feet, for a stray bit of gravel to slide beneath his bootheel, so the pain erupted afresh throughout his body. Whatever swamp the god had hid out in seemed to flood his lungs and catch fire, consuming him from the inside. He crashed on his side, so the stone bruised his shoulder and hip. The shrieking, twisting agony of torn ligaments and tendons spread through his entire frame. No matter which way he rolled, the pain intensified, 'til his teeth chattered, threatening to shatter against each other.

Too late now, you little whelp. Did you ever think you had a choice? The only choice you ever had was whether it has to hurt or not. Now feel me *seeping through everything you've ever been, anything you ever could have been, absorbing you into myself, before I—*

Hey, Sheldon, why are you listening to this bitch?

"Janie?" he shuddered.

Of course it's me. Damn, you got any idea how boring it's been, stuck here waiting for you, over an eternity? I gotta admit, I was scared when Remelea first suggested it. I still don't quite understand what all this is, or how it's happening. Stuck here all this time, though, I've just gotten...yeah, just bored!

You little bitch! Didn't I tell you to shut up?

Yeah, you did, and I'm ignoring you completely. Because you're nothing. Sheldon, it's okay, love. I'm here. Just take my hand.

Sheldon reached up through the ether and took Janie's hand.

Stop doing that, shrieked the last of the Spirelight gods.

"You don't get any say in this matter," said Sheldon. "Didn't you notice? You're just another god. I just stabbed you straight through the heart, right along with the rest of them."

As the god receded into oblivion, Sheldon rose towards the surface of the ethereal water, still clutching Janie's hand. He felt cold. His eyes fluttered open, except they weren't his eyes. This whole body didn't feel like his. It was smaller and less muscular, and weirder still, had a whole different set of parts in certain areas than what he was used to...well, at least from this end.

Remelea rushed into the stone enclosure and stared down at him. "Oh, shit, girl, I'm sorry...Janie?"

Sheldon stared up at Remelea. He felt Janie's lips and throat-muscles move. "Take me back to the Brooks House."

Remelea's face quirked quizzically. "Janie...?"

"Take me back to the Brooks House."

CHANGING OF THE GUARDS

ONE

Jesse leaned back in the front passenger seat while Zane floored it. The Big Red Beast blasted down Cedar Street. Once they turned onto High Street, there were a lot fewer mutant freaks to bounce off the front grill and splatter across the windshield. The wipers sure had gotten a workout today. When was the last time Jesse had lost this much blood? He'd forgotten just how distant and dreamlike everything got. He lifted and looked at his haphazardly bandaged hand, his arm still red and sticky to the elbow. Somehow not seeing the extent of the damage made it feel worse, like the exposed bone and flaps of shredded meat were three times the size of his whole hand.

"You know what, Zane?"

Zane kept his eyes on the road. "What's that, brother?"

"I think we might finally be getting too old for this shit." He giggled deliriously.

Zane glanced over. "That hand ain't looking good, man. We get through this, it's probably gonna have to come off."

"You remember what happened to those sawbones back in the Union Army who told me that, right?"

"Yeah. That's why I ain't looking forward to having to hold your ass down. Figure I'll have Remelea do the sawing."

"Damn. This was the hand I jerked off with, too."

"Speaking of Remelea…" Zane peered out along High Street. "Hey. You notice something funny, man?"

"I'm not noticing much of anything around here."

"That's the funny thing. Fighting ain't half as bad down this way as I expected. Shit, it's almost like—"

"Hey now, what's that?"

"What?"

Zane slowed the van to a crawl. "Down there, along the sidewalk." Now Zane's voice sounded muddled, too.

Jesse squinted. "What the fuck's Sheldon doing back here?"

"Sheldon? Man, what are you…That ain't Sheldon. It's Janie. Janie and Remelea."

"What are they doing here?" Janie was supposed to be up in the Brooks House. Remelea was supposed to be holding the bridge. Jesse started to think he'd already passed out and all this was a dream.

Some weird light bathed Janie, like the sky had changed colors just for her. Except it wasn't the light around her that was weird. It was the light that came *from* her. Through the haze, Jesse realized it wasn't exactly *light* she gave off, wasn't anything the eyes saw. He remembered the energy Sally used to emit, filling the United Deschembines and drawing them closer together. This was like that, except so much stronger, more *palpable*.

All around the two ladies, people stopped fighting and drew aside, trembling tearfully. Zane had pulled the van over, Jesse noticed. They were both trembling, staring in baffled awe, just like everyone else. Something had changed, not just in here, but outside, too. The ladies walked into the Brooks House together. Everything out here stayed the same as they'd left it.

Two

Sally had once told Janie how Rob used to have conversations with his dead best friend. Whatever was happening between her and Sheldon now, it must feel like that, except even weirder physically. From head to toe, she still felt her girl body around her, but also a boy's body, familiar as though she'd lived her whole life encased in it. *Damn, external genitalia is weird.*

She'd never met Rob, but it sounded like he'd lived at the center of his madness, waiting eagerly for it to close in. He'd sounded like one scary dude, someone she didn't want to meet. Considering this sudden experience, she almost wished he was here to give her some pointers.

Uh, no, trust me, that'd be a bad idea. Just breathe, Janie. You still have friends out there who love you. In case you ever doubted it, you should know now how much I love you. And I won't let you die.

"That's not what this is about anymore, though, is it, Sheldon? It's about us not letting them die."

Yeah. If we time this right, none of them need to. I think...we can bring them into it with us.

It was harder than either of them would have expected, staying physically coordinated with two minds fully awake within the same body. Good thing Remelea was there to help. She led them up to the final flight of stairs, opened the door and said, "Okay. Go do what you need to do. Both of you."

The final door opened into a small octagonal room with windows on all sides...the looming old cupola atop the tower at the corner of the Brooks House building, facing the intersection of Main and High Street. Janie had always wanted to come up here. Through the windows, the gray winter sky had disappeared, in every direction for as far as the eye could see. She knew no words for the vast swirling limbo, full of colors from an alien light-spectrum, as though earth's whole atmosphere had been torn away like a curtain, so the planet drifted through an alien solar system.

Yeah, that's...pretty much exactly what's happening.

She barely caught her breath to say, "Where are we?"

Where I am. I've brought you here, all of you. They all see it, but from up here, you, Janie, can have their undivided attention...because who else down there's gonna find it in them to talk while looking up and seeing that?

She looked out into the streets below. All the fighting had stopped. Everyone stared at the sky, frozen. She worked at the rusty old latch of the window. When it swung open, it echoed down into the streets. Many gazes drifted up her way. It was the only sound left in the world, after all.

At first, it had been beyond rattling, realizing that was really Sheldon, responding conversationally to her innermost thoughts, like an entity with the worst grasp of personal boundaries ever. As she got used to it, though, she realized she now shared his mind, too. His new godlike knowledge was her new godlike knowledge. It felt like it had always been there, in her mind and soul, somewhere. She didn't just physically know what it felt like to be a man. She knew what it was to be a *Spirelight* man...and a Spirelight woman, along with every other kind of man or woman or anyone else out there. Only in this cosmic place, together, could her consciousness and his contain such immensity.

She looked down at the crowd and whispered, "What am I supposed to say?"

You have it all in your head already. You have their undivided attention. So just…open your mouth and let out what we feel.

When she opened her mouth and shouted down to the crowd, the words were neither his nor hers, but both. The energy on which the words flowed had once belonged to gods, but Sheldon had taken it from them, as simply and sneakily as he'd stolen Claudette's book as a present for Janie. The words belonged to everyone who was there to hear.

"People of the Schomites and Crimbone. People of the Spirelights. People of the Earth-line. Your fighting stems from the will of gods in another world. Whatever you tell yourself you fight for, you bring only laughter to their lips and dying blood to yours. The gods are no longer here to laugh at your death. It is time for you to live instead. Forget the gods you've fought and killed for. Look at the people around you. They're the ones that matter. *You're* the ones that matter. The land around you gives you life. Tread its soil with love, side by side. Sheldon Wildfire has cut the strings of the gods of hate from your backs. You cannot see Sheldon Wildfire. You cannot feel Sheldon Wildfire. You've never even heard of Sheldon Wildfire. When you wake from this dream, it will live on within each of your souls, to carry with you throughout this new world, letting it sooth and heal everyone you meet, so that you may all find your new ways, whatever those may be. It's not for me to decide, any more than it was ever any gods' place to decide. First, though, get yourselves together then clean up this stinking mess."

Down in the streets, everyone milled in a languid daze. Janie's voice had carried far and wide throughout the town. In the coming days, its echo would spread further still, from voice to voice, from soul to soul, from land to land. No one could say when the alien cosmic swirl receded, or when the sky of this world returned. Slowly, everyone drifted away and dispersed like an ebbing tide, from the heat and stink of carnage that choked the streets.

Up in the tower, Janie blinked and swayed. An icy winter gust whistled in against her. She hugged herself against it. "Sheldon?"

He didn't answer. He wasn't here anymore. She closed the window and gazed out through the glass across the rooftops, at the mountains beyond on a gloomy, quiet Winter afternoon in Brattleboro, Vermont.

Janie sat down against the wall. Her achy, trauma-jangled muscles collapsed. For the first time since Mom died, she actually relaxed. Before she knew it, she closed her eyes and dreamed the dream she and Sheldon had given to the rest of them. It was hours before anyone found her.

THREE

Sheldon awoke on the chapel floor. The temple no longer felt like something outside of time and space. It was just a big room, made of shimmering Deschembine crystal and stone. When he dragged himself up, his fucked-up knee shrieked at him, so he fell back down on his ass. Eventually, he managed to steady himself. The podium still stood with the massive old book resting on it. Even now, he didn't bother to open it. He wouldn't know how to read it anyway. It would be ages before anyone would take interest in this place or the book again. The holes he'd made in the altar were still there, but the knives had crumbled to dust like the black weapons of a slain Crimbone.

He limped out of the temple. Climbing the hillside turned out to be a whole new exercise in humiliating agony. Atop the ridge, he gasped, sat down, and tended his wounds. There was little he could do for it, other than stand up slowly and limp along cautiously, shifting his weight awkwardly. Mere moments had passed since he'd entered the temple. Out across the distance, Spiralla still burned. He found his small bag of supplies, hoisted it, and limped downhill, back into the misty valley. He met no more of the beetle-monkeys, though he wouldn't much care if he had. They were still out there, chirping and screeching wickedly, but they seemed interested in other things, probably hunting and feasting on whatever there was to eat down here.

By the time the sun set, the mist seemed thinner. When it rose, Sheldon climbed the last hill and spotted the tracks of Kashen and Cassella's pack. He moved onward as a phantom through Deschemb, following the tracks he'd made with Kashen. Dragons soared overhead, out across the eight winds, towards war.

After many days and nights, Sheldon entered the first Deschembine forest he and Rob had explored together. He passed through the flourishing botanical cities the Schomites now grew from the earth. Food was plentiful here, and no one bothered him when he stopped and sat to eat his fill. Civilian Schomites already populated the cities, while Crimbone guarded the edges. They looked at the lone, limping vagabond, sensed nothing threatening from him, so they shrugged and let him pass. He crossed paths with a few Crimbone encampments. They spoke excitedly of their wondrous new chief, who united all races who dared to stand against the Spirelights and crushed all that stood with the oppressors.

Sheldon didn't mention that he'd killed their chief. They probably wouldn't believe him anyway. He wandered further and met Spirelight armies who marched to avenge Spiralla. None of them seemed to recognize him as a fellow Spirelight, but they still spouted the same old evangelical shit his own family had long ago drilled into him since birth. All the Priest Kings were dead, they said, collapsing their Empire into chaos and infighting, but they couldn't let themselves despair. The gods would guide them along the righteous path. Sheldon didn't mention that he'd killed their gods.

Finally, he reached the banks of the sea where he'd first set foot in Valaka…in the land of Deschemb. The sky above stretched brightly into infinity. What other shores lay at the end of forever? He might as well find out. For a few weeks, he camped out on the edge of the forest. He'd stolen a small survival knife from one of the encampments that had sheltered him. When he wasn't hunting or scavenging food, he carved and wove a boat from whichever trees gave willingly. There were others in the forest around him, whole camps of vagabonds, also building boats. He never bothered making contact with them 'til his own long, narrow craft was ready.

"Who are you guys?" he asked.

"Refugees of Spiralla," someone panted, dragging a craft into the surf while others followed to jump in. "Valaka is no longer habitable for Spirelights. Haven't you heard? The armies of the new Crimbone chief already march this way! Here's to finding friendlier shores."

Sheldon doubted they would, even before he saw the great blackness settling through the sky ahead, above a different ocean than the one he'd shoved his boat into. The old legends said the black sky covered the shores of Deschemb. The land surrounding those shores was supposed to be bleak and dead for miles around. It had been a long time since that had been the case, and it would be longer before it was again. Then again, these might not even be the same shores. The other boat went into the black ocean side by side with his. He soon lost sight of it. Whatever land for which they headed, the shores they reached would be far from those he found. That was comforting.

Sheldon rowed aimlessly through the quiet blackness. Eventually, light cut through it. Two figures waited on a torch-lit sandstone dock.

"I thought it would end here," Sheldon heard himself say as he looked them over. "No, I remember now…Yeah, I'm supposed to take you boys across, aren't I? Yeah, that's right. You'll see the land of Deschemb, and you'll start to discover…"

"What'll we discover?" asked one of the figures.

Sheldon heard himself say, "How it happened there, why our ancestors crossed these same waters."

FOUR

So tell me about the Old World.

How would I know?

You grew up knowing, hearing stories about it, right?

The Old World…Vast! Rob, it was vast! I used to read and hear the stories…Hey, don't distract me. I'm trying to tell you a story…The Old World…I've heard of it and I've dreamed of it. I've dreamed about its giant lakes that were miles deep, yet so clear…You could dive from the immense cliffs. The air there was different from anywhere else. You could leap into it and just glide down for miles, not too fast, almost flying but not quite. Then finally, you'd splash into the water. It was so clear you could look down through it and see the stone ruins of the ancestors far below, covered in every color of glowing moss. The people of the Old World…they say some of them could actually hold their breath long enough to swim down through all those miles and through the ruins.

Yeah… and in the ruins, the walls told stories. Sally, the walls told stories!

You read that in your book?

No. The book doesn't describe things like that. But Sally, when you do, I see it…I walk the ancient halls, and there are others there, both Schomite and Spirelight. I still know I'm Crimbone, and everyone around me knows too. But that doesn't matter as much, even among the Spirelights. I guess it's before the wars got so bad, before the blood-hate got so strong. I look at the walls and it's amazing! The walls tell the stories of everything they've seen, not in paintings or carvings or even writing, but…in the elemental swirl of the matter itself. I don't know, it's…

Like if you look at it right, you can see all of history in the stones of the old halls. In those sacred places, all time, all things can truly be one to you, if you know how to see it…

…And I keep looking deeper and deeper, further and further back, and I keep thinking I'm about to see the beginning of everything, and then…

He landed and shattered on the rocks, like one of those Spirelights the dragons had shaken off its back in Spiralla. No, his body was still in one piece, much as it hurt. A pulsing, blazing trail ran through his midsection, left by a blade forged from the essence of his enemies. When it had passed through him, he'd sucked that essence from it, out through himself, feeding on it as he did whenever he drove his own blades through those enemies. The black blades were still in his hands. He made it to his feet. The glow from the Spirelight blade kept him alive. He was the strongest of his kind to ever live, and he'd drink many more glows, making himself stronger still.

Now he wandered the deadly misty valley, hunched over, one arm pressed across his midsection, against the sundered guts he wouldn't let kill him. His whole body shook and contorted with agony, so he wanted to drop beneath its weight. The lands wouldn't let him, though.

This valley was dead. The minions of the gods had worked their dark spells to keep the spirits of life at bay. He sent out his call to the lands above…a *new* Call, a *Fourth* Call, known only to the Crimbone High Natural.

He had stepped forward. He had taken up his teeth and claws. He had proven his devotion to the will of the lands. Now, for the first time, he made his will *truly one* with *this* land, and invoked it. The mist thinned. The half-living monstrosities inhabiting it screeched and scurried in a panic. Sunlight, then moonlight leaked into the valley, so the creatures breathed unpolluted air. One by one, they writhed and died, poisoned by it.

He trudged on, sure that at any moment, the lands would deem his duty fulfilled, and his body and spirit would part ways as they returned to those lands. His boots met and climbed another hillside. The rocks grew large and steep enough that he had to scale parts of them with both hands and feet. His deep wound sucked and tore at him. If he lost too much blood, there was now something else to pump in its place.

As he reached level ground, his blurred vision made out a decrepit Crimbone campsite. Inactivity had brought this pack low, held captive on this hill by the legions of monsters. These Crimbone were unlike the others he'd seen in this world. Their skin was ashen, making no effort to blend with the thin grass and stale earth around them, draped in tattered rags or no clothes at all. Only a few jutting, leaning rocks sheltered them. Their bodies remained hard and lithe, though, with purposeful suppleness. Even in their half-madness, their eyes were clear. One by one, they slunk forward, staring at him with a curiosity that gave way to awe.

Their chief was a tall, wiry, scruffy man with tight narrow shoulders, clad only in tattered britches. His name was Havard, known throughout Deschemb as the mad Crimbone poet. His wild, questing blue eyes met those of the man who'd climbed from the valley, and he smiled. Now it was Havard's mind that cleared, as though all the swirling flames of his brain had drawn together before him, materializing into what would be his greatest song yet. Through Havard's poetry, this meeting would be remembered, through every Crimbone artist who etched the visions the poetry painted in their minds. Havard asked the High Natural's name.

With a madman's laugh, the High Natural roared, "Magur Sevi!"

With that, the mists rolled away behind him, along with his memories of the temple or what he'd meant to do there. The lands of Deschemb had shown in a new age, calling forth nothing less than Magur Sevi against the unchecked threat of the Spirah gods.

When Rob and Sheldon had arrived in Deschemb, no one they'd met had heard of Magur Sevi, because no one by that name had ever existed, until now. They'd known they were going to the Old World. They just hadn't known *when*. It would be a long time before the trail of the beast wound towards the road to peace. Long after the days of Magur Sevi, his descendants would find another world, across a vast dark ocean, where time flowed differently. There, they and their enemies would secretly share the Earth-line history. Somewhere in the ages ahead, on an Autumn afternoon, in a coffee shop in Brattleboro, Vermont, a boy named Rob met a girl named Sally.

EPILOGUE

ONE

"*Welcome home, little brother.*"

That was the last thing the boatman had heard Rob Coscan say to Sheldon Wildfire before shoving off from Deschembine shores for the second time. Now, after another, quieter journey, the same sandstone dock came into sight once again. The torches still burned, but no one sat waiting this time. He hadn't expected to reach this place again. Maybe he'd expected to row forever, through that empty black dream outside of time. It had been peaceful while it lasted.

Now he remembered those long-ago words and sighed, "No...*Now* I'm home." His voice sounded like an old man's. Before climbing out, he glanced at the floor of the boat. "Now what in the...? Oh, right. Those two nice young men forgot their backpacks." Without quite knowing why, he hauled up the bags and brought them along.

He climbed back up the winding stairs, shoved the rusty old door open, and looked out onto a bright spring afternoon, at a Vermont forest of green and gold. He breathed the air of the land where he'd been born, the sweetest air he'd ever tasted. It was cleaner than he remembered. When he stepped out and looked back through the doorway, the vast, dark room no longer stretched back to the stairwell. There was just a little circular room full of dirt and rocks. When he stuck his head back in and looked up, light spilled in from the top, around some broken, rotted boards of the old staircase, still clinging to the sides.

The forest was the same as he wandered through it, except much of the plant life looked different, something between what he remembered here and what he'd seen in Deschemb. When he found the road, there were fewer houses. Lush natural gardens flourished in the burnt-out ruins, in new, vibrant, ethereal shades. They blended peacefully with the old native flora.

Strange birds flitted through the ruins…if you could call them birds. They looked like fat bald pigeons, only with bigger, wilier eyes and floppy dog-like ears. Further on, folks gathered food from the gardens in the ruins. Through the leaves of the crops, there peered the small mischievous eyes of people who'd stand no taller than the gardeners' knees. As he walked further into the town, he recognized some of the folks who were out and about. None of them seemed to recognize him.

He found his way to Main Street. A thousand clear, pure rainfalls had long since washed all the bloodstains away. Some of the businesses were open. None of them were the same establishments he'd seen here before.

Past the old Latchis building, he crossed the bridge to an intersection that led uphill. It was nice without all the automobile traffic. An old street sign swayed towards him, next to an empty old diner. Through the rust, he made out the words *South Main Street*. Further uphill, he passed an old graveyard. On the other side of the street was another rusty sign that used to read *Washington Street*. He peered down it. The house he looked for was gone, along with most of the rest.

Two

Edging towards three in the afternoon, and Louis Coscan-Karn climbed atop his desk to reach the electrical socket that rested inexplicably in the corner of his bedroom ceiling.

Ever since Uncle Zane had finished wiring the house with electricity from solar panels, Louis had been determined to find a use for that socket, just for shits and giggles. Now he plugged in the old device called a *speaker*. The cord ran to another hanging speaker then down to the vinyl music box Zane had given him for his birthday back in September, along with a stack of old, black, wax-coated cylinders that poured out music like the musicians were right there in the room with you. Uncle Zane had taught him all about how the sound lived in the wax.

Louis double-checked the hookup, then put on one of the cylinders and set the needle on the spinning edge. Music filled his room. Pink Floyd sang about learning to fly. Louis wanted to listen to all these songs on all these records, but it was too nice a day to stay inside. He'd first heard of some of these artists from Mom, some from Dad, some from Uncle Zane, some through their old friends who came around.

Uncle Zane said the old musicians were the chroniclers of the world that had ended just before Louis was born. Mom said he'd been born with the world they lived in now, which was very lucky. Uncle Zane was right, though, she said. He needed to know his history, and everyone agreed, there was no better starting point than the music. He and this new world were growing up together, Mom said, him and his best friends Emil and

Lilly, and the rest of the kids. All the grownups were discovering it and figuring it out right along with the youngsters. Louis and his friends would one day decide what came next.

Music was the most effective form of time-travel, Mom liked to say. An old friend of hers named Rob used to say that a lot, she said. Whenever the grownups spoke of Rob, sometimes it sounded like they were talking about a good guy, sometimes a bad guy. Whenever Louis asked about him, they got weird and awkward. They said they'd explain it when he was older. That irritated him, when they thought he wasn't ready to understand. Lately, he'd come to suspect it was because they hadn't figured it out either.

Good thing Mom and Zane had talked Dad into letting Zane fix the house up with solar panels. Electricity was something that had flourished in the world that had ended, and Dad had been glad to see it go. Sometimes people still managed to acquire it, though, in scattered places like this. Dad and Mom and Uncle Zane had spent years renovating this house from a weirdly painted wreck. It was one of the few places that had gone untouched in the great battle where Mom and Dad had first gotten to know each other.

Sometimes Uncle Zane told him stories. Whenever he finished, he patted Louis on the shoulder, grinned and whispered, "Now don't mention all that to your mom and dad. They don't figure you're old enough to hear it, see. But you and me, we figure better, don't we?" Louis and Zane always winked and bumped fists at those moments.

Louis went downstairs and outside. Dad and Zane sat on the screened-in porch, sipping mead from the home-brewed cask Emil's dad had given them. "Ah, good shit," they'd sometimes say. "What I wouldn't give sometimes for a good ol' fashioned Heineken, though." Mom teased them for missing that frog-piss. Now she came out with a glass of mead of her own. She rubbed Dad's thick, scarred neck, then she rested her elbows on his big shoulders and watched Louis play in the yard.

Across the back yard rested another house that had come with the property, which Mom and Dad and Zane had also renovated. No one had moved into it yet. Trees grew high above its roof. The sun hovered over the branches and the distant mountain across the river. These days, Dad sat around on the porch a lot, looking more and more like an old man. So did Uncle Zane.

"Y'know," said Uncle Zane, "I sure could go for some smokes to wash this beer down with. Saw some plants the other day on the outskirts, looked sort of like tobacco." He looked left and right at Mom and Dad. "Either of you two wanna try it out with me?"

Dad laughed and rolled his eyes. "If you two decide to *smoke* that weird new shit, do it at Zane's place, hear?"

"That what the kids used to call a *hall-pass*, brother?"

Mom laughed and punched Uncle Zane in the shoulder. "Keep dreaming, stud."

While the three of them laughed it out, Louis slipped down alongside the house. He found the rusted remains of the big red vehicle that didn't run anymore, the one Dad and Zane used to ride around in, back when they were getting into adventures all the time. One of the rear doors hung loose. Louis rooted through the back 'til he found a long black iron pipe. He drew it out cautiously, so as not to upset any of the other dusty artifacts. The pipe was nearly the length of his body. He swung it around some, got a feel for it, and began going through athletic motions. He pretended it was one of the ancient black metal weapons Mom and Dad and Zane all still had tucked away somewhere.

Sometimes the younger grownups—those leading the reconstruction—came to consult Mom, Dad and

Uncle Zane. They kept calling them *living legends*. There was some sort of big community meeting downtown tonight, in the old Stone Church, presided over by Mom, along with Emil's dad Liam and his friend Bird, two of the few Earth-line guys who'd survived what everyone called *the Battle of Brattleboro*.

Uncle Zane kept saying how he wished all those young punks would leave them the hell alone. They still always wound up going to those meetings, but they never took Louis along. Earlier today, he'd overheard them arguing over whether or not it was time to bring him to his first such meeting. He hoped they would.

Louis wandered back up through the yard, swinging and pivoting with the long heavy pipe.

Dad called out, "Hey, boy, where'd you find that?"

"In the Old Red Beast!"

"Be careful where you go digging around, huh. I don't like you going through all that sharp, rusty old mess!"

"Can I keep this, though?" He brandished the black iron pipe.

Through the porch screen, Dad's face contorted uncertainly. Mom and Uncle Zane smirked at each other, then Zane leaned sideways and nudged them both with his elbow. Dad lifted a suspicious eyebrow, then grunted and settled back to finish his drink.

"Sure, just be careful with it," Dad said. "Don't go through places like that without asking us first."

"Hey," Mom shouted, "give us a few minutes, then what do you say we all go for a walk in the woods?"

Louis's face brightened. He loved it when Mom took him for her long walks in the woods, on her *scouting trails*, as she called them. She didn't take him on her longer excursions, where she was sometimes gone exploring for a day or more at a time, but she took him out further and further, the older he got. He loved it best, though, when all four of them went for hikes together. Maybe they'd run into Emil and his family, or maybe Lilly and her mom.

For now, Louis's daydreaming pantomime brought him up near the street. A tall, rough, dark, weather-beaten figure came along the sidewalk. Something in Louis tingled with awe. The stranger looked like he'd stepped right out of the raging winds of one of Uncle Zane's wildest stories. On one shoulder, he hauled two heavy-looking old-fashioned backpacks. He passed the porch, then paused and peered over. Louis glanced back with him. Mom drew up breathlessly as the stranger met her eyes, like she thought she recognized someone.

The stranger noticed Louis and stared uncertainly. Louis planted the iron pipe on the ground and leaned against it, like he'd just brought it wearily from one of those ancient battlefields of old lore.

"Hi," said Louis.

"Hey, kid. That's a tough looking piece of equipment you got there. You training to be a Crimbone or something?"

"Yep!"

"Oh, are you, now? So what's that all about, huh? To be a Crimbone, I mean?"

"A Crimbone's a champion to *all* people in need, someone who pulls us all together when the bad times come, to keep everyone united, with the strength of the land." Louis nodded at the porch. "That's my mom and dad and uncle over there. They all used to be great Crimbone warriors. You wanna come up, sit and talk with us, tell us where all you've been and what you've seen?"

The stranger's eyes glistened. "That's okay. Maybe some other time." He paused and studied Louis's face. "So that's the man you call your dad, huh? That's good. What's your name?"

"Louis Coscan-Karn."

"I remember another guy named Louis Karn from around here, lots of years back. He was a cool guy."

"That's what everyone says. He was my brother—my dad's other son—but he died long before I was born. He was the best friend of my mom's old friend, Rob Coscan. I carry on both their names."

"That's good. How old are you, Louis?"

"Eleven."

"Eleven's a good age to be learning things like that. It's good for you to practice with weapons. Hopefully you'll never have to use them to actually hurt someone. It's a good way to learn discipline, though, mentally, physically and emotionally, stuff like that."

"That's what Dad always says."

"Your dad sounds like a smart guy." The stranger smiled. "Hey, I think I recognize that piece of metal you're practicing with. It belonged to someone named Sally."

"You mean Sally Wildfire?"

"You've heard of her?"

"Yeah, Miss Janie talks about her all the time!"

"Janie?"

"Yeah, she's real nice. She's our town's blend-lady historian."

"Historian, huh? I'd like to talk to her. You know where I could find her?"

"Oh, sure. Just go to the last little house on the left, before the hill. It's about half a mile from here. She might not be home right now, though. She spends lots of her time during the day wandering around in the woods alone."

"Thanks, Louis. It was good to meet you."

With that, the stranger headed along up the street, quicker and lighter on his feet than before. Louis watched him pass from view, then went back to the house. He leaned the pipe respectfully against the porch, then climbed the steps to Mom and Dad and Uncle Zane.

Dad stood and placed his one hand on Louis's shoulder. "Ready for that walk in the woods, kiddo?"

"Yeah!" If they met up with Janie in the woods—as they often did—Louis would have to tell her about her old friend who was looking for her.

The four of them filed down off the porch. Louis' eyes darted to the top of the old telephone pole at the edge of the yard. For an instant, he thought he spotted a strange, bulbous, bat-like shape perched up there. In the blink of an eye, the creature vanished. Louis shrugged and headed off with his family into the woods.

THREE

Puttergong soars off towards the clouds ahead, which finally spread to show him the way home. Since that big ol' fight years back, he's quit botherin' to wonder why he's still stuck here. To keep from gettin' lonesome, he's had to get friendly with them fat fuckin' pigeons no less. Other than that, shit's worked out pretty good, all things considered. Definitely different than anything he ever had in mind, but hey, no sense complainin'.

Now Puttergong finally feels the body he's lived in, over the years in this here world, start to dissolve around his mind, and he finally gets an idea why it's taken so damn long. So Cop-Boy finally showed back up, lookin' all old an' weather-beaten an' shit, and the little Biter-Boy came up and talked to him. For a second there, Puttergong was scared the kid would go sensin' whatever was left of the ol' *Spirelight glow*, so he'd have some kinda *First Call* of his own. That would'a left Puttergong stuck for another go-round with *another* pain-up-the-ass Biter-Boy! So maybe Puttergong's the one been keepin' himself 'round these parts, just to make sure that didn't happen. He's glad to see that it ain't.

Hey, whatever. Hopefully Cop-Boy'll get himself a nice, slow, sweet Welcome Home present from his lil' Injun girl, whenever them two run back into each other. Puttergong figures it's time he gave 'em some privacy. He'd sure better have a nice big Welcome Home party of his own, waitin' for him back at the big ol' tree in the Ephemeral Realms. In the haze ahead, he can almost see it comin'.

Okay, guess that about wraps 'er up. Take it easy, folks. Happy trails.

THE END

Matt Spencer is the author of seven novels, two collections, and numerous novellas and short stories. He's been a journalist, New Orleans restaurant cook, factory worker, radio DJ, and a no-good ramblin' bum. He's also a song lyricist, playwright, actor, and martial artist. He lives in Vermont with his wife and two cats. Check him out online at http://mattspencerauthor.wordpress.com, on Twitter at @MattSpencerFSFH, and on Facebook at Books by Matt Spencer.

Thanks for reading, folks. Hope you enjoyed the ride. Now don't forget to go to let everyone else know what you thought! Be sure to pop over to Amazon, Goodreads, your blog, and whatever social media you frequent, and drop a short review (or a long one, if you feel like it).

www.ingramcontent.com/pod-product-compliance
Lightning Source LLC
Chambersburg PA
CBHW061923130726
47909CB00012B/31